This was the crea  ht
to bay with his feebl s,
pitiless, infinite dem s
body began to trembl
But he *had* brought it m
the moment he entered .... He forced his quavering
voice to carry boldly, "I'm here. Where is my armor?"

*My scales are my strength. Lie among them and
cover yourself with them. But if you wear my mail and
share my power, you may find them hard to put off
again. Do you accept that?*

"Why would I ever want to get rid of power? I
accept it! Power is the center of everything!"

*But power has its price, and we do not always know
how high it will be.* The dragon stirred restlessly, remembering the price of power as the water on the
cavern floor seeped up through its shifting bed.

—from "The Storm King"

A wall of blind hate slammed into me, locking me
out. Hopeless pain was all that was left, all that was
real to her now, eating her alive from inside. She
wanted to die; and she would. I had to break through
before everything imploded.

"If you have to hate," I shouted, "remember who
did this to you, who turned your gift into something
sick and dirty. *Don't let them win! We don't have to let
the goddamn scum of the universe destroy us.* Let me
in—"

Ineh jerked upright. And screamed. The scream went
on and on, pouring out of her like blood.

My mind burst open as the images smashed into me,
losing all control as she lost all control. Not even my
own mind any more, I was but a stage in darkness for
the Dreamweaver's nightmares.

—from "Psiren"

Petra swallowed, wetting her dry throat. "Oh, God . . . I wonder if our medical plan covers blowing yourself up while mind-controlled by an alien."

"Allah! Can't you do anything but make jokes—"

She laughed uncertainly. "If I have to die, I'd rather die laughing." She felt her knees give way and she knelt, paralyzed. "It's a good position for prayer, at least . . ."

Shiraz laughed this time. "Where's Earth? I've lost track of Mecca."

"You can't see it from here. If you had a last wish, what would it be?"

"That I was somewhere else." Shiraz pressed the button.

Petra stared in agonized disbelief as a blinding ball of orange light blotted out the silver dome. A fist of smoke and shock swept toward them—struck her with sickening force, throwing her over the rim of the canyon like a rag toy.

—from "Voices From the Dust"

At dusk Etaa came to me where I crouched in the doorway, watching the luminous fantasy-face of Cyclops wink behind the clouds. I heard her baby murmur as he slept, somewhere in the firelight behind us.

At last she said, "It's true, isn't it, Tam? That we're not on the Earth anymore. That we're on Laa Merth? And that little speck, passing over the face of Cyclops like a fly . . . that's the Earth?"

"Yes. It's all true."

"But our legends say the Mother is the center of all things, greater than all things. How can She be a speck on the face of the Cyclops? Tam . . ." Her fingers scraped my rough hide. "I know nothing; it is all lost on the wind. Tell me what is true, Tam." She sank down beside me, her eyes wild. "What shall I believe in now?"

—from "Mother and Child"

JOAN D. VINGE

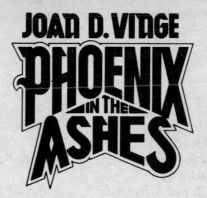

PHOENIX IN THE ASHES

A TOM DOHERTY ASSOCIATES BOOK

PHOENIX IN THE ASHES

Copyright © 1985 by Joan D. Vinge

Reprinted by arrangement with Bluejay Books, Inc.

First Tor printing: March 1986

A TOR Book

Published by Tom Doherty Associates
49 West 24 Street
New York, N.Y. 10010

Cover art by Susan Collins

ISBN: 0-812-55713-1
CAN. ED.: 0-812-55714-X

Printed in the United States of America

0 9 8 7 6 5 4 3 2 1

ACKNOWLEDGMENTS

All stories reprinted by permission of the author.

"Phoenix in the Ashes" was originally published in *Millennial Women*, Delacorte Press, 1978. Copyright © 1978 by Joan D. Vinge.

"Voices From the Dust" was originally published in *Destinies*, Volume 2, Number 2, Spring 1980 issue, Ace Books. Copyright © 1980 by Joan D. Vinge.

"The Storm King" was originally published in *Isaac Asimov's Science Fiction Magazine*, April 1980, Volume 4, Number 4. Copyright © 1980 by Joan D. Vinge.

"The Peddler's Apprentice" by Joan D. Vinge and Vernor Vinge was originally published in *Analog*, August 1975 issue, Volume XCV, Number 8. Copyright © 1975 by Joan Vinge and Vernor Vinge. Reprinted by permission of Joan D. Vinge and Vernor Vinge.

"Psiren" was originally published in *New Voices 4* edited by George R.R. Martin. Berkley Books, 1981. Copyright © 1981 by Joan D. Vinge.

"Mother and Child" was originally published in *Orbit 16*, edited by Damon Knight. Harper & Row, Publishers. Copyright © 1975 by Damon Knight.

For my father,
S.W. Dennison
1912–1984
with love

Table of Contents

Phoenix in the Ashes   1

Voices From the Dust   45

The Storm King   68

The Peddler's Apprentice   102

Psiren   148

Mother and Child   206

PHOENIX IN THE ASHES

The sun's blind, burning face pushed upward past the scarred rim of the river canyon; brands of light seared Hoffmann's closed eyelids. He stirred, and sighed. The temperature rose with the sun; flies and red ants took the day shift from the mosquitoes.

Hoffmann kicked free of the blankets and sat up. He brushed flies from his face, sand from his watch crystal. "Six A.M. . . ." Something stung his foot. "God damn!" He crushed an ant, felt the familiar throbbing begin to spread up his foot; he was allergic to ants. There was no antidote—it meant half a day's nagging pain and nausea. He put on his pants, hobbled down to the river to splash his head and shoulders with the still-cool waters of dawn. The river moved sluggishly past him, only two hundred kilometers from the Gulf; the water was silted to the color of coffee with too much cream. But Colorado meant "the color red." He wondered whether it had been different, in the past, or whether, somewhere upstream, the river still ran red. . . . "Someday we'll get to find out, Hoffmann." He stood up, dripping, noticed a piece of scrap metal half-buried in the sand. He squatted down again, dug with his fingers. "Steel . . . talk about the middle of nowhere! Yeah. Looks good. . . ." He went back up the bank.

He gathered brush for a fire, cooked rehydrated eggs and bacon. A final bat surrendered to the day, chirping shrilly

1

overhead on its erratic return to the shadowed caves on the far canyon wall. Sparrows rustled in the dusty trees behind him. He tossed out stale bread, watched the birds drop down to peck and wrestle; the sun's heat burned away the wetness on his back, faded the ends of his dark, shaggy hair. He studied the roll of USGS map reproductions again, laboriously translating from the English. "Huh! Los Angeles basin! San Pedro; nice bay . . . wonder what it looks like now? Probably like a crater, Cristovão: navy yards, at Long Beach." He pronounced it "Lona Becha." "Well, we'll know by nightfall, anyhow . . ." He laughed suddenly, mocking. "They say talking to yourself means you're crazy, Hoffmann. Hell, no—only if you answer yourself."

He forced his swollen foot into a hiking boot, pulled on his wrinkled shirt and drooping leather hat, and threw his bedroll into the cockpit behind the 'copter's single seat. The bulge of oversized fuel tanks made the 'copter look pregnant: He called it the *Careless Love*. He brushed the blazing metal of the door. "Don't short on me again, machine—they didn't build you to give me trouble. Get me to the basin, one more day, then I'll check the wiring; promise. . . ." His eyes found the starry heavens in the Brasilian flag on the door. He looked past the ship at the smoothly rising gravel of the slope, toward the barren, tortured peaks, basalt black or the yellow-gray of weathered bone. He remembered pictures of the moon; pictured himself there, the first man to walk another world since before the Holocaust; the first man in two hundred and fifty years. . . . He smiled.

As he climbed into the cockpit, he struck his aching foot on the door frame. "Mother of God!" He dropped into the pilot's seat, grimacing. "This day can only get better." He started the engine. The 'copter rose into the sky in a swirling storm of sand.

Amanda sipped tea, watched sun sparks move on the water of the bay through the unshuttered window of her sister's house. She set down her beaker, returned to brushing the dark, silken hair of Alicia, her niece. Red highlights flickered between her dye-stained fingers like light on the water, a mahogany echo of the auburn strands that escaped around the edges of her own head-covering. Alicia twisted on her lap; sudden impatience showed on the small snub-nosed face. "Ow! Aunt Amanda, tell us another story, please?" She tugged at the laces of Amanda's leather bodice, untying them.

Amanda shook her head. "No, Alicita, I can't think of any more stories; I've already told you three. Take Dog outside, you and Mano can make him chase sticks." She slid the little girl down, steadied small, bare feet on the floor, and retied the laces of her vest. Dog whined under the table as the children pulled at the scruff of his neck. He raised a bristled yellow face, his jaws snapped shut over a yawn with a *clack* of meeting teeth. He scratched, and sighed, and obeyed. She heard his toenails clicking on the floor tiles, and then happy laughter in the courtyard: sounds she seldom heard.

Her sister returned from the fire, moving slowly because of the clubfoot invisible beneath her long dress. She propped her crutch against the table and sat down again in the high-backed chair. "Are you sure it's all right for them to play with Dog, Amanda? After all, he was . . . well—"

Amanda smiled. He was a snarling, starving mongrel when she had hurled rocks at him for stealing eggs and broken his leg. And then, in remorse, she had thrown out food to him, and given him shelter. When he stood on his hind legs he was as tall as she was; his mustard-brown hide was netted with battle scars, his flopping ears were torn. He would attack any man who gave her trouble, and that was why she kept him. . . . But he slept peacefully at her feet through the long, empty hours, and rested his ugly head against her knee as she sat at her loom; and whomever she loved, he loved . . . and that was also why she kept him. "It's all right, Teresa. I'm sure."

Her sister nodded, turning her cup on the plate. Rainbows revolved in the beaker's opalescent glaze. Teresa put her hands to her bulging stomach suddenly. "Ah! I'm kicked night and day. The little devil . . . I have bruises, would you believe it?" She sighed.

Amanda laughed sympathetically, covered her envy, because Teresa tried to cover her pride.

"How do you ever think of those stories you tell the children?" Teresa pressed on, too brightly; Amanda felt her own smile pinch. "All those wondrous cities and strange sights, balloons big enough to carry men in a basket . . . honestly, Amanda! Sometimes I think José enjoys them more than the children. . . . You're so good with children. . . .'' Amanda watched the brightness break apart. "Oh, Amanda, why didn't you obey Father! You'd have children too, and a husband—''

"Let's not bring that up, little sister. Let's not spoil the afternoon—'' Amanda studied the dark wood of the tabletop; the fine lace of the cloth Teresa had made by hand caught on her calloused fingers. *To have the money, to have the time. . . .* "I made my choice; I've learned to live with it." *Even if it was wrong.* She looked away abruptly, out the window at the sea.

"I know. But you're wasting away . . . it breaks my heart to see you." Teresa's brown eyes rested on Amanda's hands and were suddenly too bright again with brimming tears. "You were always so thin."

But once there was a man who had called her beautiful; and when he touched her—Amanda felt her cheeks redden with shame. "By the Word, Teresa; it's been eight years! I'm not wasting away." Teresa jerked slightly at her oath. Embarrassed, she picked up her beaker.

"I'm sorry. I'm very . . . moody, these days."

"No . . . Teresa . . . I don't know what I would ever have done without you and José. You've been so kind, so generous to me. I never would have managed." No resentment moved in her.

"It was only justice." Old indignation flickered on Teresa's face. "After all, Father gave me your dowry as well as mine; it wasn't fair. I wish you'd let us do more—''

"I've taken enough already. Truly. It was more than I deserved that Father lets me have the cottage. And that José lets you give away his possessions like you do. He's a kind man."

Teresa patted her stomach, smiled again. "He treats me very well. I don't know why I deserve it."

"I do." Amanda smiled with her, without pain. The wind carried the sound of bells from the temple tower in Sanpedro town.

"The evening bells; José should be coming home . . . now." Teresa reached for her crutch, pushed herself up from the chair. Amanda rose, pulling up her veil as she heard a commotion in the courtyard, shrill delighted voices and a barking dog. José came in through the hall, dark and smiling, a child trailing on each arm. Amanda dropped her eyes, as Teresa did, peeked upward to see José gently raise his wife's chin with a fingertip. Longing pierced her; she pressed her own rough hands against the lavender weave of her shapeless dress.

"My husband . . ."

"My wife. And Amanda: it's good to see you, wife's sister."

She raised her eyes, looked down again, made awkward as she always was by the warm concern in his eyes. "José. Thank you."

Two more figures entered, crowding the small room. Amanda's breath caught on anger as she recognized her other sister, Estella, with her husband Houardo.

"José, why didn't you tell me we're having more guests!" Teresa pulled at her veil, flustered.

"I thought since Amanda would be here, Wife, there'd be plenty to eat for two more." José beamed at his unsubtle inspiration.

"Yes, there will be, José," Amanda said, meeting his gaze directly, made reckless by resentment. "I can't stay. I have too much . . . work . . . to do." She glanced away, at Estella. She could only see the eyes, scornful, beautiful and coal-black, above the fine cloth of Estella's veil. Memory filled in the face, pale, moonlike, flawless; the body, soft, sensually cushioned, with none of the sharp, bony angles of her own. Estella was two years older, but looked two years younger now. Houardo's hand was on Estella's shoulder, possessively, as always, a touch that stirred no longing in her. Teresa had said that Houardo beat his wife, without cause, in fits of jealousy.

But if there was no longing, there was also no sympathy in her now, as she endured their stares. Estella had loved not well, but wisely, marrying the son of the town's wealthiest

merchant; a thing which she never let her disinherited sister
forget. Amanda noticed that the rich cloth of Estella's dress
was the muddy rose color of imitation, not the pure, fragile
lavender-blue that only her own dye could produce. She
smiled, safe behind her veil. "I have to finish a piece of
cloth, if I'm to get it to market."

"Amanda . . ." Teresa started forward, leaning on José's
shoulder.

"Good-bye, Alicita, Manolito . . ." She slipped out through
the hallway, into the fading heat of the desert afternoon. Dog
joined her as she left the shaded courtyard, licked at her
hands and her bare, dusty feet. She stroked his bony back.
Dog would not share a room with Houardo.

Amanda followed the palm-lined road that led to her father's fields, her toes bunching in the warm dirt; trying to
outdistance her own futile resentment. She slowed at last,
breathing hard, a cramp burning her side from the long rise of
the road. She looked back over the bay, saw ships, like toys,
moving under the wind. *And they go away, forever.* . . . "He
will come back!"

Dog barked, his tail waving.

She looked down, her shoulders drooped as she reached to
pat his head. "And what would he find, if he did . . . ?" Her
calloused hands knotted, loosened. *They go away forever.*
But the futility, the bitterness, the sorrow and the dreams
never left her, never gave her rest. Still looking down, she
saw a wrinkled, thumb-sized lump in the dirt; she crouched to
pick it up, seeing more scattered across the road in the
reaching shadows. Dates hung in bulging clusters below the
green frond-crests, in the trees above her head. The crop was
turning, the earliest to ripen were already falling along the
road. She picked them from the dirt eagerly, filling the
pockets she had sewn into the seams of her dress.

As the track wound through the last of the fields before the
pasture, she saw her father standing in the road. She stopped;
he was not alone, but with three other men. Other merchants,
she supposed, come to dicker about the shipment of his
grain. . . . She saw that one wore the inlaid ornamental chain
of the mayor: he had come to designate the tribute to be sent to

the fortress in the hills of Palos Verdes. Her heart lurched; the men of the mayor sometimes took women, as well, for tribute. But they had seen her; she could not turn back now. She moved toward them again, walking on hot coals.

The agent of the mayor turned back to the fields, disinterested, as she drew closer. She felt the other men's eyes on her, vaguely curious, and on her father's broad, unyielding back. He had not looked at her; would not look at her, or speak, ever again. She kept her eyes carefully downcast, seeing only the edge of his long vest, the rich earth-red of his longer robe beneath it, his sandaled feet. *I have only two daughters,* he had said. She did not exist, he would not speak to her, and so she could never speak to him again. Her feet made no sound in the road; the men began to talk of wheat as she passed them.

Suddenly they fell silent again. Amanda raised her head, looking out across the fields toward the river. A high, throbbing sound in the air; she frowned, searched her memory, but no recognition came. One of the men muttered something. She saw him point, saw a dark spot on the sky, a bird's form, growing larger and larger, until it was no longer a bird form or the form of anything she knew. The noise grew with it, until she imagined that the air itself broke against her eardrums like the sea. She covered them with her hands, frozen inside her terror, as the monster swept over the green leaf-wall of the olive orchards. The workers in the field began to break and run, their shining scythes falling in the wheat, their shouts lost in monstrous thunder . . . that ceased, abruptly, leaving a shattered silence.

The monster plummeted toward the half-mown wheat, keening a death song. At the last moment a tearing cough came from it, it jerked upward, its wings a blur . . . and smashed down again into the field, with the grinding crunch of a ship gutted on the rocks. Fingers of sudden flame probed the crumpled corpse, pale smoke spiraled. In the eternity of a heartbeat, she realized that the broken thing was not alive, that it was a ship that flew, like the balloon-ships in the south. And then she saw a new movement, saw the flames give birth to a human form. The man fell, fire eating his arm,

crawled, ran desperately. Behind him the flames spread over
the ship, the stink of burning reached her, and a cracking
noise. The machine exploded, split by God's lightning, im-
paling on her eyes the image of the running man struck down
by a mighty, formless hand. Blinded and deafened, she top-
pled in the road, while the sky rained blazing debris. "Mercy
. . . have mercy on us, sweet Ángel . . . !" Dog began to
howl.

One of the merchants came to take her arms, helped her to
her feet. She blinked at his stunned face, lost to her behind
splotches of dark brilliance as he let her go.

"Are—are you all right, maid?"

She could barely hear him. She nodded, hearing other
voices fogged by her deafness.

"Ángel, Son of God—" Her father turned away as she
looked toward him. "Did you . . . it, Julio? An accursed
thing . . . down by God in my own field! My wheat field;
why did this—miracle happen in my field?" He shook his
head, to clear his eyes, or his regret. The others shook their
heads with him, murmuring things she couldn't hear. The
mayor's man stood at the edge of the irrigation ditch, his face
gray with shock.

Amanda looked out across the field again at the smoking
ruins of the machine spread over the flattened wheat. There
were no field-workers at all that she could see now, only the
sprawled form of the man struck down by God. Her hands
wadded the cloth at her stomach as a sound pierced the fog of
her ears, and the man in the field lifted his head. She saw
only redness—her blindness, or blood.

". . . help . . ."

She shut her eyes.

"Look! Listen—" The mayor's man pointed. "He's still
alive, in the field. We'll have to kill him."

"No!" her father said. "You'll make my field barren if
you shed blood." He shriveled slightly as the other turned
back coldly toward him. "He'll die anyway. Let God punish
him as He sees fit. Let him die slowly; he's a sorcerer, he
deserves to suffer for it."

Amanda's fingers twisted on her dress, sweat tickled her

ribs. The stranger's head fell forward, his hands moved, clutching at the golden, broken grass.

". . . help me . . . for Christ's sake . . . help me . . ."

"Listen! He's calling on devils," one of the merchants said. "If you go into the field, he might lay a curse on you."

"God will punish him."

"The metal thing—"

". . . *ayuda* . . ."

"Don't go near it! God only knows what demons are still left inside it . . ."

". . . please . . ."

Amanda heard a sob, choked back her own sob of anguish. *Father, he sees us! Please, help him—* She turned imploringly, but no one looked at her.

". . . that such a thing happened here. We must consult the Prophet's Book . . ." Their voices droned on, the cries from the field grew weaker, broken by hopeless silences.

". . . *pelo armo de Deus,* please . . ."

Amanda started toward the ditch. She heard an oath, looked back at the startled faces of the men, froze as she saw her father's face. *Will you humiliate me again, Amanda, before the mayor and God?* She stopped, stepped back into the road, her head down.

The merchant who had helped her up came toward her, said kindly, "This is no place for you, maid; there is evil here, these things are too strong for a woman's mind. Go home."

She faltered; she glanced again at her father, signaled to Dog and turned away down the road.

Amanda entered the cool, shuttered darkness of her cottage. She slammed the bottom half of the door, leaned against the lime-washed adobe of the wall, feeling the bricks erode under her fingers, tiny flecks of clay. In the yard Dog harried chickens, barking. "Dog, stop it!" He stopped, silence fell around the fading clutter of the chickens. She heard a gull's cry, as it wheeled above the river, heard in it the cry of the man in her father's field. *It isn't right—*

But it wasn't right for her to feel this way: It was a sin to meddle with magic, to harness the power of demons. It was

unnatural. The Book of the Prophet Ángel taught that these
things must be denied, they had been damned by God. And
surely she had seen the stranger struck down, before her eyes,
by God's wrath. Surely—

She moved away from the door, pulled down her veil,
unfastened the ties of her stiff, constricting bodice. The damp
folds of her worn dress beneath it fell free. She sighed in
relief, stretching. The weaving must be finished tonight, or
she would never have the cloth dyed by market day. . . .

He woke in darkness, retched with the blinding pain in his
head. The matted wheat was sodden with blood under his
cheek. Weakness settled his stomach; he lay without moving,
shivering in the warm air, staring at his own groping hand.
There was one memory, like a beacon on a black sea of pain:
They would not help him. . . . His eyes closed, the wheat
between his fingers became the stuff of dreams, became the
endless, rippling grass of the Pampas:

He was fifteen, living on his uncle's ranch in the Argentine
province. His cousins had gotten him drunk on the nameless
liquor that the ranch hands sucked out of hollow gourds. He
had bragged, and they had saddled the half-wild mare who
was the color of blood. . . . And she had reared and thrown
herself over on top of him, spraining his back.

He lay in the crumpled grass, every breath searing in his
chest; stared at his uncle's black, gleaming boots, like bars
against the endless freedom of the sky. "Help me, Uncle
Josef—"

Get up, Cristovão.

"I can't; it hurts too much, please help me."

*Help yourself, Cristovão. You must learn to be strong, like
my sons. You must be independent. Get up.*

"I can't. I can't."

Get up. The boot lifted his shoulder; he cried out.

"I can't!"

Get up, Cristovão. You can do anything you have to do.

"Please help me."

Get up.

"Please . . ."

Get up. Get up—!

* * *

Amanda rose from her stool, began to work the finished piece of cloth free from the loom at last. The candles flickered, her shadow danced with her on the wall. The weaving soothed her in the quiet hours of the evening, patterned her thoughts with its peaceful rhythm. Often she sang, with no one but Dog to hear, and the crickets in the yard for a chorus.

She folded the cloth carefully, kept the edge from sweeping the floor . . . and noticed that the crickets were silent. She stood still, listening, heard an unidentifiable noise in the yard. Dog stirred where he lay sleeping, growled softly. He climbed to his feet, went to the door and snuffled at the crack. Another small sound, closer to the cottage. Dog's hackles rose, her skin prickled. A coyote or wildcat out of the desert, hunting . . . a drunken herder or field hand, who knew she lived alone—

Something struck the door, struck it again. Dog began to bark, drowning her cry of surprise. "Dog, be quiet! Who's there? What do you want?" No answer came. "Go away then! Leave me alone or I'll set my dog on you!"

She heard a fumbling, a scratching, slide along the wood, and a sound that might have been human. She moved toward the door stiffly, caught in a sudden, terrifying prescience. Her hand shook as she unlatched the top of the door, pulled it open—"No!" Her hands covered her unveiled face, denying the nightmare that was the face before her.

The man from her father's field clung to the lower door with blistered, blackened hands. A gash opened the side of his head, slashed his cheek, oozing sluggish red; his eyes showed white in a death mask of crusted blood and filth.

"Sweet Ángel!" Amanda whispered, stumbled back, hands still covering her face. "I can't help you! Go away, go away—" Dog crouched, his muscles coiled.

"Please . . ." Tears spilled down the stranger's face, runneling the crusted mask. She wondered if he even saw her. "Please."

She dropped a hand to Dog's neck, rubbed it, felt his crouching tension ease. She unlatched the bottom door and pulled it open.

The stranger stumbled forward into the room. Amanda caught the bruising burden of his weight, led him to her pallet and let him slip down her arms onto the blanket that covered the straw. He lay weeping mindlessly, like a child, *"Obrigado, obrigado . . ."* Dog nosed his tangled legs.

She poured water into a bowl from the *olla* by the door, crossed the room again and took up the newly woven cloth from the loom's stool. *He'll die anyway*— She hesitated, looking back; then biting her lip, she began to tear the cloth into strips.

He sank through twisting corridors of smoke, lost in the endless halls of dream, where every convolution turned him back into the past and there was no future. He opened the doors of his life, and passed through. . . .

He opened the door to the crowded outer office, pushed his way through the confusion of milling recruits around the counter. He felt his blood pressure rise with every jarring contact, at every sight of an army uniform. He broke through, almost ran down the hall to Mario Coelho's office.

"Where the hell is Hoffmann?"

He slowed, hearing his name, and the voice of Esteban Vaca from the Corps of Engineers.

"Relax," Coelho said. "If he's half an hour late, he's early; you know that. I think he makes a point of it."

"Mother of God; I just don't understand why you put up with it!"

"You know why I put up with it. He's the best damned prospector I've ever seen; he knows more about metals than half the chemists in Brasil. He's uncanny at ferreting out deposits . . ." Coelho's chair squeaked.

"How much of an instinct does he need to find the Los Angeles basin? I suppose only some crazy fool who talks to himself in a crowd would even want to go look for it."

Laughter.

"You'd talk to yourself, too," Coelho said, "if you spent most of your life in the middle of nowhere. . . ."

"And besides, I know I'll never talk behind my back." Hoffmann grinned as he entered the room, saw Coelho's thick neck redden with embarrassment. "So, you want me to scout the Los Angeles basin." He straddled a chair, resting his arms on the hard back. "That's news. I thought we didn't have the fossil-fuel resources to mine clear up in the Northwest Territory. Or did we take over Venezuela while I was asleep?" *The Los Angeles basin.* . . . He felt a sudden eagerness, the sense of freedom and fulfillment that only prospecting brought into his life.

"We didn't; but they estimate it won't take us much longer. If that's so, the Corps of Engineers is thinking of reopening the Panama Canal: If it's feasible we've solved the transportation problem. And the coast's inhabited—which gives us a local pool of gook labor, to do the dirty work in the ruins." Vaca smiled.

"You stink, Vaca," Hoffmann mumbled. Vaca looked up sharply.

"Come on, Hoffmann." Coelho tapped his fountain pen wearily on the blotter. "Nobody makes you work for us. All we need from you is a report on whether the Los Angeles basin is worth our while."

Hoffmann shrugged unapologetically, felt them assessing his rumpled civilian clothes, the battered hat jammed down over his shaggy hair, his muddy desert boots. Even Coelho, who ought to be used to it, and to him, by now. Hoffmann said absently, "I use you, you use me. . . ."

They looked at him.

"All right, I do want the job. I'm ready whenever you are. What background stuff can you . . ." He watched as Coelho's face dissolved into the milky white globe of a street lamp; got up, staring as Vaca's face became the face of his uncle. The desk was a spreading, formless darkness, a gaping mouth to swallow him. Ragged teeth tore into his flesh as he fell through the doorway of another dream. . . .

Amanda started out of a nodding dream at the stranger's cry. The candle before her on the bare wooden table was half burned away, like the night beyond the door. She got up from her stool, stumbling over Dog at her feet, and went to kneel again beside the pallet. She had stripped off the bloody rags of the stranger's clothing and bathed him, picked metal from his torn flesh, bound his wounds and burns with the healing pith of aloe vera leaves broken from the serrated bush in the yard. And she had prayed, as she worked, that he would die, and God would take away the torment of his suffering from them both. . . .

But he did not die, and he lay now huddled between her blankets, shivering and sweating, his face on fire under her hand. She wiped it again with cool water, saw fresh blood on the white linen that swathed his head. He mumbled words that she almost understood, altered strangely. She whispered reassurance, tried to still his restless motion. His blistered hand closed spasmodically on her dress, jerking her down. *"Mãe,* I'm cold . . . s-so cold, *mãe* . . . '' She struggled as his other hand trapped her wrist, and she heard the threadbare cloth begin to tear. '' . . . cold . . .''

She went limp on the straw beside him to save her dress, shuddered as he pressed against her. "No—" She felt the fever heat even through her clothing; but there were no more blankets to keep him warm. "Ángel, Son of God, forgive me. . . .'' She put her arms around him and let him find the comfort of her own warmth. He sighed, and quieted, touching her in his delirium as a child seeks its mother, as a husband seeks his wife. Amanda heard the steeple bells sound midnight in the town below, remembered them on too many nights, when she lay alone with sleepless sorrow. Slowly her rigidness softened; her hair slipped free of its cloth as she moved her head, and spread across her shoulders. Memory caressed her with a stranger's unknowing hands, and Amanda began to weep. . . .

Diego Montoya was a merchant, dealing with the captains of the ships that sailed the long coast to the southern lands. He had no sons but only the burden of three daughters who must be dowried for marriage. But he was a wealthy man, by the standards of Sanpedro, and he had determined that his daughters would marry well . . . and so recover his losses in giving them away. His eldest daughter, Estella, was a beauty, and he had managed to match her to the wealthiest heir in town. And then he had begun to negotiate a match for his second daughter, awkward, reed-thin Amanda.

He had protected his daughters, like the valuable property they were, particularly keeping them from the sailors with whom he dealt and whom he knew too well. Again and again he impressed on his daughters the need for chasteness and obedience, the Prophet's warnings about the sins against natural law that damned the souls of the footloose sailors and their women.

But Amanda had drawn water from the well in the courtyard, and the handsome, black-haired boy drank as he waited while his captain spoke with her father inside. He was different from the sailors she had seen, somehow in her heart she felt he was not like any man she had ever seen—and he looked at her over the cup's edge in a way no man ever had, hesitantly, with pleasure. She stole glances at him, at his bare brown arms, his rough gray tunic, the laces of his sandals hugging his calves. He wore golden plugs stretching his earlobes.

"Thank you, maid." He set down the cup, caught at her with his eyes as she began to turn away. "Are you"—he seemed to be trying to think of something to say—"are you the daughter of this house?" He looked embarrassed, as if he'd hoped it would be something more profound.

"The second daughter." Knowing that she should not, she stayed and answered him.

"What's your name? I'm Miguel," he acknowledged his effrontery with a bob of his head. "I—I think you are very fair."

She blushed, looking down again, twisting the soft laces of her bodice. "You shouldn't say that."

"I know . . ."

"My—name is Amanda."

Her father saw them together by the well as he came to the doorway and ordered her sharply into the house.

But the next afternoon she slipped away, to meet Miguel on the path that wound along the river, and every afternoon, through the week that his ship was in port. Miguel answered questions her heart had never known how to ask, that had nothing to do with the limits of the world she knew. He was eighteen, hardly older than she was, but he had left his home in the far south years before, longing to see what lay beyond the headlands of the harbor. He told her tales of the peoples of the south and their strange cities, strange customs, strange beasts. He told her of men who flew, suspended beneath great bags of air; who crossed mountains higher than the shimmering peaks she could see at the desert's limits, to visit the southern lands. He said that they came from a land where there were wonders even he could not imagine, boasted that someday he would find a way to steal aboard one of the airships and explore all the new wonders that hid behind the mountain wall.

Amanda found herself dreaming with him; dreaming that she would be with him forever, share in his adventure, have his love, and his children. . . . For she had always been afraid of the things that passed between a man and wife, things a maiden hardly dared to whisper about. But lying on the warm riverbank, he had unfastened her veil to kiss her lips, freed her hair from its covering, sighing in wonder and calling it flame. And his fingers had touched her breast through the cloth of her gown, and started another flame, inside her. That night she had gone to the temple, heavy with guilt, and prayed to God for guidance. But the next afternoon, she let him touch her again . . . and only the impossibly knotted cord that pinioned her cotton drawers kept her a maiden, at last.

And then, suddenly, the week they had shared was gone, and they clung together in the shadowed heat of the olive grove. "How can I leave without you, Amanda? Come with me—" His fingers lifted tendrils of her hair.

"Stay here, with me, Miguel! Let me speak to Father, he'll let us marry—"

"I can't. I can't stay in one place, there are too many places I still haven't seen. Come away with me, let me share them with you. . . . You want to see them, too; I see them in your eyes! I'll buy you strings of opals, to match the fire in your hair . . . sky-blue butterfly wings that shine with their own light. . . . We'll cross the mountain wall in a balloon. Come away with me, Amanda!" He caught her hands, kissed her hungrily, drawing her toward the road.

The temple bells began to sound for evening prayer in the village. She pulled free, tears welling in her eyes. "I can't—the Prophet forbids it!" Afraid of God's wrath, and her father's, afraid of the shame it would bring on her family, and to her . . . afraid that none of those things mattered enough to keep her from his arms, she ran, sobbing, back through the trees.

"Amanda . . . I love you! I'll come back; wait for me! Please wait for me—"

Amanda woke up, aching with stiffness and remembered grief, to the sound of the morning bells. She gasped as she focused on the stranger's naked side lying against her own; stilled her urge to leap away, as memory stilled her terror. His head rested on her shoulder, pillowed on her spreading hair; the stains on the bandage were dark now, but his face still burned with fever. He lay quietly, his ribs barely rising, falling. With infinite care she drew her numbed arm from beneath him, covered him again and stood up. Dog scratched at the door; she let him out into the dawn, let in the pungent, sage-scented air to cleanse the smell of sickness. She noticed a line of dark stains across the hard dirt floor, tracing the stranger's path from door to bed. *Oh God, why must you send me this new trial?*

The stranger lived, on the edge of death, through the long day; and that night again she held him in her arms, startled from her sleep by the ghosts of his haunted fever dreams. Names of people, cities and objects, words in a meaningless tongue, filled her own unquiet rest with strange, unnatural dreams. And yet, time and again he spoke the names of places she knew: Losangeles, Palos Verdes, her own Sanpedro.

The dreams clung to him like death's shroud while two days passed, and three, and four. Amanda carried water from the river, heated it, washed bandages and dressed his wounds. She bathed his parched body, forced liquids down his throat. He was damned, but in his willfulness and sinful pride he struggled for his own destiny, defying the powers of nature and God. She shared in his defiance of fate, afraid to stop and question why.

At last a night came when he slept in her arms breathing quietly and deeply, unharrowed by dreams; and, touching his face in the morning, she knew that he had won. She cried again, as she had cried on the first night.

Late in the afternoon the stranger woke: Amanda looked up from her loom to find him staring silently at her face. She pulled up her veil self-consciously, wondered how long she had been sitting revealed to him, and went to kneel down at his side. He tried to speak, a raw noise caught in his throat; she gave him water and he drank, gratefully.

"Where . . . where am I?" The words were thick, like his swollen tongue.

"You are in my house." Habitually she answered what a man asked, and no more.

His hand moved under the blanket, discovering his nakedness. He looked back at her, confused. "Have I been . . . were we—? I mean, are you a—" She flushed, stiffening upright. "I'm sorry . . . I can't seem to remember, my head—" He lifted his hand with an effort; his fingers grew rigid as they brushed the thick, swathing bandages. He stared at his hand, also bandaged. *"Meu Deus* . . . an accident? Was I in an accident?" He looked away, taking in the small, windowless room, the streaming dusty light that struck her loom from the open door. "Where is this place?"

"This is the village of Sanpedro." She hesitated. "You fell from the sky, into my father's field. God . . . God struck you down. You nearly died."

"I did?" He sighed suddenly, closing the eye not covered by bandage. "I can believe it." He was quiet for a long time; she thought he had fallen asleep. She started to get up; his eye opened. "Wait! Wait . . . don't go—"

She kneeled down again, feeling the tension in his voice.

"Who are you?"

"Amanda. Amanda Montoya."

"Who am I?"

She blinked, shook her head. "I don't know."

"I don't know either . . ." His hand pressed his head again, the words faded. "Christ . . . I don't remember anything. Not anything—" He broke off. "Except . . . except

. . . the field; people, standing in a road, looking at me . . . but they wouldn't help me. They saw me, they knew, but they wouldn't help me.'' He trembled. "God . . . they wouldn't help me. . . .'' And he slept.

"I know the name San Pedro . . ." he said stubbornly between sips of broth as she fed him. She had killed a chicken while he slept, and made soup to give him strength. "I saw it, somewhere . . . the Los Angeles basin? Does that mean anything?" He looked up at her, hopeful, swallowed another mouthful of soup. His eye was as gray as sorrow in the candlelight, and fear lurked in it.

"Yes. It's the desert, all around us, to the north, to the mountains— We only go into it for metals.''

"Metals!" He pushed up onto his elbows, spilling soup, sank back with a groan. "Metals—'' His hand reached for something, found it gone. She wiped soup from his half-grown beard and his chest. "Damn it," he whispered, "it will come back. It will. When I'm stronger I'll go to the—the place where it happened, and I'll remember.''

"Yes," Amanda said softly, thinking he expected an answer. "Yes, I'm sure you will.''

The gray eye glanced at her, surprised; she realized that he had not been speaking to her. She offered him more soup; he shook his head carefully. "Why do you cover your face— Amanda? You didn't before . . . or your hair; I remember, your hair is red.''

"You weren't supposed to see it!" She wondered, mortified, what else he remembered. "The prophet Ángel teaches us that it isn't modest for a woman to show herself to a man who is not her husband.''

He smiled stiffly with one side of his mouth. "I'm sleeping in your bed, but you won't let me look at your face. . . . Who is this 'Ángel'?''

She felt irritation prick her at the tone of his voice. "No wonder you practice sorcery, if you've never received his Word. Ángel is the son of God, who led our people here from the south. He revealed that the only true and righteous life is one within the pattern of nature, the life all creatures were meant to live. To do sorcery, to try to put yourself in the place of God, from false pride, is to bring down ruin—as you were shown. That's why my father and the other men wouldn't help you. It was God's punishment.''

His expression doubted her, changed. ''You were there—''

''Yes.'' She looked down.

He took a deep breath, held it. ''But—when I came down to your door, you helped me. Why? Weren't you afraid of God's punishment, too?''

She smiled. ''There's little more that God could do to me, or I to God. . . .'' She got up and moved away, gave the last of the soup to Dog where he lay under the table, her own hunger forgotten.

''Amanda?''

She straightened up, looked back at the stranger.

''When I'm well—''

''Then you must leave.'' She rubbed her arms inside the loose sleeves of her dress. ''Or people will call me a harlot.'' *And they call me too many things already.*

''But what if I can't—'' He didn't finish it.

She went back to her loom. When she looked up again, he was sleeping.

Days passed; the swollen redness slowly went out of his wounds, the sight of his blistered arm no longer turned her stomach. But still he sometimes dropped off to sleep in the middle of a sentence, to wake minutes or hours later, out of a mumbling, delirious dream; a dream that he could never remember. He pressed her angrily, almost desperately, for the details of his dreams, old ones and new, swearing at her once because she couldn't write them down.

''Women are not taught to write,'' she had snapped. ''Women are taught to serve their husbands, and—and their fathers. Only men have a need to write.''

''What kind of garbage is that?'' He struggled to sit up, propping his back against the cool wall. *''You* need to write, so you can tell me what I say! This place is the damnedest, most backward piece of real estate in the entire Northwest Territory!'' He frowned, analyzing. ''In what's left of it—''

She glared at him. ''Then it's a pity you'll have to stay

here. Perhaps that's God's final punishment to you." She dared many things, in her speech with this stranger, that she would never have dared with a man of her own village or one strong enough to strike her.

He looked up sullenly. "What makes you think I'll stay in San Pedro?"

"Because your flying ship is broken. You'll never get back to wherever you came from, across the desert and the mountain, without it."

He was silent; she saw tension drawing the muscles of his hollowed cheek. "I see," he said finally. "What . . . what happens to 'sorcerers' in San Pedro?"

"Anything." She hardened her voice, and her heart. "They're outcasts. They can pray for forgiveness, and do penance at the temple, if someone will sponsor them. But you're an outsider. You have no family, and no money; no one will protect you. If you offend people, they will stone you. If not, they'll ignore you; you'll have to beg to live. Some walk out into the desert, and never come back—" *The silent, burning mirror of light; the scented, fevered wind; the shimmering, unattainable peaks of Sangabriel. . . .* It had drawn her away, as she gathered brush, more than once; but never far enough.

The stranger sat, stricken, his uncovered eye expressionless with the confusion of his emotions. Almost defiantly he said, "What if I won't leave here?"

"Then Dog will tear your throat out."

He slid down the wall onto the straw, pulling the blanket up over his shoulders, and turned his back on her. That night she lay sleepless on her own new pallet of straw, hearing the hard, bitter voices of the midnight bells.

The next morning she knelt at her *metate,* watching the sun rise over the distant peaks as she ground the grain she had gleaned from her father's fields. Dog lay stretched on the cool dirt, tongue lolling, looking half-dead in his eye-rolling ecstasy. She smiled, glanced up as he raised his head and barked once, inquiringly.

The stranger stood in the doorway of the cottage, wearing his torn, close-fitting pants and nothing else. The pants hung precariously around his hips; his ribs showed. He sat down abruptly against the house, sighed in satisfaction, smiled at her. "It's a beautiful morning."

She looked down, watching the motion of the smooth granite *mano* beneath her palms, made ashamed at the sight of him and by the memory of her cruelty.

But if he was angry, or afraid, he showed no sign, only stretched his scarred limbs gingerly in the soothing heat of the early sun. He watched her form the flat, gritty loaves of unleavened bread. "Can I help?"

"No," she said, startled. "No, enjoy the sun. You—you need to go slowly, to recover your strength. Besides, this is woman's work." She chided, mildly.

"It doesn't look too complicated. I expect I could learn."

"Why should you want to?" She wondered if the blow on the head had driven him mad, as well. "It's unnatural for a man to want to do women's work. Don't you remember anything?"

"I don't remember that. But then," he shrugged, "I don't think I was ever an Ángelino, either. I only thought—maybe I could help out with some of the work around here. You never seem to rest. . . . You'd have more time for your hobby." His voice was oddly cajoling.

"Hobby?" She struck her flint against the bar of steel, saw sparks catch in the tinder-dry brush beneath the oven. "What hobby?"

"Your weaving." He scratched his bandaged head, smiling cheerfully. "Mother of God, this itches." He scratched too hard, winced.

She turned to stare at him, at the linen that bound his head, in stunned disbelief. "It's not my hobby! It's how I stay alive: by weaving cloth. It took me two months to finish the piece I tore into rags, to bind your wounds!"

His hand froze against his head. "I'm sorry. I didn't know that—people wove cloth by hand. . . ." He looked down at his pants. "Let me make it up to you, Amanda. Let me work while you weave; it doesn't matter if it's women's work. I'm just grateful to have my life."

Smoke blew into Amanda's eyes, brought stinging tears. She wiped them away and didn't answer.

But she let him help her with the endless, wearying tasks that wove the pattern of her life, so that she could weave cloth, instead. At first he was too weak to do more than toss the sparse handful of grain to the sparse handful of scrawny chickens, hunt for their occasional eggs, sit on a stool in the sun tending her cooking pot. He ate ravenously, never quite seeming to realize how little there was, and she was glad that it was the autumn harvest, when the little was more than usual. And she was glad that he would soon be gone. . . .

But as his strength returned he began to do more, though he still collapsed into dreaming trances sometimes while he worked. He mumbled to himself, too, as though he really were a little mad, as he fetched water up the long slope from the river, walked out across the brown pastures to the desert's edge, bringing back brush and deadwood to chop up for her fire. She was afraid to send him to town, or even into her father's fields to glean—for his own sake, or hers, she didn't know. But, of his own accord, he began to fish from the riverbank: He gutted and scaled his glassy-eyed catches, spitted them over the fire for her dinner; and as the days passed she began to feel a trace of softness cushioning the sharp edges of her bones. She watched the stranger's own emaciated body fill out, saw, unwillingly, that he had a strong and graceful build. She cut a slit in one of her blankets to make him a poncho; to protect him from the hot sun, to protect herself from the shameful embers the sight of him began to stir within her.

At last, as though he had postponed it as long as he dared, the stranger asked her to take him to the place where he had fallen to earth. She led him back through the rustling shadows along the palm-lined track, to the field where his machine lay in pieces in the amber sea of grain. He stopped in the road, stared, his face burning with hope . . . but he only shook his head and crossed the irrigation ditch, dry now, into the field. He began to search through the grasses, forgetting her, hunting for his past as Dog hunted for squirrels.

She followed him, strangely excited, afraid to interfere, and heard his sudden exclamation. "What is it?" She came hesitantly to his side, tugging at her snagged skirts.

"I don't know. . . ." He kneeled down by a flat piece of metal, warped at one end. She saw a rectangle of green paint, a yellow diamond inside it, a blue circle filled with stars. A band of white, with lettering, arced across the sky. "But that," he pointed at the rectangle, "is the Brasilian flag!"

"What's Brasil?"

"A place. A country."

"Where? Beyond the mountains? Is it like the mayor's domain?"

"I don't know." He frowned. "That's all I can remember. But the words *Ordem e Progresso:* that means 'order and progress' . . . I think it does. Brasilian must be the other language I speak—for whatever good that does me." He got up.

Dog came bounding to them, something large and brown flopping in his jaws. Amanda grimaced, "Dog! Don't bring your carcasses to me—!"

"No, wait, it's not an animal. Come here, Dog! Bring it here, good boy . . ." The stranger held out his hand; Dog came to him obediently, tail beating. Amanda wondered if Dog knew a fellow outcast by instinct, or why he gave this one other person his trust. "It looks like a hat—" The stranger pried it loose from Dog's massive jaws, pounded his back in appreciation. Dog smiled, panting. "Could it be from around here?"

She shook her head.

He turned it in his hands: "It must be mine," and he looked inside. His breath caught. " 'Cristovão Hoffman,' " he said quietly. "Cristovão . . . I'm Cristovão Hoffmann!"

"Do you remember—?"

"No." His mouth pulled down. "No, I don't remember! Hell, for all I know Cristovão Hoffmann's the man who made that hat!" He looked back at her, defeated, set the hat on top of his bandages; it fell off. "But it doesn't matter. I'll be Cristovão Hoffmann; it doesn't feel so bad. I have to be somebody. Christ, maybe *I* made the hat." He started away across the field to the main wreckage, the mutilated skeleton of the flying ship. She picked up his hat, began to strip wheat from the stalks to fill it up.

When she reached the charred hulk of the flying ship, she found him lying senseless in the grass.

The clouds closed around him like soft wings as he reached the wreck, stealing him away from the dream world of his waking reality, back into the reality of his dreams. He chose a door: The clouds parted, and he was flying. . . .

Hoffmann followed the frayed brown-green ribbon of the river out of the mountains, looking down on the sun's anvil pocked with skeletal shrubs: the desert that stretched to the sea. "If anybody's crazy enough to live here now, they've got to be sane enough to stay by the water. . . ." On every side, for as far as he could see, a faint rectangular gridwork patterned the desolation. He caught occasional flickers of blinding whiteness, the sun mirrored on metal and glass. This was the Los Angeles basin: hundreds of square miles of accessible aluminum, steel and iron . . . copper, tungsten, rare earth elements . . . all the riches of a benevolent nature, waiting for discovery and recognition. Waiting for him. Waiting for him. . . . His skin itched with desire; tomorrow he would begin to explore.

But with the desperate scarcity of one thing—fossil fuels—no one would ever make use of his discovered bounty, unless there was an available pool of local labor to do what machines could not. He knew small primitive villages and colonies stretched northward up the coast from the South American continent, cut off from all but the most fragmentary dirigible contact with the Brasilian Hegemony: Today he would search for those. If there was an available subsistence agriculture the specialists could upgrade, then the local population, and even imported laborers, could be put to work mining the treacherous, possibly radioactive ruins. The people would have more food, better medical care—and lose their freedom of choice, and their lives, in grueling servitude to the government. It had been the way of governments since the first city-state, and though it troubled Hoffmann somewhat that he had a part in it now, he seldom thought about why. Prospecting was the one thing that gave any real meaning to his life, that evoked any real emotion in him: He endured his fellow men to the extent

that they made it possible for him to live the way he did;
beyond that, he chose to live without them.

He began to see the form of San Pedro Bay, promising for
shipping. From the air, the land was visibly patterned by ruins
beneath the amorphous sandpiled pavement of desert. The
bay was more deeply incut than he remembered on the maps,
with a scalloped rim. " 'Like a crater, Cristovão. . . .' " he
repeated. "Jesus, what a beautiful harbor!" He could see
signs of habitation now, a small mud-brick town, bright sails
in the harbor, fields and pasturage along the river. He used
his binoculars, thought he detected other signs of habitation
farther along the northwestward curve of the coast; pleased,
he dropped lower, buzzing the fields. "Some irrigation, primitive . . . bet they don't rotate their crops. . . ." Tiny figures
huddled, staring up at him, or fled the 'copter's shadow in
terror. They were as nonessential to him as the rest of humanity, less real than the shining, lifeless wilderness of the
desert.

And then, abruptly, the umbilical of vibrating roar that
gave him life within his glass-and-metal womb was cut. Faint
cries of fear and disbelief reached him through the windshield
glass, echoed in his mind, as he began to fall. . . .

The stranger jerked awake, sitting up from Amanda's lap in
the shade of the broken ship. His breath came hard; he rubbed
his sweating face. *"Mãe do Deus. . . ."* He looked back at
her, at the shadowing hull above them. "It happened again?"

She nodded.

"I was falling . . . *that* was falling, the—the *Careless
Love*. The electrical system was . . . was. . . . Damn it! Damn
it! It's in there, my whole life! But every time I reach for it, it
slips between my fingers . . . like mercury. . . ."

"Maybe if you didn't try, it would come. Maybe you try
too hard." She wondered what good it would do him to
know, but knew that even she would need to know.

"How am I supposed to stop trying?" He covered the
frustration in his voice. "Did I—say anything?"

"You said, 'Cristoval.' " The name wasn't quite the same,
when he pronounced it. "You said, 'Craters.' And that we

didn't . . . turn our crops around." She made circling motions with her hand.

"Rotate your crops," he said absently. "Alternate them, from field to field, season to season, to let the fields rest. It's good for the soil. . . ." He stopped. "Maybe I was some kind of advisor. Maybe I could teach your father better farming methods—"

A small, sharp laugh escaped her. "I don't think he'd listen to you. Not after he watched you struck down by God."

He grimaced, got up, staring at the burned-out wreck. He leaned down to pick up a handful of charred papers. "Maps. They're in English . . . but I can't read it anymore." He bunched them in his hand, didn't drop them, looking south across the bay. "It's a good harbor. And that's important. . . ."

"Yes, it is." She answered, knowing now that he didn't need an answer.

"Where do the ships go from here?"

"Mostly south, for a long way. In the southern lands there are airships that fly with balloons, not sorcery, and cross the mountains to a strange land." Her heart constricted.

"There are?" he said, suddenly excited. "If I could find a ship in port, to take me—"

"Not unless you could pay for it."

"How much?"

"More than nothing, which is all you have. And all I have."

"How am I supposed to get the money? I can't *do* anything!" His hand struck the blackened frame. *"Tamates!* I can't do anything . . . it's never going to come back. Let's go." He started abruptly back toward the road.

When they returned to the cottage, he took the leather hat and stood before the broken mirror on the wall. He began to unwrap the bandages that covered his head. As he pulled the final clinging strips away from his skin, she saw his hands drop, nerveless, to his sides; the streamer of bandage fluttered down. She saw his face in the mirror: the half-healed scar that gaped along his cheek and scalp, the stunned revulsion in his eyes.

"Cristoval," she whispered, "it was worse, before. It will be much better, in time. Much better. . . ." She met his eyes in the mirror, eyes as gray as sorrow.

He looked away; went to the door, and out, wordlessly.

She sat weaving, waiting, through the hot autumn afternoon, but he did not return. She watched the cloth grow as she passed the shuttle back, and back again, through the taut threads; thinking how much it had grown, in so short a time, because the stranger had come into her life. She went down to the river, but he was not there; she bathed, and washed her hair. Suppertime came, and passed. Dog sat in the doorway, whining into the twilight. Hungry for broiled fish, she drank water and ate dry bread. . . . He would fell the dead orange tree, he had said, before it fell on her house . . . he would build her a palmleaf canopy in the yard to shade her while she cooked. A fence of adobe bricks . . . a henhouse . . . a shower . . . a real bed. A life for a life. . . .

She blew out the candle, lay down on her pallet of straw and in the darkness remembered the feel of his body against her, the touch of his hands. He had gone out into the desert; he would walk toward the unreachable mountains, trying to go home. And he would lie down at last and die, alone, and the buzzards would pick his bones. She heard the tolling of the midnight bells: Pitiless and unforgiving, they mocked her, and named her, *Amanda, Amanda.* . . .

"Amanda?" The door rattled; Dog leaped to his feet, barking joyfully. "Amanda? Will you let me in?"

She ran to the door, wrapped in her blanket, her hair streaming. She unbolted it, threw it open; the light of the full moon struck her face. Cristoval's shadowed eyes looked long on her, in silence. At last he stepped forward, into the house. She lit a candle as he bolted the door, brought him bread and a pitcher of water. He drank deeply, sighed. She sat across from him at the table, covering her face with a corner of her blanket, but feeling no embarrassment. She didn't ask where he had been, he didn't tell her; he kept his face slightly averted, hiding his scar.

"Amanda—" He finished the bread, drank again. "Tell me why you're not married."

She started. "What, now?"

"Yes, now. Please."

"I have no dowry," she said simply, hoping he would understand that much and let it go. "No man would take me."

An unreadable expression crossed his face. "But your father must be a wealthy man, he owns all these fields—why does he treat you like this; why do you live in this hovel?"

She reddened. "He's very generous to let me live here! I defied him, and he disowned me. He didn't have to give me anything; I would have been like you. But he lets me stay in this cottage, and glean in his fields. I suppose he would have been ashamed to watch his daughter become a beggar or a whore."

"Why did you disobey him? What did you do?"

"I wouldn't marry the man chosen for me. He was a good man; but I thought—I thought I was in love. . . ." She tasted bitterness, remembering the red-haired girl she had once been: who sat with her embroidery for hours at the window, gazing out over the bay, who wept with unconsolable loss, for her heart had been stolen, and she had not had the strength to follow it; who found that the staid ritual of life in Sanpedro was suffocating her, and her dreams were dying. *He said he would come back* . . . and she had believed him, and vowed that she would wait for him.

But her father had known none of that, thinking only that his spindly, homely daughter longed to marry any man; that it was high time to get her a husband, to make order out of her foolish maiden's fancies. And when he had told her of the match, she had run sobbing from the room and sworn that she would never marry. Her father raged, her mother scolded, her sisters wept and pleaded. But she sat as still and unreachable as her aged grandmother, who rocked endlessly by the fire, blind with cataracts, and deaf: who had had hair of flame, like her own, once, in youth. . . .

And at last her father had given her an ultimatum, and in her childish vanity she had spurned the marriage, and he had disowned her. He had given her dowry to Teresa, ungainly of body but fair of heart, and for Teresa he had chosen well—a man who desired her for her soul, and not for her riches.

"And so I came to live here, and learned what it is to be poor. My vanity starved to death, long ago. But by then it was too late." She glanced down at the rough hand holding the blanket edge. "There is no end to my sin, no end to my punishment, now." Her hand slid down, taking the blanket with it; Cristoval looked at her strangely. She pulled it back up, defensive. "I am still a virgin; my marriage sheets would not dishonor my husband. But I don't have a maiden's soul . . ." She felt her words fading. "In my mind, lying alone at night, I have sinned, and sinned. . . ." She reddened again, remembering her thoughts this night. "Sweet Ángel; I'm so tired!" Her voice shook. "I would gladly have married, a hundred times over, by now! But what man would have me now?"

She heard Cristoval draw a long breath. "I would have you. Amanda . . . will you marry me?"

Her blush deepened with anger. "You! Do you think I don't know why you're asking me? I may be just a woman, but I'm not such a fool that I can't see what you've been trying to do to me. You've smiled, and wheedled, and tried to make me depend on you, so that when you were well I wouldn't make you leave. And so you'd even marry me, to save yourself?"

"Well, what the hell's wrong with that?" His scarred hand knotted on the table. "You just told me you'd marry anybody, to save yourself from the hardship, and the loneliness. Why is it wrong for me to want the same thing? I don't want to die a friendless beggar in this self-righteous hell, either! I'm not asking you to love me—I don't love you. I want to marry you to save myself, because there's no other way I can; that's all. If you accept, take me out of your own need. I'll be a good husband to you. I'll carry my share of the weight. Together, maybe we could even make a decent life for ourselves." He glanced down, turned his face squarely to her in the light. "God knows I'm not much to look at, now, Amanda. But . . . but in the dark—"

She studied his face, her eyes catching only once on the scar, used to it from dressing his wound. Apart from it his face was pleasant, almost handsome now with familiarity, under the short, sun-faded hair. He was no more than thirty, perhaps no older than herself: He was strong and, behind the strangeness of his peculiar habits, somehow gentle. She did not think he would beat her. And— "And I'm not . . . much to look at, either, now; I know." She sighed. "Love is not a right to demand in marriage. Love is a reward. Yes, then, Cristoval; I will be your wife. Tomorrow we will go to see my father." Her shoulders sagged; pulling the blanket close around her, she rose and went to her bed.

Cristoval followed her with his eyes before he blew out the candle. She heard him lie down on his own pallet, heard his voice in the darkness: "Thank you."

They walked slowly along the road to town, silently. Amanda listened to the creaking gulls and the twittering waking sparrows. *This is my wedding day*, she thought, surprised. *Will I be different tomorrow, if we're wed? Will he?* She glanced at Cristoval, his face turned away toward the sea. He didn't touch her but walked as though he were entirely alone, brooding. *Everything will be different. I've lived alone for so long. . . .*

"Amanda," he said suddenly, startling her. "Do we have to go to your father?" Her breath caught; she saw that they were passing the field where his ruined ship lay. "I mean, isn't there—a priest, or somebody, who could just marry us quietly, instead?"

She saw the unhealed wound that still lay behind his eyes, felt her own fear drain out of her. "Each man is his own priest, with the Prophet's Book to guide him. My father must give us his blessing, or we will be living in sin, and no better off than we were alone. We'll go to my sister first, she can speak to Father for me; and, I hope, make him listen—"

He sighed, nodded. " *'Casamento e mortalha, no céu se talha. . . .'* "

"What?" She looked up at him.

He shrugged. " 'Marriages and shrouds are made in heaven.' "

José came to the door of his house; surprise showed on his face, and then incredulity. "Ámanda!"

"José. This is . . . this is my bethrothed, Cristoval . . . Hoffmann." She struggled with the word.

"By the Book. . . . Teresa! Amanda's here. And"—he laughed—"by the Prophet Ángel, she's brought a man with her!"

Teresa, José, and the laughing children went ahead of her as they reached her father's courtyard at last; Cristoval walked grimly beside her. Her heart fluttered like bird wings under the wedding vest, beaded with pearls, that Teresa had given her to cover her faded dress. Cristoval wore one of José's robes, a vest and head-covering, in place of his poncho and his flopping hat. He could pass for a townsman; but she knew that it would not fool her father. The sun's heat made her suddenly giddy.

The heavy door of the house swung open, and Diego Montoya came out into the yard. His broad, jowled face widened with a smile at the sight of his grandchildren; they danced around him, chanting, "Aunt Amanda's getting married!"

Her father's obsidian eyes flickered up, seeing her in her wedding vest, seeing the scarred stranger beside her. "Teresa, what's the meaning of this?" Behind him her mother came to the door, and her sister Estella.

Teresa hung on her husband's shoulder, his arm around her waist, steadying her. "Father, Amanda has asked me to speak to you for her. This man would take her for his wife, even though she hasn't any dowry. Please, Father, she begs your forgiveness for the past; she asks you to give her in marriage, so that she may live as a dutiful wife, and—and make amends for the grief that her willfulness has caused you."

Her father stared at Cristoval, the words lost in the rising fury of his realization. "Amanda!" He spoke directly to her for the first time in eight years; she dropped her eyes, despairing. "What new mockery is this?" He came toward them; his hand closed on the cloth of Cristoval's head-covering. He jerked it off, revealing the ragged wound and the short, sun-faded hair. Her father threw the cloth to the ground, disgusted, moved away again. "Why do you shame me this way?'' He turned back, his voice agonized. "How have I offended God, that such a creature was born a child of mine? How can you come here, and tell me you would marry this—" He gestured, his hand constricted into a fist.

"Father!" Teresa said, appalled, not understanding. The children hung on her skirts, eyes wide.

"By the Son of God, I won't stand for it! No more; no more humiliation, Amanda!" He reached down, caught up a stone. He lifted his hand.

Amanda cried out, cringing. Cristoval pressed against her, his body as rigid as metal.

José moved forward, caught his father-in-law's arm. "Father, no!" He pulled the hand down, his arm straining; Montoya glared at him. "Forgive me, Father. But I won't let you do such a thing before the children." He shook his head. "What's this man done to make you hate him?"

Amanda's father looked at the stone. "He's the sorcerer whose machine fell into my field. He is despised by God; it was God's will that he should die; no man would raise a hand to help him. But my—daughter," the word cut her, she flinched, "would defy natural law, defy God, again, to help him. And now she asks to marry him. Marry him! God should strike them both dead!"

"Perhaps He's punished them enough," José said quietly. "Even a sorcerer can repent and be forgiven."

Cristoval put his arm around Amanda. "Sir—" She heard a tremor in his voice, very faint. "God—God has stripped the evil thoughts from my mind; I can't remember anything of what I was." He touched his head. "I only want to marry your daughter, and live quietly; nothing more."

"Nothing?" Montoya said sourly.

"I don't demand a dowry. In fact, I'll give you a . . . a bride payment for her, instead."

Amanda's eyes widened; she saw every face turn to stare at her, at Cristoval.

"What kind of a payment?" The merchant pressed forward into her father's eyes.

"You use metals, don't you? Aluminum? Steel? I'll give you my ship in the field, what's left of it."

"It's accursed; it's full of demons."

"You have rituals to purify metals. If the ship was your own to make into . . . natural objects, the curse could be lifted. . . ."

The merchant weighed and considered.

"There must be at least half a ton of usable scrap metals left there. Maybe more."

"Oh, please, Father!" Teresa burst out. "Think of the honor it does you. No one has ever made such an offer, for anyone's daughter!" Amanda saw tears wetting her mother's veil, felt the look of astonished envy in Estella's dark and perfect eyes. She suddenly saw that one of the eyes was not perfect, swollen by a black-and-purple bruise. Amanda looked away.

"Half a ton . . . ?" her father was saying. He drew himself up. "The mayor's men came here looking for you, you know. In case you were still alive."

"No," Cristoval said. "I didn't know." His hand tightened on Amanda's shoulder. "Why? What does that mean?"

"Nothing." Her father shrugged. "Your body was gone from the field. I told them God had taken it away to hell— what else could I say? I thought you were dead. So did they; they seemed relieved." A smile struggled in the folds of his face. "The mayor has halved my field tribute this harvest, because of the miracle." He dropped the stone, sighed. "Half a ton. It must surely be God's will in the matter. . . . All right, Amanda, I will see you wed. But that is all. We'll go to the temple now. And then I will call a gathering, to bless the machine."

Amanda knelt by Cristoval before the altar in the silent temple while her father pronounced the words above them, and her family looked on. There would be no ritual, no feasting, no celebration. It was nothing like her dreams. . . . *But the dreams go away forever.* She remembered how long it had been since she had prayed in the temple; it had been too far to walk into town, to be met by stares and whispered scorn. She gazed without emotion at the rainbow of light that broke across the dusty tiles, below the altar window fused from colored shards of glass.

And then she followed her husband home, walking two paces behind him, eyes downcast.

He caught fish for their wedding supper while she finished the new piece of cloth on her loom, trying to recall the habits of a dutiful wife. Silent, patient, obedient . . . she had not been any of those, to her stranger-husband, until now. She must please him, now, and learn to make the best of it.

But as the evening passed she felt his irritation at her awkward deference, and, not understanding, she tried harder; felt her tension grow, and her resentment.

"Damn it, Amanda, what's the matter with you!"

She looked up at him meekly. "Forgive me, my husband. Have I displeased you?"

"Yes." He frowned from his seat at the table. "What the hell is this silent treatment? And why wouldn't you walk beside me today?" His hand covered his cheek, unconsciously. "Are you that ashamed to be married to me?"

"No!" Tears of exasperation blurred her eyes. "No. You've honored me greatly, in the eyes of my family. But it's proper for a woman to defer to a man, in speech, in actions . . . in all things."

"Even if he's wrong?"

"Yes." Her hands clenched on the cloth of her dress. "But, of course, a man is never wrong."

"Mother of God, Amanda—you don't believe that?" He looked at her. "I'm a man. Up until now I've made plenty of mistakes, and you haven't been afraid to let me know about them."

"I—I'm sorry. It's just that I've lived alone for so long . . . but I'll change. I want to be a good wife to you." A tear burned her cheek, caught on her veil.

"You can be; just stay the way you were. Do what you want, talk when you feel like it. Don't hang on me! I haven't got the patience for it. I—I think I've lived alone for a long time, too, Amanda, and I don't want to have to change my habits; I don't expect you to change yours. We're sharing space in time, that's all. Let's do it as painlessly as possible."

"If that is what you wish, my husband . . ."

"Amanda!" His anger slapped her. "None of this 'my

husband,' 'my wife.' It's just Cristovão, and Amanda. And in the future, walk with me, not behind me; I felt like I owned a servant, a slave. . . .'' He rubbed his head, staring into space.

"But it's the custom; every wife follows her husband." She felt a terrible relief begin to loosen her knotted muscles.

"Not your sister Teresa."

"She's crippled. José has to help her walk."

"She does fine on a crutch. I don't think that's why he does it at all. I think it's because he wants her there."

Amanda wiped her eyes, startled, amazed. "But—but, you and I, people would . . . laugh at us."

"So what? After a while they won't even notice us anymore." He stood up, came toward her; her heart beat faster. "And the veil—"

She jerked away from him, appalled. "Would you humiliate me so, before every man in town—?"

"No." He caught her arm. "No, Amanda. But in our home you can let me see your face, can't you? You *are* my wife, now." He drew her veil down gently, pulled the cloth from her hair. Her hair came undone, spilled loose over her shoulders; he filled his hands with it. "Like spun copper . . . spun gold . . . like flame. . . .'' She stood very still. His hands found the laces of her leather vest, untied them; his voice was husky. "I . . . just want you to know that, in town today, you were the most beautiful woman I saw."

Like flame. . . . She heard nothing more. On her wedding night she lay at last with her husband, and dreamed that the man who made love to her was someone else.

The days passed, and the weeks, and the months; Sanpedro entered the gentle season of winter. Amanda did as her husband wished by doing as she always did, self-consciously at first, but easily and gratefully again, in time, as she came to realize how much her independence had grown to be a part of her, a source of pride and integrity, a defense against the indignities of life.

As he had promised, Cristoval worked hard, sharing the endless tasks of her daily existence and freeing her to make the cloth that was their only item of trade for the village market. He walked with her, too, for miles along the sea's shining edge, on the days when she gathered the tiny fluted shells she used to make lavender dye. He questioned her about her discovery; she told him how she had boiled them in salty water, desperate with hunger; how the tiny sea snails had been inedible, but how, because they turned the water purple, she had never been as hungry again. Cristoval had looked out across the bay, where Dog plunged beside them, shattering the foam. "You'll never be hungry again, Amanda; we'll never be hungry, if I can help it."

Farther along the beach they had come on a dead fish mired in a clot of greasy black scum. Cristoval squatted down beside it, took some on his fingers and sniffed it, fascinated.

"It's the sea filth, that fouls the water's surface and can kill fish and birds." She waved Dog back. "It happens farther up the coast, too; at Santabarbara."

Cristoval wiped his fingers on the sand. "Does it?" His voice was wondering. "But that's good! It's oil, Amanda; don't you know what that means? It means they can establish a major outpost here, they can put in wells . . . they can mine metals with—with gook labor. . . ."

"Who can?" she asked, frightened.

He stopped, staring at her strangely. He touched her arm for a moment, as though to reassure her, or reassure himself of her reality. "I don't know," he muttered. "Nobody, I hope."

Late in the winter he had gone to her father and asked permission to till a part of the grassy pastureland adjoining the wheat fields in return for half the crop. Amanda had protested unhappily, saying they could glean enough to get by on and that it was too much extra work. But he had said it would be an investment in the future and worth it a hundred-fold: "You were right in what you told me once, Amanda. With a man like your father, you don't tell him things. You show him. . . ."

And when the wheat grew up past her knees, past her waist, almost up to her breasts, she had begun to understand the method in the madness of tilling fresh ground. And the method had not escaped the merchant's eye of her father, either, for he began to ask Cristoval questions, rewarding them with a cow and, in time, even asking them into his home.

Amanda had blossomed with the spring, the ache of hunger forgotten, and the aching weariness that had aged her before her time. She would never be plump and comely like her sisters, but she took a secret pleasure in the new soft curves that she discovered in the broken mirror on the wall. Cristoval fished and worked their field; she wove and tended the green sprouts in the garden patch; the work was still unending, but now it filled her with hope and pride instead of hopeless despair. At night she no longer lay sleepless hearing the midnight bells, but fell into dreams quickly and easily. And if in her dreams she sometimes found a face that she reached for with longing and could never forget, she knew that her regret was nothing to her husband's in his longing for the things he might never remember. He was a thoughtful and satisfying lover; he brought peace and fulfillment to her body, if not her soul.

The sudden fits of haunted sleep that took him through the locked doors of his mind to walk in his forgotten past grew more and more infrequent; though his hair grew in pure white along the seam of the scar. As the dreams faded, his interest in them seemed almost to fade as well. He no longer grew angry because she couldn't describe their details to him, and the projects and problems of his new life left him little strength or time for seeking after the old one.

But as he stopped pressing to remember, more and more bits and fragments of his life began to rise unbidden to the surface of his mind. A rare animation would take him, and carry her with him, when he remembered a place he had traveled to see and described to her the brief, bright flashes of its terrifying wonder: A forest of tree and shrub that grew so densely that he had hacked his way through it with a hatchet, to find a gleaming mound of shattered glass, stitched with vine, embroidered by fragile blossoms in the colors of dawn. . . . A ruined city filled with bones, on a treeless plain beneath a sullen, metallic sky; a wind so bitterly cold that the rain froze into stinging pellets. . . . The shadow of a man long dead, imprisoned by some ancient sorcery forever in the surface of a building wall. . . .

He rarely mentioned people or memories of his own land, only the memories of searching the strange and alien ruins of the "Northern Hemisphere." He never seemed to wonder whether someone was searching for him, or waiting for him, or mourning for him. She wondered whether he chose not to tell her of a wife or lover or friends, or whether there was truly no one he wanted to remember. For, at first, he had seldom spoken to her at all about things that didn't directly concern her. Instead he would mumble to himself, answering himself, oblivious. She discovered gradually that it was not because he believed that, being a woman, she would have nothing to say; but rather because he lived, somehow, completely within himself—as though two men lived together in one, behind his eyes: Perhaps, she thought, there were two men; the old one, and the new.

But his solitary conversations aggravated her, as her own traditional behavior had aggravated him. She had learned not to be silent, and so she began to answer him, stubbornly, chipping at the shell of his isolation. And after a time, as though, like herself, he had had to learn that he could, he began to talk to her instead; became a companion for her lonely days, and not just a silent presence in her house.

Spring passed into summer, blistering summer moved again into fall. Amanda let herself be carried by the flow of unnumbered days, thoughtlessly, unquestioningly. At last one day she left the marketplace in the heat of noon, climbing slowly past the shuttered houses along the curving street. The sea breeze was strong, tangy with salt and the tartness of seaweed, sweeping her skirts ahead of her. She was poorer by one piece of cloth, richer by a basket of fruits and cheese, a razor and a new pair of leather sandals for Cristoval, a bangle of copper and colored stones: She looked down at her wrist, bare for so many years; touched the bracelet, feeling as light-footed as a girl with joy. Brightness danced along it like sunlight across the sea; she kept her eyes on it and forgot the hot, weary journey home to the cottage.

She looked up only once, stopping in the shadow of the date palms to gaze out at the field where Cristoval's airship had lain. There was no sign now that it had ever existed; the freshly turned earth lay waiting for the winter crop. She smiled briefly and went on her way.

She opened the gate in the new-made fence, her eyes searching the yard for Cristoval . . . heard voices from behind the cottage, strangers' voices. She walked quietly through the shadow beside the house, looked out again into brightness, shielding her eyes. She saw Cristoval sitting on the milking stool beside the spotted cow, listening to two men she had never seen before. Dog lay warily beside him.

" . . . report to the Brasilian government on the feasibility of mining the Los Angeles basin. But you never came back, and so we came looking . . ."

Amanda dropped her basket. Her hand rose to her mouth; she bit her knuckles to keep from crying out.

" . . . the fossil-fuel situation is too critical, we can't afford to clean out the canal now. The Venezuelan war's reached a stalemate; we'll have to stop all further plans for expansion of our mining operations, unless someone like you can discover an independent source of oil or coal—" The speaker looked at Cristoval hopefully.

Cristoval shrugged, his face polite and expressionless, his hand covering his scar. "How did you—find me, here?"

"The 'miracle' of your crash filtered down the coast. We didn't know if we'd find you alive or dead, or not at all. But we had to come and see; you're that important, Hoffmann."

He laughed uncomfortably. "I don't know why . . ."

"Because you're the best damned prospector in Brasil—"

"It doesn't matter, for Christ's sake," the second man said. "You know you don't belong here, Hoffmann. Let us get you out of this dirty, godforsaken hole. There are doctors in Brasil who can treat your problem; you'll remember everything, in time. At least you'll be back in civilization again, living like a human being, and not like a dog." He glanced down, his disgust showing.

Cristoval stood up slowly.

Amanda shut her eyes; Cristoval's face patterned on her eyelids. And in her mind she saw him clearly for the first time: her husband; the strange and gentle stranger who had come to her door, accursed, hopeless, and changed her own accursed, hopeless life forever. She pressed back against the warm wall, not breathing.

"No. I'm sorry." Cristoval shook his head. "I'm not going with you."

"Diablo!" the first man said. "Why not? Coelho didn't risk coming six thousand kilometers on a sailing ship, dressed like a peon, for you to turn him down!"

"He didn't come for me at all. He came for the . . . government."

"We need you, Hoffmann. We can force you to go with us—"

Dog growled where he lay, the hair on his back ridging.

"I don't think so." Cristoval smiled faintly. "I don't know what you want of me; I don't think I ever will. I don't even know what oil looks like anymore. I might as well be dead, for all the good I'd be to you. I'm content here; let's just leave it at that."

"Hoffmann." The second man looked at him with pity and dismay. "Can't you *feel* what you're giving up? If you could only know what your old life meant to you: Can't you remember, don't you know the discoveries you've made; the things you must have seen; the knowledge that's still locked inside your mind . . . how important you were to your people?"

Cristoval kept his smile. "I only know how important I am, to someone, now—and someone is to me."

The second man looked puzzled. He produced something from inside his sleeveless coat. "You're right; you might as well be dead. Take this, then; in case you ever . . . remember, and want a way out. It's a distress beacon; they'll pick it up in El Paso. We'll try to send someone to you."

"All right." Cristoval took the dark, hand-sized box.

"Seja feliz, Hoffmann. Adeus."

"Good-bye."

The two men turned, started back across the yard toward her. Amanda picked up her basket, stood stiffly, with dignity, as they noticed her and, staring, passed on by.

"Hoffmann's?" the first man said, incredulous.

"Será possível—!" the second man murmured, looking at her, shaking his head. *"Deus dá o frio conforme a roupa. . . ."*

When they were gone from the yard, she ran to Cristoval,

clung to him, wordless. The strange box jabbed her back as he put his arms around her.

"Amanda! What's the matter?"

"Oh, my husband." She sighed, against his robe. "Who—who were those men?" She glanced up, watching his face.

"Nobody . . . nobody important." He smiled; but the old sorrow showed in his eyes, like a colorless flame. He pried himself loose from her gently, looked down at the hard, almost featureless box still clutched in his hand. He threw it away over the fence. "Nobody who'll ever hurt you now. My prospecting days are over. . . ." He sighed, put his arm around her again, drew her close; he reached down to scratch Dog's leathery ears. "But you know, Amanda, in time, if we ever have any money, we could take a ship along the coast, see the south. Maybe we'd even find those balloon airships of yours." He laughed. "But we won't take a ride in one! Would you like that?"

She nodded, resting her head on his shoulder. "Yes, my husband; I'd like that very much."

"Amanda . . ." he said, surprised, wonderingly. "My wife. My wife."

AFTERWORD—
PHOENIX IN THE ASHES

This story was described by one reviewer as "a Southern California love story with a difference."

I often get the inspiration for a story from a song. This story was inspired by two different songs, one by Judy Collins, called "Albatross," and the other an old folk song called "Take Me Out of Pity." The former is a haunting love song that I'd always imagined taking place in a kind of Arthur Rackham fantasy world; but a friend of mine envisioned it as happening in New England, and there is a line in it about "a Spanish friend of the family." The other song, also known as "The Old Maid's Lament," is a traditional song with a much more pragmatic outlook. Somehow the two songs and all the disparate images fused in my mind, and with further input from my first husband, Vernor, as I was trying to plot a story around them, the novelette ended up taking place in Southern California after a nuclear war. (Two potential alternate scenarios involved a woman in colonial times becoming involved with a humanoid alien stranded on Earth, or a war between populations of a double planet system. I still wonder sometimes what the story would have turned into if I'd followed either of those ideas through; they may yet mutate into something else and turn up in some future story I write.)

Originally I'd intended to call the story "Take Me Out of Pity," which I saw as having a nice double meaning, in the context. But my editor asked me to reconsider, saying that if some critic happened to dislike the story, calling it "Take Me Out of Pity" was like "putting your head on the block and handing someone the ax." I changed the title. (I seem to have a knack for picking arcane titles. I originally wanted to call my novel The Snow Queen "Carbuncle," after the city in which most of the action takes place. I liked the ambience of a word that meant either "jewel" or "fester" —the city being both—but unfortunately people who only know the meaning "fester" seem to far outnumber the ones who know both meanings. I got very mixed reactions when I told people what I was calling the book ... some nods and smiles, a lot of blanching. I was finally convinced, by another editor, not to call my novel Fester. Now, quite frankly, even I can't imagine why I ever wanted to.)

VOICES FROM THE DUST

4:30. 4:30 in the morning. 4:30 and fifteen Martian seconds. . . . Petra Greenfeld picked up the wood-grained electric clock and shook it. *Hurry up! Hurry up . . . or else stop.* She set it down on the desk again, too hard in the low gravity, and rubbed her eyes. *To think I've been up all night, and there isn't even a man in my room. I really must be crazy.* She laughed, weakly. *How can I be crazy and have a sense of the absurd?*

But then why was she sitting here, if she wasn't crazy? Why had she been sitting here all night, like someone condemned, waiting for the dawn? Why wasn't she asleep in her bed like any normal human being—? She swiveled her chair to look at the rumpled sleeping bag on the cot. Because when she slept the pull was stronger, it pried open her dreams and painted the walls of her mind with the red walls of the Valley, and led her, again and again, to an unknown destination. . . .

"Oh, *stop* it." She shut her eyes, and turned back to the desk. She wasn't obsessed; she was just upset. Why shouldn't she be upset—that damned Mitradati! Her fist tightened on the graffiti-covered blotter. That egotistical tin god. So he was sending her back to "civilization" today, was he? So her poor, frail little mind needed a rest, did it? Just wait until she got back to Little Earth and made her complaint. They'd let her conduct her investigation without interference, they'd see that her judgments weren't irrational. And that narrow-minded

45

apeman could go suck an egg. . . . Better yet, why couldn't
she take one of the buggies, and go to the place first? She'd
find her proof, she knew where to look, exactly where—

She got up from her chair, shaking her head, and began to
move restlessly around the small room. Think about something else, anything else. . . . *My God, am I really losing my
mind? This isn't normal.* Maybe it would be best to get away
from here, for a while; from Mitradati, from—the artifact.
She hadn't been up to the pole in weeks, hadn't seen a movie,
or had a decent dinner, or called Fred. And stuck here with
this baker's half-dozen of impossible— No. She couldn't
really blame them. Who had been more impossible than she
had, these past two weeks?

She looked over at Elke's unused bed, under the curve
where the ceiling became the outer wall. Elke had been
sleeping with Sergei lately, and she suspected it was as much
from uneasiness about her as it was from passion. At least
Elke was sympathetic, and supportive . . . but Elke was a
meteorologist, not a geologist, and what did she know? And
Sergei, with his damned Russian obsession about parapsy-
chology; making the whole idea sound like something out of a
Grade Z science fiction movie. She was glad he had Elke to
distract him, before his endless prying curiosity made her do
something she would regret.

She saw the cigarettes and lighter Elke had left on the stool
by her cot. She picked up the pack mindlessly, took out a
cigarette, lit it, inhaled—and, coughing disgustedly, ground it
out with her slipper on the cold metal floor. *At least I haven't
gone completely insane.* She went back to the desk, looked at
the clock again. 4:43. Dawn . . . soon it would be dawn. But
why was dawn so important? The hopper wouldn't be going
to the north pole until afternoon, on their bi-weekly supply
run; this time taking her along in disgrace at Mitradati's
order. That was why she was upset, and angry, why she
couldn't stop thinking about the artifact—

The artifact: she had seen it lying like a diamond in the
rubbly detritus along a canyon wall, twelve days ago, as she
and Mitradati had collected rock specimens. And the moment
she had seen it, touched it, she had known, she had *known*—
It appeared to be a lump of fused ore, unusual, but not

extraordinary. Yet somehow she had sensed an unrightness about it, an unnaturalness. And when she had tested it and found an alloy that had never been known to form outside of a laboratory, she had dared to tell the others about her suspicion . . . about her belief: That this piece of metal could never have been produced by natural geologic processes, that it had been made by an intelligent, alien life-form. And furthermore, that its presence could be a key to an even greater discovery—proof that humanity was not alone.

The reaction had been immediate, and negative. Even she had realized—still realized—that the idea was incredible. Some of the others, Taro, Shailung, hadn't been totally unreasonable; suggesting that it might be a piece of space junk, something from their orbital lab. But Shiraz Mitradati had rejected the idea coldly, in spite of having no better explanation—calling it, and by implication her judgment, irrational. She had argued with him, pointing out that her past work with an archeological crew had given her a feel for geological samples that were something more . . . that even a conservative estimate claimed observers from another star system would visit this one once in every million years; no time at all, in geologic terms.

She had gone on arguing with him, continuously, while her conviction grew that the most valuable discovery they would ever make on Mars must lie somewhere here in the Mariner Valley. And as her conviction grew that out in the thousands of square kilometers of this tremendous canyon system, she alone could find that proof . . .

Petra wrapped the collar of her bathrobe tightly under her chin. Even though this small temporary base was buried under two meters of insulating soil, the determined Martian cold crept in, and it was always coldest just before the dawn. *And darkest.* Anger drove the chill out of her again as she remembered Mitradati's contemptuous sarcasm, the hostility lying so clearly below the surface of his 'rational' mind: "Simply because it's 2001, Petra, that doesn't mean an alien monolith is waiting for us." The taunt still stung her. . . . No: Haunted her. *Haunted*— She remembered the look on his face, as though he hadn't expected to say the words himself. And she remembered the almost physical pain as the words burst into stars behind her eyes. In that instant certainty had crystalized out of the vague urges moving her forward, and she had *known* what she had to do. As she knew it now. . . .

Petra swore softly and crossed the room to her dresser, pulled open a drawer. The first time she had seen Shiraz Mitradati, among the scientists awaiting departure from L2 for the journey to Mars, she had been strongly attracted to him. But it had been purely a physical attraction, and abruptly short-circuited. Mitradati was an Iranian: although Iran had used its oil money to catch up with the 20th Century (before clean hydrogen fusion had made oil obsolete), she had discovered that social progress—at least as far as Mitradati was concerned—had not kept up with technological progress. He was a believer in Iran's old regime, who would have been much happier in her presence, she suspected, if she'd been wearing a veil.

But once they reached Little Earth on Mars they had gone their separate ways, on separate research projects; up until three months ago, when she had joined this particular geological team, a team that Shiraz Mitradati was nominally in charge of. Neither Elke nor Shai-lung seemed to feel the same irritation with Mitradati that she did, and she had wondered whether it was all her own fault, her own outspokenness, her own opinionation. . . . *Damn it! I'm teaching at Harvard because I happen to have something to say.* It took two to make an argument. Shiraz had refused a perfectly reasonable request to let her investigate her find more fully, and his growing irrational hostility had nothing to do with 'reason' or 'logic.' It was no wonder her own conviction had hardened into an obsession; that even while she was awake the need to go on with her search filled her mind. He had no right to stop her; why should she let him stand in her way, she didn't have to—

Petra blinked, shivering violently; found herself half-naked, in the act of getting dressed. She stood for a moment staring down at the bulky red sweater clutched between her hands in a death-grip, watched her hands begin to tremble. Then she pulled the sweater roughly on over her head, fastened her pants, and sat down to put on her worn sneakers. She could see the clock on the desk: almost 5:00. A quarter of an hour left until dawn; now was the time, before anyone else was awake. She couldn't afford to have anyone stop her now—she stood at the mirror, folding her straight black hair into a knot at the back of her head, fastening it with a clip; moving methodically now, her face frozen into placidity. Dark eyes stared back at her from the mirror, her own eyes, screaming at her silently, *What are you doing to me?* She shook her head at the caged image, *"Oy, Gottenyu,* Petra—" She picked up her flashlight and left the room.

She walked silently down the dim hallway, knowing that the room partitions were paper thin. She slipped into the dark stairwell midway along it, switched on her flashlight and went down the steps into the storage area. She needed a vehicle, her pressure suit, and—the other thing she had to find. She moved cautiously among piled crates and equipment, following a thin streamer of light through the dark room, and through the blackness that clotted her brain. This was the right thing, the only rational thing to do . . . *then why am I so afraid?*

The room filled with light, an explosion against her senses. She cried out in surprise and protest, turning—

"Shiraz!" Squinting against the sudden brightness she pulled the figure into focus. She raised her hand with the flashlight to shield her eyes, half threatening. "What are you doing here?" An accusation.

"I might ask the same of you." She thought there was a trace of sullenness in his accented Oxford English.

"I'm going to prove I'm right. I'm going out to find . . . to find—it." She glanced down, confused, as the image slipped away from her. She looked up again, brandishing the heavy flashlight as he moved. "Don't get in my way, Shiraz! I'll kill you if I have to," knowing, desperately, that she meant every word of it.

"I know you will. I'd do the same, to you, to anybody, now." He moved away from the out-curve of the wall, coming toward her, his hands open and empty. "Petra, listen to me. I'm not here to stop you. I've come for the same reason you have."

"Don't try to humor me, Shiraz. It won't work."

"Humor you! For God's sake! Do I look like I want to be

here?'' He was close enough now that she could see his eyes, see the fury and the desperation that mirrored her own. ''I don't want to be here! But I couldn't help myself . . . I couldn't stop it. Could you—?'' with something in his voice that she had never heard before.

''No.'' She shook her head, her hand dropped to her side. ''I couldn't stop it, either. . . . But all this time, you denied it! Why?''

''How could I admit to a thing like that? That I heard 'voices' whispering in my head—like some bloody lunatic. People would have thought I was mad!'' She saw his fists tighten, and waited for the outburst. But he only said at last, wearily, ''I'm sorry.''

She looked down, rubbing her hand across her mouth. ''Yes, so am I. We should try not to make this any harder than it is.'' She realized for the first time that he was already wearing his pressure suit. She turned away, picking a path through the boxes and equipment to the locker, to take out her own suit. She watched her tiny, crumpled image reflecting over and over as she pulled it on. ''We'll have to hurry if we want to get out of here before anyone wakes up.'' She listened to her mind, watching her body obey it unquestioningly—the way a stranger would, the way she watched her reflections move, echoes of her self.

''I know.'' Shiraz tested his air tanks.

''We have explosives here, don't we? Where are they? We'll need them—''

''It's taken care of. I've already put what we want in the back of the buggy.''

''Good.'' She nodded, checking her own suit. ''Do you—do you know why?''

''No. Do you?''

''No.'' She looked away, down the long half-cylinder of the lower level, toward the air lock. ''I don't like being somebody's golem.''

She walked slowly along the floor platform, awkward in her insulated suit, to the balloon-tired exploration vehicles parked side by side. ''Which one?''

Shiraz followed. ''The first one. That's where I put the bomb.''

She opened the door and climbed in on the driver's side; he got in on the other, without protest. She wondered whether he was too tense to drive; managed a brief sympathy for the extra strain his inability to accept this nightmarish loss of control must add to the tangle of emotions that already held them both. She leaned past the seat's headrest, glanced into the back of the pressurized cab; saw the drab, unremarkable metal container waiting, and the red radiation trefoil on its side. "Oh, my God . . ." They had set off small, clean atomic blasts to create measurable seismic tremors in their analysis of the planet's core. *But why do we need one now?* She turned back, fastening her safety harness. "Do you know how to detonate one of these? I've never—worked with one."

He shrugged, wiping away sweat. "I've watched it done."

She nodded. She checked the fuel gauge, not sure how far they were going: Full, as usual, a full one liter of water. She started the fusion power unit.

They passed through the lock and up onto the flat, wind-scoured surface of the still-dark canyon floor. The canyon was more like a plain, more immense than any she had ever seen on Earth. Here, where the sub-canyons of Capri Chasm and Gangis Chasm intersected, the floor of the Mariner Valley was nearly two hundred kilometers wide; wide enough that the distant two-kilometer wall bounding this trisection of the floor seemed more like a line of distant mountains dancing at a desert's edge. She turned almost due west, toward the mouth of Gangis Chasm, knowing as she had known for so long, with such aching certainty, that this was where her destiny lay.

"*Kismet,*" Shiraz said absently, not even looking at her.

"Kind of florid; isn't it?" She managed a smile.

He managed laughter. "Perhaps there is a monolith waiting for us, after all."

The headlight spilled out like bright fluid, highlighting the stone-studded ground. The dim brown of the undifferentiated surface still in darkness stretched to the far canyon wall, which became a gleaming band of gold as the sun rose behind them. Petra glanced at the side mirror; seeing the unnatural cylindrical hummock of their buried lab silhouetted with the

low, conical hills that lay scattered like a case of hives over
the flatness. She looked out again at the slowly brightening
plain, and at Shiraz's dark, tense profile at the corner of her
sight. She had meditated often enough on the symbolism of
his name, finding it more than fitting in her aggravation—
Mitradati, from Mithra, the mace-wielding Persian god of
war, the paternalistic Protector of his People. . . . Now suddenly she remembered another of Mithra's aspects: god of the
light that precedes the dawn. She let her mind probe the
possibilities, searching for one that might be a symbol of
hope.

The jouncing vibration of their progress increased uncomfortably; she eased her foot on the accelerator. In Mars'
lighter gravity every bounce and swerve was accentuated, but
the jarring that followed it was gentler than on Earth. She
remembered her first painful ride, years before, in a dune
buggy: the grotesque, frivolous Earthside hybrid that had
become so indispensable to her work in the desert, and to the
exploration of Mars . . . remembering the stark fantasy of the
desert, and the tennis ball-sized bruises the seatbelt had left
on her hip-bones. She felt suddenly, unbearably homesick.

Why me? . . . why us? Why were they doing this; why
couldn't they at least understand. . . . *Because it doesn't have
to let us understand anything.* She tried to focus her resentment against the straitjacket bonds that held her free will
prisoner. Even terror, even fear—anything to give her strength.
But emotion dissipated the way the paper-thin film of frost
sublimed as the ground warmed. It was useless, it was pointless.

The day opened onto the full rust-red brilliance of the
endless Martian desert. The dusty sky was salmon pink now
around the horizon, deepening rapidly to a black-red zenith.
The cloud of fine dust lifting behind them became an auburn
haze against the sunlight. She turned southward, slightly, to
take them through the gap of flat desert pavement between a
tremendous black-sand dunefield to her left, and the kilometers-
long slope of slumped earth and talus that fanned from the
canyon's north rim on her right. Above the jumbled slope she
could see the pit in the profile of the sheer canyon wall,
where the rim of a shallow crater had fallen away with the
collapsing cliff-face.

She could picture the canyon and the cratered plains that lay above it as they looked from the air. She had seen them coming here from the polar base, from the southeastward descending arc of the shuttle's trajectory from pole to equator. She pictured the chain of magnificent volcanoes that were the Tharsis Mountains lying beyond the far end of the Valley, four thousand kilometers to the west—those mountains that dwarfed any on Earth, as the great rift valley itself almost defied her attempts to comprehend its scale. She had been deeply moved by the wonders of this alien world, where geology existed on such a grand scale: loved its strangeness and its familiarity, with the breadth of emotion that belonged to all who loved the faces and forces of the natural world, and the depth of emotion that belonged to those who truly understand them. *And never more than now: Where am I going? Will I ever see them again?*

Or ever see Earth again. . . . The limonite-stained cliffs were much closer on their left, now; the red, convoluted walls reminded her of the Near East, her journey to Petra, the City in the Rock—her namesake. She saw in her mind the ancient city, hidden in a cleft of red sandstone, its temples and dwellings built from and into the rock itself: a timeless thing, a part of the earth. . . . And the sun-bleached mudbrick villages that had not changed in a thousand years, or two, or three; that lay drowsing on parched hillsides an hour's drive from some twenty-first century metropolis. An hour's drive, in an air-conditioned time machine . . . She had spent three years in Israel, as the geologist for a Harvard-sponsored archeological crew, and they had been in Tel Aviv during Israel's Fiftieth Anniversary celebrations, laughing, drinking, dancing, embracing and being embraced by joyful total strangers.

Yesterday and today . . . and tomorrow: She was here on Mars, now, as a part of this project that celebrated the turning of a new millennium. Enough honor for a lifetime. . . . *But I'm not ready for it to end! Will there really be a tomorrow? And what kind will it be—none that I ever imagined* . . . She saw suddenly in her mind the smiling, freckled face of Fred Haswell, astronomer; who has been so much a part of this place, become so much more than just a friend to her, before

his stay here had ended four months ago. Now, not knowing
whether she would ever see him again, or touch him or feel a
man. . . . *Oh, Lord; this is no time to get horny!* She bit her
lip.

"A penny for your thoughts?" Mitradati said.

She looked away instead of at him; at the menhirs of dark
volcanic stone that crouched like confused giants along their
path, casting long shadow-fingers across the black sand. There
were red anti-shadows stretched in opposition, where the
ground was free of sand in the wind's lee. "I . . . I was
watching my whole life pass before my eyes, I think." She
felt herself begin to blush, and kept her face turned away.

"Isn't that what you're supposed to do before you die?"
Softly.

"I guess so. But I hope not." Her gloved hands tightened
on the wheel. "There—isn't much else to think about. Or to
say. Is there?" She looked back at him, at last.

"No." He shook his head, leaned back against the headrest, his own hands closing over his elbows. "Turn up the
heater, will you? I'm feeling rather cold."

She turned up the heater. Up ahead, beyond the field of
black sand, she could see another, smaller avalanche of dirt
and rock spilling down from the opposite wall of the canyon.
She looked back at him as his gaze left her. *Mind control
makes strange bedfellows.* She sighed, studying his profile
again, his close-cut, curly hair, the bushy, drooping mous-
tache that had so fascinated her the first time she saw him.
She smiled unhappily, looking away again, paying attention
once more to their progress up the canyon. Her interests and
his were similar; their heritage, reaching back over thousands
of years, was similar. But their personalities were still poles
apart. Or were they too much alike—?

"Have you ever been to see Persepolis?"

"No." She shook her head, loosened her stiffening neck
muscles. "I wish I'd had the chance to . . ." She went on,
determinedly, "I will see it, the next time I work in the Near
East. I want to climb those magnificent stairs."

"And see those columns standing like sentinels above the
past, against a *blue* sky—" He stared out at the glaring
red-black dome above them. Petra saw a handful of tiny

clouds, very high up, their whiteness tinted faintly pink by the haze of dust. "Did you know that some of the beliefs in the Old Testament were influenced by the teachings of Zoroaster?"

She smiled, nodding. "The name of the Pharisees probably came from the word for 'Persian.' "

"How far do you think we're going?"

"I don't know either."

"If you get tired of driving, let me know, and I'll change with you."

"All right. Thanks." She realized, with a selfish possessiveness, that she was grateful to have even the driving to help keep her mind occupied.

They reached the end of the gigantic slope of fallen cliff-face at last, and she angled their track across the canyon floor again, closing with the northern wall. She watched the wall come at them, inexorably, rising and rising, a rippling tidal wave of stone; she imagined herself drowning. Hours had passed already, and continued to pass. The sun rose to its zenith behind them and began to drop forward, getting into her eyes, as she followed their unchosen course along the foot of the canyon wall. They had brought no food with them, but she was not hungry or thirsty, not even tired. Mitradati said little and she said less; her self-awareness ebbed. She felt herself slipping further into a kind of fatalistic boredom, her thoughts almost formless, meaningless.

She could not remember anything she had been thinking, when at last she was able to realize it. They were passing the point of a protruding arm of the red-stained cliff; she began to see another of the endless side canyons that crenelated the heights. But a sudden emotion, utterly unexpected, filled her as the new subcanyon emerged before them: Anticipation? Excitement? Recognition. . . . Inexplicable knowledge that they were reaching the journey's end at last.

Shiraz stirred in his seat, leaning forward, peering out with what looked like eagerness. "We're almost there!"

"Yes—" And the alien emotion, or lack of emotion, within her became recognizable longing again. The shapeless fears that had dulled her desire to reach this goal fell away and were forgotten. This canyon was broader and deeper than most; she studied it for a way up into its network of dry channels and tumbled rock. The canyon became a sheer cleft about a kilometer above them, above an outcropping of resistant strata; but below that point the wall had been undercut, when water, and later windblown sand, had eaten away the weaker rock beneath it to form a natural shelter. Her eyes lingered on that hollow in the rock, a memory of the cliff-dwellings of the American Southwest moving across it like a cloud shadow. She could see nothing up there, yet. . . . And yet she was certain now that something was there, something more important than anything a human being had ever discovered—

"Can't you get up there any faster?" Shiraz's voice was sharp with frustration.

She got them up there, as fast as she could, over terrain and past obstacles that she would never have dared if she had had any freedom to make a judgment. She stopped the buggy at last, twenty meters below the final ledge that was their destination. "I can't get us any closer than this. We'll have to climb from here."

"All right."

Shiraz picked his helmet up from the floor, and she picked up her own, catching it on the steering wheel in her haste. She settled it on, barely latching it in place in time before they were unsealing the doors and leaping down into the thick, talc-fine, cloying dust. The red-stained dust was darker and duller where it had been disturbed, making her think of midden soil. Making her realize that they were about to unearth a greater mystery, and gaze on the future/past. . . . She saw Shiraz haul the drab, rectangular container that was the bomb out of the back seat, and felt dark doubt gnaw at the edges of her desire. "Do you think anyone will come after us? Maybe they're already searching—they must wonder where we've gone." She realized for the first time that she had never switched on the radio, never even thought to try. An unfamiliar heaviness clogged her chest.

"Probably. They know something is wrong by now. But we must have a big lead on them, whatever they decide to do. It won't make any difference." Doubt clouded his own face again.

They struggled up the final slope, pushing and lifting and dragging the metal box and each other; until they stood finally on the wide ledge below the overhang of ancient basalt. Petra turned slowly, breathing hard, her heart pounding with exertion and excitement.

The compulsion that had drawn them here by an invisible thread intensified stunningly inside her; as though she had passed through a doorway, letting the psychic pull she had known only as a deep, formless vibration burst over her, reverberate through her. She was dimly aware of a human sound, a grunt of astonishment, had no idea whether it had come from Shiraz's throat or her own. She was frozen in the moment, utterly absorbed in the awareness of what was happening to her, a thing that no human being had ever experienced before: the communication of an alien mind. The presence grew and grew inside her own mind, taking form, focusing. She strained toward it with all her will, straining to understand—

And suddenly she did understand, as the swollen presence clogged her brain and paralyzed her synapses: a cold, unfeeling radiation, without meaning, without—life. Like a machine . . . a machine programmed to lie in wait for centuries; but not in order to share with humankind the secrets of an interstellar society. There was no intelligence here, there would be no answer, no revelation, just—

A pile of ruins. Across the plateau, a jumble of red native stone, a warren of broken circles and irregularities filled with rubble, reaching back and back into the russet shadows below the overhang. *A ruin.* A cypher, empty of meaning, long since empty of life. Still she did not *know*—and she realized that she would never know; never feel illumination break the heavy clouds of compulsion. . . . The Unknown held her in bondage, and she meant less than nothing to it. The emotion that swelled in her, straining at her bonds, was not alien any longer—it was not even fear, but anger. Her eyes burned with fierce disappointment, and fiercer determination: She *would* know, she would find out! She moved forward, unexpectedly free to move, taking easy, unresisted bounds across the level surface. Shiraz called after her and she felt him follow. She reached the ruins ahead of him, found that they were even more immense than she had realized. The broken walls were twice her height, wearing deep skirts of dust, and they stretched away for hundreds of meters. She ran her gloved hands over the dust-filmed wall, along the line that age was etching between perfectly-matched precision-cut surfaces of stone. The ruining of this place had taken a long time. She was suddenly, totally certain that it was an ancient thing; that it had been waiting, waiting for millennia. But not for her . . .

Shiraz stopped beside her, bent over to set the bomb container down against the wall. When he straightened again she saw the despair on his face. And she knew then, just as certainly, that this was all they would ever know, all that they had ever been meant to understand. . . . They had not been chosen receivers of an alien secret to be shared with all of humanity; they were the chosen destroyers, because humanity had never been intended to know of this. "We're going to blow it up." Not a question. "Nothing will be left." And the mindless presence within her reveled at her understanding—at its own victory, and their defeat—without any comprehension of the significance of the act.

He nodded wordlessly, prying the lid loose on the box. He lifted out a small remote control unit and set it aside; the detonator, she supposed. She watched him begin to flick a switch, twist a knob, inside the box.

"Is the process very complicated?"

He shrugged, flicking another switch. "A bit. Not terribly."

"Is there any chance of making a mistake—?"

He looked up at her, bitterly. "Not intentionally." He looked down again, a stiff, resisted movement. "I have to concentrate. . . ."

She turned to gaze out over the rim of the ledge, down the valley, seeing the sunwashed canyon floor beyond like the ruddy golden fields of heaven. Searching for movement, fruitlessly.

"All right." He stood up finally, dust coating his knees. The detonator was in his hand. "Let's get out of here."

They began to walk back toward the sunlit rim of the ledge, toward the buggy waiting below, toward safety. And every step became slower, more leaden, more difficult . . . more impossible. "Shiraz?" Her panic leaped with the terror she heard in her own voice. She stood straining like an animal at the end of a leash.

"Petra . . . I can't go any further. I can't—" She saw his empty hand reaching as his body jerked around to face her. Five meters beyond him lay the path down to the buggy, and escape.

But they would not be allowed to use it. "No witnesses?" she said softly, meeting his eyes.

"No . . ." He looked down at the detonator in his hand. She watched him try to throw it away, and fail.

She swallowed, wetting her dry throat. "Oh, God. I wonder if our medical plan covers blowing yourself up while mind-controlled?"

"Allah! Can't you do anything but make jokes—"

She laughed uncertainly. "I've either got to laugh or cry, and if I have to die I'd rather die laughing."

He made a noise that was either amused or disgusted. "What are the rules of this game? I wonder if we're allowed to lie down flat?"

"Try." She fought her trembling body with one last, frantic calling-up of outrage and fear; felt her knees give way, dropping her painfully onto the rocks. But her spine was a steel rod and she knelt, paralyzed, watching Shiraz struggle to do the same. "It's a good position for prayer, at least . . ."

Help me, God, help me—

She was sure it was a laugh, this time. "Where's Earth; I've lost track of Mecca."

"You can't see it from here." She twisted, trying for one more glimpse down the canyon. "If you had a last wish, what would it be?"

"That I was somewhere else."

"Scared?" Her own voice broke.

"Shitless." He raised his hands unsteadily, holding the detonator out like an offering, kneeling in this alien temple where they were about to become a human sacrifice. . . . He murmured something in a language she didn't understand. And he pressed the button.

She kept her eyes open, staring in agonized disbelief: As a blinding ball of orange light blotted out the silver dome, a cloud of smoke and rubble rose to blot out the fire, a fist of

smoke and shock and sound swept toward them through a
split-second's eternity—struck her with sickening force, throwing her back and over the rim of the ledge like a rag toy.

Awake, aware, she found herself lying dazed on the slope.
Still alive. She felt her body with her mind: sprawling twisted
on its side, head down, faceplate down in the red dust. Stones
and pebbles still pelted her. She thought she heard, dimly, the
bang of a stone on metal; tried to raise her head, gasped as
pain like an electric shock stabbed at the base of her neck.
But before her head dropped forward again she saw the
buggy, barely three meters below her, and the still body
wedged against it. . . .

"Shiraz?" She lay face down again, putting all her strength
into the one word. "Shiraz—?" No answer. Grimly she drew
a leg in, pushed off; crawled and slid on her stomach down
the slope, whimpering and cursing. She reached his side, saw
his face through his helmet glass, saw blood on it. And his
eyes shut, no response. She couldn't tell whether his bulky,
insulated suit was still pressurized, whether he was even still
alive. But one leg lay crumpled beneath him, like a twisted
branch, like nothing that belonged to a human being. She
almost shut her eyes; didn't, as she focused on the faintest
whisper of whiteness in the air above it. A tiny, fragile cloud
of condensing moisture . . . the suit had torn. She fell back,
bright fire exploding in her head as she struggled to release
the catch on the equipment belt at her waist. She pulled it
loose, forced it under his suited leg above the tear, not even
aware that she was sobbing now. She drew it tight and jammed
the catch, barely able to see her hands through golden fog,
the rushing water of noise that drowned her senses. *The
radio.* If she could only get to the radio. She tried to push
herself up, to reach the door handle. But the one meter to the
door handle might as well have been the distance to the sun.
She collapsed helplessly across his legs, her strength gone.

But she knew, with ironic grief, before her senses left her
too, that she was free to use it if she could. That her mind
was free of the compulsion at last, that at least she would be
free forever when she died. . . .

*   *   *

"Hello, Shiraz." Petra entered the quiet, dim-lit room where Shiraz Mitradati lay, sat down in the chair at his bedside with exquisite care. "Dr. Leidu told me you felt like talking. I'm glad. So do I." She drew the collar of her robe closer around the thick, white neck brace. "There's not really anyone else who understands. . . ."

"I know." He smiled at her from the pillows, his face hollow and tired. "Thanks for coming. It's good to see you—up and around already."

"All it took was a little chicken soup. It works miracles. You should try it." Her mouth twitched, still not quite ready for laughter. Her head hurt, as it had hurt for the past four days, relentlessly. "It will be good to see you up and around again, too."

"Not for a bit, I'm afraid."

She glanced down, uncomfortably.

"But I'd never be up again at all if you hadn't stopped that leak in my suit. I want you to know how grateful I am for that."

She looked up again, smiling, embarrassed. "I never believed they'd ever find us, anyway; not in time. But they saw the dust cloud from the explosion. The thing that almost killed us saved us, in the end."

"But why didn't it kill us in the first place? We had no right to survive; it was impossible, we should have been incinerated—"

"Didn't they tell you?" She turned her head too quickly, felt the drug-dulled ache flare up, making her wince.

"Tell me what? . . . I haven't been in the mood for much conversation since I woke up." His hand moved along the cold metal rail at the edge of the bed, tightened.

"That you made a mistake." Her smile felt real, and warm, and right to her this time. "You never disengaged the fail-safe on the bomb; only the core explosive went off, there was no atomic blast. That's the only reason we're still in— still here to talk about it."

"Well." Faint humor brightened his eyes. "No one's perfect, after all—not even me. What about the ruin?"

"Partly buried. Part of the overhang came down on it. A team is there excavating already."

"Has anyone else had any—trouble, working with it?"

"No. No more trouble." She settled back in the plastic chair, trying to find the position that hurt the least.

"Can anyone explain what happened to us? How some—alien *thing* we never even saw could turn us into time bombs?" His voice grew more agitated.

"They found the thing that did it." She felt him look at her abruptly. "Just a machine." *Just a thing.* "Nothing more than a twisted-up mess of ceramic and metal. There was still a little 'life' in it; enough to pick up on instruments once our people started searching the rubble for it. . . ." She saw him tense. "But the blast broke its back." Her hands felt her neck brace unconsciously. "I knew that, I felt it, even before we were rescued—that we were finally free."

"How—how does it work?"

She tried to shrug. "They have no idea . . . yet." She wondered suddenly what would happen to humanity if they ever found out. "But I told them everything I remembered. Enright figures the thing must have been left there on purpose, like—like a mousetrap, for any sentient creatures that might pose a threat. He says it must set up a feedback in the mind; in a way, you yourself provide your own mind control. What appeals to you draws you, and helps tune out your willpower."

"But why? Why would someone leave something like that in a ruin? And—why *us?* Why were we the victims?" He pushed himself up from the pillows, hurling his anger against an unreachable persecutor, an unrightable wrong.

"We found the bait, the piece of cheese—that artifact." It seemed to her as though it had happened a lifetime ago. She wondered how many other treacherous clues were scattered through the Mariner Valley; harmlessly, now. "Maybe we were the most curious; I don't know." Lines tightened between her eyes. "Just lucky, I guess." Trying to keep it light, she heard her own unhealed fear betray her. "But why the ruin was left boobytrapped. . . . Do you remember what it—what it felt like, that *thing*," her own voice attacked it, "when it got into our minds?"

He nodded, tight-lipped. "Ruthless. Arrogant. Megalomaniacal . . . as though the ones who set it up would have enjoyed making us grovel, watching us destroy ourselves.''

She wrapped the tie of her bathrobe around her fingers. ''Yes. . . . Ironic, isn't it, that after all its arrogance we were too dumb to destroy ourselves. But a—feeling like that belongs to an invading army, a military outpost; assuming they were anything like us. . . .''

''*Are* anything like us.''

''Were.'' She moved her head cautiously from side to side. ''Those ruins have been there for three millennia, at least. Maybe they were boobytrapped because the Martian Foreign Legion was being forced to retreat. The way the place was built of native stone—and it extends underground, too; as if it was designed to stay hidden. Maybe they expected a visit from the Other Side.''

''Or from us. They wouldn't have bothered to be so subtle with an active aggressor, I'm sure.''

''Maybe not. No one else ever found it, or came back to reclaim it, anyway.''

His head fell back against the pillow, he stared at the ceiling. ''I was just thinking. . . .''

''What?''

''About 'flying saucers' . . . and Ezekiel's 'wheels in the air.' Good Lord. What kept them from tampering with humanity, I wonder?''

''Maybe they did.''

He grimaced.

She smiled faintly. ''And a lousy mess they made of it, if so.''

''But that's all meaningless, now, anyway. The only real proof we have of other life in our system—or in the galaxy—is here on Mars: these ruins, left by some ruthless monsters who have been dead for thousands of years. A relic, a curiosity, a problem for the academics.'' His hands bunched the blankets. ''It isn't worth it! It isn't worth dying for. It isn't even worth . . . having survived.'' He looked down along the bed at his hidden body. ''They told you, about my—about my leg?''

She followed his pointing hand unwillingly, saw the terrible lack of symmetry that she had tried not to see beneath the blankets. His broken leg had been injured too badly; without the sophisticated medical care available on Earth, they had not been able to save it. Dizzy, she said evenly, "Yes, they told me. I'm very sorry." She met his gaze until he looked away. "But it *was* worth it, Shiraz." A part of her own mind shouted that she lied, that the price he had paid—they both had paid—in suffering and terror was too high. For the sake of his sanity and her own, she let her voice drown it out: "We *won*, even by default. We're alive, we have their artifacts to study, we'll learn their secrets!" *What secrets, from an abandoned outpost? Cooking pots and dirty underwear?* "We are going to learn what it was all about, after all. Our monolith, our alien treasure. . . . God, I can't wait to get at it! Proof that other intelligent beings exist in the universe. It really is a treasure of knowledge—" finding to her surprise that she was geniunely beginning to feel the enthusiasm she forced into her voice. She saw a spark of belief begin to catch in the cold emptiness of Shiraz's eyes; reached out to him, stretching forward. "Oh!" She sank back, raised her hands to her head, dazzled by pain-stars. "Such a headache I never had in my life; like a dozen hangovers piled on top of each other." She lowered her hands to the neck brace, swallowing her pain, because his trace of a smile had disappeared. "And how do you like my horse collar? I feel like I should be pulling a plow."

"At least it's something you'll be able to get rid of. I expect you'll be able to get back to your work quite soon. I wish I could be as lucky. That's the only real regret I have— that the rest of my stay here will be wasted. I won't be able to finish my work . . ."

"*Dreck,*" she said sharply. "I don't see why not. It's not your mind that you've lost." He looked back at her, frowning. She put out her hand, carefully this time, and touched his arm. "You'll get around perfectly well with a cane in one-third gee. And with a prosthesis, back on Earth, you'll be better than new. Wait and see . . . you'll want to get back to work. This is *our* discovery, yours and mine. You won't be able to stay away—not from the discovery of a lifetime. I know you; and believe me, you're much too vain for that, Shiraz."

"Am I?" The frown eased into an uncertain bemusement;

he lay back. "I know, thousands of other people have had to live with it. I suppose I shall go on living too; like it or not. . . . Maybe a missing leg will give me a certain exotic mystery, like an eye patch; and make me more attractive to the ladies—"

She saw suddenly that he had lied when he said that he had only one regret. "Especially when you tell them that story about being kidnapped by aliens. Aliens who haven't been here for thousands of years."

"Maybe it might even make me more attractive to you." He held her eyes, with an expression she couldn't read.

She blinked, silent with surprise.

"Maybe when we're both back on Earth, when you come to see Persepolis, you'd go to dinner with me?"

"Why do we need to put it off for years?" She let a smile form slowly, hesitantly; was glad, when she saw his smile answer it at last. "Afterwards, we could go up to my place, sip a little wine, watch our own private Late Show. . . . I could even check out *2001* at the tape library—"

For a moment, they stopped smiling.

AFTERWORD—
VOICES FROM THE DUST

This is one of only three short stories that I've written. Most of my "short" works have been either novelettes or novellas. A lot has been written about the novella, in particular, being a length uniquely suited to science fiction, and one in which science fiction writers work far more often than mainstream writers. The reason seems to be that science fiction writers are dealing with societies and backgrounds that are new and strange to the average reader, and these elements of the story have to be developed along with the basic plot and character—a complication that mainstream writers generally don't have to deal with. This makes it very difficult to set up every point that needs to be established in under 7500 words, the official length of a short story. Occasionally I've been able to do it, when the basic story is straightforward enough; this was one of the results. (I calculate that it is just about exactly 7500 words, in fact.)

The setting of this story is an actual area of Mars, which I have tried to describe as realistically as possible, using information gained from the Mariner missions. There is also an element of the past in its creation, however. I have a background in anthropology, and specifically in archeology, and I found the original title, Voices from the Dust, which inspired this story on an archeology textbook I saw while browsing in a used book store. I'd originally wanted to make the protagonist, Petra Greenfeld, an archeologist, but couldn't justify sending her to Mars (as opposed to, say, Barsoom), so I had to be content with making her a geologist with archeological experience.

THE STORM KING

They said that in those days the lands were cursed that lay in the shadow of the Storm King. The peak thrust up from the gently rolling hills and fertile farmlands like an impossible wave cresting on the open sea, a brooding finger probing the secrets of heaven. Once it had vomited fire and fumes; ash and molten stone had poured from its throat. The distant ancestors of the people who lived beneath it now had died of its wrath. But the Earth had spent Her fury in one final cataclysm, and now the mountain lay quiet, dark, and cold, its mouth choked with congealed stone.

And yet still the people lived in fear. No one among them remembered having seen its summit, which was always crowned by cloud. Lightning played in the purple, shrouding robes, and distant thunder filled the dreams of the folk who slept below with the roaring of dragons.

For it was a dragon who had come to dwell among the crags: that elemental focus of all storm and fire carried on the wind, drawn to a place where the Earth's fire had died, a place still haunted by ancient grief. And sharing the spirit of fire, the dragon knew no law and obeyed no power except its own. By day or night it would rise on furious wings of wind and sweep over the land, inundating the crops with rain, blasting trees with its lightning, battering walls and tearing away rooftops; terrifying rich and poor, man and beast, for the sheer pleasure of destruction, the exaltation of uncontrolled power. The people had prayed to the new gods who had replaced their worship of the Earth to deliver them; but the new gods made Their home in the sky, and seemed to be beyond hearing.

By now the people had made Their names into curses, as they pried their oxcarts from the mud or looked out over fields of broken grain and felt their bellies and their children's bellies tighten with hunger. And they would look toward the distant peak and curse the Storm King, naming the peak and the dragon both; but always in whispers and mutters, for fear the wind would hear them, and bring the dark storm sweeping down on them again.

The storm-wracked town of Wyddon and its people looked up only briefly in their sullen shaking-off and shoveling-out of mud as a stranger picked his way among them. He wore the woven leather of a common soldier, his cloak and leggings were coarse and ragged, and he walked the planks laid down in the stinking street as though determination alone kept him on his feet. A woman picking through baskets of stunted leeks in the marketplace saw with vague surprise that he had entered the tiny village temple; a man putting fresh thatch on a torn-open roof saw him come out again, propelled by the indignant, orange-robed priest.

"If you want witchery, find yourself a witch! This is a holy place; the gods don't meddle in vulgar magic!"

"I can see that," the stranger muttered, staggering in ankle-deep mud. He climbed back onto the boards with some difficulty and obvious disgust. "Maybe if they did you'd have streets and not rivers of muck in this town." He turned away in anger, almost stumbled over a mud-colored girl blocking his forward progress on the boardwalk.

"You priests should bow down to the Storm King!" The girl postured insolently, looking toward the priest. "The dragon can change all our lives more in one night than your gods have done in a lifetime."

"Slut!" The priest shook his carven staff at her; its necklace of golden bells chimed like absurd laughter. "There's a witch for you, beggar. If you think she can teach you to tame the dragon, then go with her!" He turned away, disappearing into the temple. The stranger's body jerked, as though it strained against his control, wanting to strike at the priest's retreating back.

"You're a witch?" The stranger turned and glared down at the bony figure standing in his way, found her studying him back with obvious skepticism. He imagined what she saw—a foreigner, his straight black hair whacked off like a serf's, his clothes crawling with filth, his face grimed and gaunt and set in a bitter grimace. He frowned more deeply.

The girl shook her head. "No. I'm just bound to her. You have business to take up with her, I see—about the Storm King." She smirked, expecting him to believe she was privy to secret knowledge.

"As you doubtless overheard, yes." He shifted his weight from one leg to the other, trying fruitlessly to ease the pain in his back.

She shrugged, pushing her own tangled brown hair back from her face. "Well, you'd better be able to pay for it, or you've come a long way from Kwansai for nothing."

He started, before he realized that his coloring and his eyes gave that much away. "I can pay." He drew his dagger from its hidden sheath; the only weapon he had left, and the only thing of value. He let her glimpse the jeweled hilt before he pushed it back out of sight.

Her gray eyes widened briefly. "What do I call you, Prince of Thieves?" with another glance at his rags.

"Call me Your Highness," not lying, and not quite joking.

She looked up into his face again, and away. "Call me Nothing, Your Highness. Because I am nothing." She twitched a shoulder at him. "And follow me."

They passed the last houses of the village without further speech, and followed the mucky track on into the dark, dripping forest that lay at the mountain's feet. The girl stepped off the road and into the trees without warning; he followed her recklessly, half angry and half afraid that she was abandoning him. But she danced ahead of him through the pines, staying always in sight, although she was plainly impatient with his own lagging pace. The dank chill of the sunless wood gnawed his aching back and swarms of stinging gnats feasted on his exposed skin; the bare-armed girl seemed as oblivious to the insects as she was to the cold.

He pushed on grimly, as he had pushed on until now, having no choice but to keep on or die. And at last his persistence was rewarded. He saw the forest rise ahead, and buried in the flank of the hillside among the trees was a mossy hut linteled by immense stones.

The girl disappeared into the hut as he entered the clearing before it. He slowed, looking around him at the cluster of carven images pushing up like unnatural growths from the spongy ground, or dangling from tree limbs. Most of the images were subtly or blatantly obscene. He averted his eyes and limped between them to the hut's entrance.

He stepped through the doorway without waiting for an invitation, to find the girl crouched by the hearth in the hut's cramped interior, wearing the secret smile of a cat. Beside her an incredibly wrinkled, ancient woman sat on a three-legged stool. The legs were carved into shapes that made him look away again, back at the wrinkled face and the black, buried eyes that regarded him with flinty bemusement. He noticed abruptly that there was no wall behind her: the far side of the hut melted into the black volcanic stone, a natural fissure opening into the mountain's side.

"So, Your Highness, you've come all the way from Kwansai seeking the Storm King, and a way to tame its power?"

He wrapped his cloak closely about him and grimaced, the nearest thing to a smile of scorn that he could manage. "Your girl has a quick tongue. But I've come to the wrong place, it seems, for real power."

"Don't be so sure!" The old woman leaned toward him, shrill and spiteful. "You can't afford to be too sure of anything, Lassan-din. You were prince of Kwansai; you should have been king there when your father died, and overlord of these lands as well. And now you're nobody and you have no home, no friends, barely even your life. Nothing is what it seems to be . . . it never is."

Lassan-din's mouth went slack; he closed it, speechless at last. *Nothing is what it seems*. The girl called Nothing grinned up at him from the floor. He took a deep breath, shifting to ease his back again. "Then you know what I've come for, if you already know that much, witch."

The hag half-rose from her obscene stool; he glimpsed a flash of color, a brighter, finer garment hidden beneath the drab outer robe she wore—the way the inner woman still burned fiercely bright in her eyes, showing through the wasted flesh of her ancient body. "Call me no names, you prince of beggars! I am the Earth's Own. Your puny Kwansai priests, who call my sisterhood 'witch,' who destroyed our holy places and drove us into hiding, know nothing of power. They're fools; they don't believe in power and they are powerless, charlatans. You know it or you wouldn't be here!" She settled back, wheezing. "Yes, I could tell you what you want; but suppose you tell me."

"I want what's mine! I want my kingdom." He paced restlessly, two steps and then back. "I know of elementals, all the old legends. My people say that dragons are storm-bringers, born from a joining of Fire and Water and Air, three of the four Primes of Existence. Nothing but the Earth can defy their fury. And I know that if I can hold a dragon in its lair with the right spells, it must give me what I want, like the heroes of the Golden Time. I want to use its power to take back my lands."

"You don't want much, do you?" The old woman rose from her seat and turned her back on him, throwing a surreptitious handful of something into the fire, making it flare up balefully. She stirred the pot that hung from a hook above it, spitting five times into the noxious brew as she stirred. Lassandin felt his empty stomach turn over. "If you want to challenge the Storm King, you should be out there climbing, not here holding your hand out to me."

"Damn you!" His exasperation broke loose, and his hand wrenched her around to face him. "I need some spell, some magic, some way to pen a dragon up. I can't do it with my bare hands!"

She shook her head, unintimidated, and leered toothlessly at him. "My power comes to me through my body, up from the Earth Our Mother. She won't listen to a man—especially one who would destroy Her worship. Ask your priests who worship the air to teach you their empty prayers."

He saw the hatred rising in her, and felt it answered: The dagger was out of its hidden sheath and in his hand before he knew it, pressing the soft folds of her neck. "I don't believe you, witch. See this dagger—" quietly, deadly. "If you give me what I want, you'll have the jewels in its hilt. If you don't, you'll feel its blade cut your throat."

"All right, all right!" She strained back as the blade's tip began to bite. He let her go. She felt her neck; the girl sat perfectly still at their feet, watching. "I can give you something—a spell. I can't guarantee She'll listen. But you have enough hatred in you for ten men—and maybe that will make your man's voice loud enough to penetrate Her skin. This mountain is sacred to Her. She still listens through its ears, even if She no longer breathes here."

"Never mind the superstitious drivel. Just tell me how I can keep the dragon in without it striking me dead with its lightning. How I can fight fire with fire—"

"You don't fight fire with fire. You fight fire with water."

He stared at her; at the obviousness of it, and the absurdity— "The dragon is the creator of storm. How can mere water—?"

"A dragon is anathema. Remember that, prince who would be king. It is chaos, power uncontrolled; and power always has a price. That's the key to everything. I can teach you the spell for controlling the waters of the Earth; but you're the one who must use it."

He stayed with the women through the day, and learned as the hours passed to believe in the mysteries of the Earth. The crone spoke words that brought water fountaining up from the well outside her door while he looked on in amazement, his weariness and pain forgotten. As he watched she made a brook flow upstream; made the crystal droplets beading the forest pines join in a diadem to crown his head, and then with a word released them to run cold and helpless as tears into the collar of his ragged tunic.

She seized the fury that rose up in him at her insolence, and challenged him to do the same. He repeated the ungainly, ancient spellwords defiantly, arrogantly, and nothing happened. She scoffed, his anger grew; she jeered and it grew stronger. He repeated the spell again, and again, and again . . .

until at last he felt the terrifying presence of an alien power rise in his body, answering the call of his blood. The droplets on the trees began to shiver and commingle; he watched an eddy form in the swift clear water of the stream— The Earth had answered him.

His anger failed him at the unbelievable sight of his success . . . and the power failed him too. Dazed and strengthless, at last he knew his anger for the only emotion with the depth or urgency to move the body of the Earth, or even his own. But he had done the impossible—made the Earth move to a man's bidding. He had proved his right to be a king, proved that he could force the dragon to serve him as well. He laughed out loud. The old woman moaned and spat, twisting her hands that were like gnarled roots, mumbling curses. She shuffled away toward the woods as though she were in a trance; turned back abruptly as she reached the trees, pointed past him at the girl standing like a ghost in the hut's doorway. "You think you've known the Earth; that you own Her, now. You think you can take anything and make it yours. But you're as empty as that one, and as powerless!" And she was gone.

Night had fallen through the dreary wood without his realizing it. The girl Nothing led him back into the hut, shared a bowl of thick, strangely herbed soup and a piece of stale bread with him. He ate gratefully but numbly, the first warm meal he had eaten in weeks; his mind drifted into waking dreams of banqueting until dawn in royal halls.

When he had eaten his share, wiping the bowl shamelessly with a crust, he stood and walked the few paces to the hut's furthest corner. He lay down on the hard stone by the cave mouth, wrapping his cloak around him, and closed his eyes. Sleep's darker cloak settled over him.

And then, dimly, he became aware that the girl had followed him, stood above him looking down. He opened his eyes unwillingly, to see her unbelt her tunic and pull it off, kneel down naked at his side. A piece of rock crystal, perfectly transparent, perfectly formed, hung glittering coldly against her chest. He kept his eyes open, saying nothing.

"The Old One won't be back until you're gone; the sight of a man calling on the Earth was too strong for her." Her hand moved insinuatingly along his thigh.

He rolled away from her, choking on a curse as his back hurt him sharply. "I'm tired. Let me sleep."

"I can help you. She could have told you more. I'll help you tomorrow . . . if you lie with me tonight."

He looked up at her, suddenly despairing. "Take my body, then; but it won't give you much pleasure." He pulled up the back of his tunic, baring the livid scar low on his spine. "My uncle didn't make a cripple of me—but he might as well have." When he even thought of a woman there was only pain, only rage . . . only that.

She put her hand on the scar with surprising gentleness. "I can help that too . . . for tonight." She went away, returned with a small jar of ointment and rubbed the salve slowly into his scarred back. A strange, cold heat sank through him; a sensuous tingling swept away the grinding ache that had been his only companion through these long months of exile. He let his breath out in an astonished sigh, and the girl lay down beside him, pulling at his clothes.

Her thin body was as hard and bony as a boy's, but she made him forget that. She made him forget everything, except that tonight he was free from pain and sorrow; tonight he lay with a woman who desired him, no matter what her reason. He remembered lost pleasure, lost joy, lost youth, only yesterday . . . until yesterday became tomorrow.

In the morning he woke, in pain, alone and fully clothed, aching on the hard ground. *Nothing.* . . . He opened his eyes and saw her standing at the fire, stirring a kettle. A *Dream—?* The cruel betrayal that was reality returned tenfold.

They ate together in a silence that was sullen on his part and inscrutable on hers. After last night it seemed obvious to him that she was older than she looked—as obvious as the way he himself had changed from boy to old man in a span of months. And he felt an insubstantiality about her that he had not noticed before, an elusiveness that might only have been an echo of his dream. "I dreamed, last night . . ."

"I know." She climbed to her feet, cutting him off, combing her snarled hair back with her fingers. "You dream loudly." Her face was closed.

He felt a frown settle between his eyes again. "I have a

long climb. I'd better get started." He pushed himself up and moved stiffly toward the doorway. The old hag still had not returned.

"Not that way," the girl said abruptly. "This way." She pointed as he turned back, toward the cleft in the rock.

He stood still. "That will take me to the dragon?"

"Only part way. But it's easier by half. I'll show you." She jerked a brand out of the fire and started into the maw of darkness.

He went after her with only a moment's uncertainty. He had lived in fear for too long; if he was afraid to follow this witch-girl into her Goddess's womb, then he would never have the courage to challenge the Storm King.

The low-ceilinged cleft angled steeply upward, a natural tube formed millennia ago by congealing lava. The girl began to climb confidently, as though she trusted some guardian power to place her hands and feet surely—a power he could not depend on as he followed her up the shaft. The dim light of day snuffed out behind him, leaving only her torch to guide them through utter blackness, over rock that was alternately rough enough to flay the skin from his hands and slick enough to give him no purchase at all. The tunnel twisted like a worm, widening, narrowing, steepening, folding back on itself in an agony of contortion. His body protested its own agony as he dragged it up handholds in a sheer rock face, twisted it, wrenched it, battered it against the unyielding stone. The acrid smoke from the girl's torch stung his eyes and clogged his lungs; but it never seemed to slow her own tireless motion, and she took no pity on his weakness. Only the knowledge of the distance he had come kept him from demanding that they turn back; he could not believe that this could possibly be an easier way than climbing the outside of the mountain. It began to seem to him that he had been climbing through this foul blackness for all of eternity, that this was another dream like his dream last night, but one that would never end.

The girl chanted softly to herself now; he could just hear her above his own labored breathing. He wondered jealously if she was drawing strength from the very stone around them, the body of the Earth. He could feel no pulse in the cold heart of the rock; and yet after yesterday he did not doubt its presence, even wondering if the Earth sapped his own strength with preternatural malevolence. *I am a man, I will be a king!* he thought defiantly. And the way grew steeper, and his hands bled.

"Wait—!" He gasped out the word at last, as his feet went out from under him again and he barely saved himself from sliding back down the tunnel. "I can't go on."

The girl, crouched on a level spot above him, looked back and down at him and ground out the torch. His grunt of protest became a grunt of surprise as he saw her silhouetted against a growing gray-brightness. She disappeared from his view; the brightness dimmed and then strengthened.

He heaved himself up and over the final bend in the wormhole, into a space large enough to stand in if he had had the strength. He crawled forward hungrily into the brightness at the cave mouth, found the girl kneeling there, her face raised to the light. He welcomed the fresh air into his lungs, cold and cleansing; looked past her—and down.

They were dizzyingly high on the mountain's side, above the tree line, above a sheer, unscalable face of stone. A fast-falling torrent of water roared on their left, plunging out and down the cliff-face. The sun winked at him from the cloud-wreathed heights; its angle told him they had climbed for the better part of the day. He looked over at the girl.

"You're lucky," she said, without looking back at him. Before he could even laugh at the grotesque irony of the statement she raised her hand, pointing on up the mountainside. "The Storm King sleeps—another storm is past. I saw the rainbow break this sunrise."

He felt a surge of strength and hope, absorbed the indifferent blessing of the Holy Sun. "How long will it sleep?"

"Two more days, perhaps. You won't reach its den before night. Sleep here, and climb again tomorrow."

"And then?" He looked toward her expectantly.

She shrugged.

"I paid you well," not certain in what coin, anymore. "I want a fair return! How do I pen the beast?"

Her hand tightened around the crystal pendant hanging against her tunic. She glanced back into the cave mouth.

"There are many waters flowing from the heights. One of them might be diverted to fall past the entrance of its lair."

"A waterfall? I might as well hold up a rose and expect it to cower!"

"Power always has its price; as the Old One said." She looked directly at him at last. "The storm rests here in mortal form—the form of the dragon. And like all mortals, it suffers. Its strength lies in the scales that cover its skin. The rain washes them away—the storm is agony to the stormbringer. They fall like jewels, they catch the light as they fall, like a trail of rainbow. It's the only rainbow anyone here has ever seen . . . a sign of hope, because it means an end to the storm; but a curse, too, because the storm will always return, endlessly."

"Then I could have it at my mercy. . . ." He heard nothing else.

"Yes. If you can make the Earth move to your will." Her voice was flat.

His hands tightened. "I have enough hate in me for that."

"And what will you demand, to ease it?" She glanced at him again, and back at the sky. "The dragon is defiling this sacred place; it should be driven out. You could become a hero to my people, if you forced the dragon to go away. A god. They need a god who can do them some good. . . ."

He felt her somehow still watching him, measuring his response, even though she had looked away. "I came here to solve my problem, not yours. I want my own kingdom, not a kingdom of mud-men. I need the dragon's power—I didn't come here to drive that away."

The girl said nothing, still staring at the sky.

"It's a simple thing for you to move the waters—why haven't you driven the dragon away yourself, then?" His voice rasped in his parched throat, sharp with unrecognized guilt.

"I'm Nothing. I have no power—the Old One holds my soul." She looked down at the crystal.

"Then why won't the Old One do it?"

"She hates, too. She hates what our people have become under the new gods, your gods. That's why she won't."

"I'd think it would give her great pleasure to prove the impotence of the new gods." His mouth stretched sourly.

"She wants to die in the Earth's time, not tomorrow." The girl folded her arms, and her own mouth twisted.

He shook his head. "I don't understand that . . . why didn't you destroy our soldiers, our priests, with your magic?"

"The Earth moves slowly to our bidding, because She is eternal. An arrow is small—but it moves swiftly."

He laughed once, appreciatively. "I understand."

"There's a cairn of stones over there." She nodded back into the darkness. "Food is under it." He realized that this must have been a place of refuge for the women in times of persecution. "The rest is up to you." She turned, merging abruptly into the shadows.

"Wait!" he called, surprising himself. "You must be tired."

She shook her head, a deeper shadow against darkness.

"Stay with me—until morning." It was not quite a demand, not quite a question.

"Why?" He thought he saw her eyes catch light and reflect it back at him, like a wild thing's.

Because I had a dream. He did not say it, did not say anything else.

"Our debts have balanced." She moved slightly, and something landed on the ground at his feet: his dagger. The hilt was pock-marked with empty jewel settings; stripped clean. He leaned down to pick it up. When he straightened again she was gone.

"You need a light—!" he called after her again.

Her voice came back to him, from a great distance: "May you get what you deserve!" And then silence, except for the roaring of the falls.

He ate, wondering whether her last words were a benediction or a curse. He slept, and the dreams that came to him were filled with the roaring of dragons.

With the light of a new day he began to climb again, following the urgent river upward toward its source that lay hidden in the waiting crown of clouds. He remembered his own crown, and lost himself in memories of the past and future, hardly aware of the harsh sobbing of his breath, of flesh and sinew strained past a sane man's endurance. Once he had been the spoiled child of privilege, his father's only son—living in the world's eye, his every whim a command. Now he was as much Nothing as the witchgirl far down the mountain. But he would live the way he had again, his every wish granted, his power absolute—he would live that way again, if he had to climb to the gates of Heaven to win back his birthright.

The hours passed endlessly, inevitably, and all he knew was that slowly, slowly, the sky lowered above him. At last the cold, moist edge of clouds enfolded his burning body, drawing him into another world of gray mist and gray silences; black, glistening surfaces of rock; the white sound of the cataract rushing down from even higher above. Drizzling fog shrouded the distances any way he turned, and he realized that he did not know where in this layer of cloud the dragon's den lay. He had assumed that it would be obvious, he had trusted the girl to tell him all he needed to know. . . . Why had he trusted her? That pagan slut—his hand gripped the rough hilt of his dagger; dropped away, trembling with fatigue. He began to climb again, keeping the sound of falling water nearby for want of any other guide. The light grew vaguer and more diffuse, until the darkness falling in the outer world penetrated the fog world and the haze of his exhaustion. He lay down at last, unable to go on, and slept beneath the shelter of an overhang of rock.

He woke stupefied by daylight. The air held a strange acridness that hurt his throat, that he could not identify. The air seemed almost to crackle; his hair ruffled, although there was no wind. He pushed himself up. He knew this feeling now: a storm was coming. A storm coming . . . a storm, here? Suddenly, fully awake, he turned on his knees, peering deeper beneath the overhang that sheltered him. And in the light of dawn he could see that it was not a simple overhang, but another opening into the mountain's side—a wider, greater one, whose depths the day could not fathom. But far down in the blackness a flickering of unnatural light showed. His hair rose in the electric breeze, he felt his skin prickle. *Yes . . . yes!* A small cry escaped him. He had found it! Without even knowing it, he had slept in the mouth of the dragon's lair all night. Habit brought a thanks to the gods to his lips, until he remembered— He muttered a *thank you* to the Earth beneath him before he climbed to his feet. A brilliant flash silhouetted him; a rumble like distant thunder made the ground vibrate, and he froze. Was the dragon waking—?

But there was no further disturbance, and he breathed again. Two days, the girl had told him, the dragon might sleep. And now he had reached his final trial, the penning of the beast. Away to his right he could hear the cataract's endless song. But would there be enough water in it to block the dragon's exit? Would that be enough to keep it prisoner, or would it strike him down in lightning and thunder, and sweep his body from the heights with torrents of rain? . . . Could he even move one droplet of water, here and now? Or would he find that all the thousand doubts that gnawed inside him were not only useless but pointless?

He shook it off, moving out and down the mist-dim slope to view the cave mouth and the river tumbling past it. A thin stream of water already trickled down the face of the opening, but the main flow was diverted by a folded knot of lava. If he could twist the water's course and hold it, for just long enough . . .

He climbed the barren face of stone at the far side of the cave mouth until he stood above it, confronting the sinuous steel and flashing white of the thing he must move. It seemed almost alive, and he felt weary, defeated, utterly insignificant at the sight of it. But the mountain on which he stood was a greater thing than even the river, and he knew that within it lay power great enough to change the water's course. But he was the conduit, his will must tap and bend the force that he had felt stir in him two days ago.

He braced his legs apart, gathered strength into himself, trying to recall the feel of magic moving in him. He recited the spell-words, the focus for the willing of power—and felt nothing. He recited the words again, putting all his concentration behind them. Again nothing. The Earth lay silent and inert beneath his feet.

Anger rose in him, at the Earth's disdain, and against the strange women who served Her—the jealous, demanding anger that had opened him to power before. And this time he did feel the power stir in him, sluggishly, feebly. But there was no sign of any change in the water's course. He threw all his conscious will toward change, *change, change*—but still the Earth's power faltered and mocked him. He let go of the ritual words at last, felt the tingling promise of energy die, having burned away all his own strength.

He sat down on the wet stone, listened to the river roar with laughter. He had been so sure that when he got here the force of his need would be strong enough. . . . *I have enough hate in me*, he had told the girl. But he wasn't reaching it now. Not the real hatred, that had carried him so far beyond the limits of his strength and experience. He began to concentrate on that hatred, and the reasons behind it: the loss, the pain, the hardship and fear. . . .

His father had been a great ruler over the lands that his ancestors had conquered. And he had loved his queen, Lassandin's mother. But when she died, his unhealing grief had turned him ruthless and iron-willed. He had become a despot, capricious, cruel, never giving an inch of his power to another man—even his spoiled and insecure son. Disease had left him wasted and witless in the end. And Lassan-din, barely come to manhood, had been helpless, unable to block his jealous uncle's treachery. He had been attacked by his own guard as he prayed in the temple (*In the temple*—his mouth pulled back), and maimed, barely escaping with his life, to find that his entire world had come to an end. He had become a hunted fugitive in his own land, friendless, trusting no one—forced to lie and steal and grovel to survive. He had eaten scraps thrown out to dogs and lain on hard stones in the rain, while the festering wound in his back kept him away from any rest. . . .

Reliving each day, each moment, of his suffering and humiliation, he felt his rage and his hunger for revenge grow hotter. The Earth hated this usurper of Her holy place, the girl had said . . . but no more than he hated the usurper of his throne. He climbed to his feet again, every muscle on fire, and held out his hands. He shouted the incantation aloud, as though it could carry all the way to his homeland. *His homeland:* he would see it again, make it his own again—

The power entered him as the final word left his mouth,

paralyzing every nerve, stopping even the breath in his throat. Fear and elation were swept up together into the maelstrom of his emotions, and power exploded like a sun behind his eyes. But through the fiery haze that blinded him, he could still see the water heaved up from its bed, a steely wall crowned with white, crumbling over and down on itself. It swept toward him, a terrifying cataclysm, until he thought that he would be drowned in the rushing flood. But it passed him by where he stood, plunging on over the outcropping roof of the cave below. Eddies of foam swirled around his feet, soaking his stained leggings.

The power left him like the water's surge falling away. He took a deep breath, and another, backing out of the flood. His body moved sluggishly, drained, abandoned, an empty husk. But his mind was full with triumph and rejoicing.

The ground beneath his feet shuddered, jarring his elation, dropping him giddily back into reality. He pressed his head with his hands as pain filled his senses, a madness crowding out coherent thought—a pain that was not his own.

(Water . . . !) Not a plea, but outrage and confusion, a horror of being trapped in a flood of molten fire. *The dragon.* He realized suddenly what had invaded his mind; realized that he had never stopped to wonder how a storm might communicate with a man: Not by human speech, but by stranger, more elemental means. Water from the fall he had created must be seeping into its lair. . . . His face twisted with satisfaction. "Dragon!" He called it with his mind and his voice together.

(Who calls? Who tortures me? Who fouls my lair? Show yourself, slave!)

"Show yourself to me, Storm King! Come out of your cave and destroy me—if you can!" The wildness of his challenge was tinged with terror.

The dragon's fury filled his head until he thought that it would burst; the ground shook beneath his feet. But the rage turned to frustration and died, as though the gates of liquid iron had bottled it up with its possessor. He gulped air, holding his body together with an effort of will. The voice of the dragon pushed aside his thoughts again, trampled them underfoot; but he knew that it could not reach him, and he endured without weakening.

(Who are you, and why have you come?)

He sensed a grudging resignation in the formless words, the feel of a ritual as eternal as the rain.

"I am a man who should have been a king. I've come to you, who are King of Storms, for help in regaining my own kingdom."

(You ask me for that? Your needs mean nothing, human. You were born to misery, born to crawl, born to struggle and be defeated by the powers of Air and Fire and Water. You are meaningless, you are less than nothing to me!)

Lassan-din felt the truth of his own insignificance, the weight of the dragon's disdain. "That may be," he said sourly. "But this insignificant human has penned you up with the Earth's blessing, and I have no reason to ever let you go unless you pledge me your aid."

The rage of the storm beast welled up in him again, so like his own rage; it rumbled and thundered in the hollow of the mountain. But again a profound agony broke its fury, and the raging storm subsided. He caught phantom images of stone walls lit by shifting light, the smell of water.

(If you have the strength of the Earth with you, why bother me for mine?)

"The Earth moves too slowly," *and too uncertainly,* but he did not say that. "I need a fury to match my own."

(Arrogant fool,) the voice whispered, (you have no measure of my fury.)

"Your fury can crumble walls and blast towers. You can destroy a fortress castle—and the men who defend it. I know what you can do," refusing to be cowed. "And if you swear to do it for me, I'll set you free."

(You want a castle ruined. Is that all?) A tone of false reason crept into the intruding thoughts.

"No. I also want for myself a share of your strength—protection from my enemies." He had spent half a hundred cold, sleepless nights planning these words; searching his memory for pieces of dragonlore, trying to guess the limits of its power.

(How can I give you that? I do not share my power, unless I strike you dead with it.)

"My people say that in the Golden Time the heroes wore

mail made from dragon scales, and were invincible. Can you give me that?'' He asked the question directly, knowing that the dragon might evade the truth, but that it was bound by immutable natural law and could not lie.

(I can give you that,) grudgingly. (Is that all you ask of me?)

Lassan-din hesitated. "No. One more thing." His father had taught him caution, if nothing else. "One request to be granted at some future time—a request within your power, but one you must obey."

The dragon muttered, deep within the mountainside, and Lassan-din sensed its growing distress as the water poured into the cave. (If it is within my power, then, yes!) Dark clouds of anger filled his mind. (Free me, and you will have everything you ask!) *And more*— Did he hear that last, or was it only the echoing of his own mind? (Free me, and enter my den.)

"What I undo, I can do again." He spoke the warning more to reassure himself than to remind the dragon. He gathered himself mentally, knowing this time what he was reaching toward with all his strength, made confident by his success. And the Earth answered him once more. He saw the river shift and heave again like a glistening serpent, cascading back into its original bed; opening the cave mouth to his sight, fanged and dripping. He stood alone on the hillside, deafened by his heartbeat and the crashing absence of the river's voice. And then, calling his own strength back, he slid and clambered down the hillside to the mouth of the dragon's cave.

The flickering illumination of the dragon's fire led him deep into a maze of stone passageways, his boots slipping on the wet rock. His hair stood on end and his fingertips tingled with static charge; the air reeked of ozone. The light grew stronger as he rounded a final corner of rock; blazed up, echoing and reechoing from the walls. He shouted in protest as it pinned him like a creeping insect against the cave wall.

The light faded gradually to a tolerable level, letting him observe as he was observed, taking in the towering, twisted, black-tar formations of congealed magma that walled this cavern . . . the sudden, heart-stopping vision they enclosed.

He looked on the Storm King in silence for a time that seemed endless.

A glistening layer of cast-off scales was its bed, and he could scarcely tell where the mound ceased and the dragon's own body began. The dragon looked nothing like the legends described, and yet just as he had expected it to (and somehow he did not find that strange): Great mailed claws like crystal kneaded the shifting opalescence of its bed; its forelegs shimmered with the flexing of its muscles. It had no hindquarters, its body tapered into the fluid coils of a snake's form woven through the glistening pile. Immense segmented wings, as leathery as a bat's, as fragile as a butterfly's, cloaked its monstrous strength. A long, sinuous neck stretched toward him; red faceted eyes shone with inner light from a face that was closest to a cat's face of all the things he knew, but fiercely fanged and grotesquely distorted. The horns of a stag sprouted from its forehead, and foxfire danced among the spines. The dragon's size was a thing that he could have described easily, and yet it was somehow immeasurable, beyond his comprehension.

This was the creature he had challenged and brought to bay with his feeble spell-casting . . . this boundless, pitiless, infinite demon of the air. His body began to tremble, having more sense than he did. But he *had* brought it to bay, taken its word-bond, and it had not blasted him the moment he entered its den. He forced his quavering voice to carry boldly, "I'm here. Where is my armor?"

(Leave your useless garments and come forward. My scales are my strength. Lie among them and cover yourself with them. But remember when you do that if you wear my mail, and share my power, you may find them hard to put off again. Do you accept that?)

"Why would I ever want to get rid of power? I accept it! Power is the center of everything."

(But power has its price, and we do not always know how high it will be.) The dragon stirred restlessly, remembering the price of power as the water still pooling on the cavern's floor seeped up through its shifting bed.

Lassan-din frowned, hearing a deceit because he expected one. He stripped off his clothing without hesitation and crossed the vast, shadow-haunted chamber to the gleaming mound. He lay down below the dragon's baleful gaze and buried himself in the cool, scintillating flecks of scale. They were damp and surprisingly light under his touch, adhering to his body like the dust rubbed from a moth's wing. When he had covered himself completely, until even his hair glistened with myriad infinitesimal lights, the dragon bent its head until the horrible mockery of a cat's face loomed above him. He cringed back as it opened its mouth, showing him row behind row of inward-turning teeth, and a glowing forge of light. It let its breath out upon him, and his sudden scream rang darkly in the chamber as lightning wrapped his unprotected body.

But the crippling lash of pain was gone as quickly as it had come, and looking at himself he found the coating of scales fused into a film of armor as supple as his own skin, and as much a part of him now. His scale-gloved hands met one another in wonder, the hands of an alien creature.

(Now come.) A great glittering wing extended, inviting him to climb. (Cling to me as your armor clings to you, and let me do your bidding and be done with it.)

He mounted the wing with elaborate caution, and at last sat astride the reptilian neck, clinging to it with an uncertainty that did not fully acknowledge its reality.

The dragon moved under him without ceremony or sign, slithering down from its dais of scales with a hiss and rumble that trembled the closed space. A wind rose around them with the movement; Lassan-din felt himself swallowed into a vortex of cold, terrifying force that took his breath away, blinding and deafening him as he was sucked out of the cave-darkness and into the outer air.

Lightning cracked and shuddered, penetrating his closed lids, splitting apart his consciousness; thunder clogged his chest, reverberating through his flesh and bones like the crashing fall of an avalanche. Rain lashed him, driving into his eyes, swallowing him whole but not dissolving or dissipating his armor of scales.

In the first wild moments of storm he had been piercingly aware of an agony that was not his own, a part of the dragon's being tied into his consciousness, while the fury of rain and storm fed back on their creator. But now there was no pain, no awareness of anything tangible; even the substantiality of the dragon's existence beneath him had faded. The elemental storm was all that existed now, he was aware only of its raw, unrelenting power surrounding him, sweeping him on to his destiny.

After an eternity lost in the storm he found his sight again, felt the dragon's rippling motion beneath his hands. The clouds parted and as his vision cleared he saw, ahead and below, the gray stone battlements of the castle fortress that had once been his . . . and was about to become his again. He shouted in half-mad exultation, feeling the dragon's surging, unconquerable strength become his own. He saw from his incredible height the tiny, terrified forms of those men who had defeated and tormented him, saw them cowering like worms before the doom descending upon them. And then the vision was torn apart again in a blinding explosion of energy, as lightning struck the stone towers again and again, and the screams of the fortress's defenders were lost in the avalanche of thunder. His own senses reeled, and he felt the dragon's solidness dissolve beneath him once more; with utter disbelief felt himself falling, like the rain. . . . "No! No—!"

But his reeling senses righted abruptly, and he found himself standing solidly on his own feet, on the smoking battlements of his castle. Storm and flame and tumbled stone were all around him, but the blackened, fear-filled faces of the beaten defenders turned as one to look up at his; their arms rose, pointing, their cries reached him dimly. An arrow struck his chest, and another struck his shoulder, staggering him; but they fell away, rattling harmlessly down his scaled body to his feet. A shaft of sunlight broke the clouds, setting afire the glittering carapace of his armor. Already the storm was beginning to dissipate; above him the dragon's retreat stained the sky with a band of rainbow scales falling. The voice of the storm touched his mind a final time, (You have what you desire. May it bring you the pleasure you deserve.)

The survivors began, one by one, to fall to their knees below him.

* * *

Lassan-din had ridden out of exile on the back of the whirlwind, and his people bowed down before him, not in welcome but in awe and terror. He reclaimed his birthright and his throne, purging his realm of those who had overthrown it with vengeful thoroughness, but never able to purge himself of the memories of what they had done to him. His treacherous uncle had been killed in the dragon's attack, robbing Lassan-din of his longed-for retribution, the payment in kind for his own crippling wound. He wore his bitterness like the glittering dragonskin, and he found that like the dragonskin it could not be cast off again. His people hated and feared him for his shining alienness; hated him all the more for his attempts to secure his place as their ruler, seeing in him the living symbol of his uncle's inhumanity, and his father's. But he knew no other way to rule them; he could only go on, as his father had done before him, proving again and again to his people that there was no escaping what he had become. Not for them, not for himself.

They called him the Storm King, and he had all the power he had ever dreamed of—but it brought him no pleasure or ease, no escape from the knowledge that he was hated or from the chronic pain of his maimed back. He was both more and less than a man, but he was no longer a man. He was only the king. His comfort and happiness mattered to no one, except that his comfort reflected their own. No thought, no word, no act affected him that was not performed out of selfishness; and more and more he withdrew from any contact with that imitation of intimacy.

He lay alone again in his chambers on a night that was black and formless, like all his nights. Lying between silken sheets he dreamed that he was starving and slept on stones.

Pain woke him. He drank port wine (as lately he drank it too often) until he slept again, and entered the dream he had had long ago in a witch's hut, a dream that might have been something more. . . . But he woke from that dream too; and waking, he remembered the witch-girl's last words to him, echoed by the storm's roaring—"May you get what you deserve."

That same day he left his fortress castle, where the new stone of its mending showed whitely against the old; left his rule in the hands of advisors cowed by threats of the dragon's return; left his homeland again on a journey to the dreary, gray-clad land of his exile.

He did not come to the village of Wydden as a hunted exile this time, but as a conqueror gathering tribute from his subject lands. No one there recognized the one in the other, or knew why he ordered the village priest thrown bodily out of his wretched temple into the muddy street. But on the dreary day when Lassan-din made his way at last into the dripping woods beneath the ancient volcanic peak, he made the final secret journey not as a conqueror. He came alone to the ragged hut pressed up against the brooding mountain wall, suffering the wet and cold like a friendless stranger.

He came upon the clearing between the trees with an unnatural suddenness, to find a figure in mud-stained, earth-brown robes standing by the well, waiting, without surprise. He knew instantly that it was not the old hag; but it took him a longer moment to realize who it was: The girl called Nothing stood before him, dressed as a woman now, her brown hair neatly plaited on top of her head and bearing herself with a woman's dignity. He stopped, throwing back the hood of his cloak to let her see his own glittering face— though he was certain she already knew him, had expected him.

She bowed to him with seeming formality. "The Storm King honors my humble shrine." Her voice was not humble in the least.

"Your shrine?" He moved forward. "Where's the old bitch?"

She folded her arms as though to ward him off. "Gone forever. As I thought you were. But I'm still here, and I serve in her place; I am Fallatha, the Earth's Own, now. And your namesake still dwells in the mountain, bringing grief to all who live in its cloud-shadow. . . . I thought you'd taken all you could from us, and gained everything you wanted. Why have you come back, and come like a beggar?"

His mouth thinned. But this once he stopped the arrogant response that came too easily to his lips—remembering that he had come here the way he had to remind himself that he must ask, and not demand. "I came because I need your help again."

"What could I possibly have to offer our great ruler? My spells are nothing compared to the storm's wrath. And you have no use for my poor body—"

He jerked at the mocking echo of his own thoughts. "Once I had, on that night we both remember—that night you gave me back the use of mine." He gambled with the words. His eyes sought the curve of her breasts, not quite hidden beneath her loose outer robe.

"It was a dream, a wish; no more. It never happened." She shook her head, her face still expressionless. But in the silence that fell between them he heard a small, uncanny sound that chilled him. Somewhere in the woods a baby was crying.

Fallatha glanced unthinkingly over her shoulder, toward the hut, and he knew then that it was her child. She made a move to stop him as he started past her; let him go, and followed resignedly. He found the child inside, an infant squalling in a blanket on a bed of fragrant pine boughs. Its hair was midnight black, its eyes were dark, its skin dusky; his own child, he knew with a certainty that went beyond simply what his eyes showed him. He knelt, unwrapping the blanket—let it drop back as he saw the baby's form. "A girl-child." His voice was dull with disappointment.

Fallatha's eyes said that she understood the implications. "Of course. I have no more use for a boy-child than you have for that one. Had it been a male child, I would have left it in the woods."

His head came up angrily, and her gaze slapped him with his own scorn. He looked down again at his infant daughter, feeling ashamed. "Then it did happen. . . ." His hands tightened by his knees. "Why?" Looking up at her again.

"Many reasons, and many you couldn't understand. . . . But one was to win my freedom from the Old One. She stole my soul, and hid it in a tree to keep me her slave. She might have died without telling me where it was. Without a soul I had no center, no strength, no reality. So I brought a new soul into myself—this one's," smiling suddenly at the wailing baby, "and used its focus to make her give me back my own.

And then with two souls," the smile hardened, "I took hers away. She wanders the forest now searching for it. But she won't find it." Fallatha touched the pendant of rock crystal that hung against her breast; what had been ice-clear before was now a deep, smoky gray color.

Lassan-din suppressed a shudder. "But why *my* child?" *My child.* His own gaze would not stay away from the baby for long. "Surely any village lout would have been glad to do you the service."

"Because you have royal blood, you were a king's son—you are a king."

"That's not necessarily proof of good breeding." He surprised himself with his own honesty.

"But you called on the Earth, and She answered you. I have never seen Her answer a man before . . . and because you were in need." Her voice softened unexpectedly. "An act of kindness begets a kind soul, they say."

"And now you hope to beget some reward for it, no doubt." He spoke the words with automatic harshness. "Greed and pity—a fitting set of godparents, to match her real ones."

She shrugged. "You will see what you want to see, I suppose. But even a blind man could see more clearly." A frown pinched her forehead. "You've come here to me for help, Lassan-din; I didn't come to you."

He rubbed his scale-bright hands together, a motion that had become a habit long since; they clicked faintly. "Does—does the baby have a name?"

"Not yet. It is not our custom to name a child before its first year. Too often they die. Especially in these times."

He looked away from her eyes. "What will you do with—our child?" Realizing suddenly that it mattered a great deal to him.

"Keep her with me, and raise her to serve the Earth, as I do."

"If you help me again, I'll take you both back to my own lands, and give you anything you desire." He searched her face for a response.

"I desire to be left in peace with my child and my goddess." She leaned down to pick the baby up, let it seek her breast.

His inspiration crystallized: "Damn it, I'll throw my own priests out, I'll make your goddess the only one and you Her high priestess!"

Her eyes brightened, and faded. "A promise easily spoken, and difficult to keep."

"What do you want, then?" He got to his feet, exasperated.

"You have a boon left with the dragon, I know. Make it leave the mountain. Send it away."

He ran his hands through his glittering hair. "No. I need it. I came here seeking help for myself, not your people."

"They're your people now—they *are* you. Help them and you help yourself! Is that so impossible for you to see?" Her own anger blazed white, incandescent with frustration.

"If you want to be rid of the dragon so much, why haven't you sent it away yourself, witch?"

"I would have." She touched the baby's tiny hand, its soft black hair. "Long ago. But until the little one no longer suckles my strength away, I lack the power to call the Earth to my purpose."

"Then you can't help me, either." His voice was flat and hopeless.

"I still have the salve that eased your back. But it won't help you now, it won't melt away your dragon's skin. . . . I couldn't help your real needs, even if I had all my power."

"What do you mean?" He thrust his face at her. "You think that's why I've come to you—to be rid of this skin? What makes you think I'd ever want to give up *my* power, my protection?" He clawed at his arms.

"It's not a man's skin that makes him a god—or a monster," Fallatha said quietly. "It's what lies beneath the skin, behind the eyes. You've lost your soul, as I lost mine; and only you know where to find it. . . . But perhaps it would do you good to shed that skin that keeps you safe from hatred; and from love and joy and mercy, all the other feelings that might pass between human beings, between your people and their king."

"Yes! Yes, I want to be free of it, by the Holy Sun!" His defiance collapsed under the weight of the truth: He saw at last that he had come here this time to rid himself of the same things he had come to rid himself of—and to find—before. "I have a last boon due me from the dragon. It made me as I am; it can unmake me.'' He ran his hands down his chest, feeling the slippery, unyielding scales hidden beneath the rich cloth of his shirt.

''You mean to seek it out again, then?''

He nodded, and his hands made fists.

She carried the baby with her to the shelf above the crooked window, took down a small earthenware pot. She opened it and held it close to the child's face still buried at her breast; the baby sagged into sleep in the crook of her arm. She turned back to his uncomprehending face. ''The little one will sleep now until I wake her. We can take the inner way, as we did before.''

''You're coming? Why?''

''You didn't ask me that before. Why ask it now?''

He wasn't sure whether it was a question or an answer. Feeling as though not only his body but his mind was an empty shell, he shrugged and kept silent.

They made the nightmare climb into blackness again, worming their way upward through the mountain's entrails; but this time she did not leave him where the mountain spewed them out, close under the weeping lid of the sky. He rested the night with the mother of his child, the two of them lying together but apart. At dawn they pushed on, Lassan-din leading now, following the river's rushing torrent upward into the past.

They came to the dragon's cave at last, gazed on it for a long while in silence, having no strength left for speech.

''Storm King!'' Lassan-din gathered the rags of his voice and his concentration for a shout. ''Hear me! I have come for my last request!''

There was an alien stirring inside his mind; the charge in the air and the dim, flickering light deep within the cave seemed to intensify.

(So you have returned to plague me.) The voice inside his head cursed him, with the weariness of the ages. He felt the stretch and play of storm-sinews rousing; remembered suddenly, dizzily, the feel of his ride on the whirlwind.

(Show yourself to me.)

They followed the winding tunnel as he had done before to

an audience in the black hall radiant with the dust of rainbows. The dragon crouched on its scaly bed, its glowering ruby eye fixed on them. Lassan-din stopped, trying to keep a semblance of self-possession. Fallatha drew her robes close together at her throat and murmured something unintelligible.

(I see that this time you have the wisdom to bring your true source of power with you . . . though she has no power in her now. Why have you come to me again? Haven't I given you all that you asked for?)

"All that and more," he said heavily. "You've doubled the weight of the griefs I brought with me before."

(I?) The dragon bent its head; its horn raked them with claw-fingered shadows in the sudden, swelling brightness. (I did nothing to you. Whatever consequences you've suffered are no concern of mine.)

Lassan-din bit back a stinging retort; said, calmly, "But you remember that you owe me one final boon. You know that I've come to collect it."

(Anything within my power.) The huge cat-face bowed ill-humoredly; Lassan-din felt his skin prickle with the static energy of the moment.

"Then take away these scales you fixed on me, that make me invulnerable to everything human!" He pulled off his drab, dark cloak and the rich, royal clothing of red and blue beneath it, so that his body shone like an echo of the dragon's own.

The dragon's faceted eyes regarded him without feeling. (I cannot.)

Lassan-din froze as the words out of his blackest nightmares turned him to stone. "What—what do you mean, you cannot? You did this to me—you can undo it!"

(I cannot. I can give you invulnerability, but I cannot take it away from you. I cannot make your scales dissolve and fall away with a breath any more than I can keep the rain from dissolving mine, or causing me exquisite pain. It is in the nature of power that those who wield it must suffer from it, even as their victims suffer. This is power's price—I tried to warn you. But you didn't listen . . . none of them have ever listened.) Lassan-din felt the sting of venom, and the ache of an ageless empathy.

He struggled to grasp the truth, knowing that the dragon could not lie. He swayed as belief struck him at last, like a blow. "Am I . . . am I to go through the rest of my life like this, then? Like a monster?" He rubbed his hands together, a useless, mindless washing motion.

(I only know that it is not in my power to give you freedom from yourself.) The dragon wagged its head, its face swelling with light, dazzling him. (Go away, then,) the thought struck him fiercely, (and suffer elsewhere!)

Lassan-din turned away, stumbling, like a beaten dog. But Fallatha caught at his glittering, naked shoulder, shook him roughly. "Your boon! It still owes you one—ask it!"

"Ask for what?" he mumbled, barely aware of her. "There's nothing I want."

"There is! Something for your people, for your child— even for you. Ask for it! Ask!"

He stared at her, saw her pale, pinched face straining with suppressed urgency and desire. He saw in her eyes the endless sunless days, the ruined crops, the sodden fields—the mud and hunger and misery the Storm King had brought to the lands below for three times her lifetime. And the realization came to him that even now, when he had lost control of his own life, he still had the power to end this land's misery.

He turned back into the sight of the dragon's hypnotically swaying head. "My last boon, then, is something else; something I know to be within your power, stormbringer. I want you to leave this mountain, leave these lands, and never return. I want you to travel seven days on your way before you seek a new settling place, if you ever do. Travel as fast as you can, and as far, without taking retribution from the lands below. That is the final thing I ask of you."

The dragon spat in blinding fury. Lassan-din shut his eyes, felt the ground shudder and roll beneath him. (You dare to command me to leave my chosen lands? You dare?)

"I claim my right!" He shouted it, his voice breaking. "Leave these lands alone—take your grief elsewhere and be done with them, and me!"

(As you wish, then—) The Storm King swelled above them until it filled the cave-space, its eyes a garish hellshine fading into the night-blackness of storm. Lightning sheeted the closing walls, thunder rumbled through the rock, a screaming whirlwind battered them down against the cavern floor. Rain poured over them until there was no breathing space, and the Storm King roared its agony inside their skulls as it suffered retribution for its vengeance. Lassan-din felt his senses leave him; thinking the storm's revenge would be the last thing he ever knew, the end of the world. . . .

But he woke again, to silence. He stirred sluggishly on the wet stone floor, filling his lungs again and again with clear air, filling his empty mind with the awareness that all was quiet now, that no storm raged for his destruction. He heard a moan, not his own, and coughing echoed hollowly in the silence. He raised his head, reached out in the darkness, groping, until he found her arm. "Fallatha—?"

"Alive . . . praise the Earth."

He felt her move, sitting up, dragging herself toward him. The Earth, the cave in which they lay, had endured the storm's rage with sublime indifference. They helped each other up, stumbled along the wall to the entrance tunnel, made their way out through the blackness onto the mountainside.

They stood together, clinging to each other for support and reassurance, blinking painfully in the glaring light of early evening. It took him long moments to realize that there was more light than he remembered, not less.

"Look!" Fallatha raised her arm, pointing. Water dripped in a silver line from the sleeve of her robe. "The sky! The sky—" She laughed, a sound that was almost a sob.

He looked up into the aching glare, saw patches that he took at first for blackness, until his eyes knew them finally for blue. It was still raining lightly, but the clouds were parting; the tyranny of gray was broken at last. For a moment he felt her joy as his own, a fleeting, wild triumph—until, looking down, he saw his hands again, and his shimmering body still scaled, monstrous, untransformed. . . . "Oh, gods—!" His fists clenched at the sound of his own curse, a useless plea to useless deities.

Fallatha turned to him, her arm still around his shoulder, her face sharing his despair. "Lassan-din, remember that my people will love you for your sacrifice. In time, even your own people may come to love you for it. . . .'' She touched his scaled cheek hesitantly, a promise.

"But all they'll ever see is how I look! And no matter what I do from now on, when they see the mark of damnation on me, they'll only remember why they hated me." He caught her arms in a bruising grip. "Fallatha, help me, please—I'll give you anything you ask!"

She shook her head, biting her lips. "I can't, Lassan-din. No more than the dragon could. You must help yourself, change yourself—I can't do that for you."

"How? How can I change this if all the magic of Earth and Sky can't do it?" He sank to his knees, feeling the rain strike the opalescent scales and trickle down—feeling it dimly, barely, as though the rain fell on someone else. . . . Through all of his life, the rain had never fallen unless it fell on him; the wind had never stirred the trees, a child had never cried in hunger, unless it was his hunger. And yet he had never truly felt any of those things—never even been aware of his own loss. . . . Until now, looking up at the mother of his only child, whose strength of feeling had forced him to drive out the dragon, the one unselfish thing he had ever done. Remorse and resolution filled the emptiness in him, as rage had filled him on this spot once before. Tears welled in his eyes and spilled over, in answer to the calling-spell of grief; ran down his face, mingling with the rain. He put up his hands, sobbing uncontrollably, unself-consciously, as though he were the last man alive in the world, and alone forever.

And as he wept he felt a change begin in the flesh that met there, face against hands. A tingling and burning, the feel of skin sleep-deadened coming alive again. He lowered his hands wonderingly, saw the scales that covered them dissolving, the skin beneath them his own olive-brown, supple and smooth. He shouted in amazement, and wept harder, pain and joy intermingled, like the tears and rain that melted the cursed scales from his body and washed them away.

He went on weeping until he had cleansed himself in body and spirit; set himself free from the prison of his own making. And then, exhausted and uncertain, he climbed to his feet again, meeting the calm, gray gaze of the Earth's gratitude in

Fallatha's eyes. He smiled and she smiled; the unexpectedness of the expression, and the sight of it, resonated in him.

Sunlight was spreading across the patchwork land far below, dressing the mountain slope in royal greens, although the rain still fell around them. He looked up almost unthinkingly, searching—found what he had not realized he sought. Fallatha followed his glance and found it with him. Her smile widened at the arching band of colors, the rainbow; not a curse any longer, or a mark of pain, but once again a promise of better days to come.

AFTERWORD—
THE STORM KING

"The Storm King" is one of two stories I've written that I consider to be pure fantasies in the classic sense. A lot of people seem to want to call most or all of my work fantasy (including a fair number of men who apparently don't want to believe women can write anything else), but despite the intentional use of certain mythological references and symbols in some of my stories, I consider myself primarily a science fiction writer. My imagination stubbornly insists that mass ratios should be equal and rocket drives at least theoretically functional; it gets nervous if a man turns into a bird, simply because they don't weigh the same. Nevertheless, I've always enjoyed reading fantasy just as much as I enjoy reading science fiction and have always wanted to try my hand at writing it.

In "The Storm King" I wanted to create something with the feel of a classic fairy tale. Most of the fairy tales we think of as children's stories are more correctly folk tales—tales passed down like folk songs, by word of mouth, through generations, in basically the same ecological niche as mythology. They are rooted in the cultures and superstitions of our ancestors, but they continue to be told, and to exert power over us, because they are about the universal aspects of human relationships. Because their roots are so ancient, some of the fairy tales we know sometimes seem grotesque or almost dreamlike now, but we still recognize the basic morality tale that lies at their heart. "The Storm King" is that sort of morality tale, told with a more modern viewpoint, but drawing on my background in anthropology to give it an archaic feel.

At the time I was working on this novelette, my life was going through another of its recent highly unsettled periods, and I had a great deal of trouble finishing the story. My alienation was so severe that the two protagonists actually had no names through the entire first draft; they were merely sets of parentheses. A trip to England helped me get a fresh start on it—the feel of being in a country with such deep layers of history, and actually seeing the beauty of the land and its ruins of ancient places (where ancestors of mine might even have lived) was literally inspiring to my muse. And I found the perfect image of the dragon in my story in a museum there. I came home and finished the story at last.

THE PEDDLER'S APPRENTICE

by Joan D. Vinge and Vernor Vinge

Lord Buckry I of Fyffe lounged on his throne, watching his two youngest sons engaged in mock battle in the empty Audience Hall. The daggers were wooden but the rivalry was real, and the smaller boy was at a disadvantage. Lord Buckry tugged on a heavy gold earring. Thin, brown-haired Hanaban was his private favorite; the boy took after his father both in appearance and turn of mind.

The lord of the Flatlands was a tall man, his own unkempt brown hair graying now at the temples. The blue eyes in his lean, foxlike face still perceived with disconcerting sharpness, though years of experience kept his own thoughts hidden. More than twenty years had passed since he had won control of his lands; he had not kept his precarious place as lord so long without good reason.

Now his eyes flashed rare approval as Hanaban cried, "Trace, look there!" and, as his brother turned, distracted, whacked him soundly on the chest.

"Gotcha!" Hanaban shrieked delightedly. Trace grimaced with disgust.

Their father chuckled, but his face changed suddenly as the sound of a commotion outside the chamber reached him. The heavy, windowed doors at the far end of the room burst open; the Flatlander courier shook off guards, crossed the high-ceilinged, echoing chamber and flung himself into a bow, his rifle clattering on the floor. "Your Lordship!"

Lord Buckry snapped his fingers; his gaping children silently fled the room. "Get up," he said impatiently. "What in tarnation is this?"

"Your Lordship." The courier raised a dusty face, wincing mentally at his lord's Highland drawl. "There's word the sea kingdoms have raised another army. They're crossing the coast mountains, and—"

"That ain't possible. We cleaned them out not half a year since."

"They've a lot of folk along the coast, Your Lordship." The horseman stood apologetically. "And Jayley Sharkstooth's made a pact this time with the Southlands."

Lord Buckry stiffened. "They've been at each other's throats long as I can remember." He frowned, pulling at his earring. "Only thing they've got in common is—me. Damn!"

He listened distractedly to the rider's report, then stood abruptly, dismissing the man as an afterthought. As the heavy doors of the hall slid shut he was already striding toward the elevator, past the shaft of the ballistic vehicle exit, unused for more than thirty years. His soft-soled Highlander boots made no sound on the cold polished floor.

From the parapet of his castle he could survey a wide stretch of his domain, the rich, utterly flat farmlands of the hundred-mile-wide valley—the lands the South and West were hungry for. The fields were dark now with turned earth, ready for the spring planting; it was no time to be calling up an army. He was sure his enemies were aware of that. The day was exceptionally clear, and at the eastern reaches of his sight he could make out the grayed purple wall of the mountains: the Highlands, that held his birthplace—and something more important to him now.

The dry wind ruffled his hair as he looked back across thirty years; his sunburned hands tightened on the seamless, ancient green-blackness of the parapet. "Damn you, Mr. Jagged," he said to the wind. "Where's your magic when I *need* it?"

* * *

The peddler came to Darkwood Corners from the east, on Wim Buckry's seventeenth birthday. It was early summer, and Wim could still see sun flashing on snow up the pine-wooded hill that towered above the Corners; the snowpack in the higher hills was melting at last, sluicing down gullies that stood dry through most of the year, changing Littlebig Creek into a cold, singing torrent tearing at the earth below the cabins on the north side of the road. Even a week ago the East Pass had lain under more than thirty feet of snow.

Something like silence came over the townspeople as they saw the peddler dragging his cart down the east road toward the Corners. His wagon was nearly ten feet tall and fifteen long, with carved, brightly painted wooden sides that bent sharply out over the wheels to meet a gabled roof. Wim gaped in wonder as he saw those wheels, spindly as willow wood yet over five feet across. Under the cart's weight they sank half a foot and more into the mud of the road, but cut through the mud without resistance, without leaving a rut.

Even so, the peddler was bent nearly double with the effort of pulling his load. The fellow was short and heavy, with skin a good deal darker than Wim had ever seen. His pointed black beard jutted at a determined angle as he staggered along the rutted track, up to his ankles in mud. Above his calves the tooled leather of his leggings gleamed black and clean. Several scrofulous dogs nosed warily around him as he plodded down the center of the road; he ignored them as he ignored the staring townsfolk.

Wim shoved his empty mug back at Ounze Rumpster, sitting nearest the tavern door. "More," he said. Ounze swore, got up from the steps, and disappeared into the tavern.

Wim's attention never left the peddler for an instant. As the dark man reached the widening in the road at the center of town, he pulled his wagon into the muddy morass where the Widow Henley's house had stood until the Littlebig Creek dragged it to destruction. The stranger had everyone's attention now. Even the town's smith had left his fire, and stood in his doorway gazing down the street at the peddler.

The peddler turned his back on them as he kicked an arresting gear down from the rear of the painted wagon and let it settle into the mud. He returned to the front of the cart and moved a small wheel set in the wood paneling: a narrow blue pennant sprouted from the peak of the gable and fluttered briskly; crisp and metallic, a pinging melody came from the wagon. That sound emptied the tavern and brought the remainder of the Corners' population onto the street. Ounze Rumpster nearly fell down the wooden steps in his haste to see the source of the music; he sat down heavily, handing the refilled mug to Wim. Wim ignored him.

As the peddler turned back to the crowd the eerie music stopped, and the creek sounded loud in the silence. Then the little man's surprising bass voice rumbled out at them. "Jagit Katchetooriantz is my name, and fine wrought goods is my trade. Needles, adze-heads, blades—you need 'em?" He pulled a latch on the wagon's wall and a panel swung out from its side, revealing rows of shining knife blades and needles so fine Wim could see only glitter where they caught the sunlight. "Step right on up, folks. Take a look, take a feel. Tell me what they might be worth to you." There was no need to repeat the invitation—in seconds he was surrounded. As the townspeople closed around him, he mounted a small step set in the side of the wagon, so that he could still be seen over the crowd.

Wim's boys were on their feet; but he sat motionless, his sharp face intent. "Set down," he said, just loudly enough. "Your eyes is near busting out of your heads. They'd skin us right fast if we try anything here. There's too many. Set!" He gave the nearest of them, Bathecar Henley, a sideways kick in the shin; they all sat. "Gimme that big ring of yours, Sothead."

Ounze Rumpster's younger brother glared at him, then extended his jeweled fist from a filthy woolen cuff. "How come you're so feisty of a sudden, Wim?" He dropped the ring peevishly into the other's hand. Wim turned away without comment, passing the massive chunk of gold to Bathecar's plump, fair girlfriend.

"All right, Emmy, you just take yourself over to that wagon and see about buying us some knife blades—not too long, say about so." He stretched his fingers. "And find out how they're fastened on the rack."

"Sure, Wim." She rose from the steps and minced away

across the muddy road toward the crowd at the peddler's
wagon. Wim grimaced, reflecting that the red knit dress
Bathecar had brought her was perhaps too small.

The peddler's spiel continued, all but drowning out the
sound of Littlebig Creek: "Just try your blades 'gin mine,
friends. Go ahead. Nary a scratch you've made on mine, see?
Now how much is it worth, friends? I'll take gold, silver. Or
craft items. And I need a horse—lost my own, coming down
those blamed trails." He waved toward the East Pass. The
townspeople were packed tightly together now as each of
them tried for a chance to test the gleaming metal, and to
make some bid that would catch the peddler's fancy. Emmy
wriggled expertly into the mass; in seconds Wim could see
her red dress right at the front of the crowd. She was happily
fondling the merchandise, competing with the rest for the
stranger's attention.

Hanaban Kroy shifted his bulk on the hard wooden step.
"Three gold pigs says that outlander is from down west. He
just come in from the east to set us all to talking. Nobody
makes knives like them east of the pass."

Wim nodded slightly. "Could be." He watched the peddler and fingered the thick gold earring half-hidden in his
shaggy brown hair.

Across the road, the merchant was engaged in a four-way
bidding session. Many of the townsfolk wanted to trade furs,
or crossbows, but Jagit Katchetooriantz wasn't interested.
This narrowed his potential clientele considerably. Even as he
argued avidly with those below him, his quick dark eyes
flickered up and down the street, took in the gang by the
tavern, impaled Wim for a long, cold instant.

The peddler lifted several blades off the rack and handed
them down, apparently receiving metal in return. Emmy got
at least two. Then he raised his arms for quiet. "Folks, I'm
real sorry for dropping in so sudden, when you all wasn't
ready for me. Let's us quit now and try again tomorrow,
when you can bring what you have to trade. I might even take
on some furs. And bring horses, too, if you want to. Seein' as
how I'm in need of one, I'll give two, maybe three adze
heads for a good horse or mule. All right?"

It wasn't. Several frustrated townsfolk tried to pry merchandise off the rack. Wim noticed that they were unsuccessful. The merchant pulled the lanyard at the front of the cart and the rack turned inward, returning carved wood paneling to the outside. As the crowd thinned, Wim saw Emmy, clutching two knives and a piece of print cloth, still talking earnestly to the peddler.

The peddler took a silvery chain from around his waist, passed it through the wheels of his cart and then around a nearby tree. Then he followed Emmy back across the road.

Ounze Rumpster snorted. "That sure is a teensy ketter. Betcha we could bust it right easy."

"Could be . . ." Wim nodded again, not listening. Anger turned his eyes to blue ice as Emmy led the peddler right to the tavern steps.

"Oh, Bathecar, just lookit the fine needles Mr. Ketchatoor sold me—"

Sothead struggled to his feet. "You stupid little—little— We told you to buy knives. Knives! And you used my ring to buy needles!" He grabbed the cloth from Emmy's hands and began ripping it up.

"Hey—!" Emmy began to pound him in useless fury, clawing after her prize. "Bathecar, make him stop!" Bathecar and Ounze pulled Sothead down, retrieved needles and cloth. Emmy pouted, "Big lout."

Wim frowned and drank, his attention fixed on the peddler. The dark man stood looking from one gang member to another, hands loosely at his sides, smiling faintly; the calm black eyes missed nothing. Eyes like that didn't belong in the face of a fat peddler. Wim shifted uncomfortably, gnawed by sudden uncertainty. He shook it off. How many chances did you get up here, to try a contest where the outcome wasn't sure— He stood and thrust out his hand. "Wim Buckry's the name, Mr. Ketchatoor. Sorry about Sothead; he's drunk all the time, 'truth."

The peddler had to reach up slightly to shake his hand. "Folks mostly call me Jagit. Pleased to meet you. Miss Emmy here tells me you and your men sometimes hire out to protect folks such as me."

Behind him, Bathecar Henley was open-mouthed. Emmy simpered; every so often, she proved that she was not as stupid as she looked. Wim nodded judiciously. "We do, and it's surely worth it to have our service. There's a sight of thieves in these hills, but most of them will back down from six good bows." He glanced at Sothead. "Five good bows."

"Well then." The pudgy little man smiled blandly, and for a moment Wim wondered how he could ever have seen anything deadly in that face. "I'd like to give you some of my business."

And so they came down out of the high hills. It was early summer, but in the Highlands more like a boisterous spring: Under the brilliant blue sky, green spread everywhere over the ground, nudging the dingy hummocks of melting snow and outcropping shelves of ancient granite. Full leaping streams sang down the alpine valleys, plunged over falls and rapids that smashed the water to white foam and spread it in glinting veils scarcely an inch deep over bedrock. The ragged peaks skirted with glacier fell further and further behind, yet the day grew no warmer; everywhere the chill water kept the air cool.

The peddler and his six "protectors" followed a winding course through deep soughing pine forest, broken by alpine meadows where bright starlike flowers bloomed and the short hummocky grass made their ankles ache with fatigue. They passed by marshes that even in the coolness swarmed with eager mosquitoes, and Wim's high moccasins squelched on the soft dank earth.

But by late afternoon the party had reached Witch Hollow Trail, and the way grew easier for the horse pulling the merchant's wagon. Somewhere ahead of them Ounze Rumpster kept the point position; off to the side were fat Hanaban, Bathecar, and Shorty, while Sothead Rumpster, now nearly sober, brought up the rear. In the Highlands even the robbers— particularly the robbers—journeyed with caution.

For most of the day Wim traveled silently, listening to the streaming water, the wind, the twittering birds among the pines—listening for sounds of human treachery. But it seemed they were alone. He had seen one farmer about four miles outside of Darkwood Corners and since then, no one.

Yesterday the peddler had questioned him about the area, and how many folk were in the vicinity of the Corners, what they did for a living. He'd seemed disappointed when he'd heard they were mostly poor, scattered farmers and trappers, saying his goods were more the kind to interest rich city folk. Wim had promptly allowed as how he was one of the few Highlanders who had ever been down into the Great Valley, all the way to the grand city of Fyffe; and that they'd be more than glad to guide him down into the Flatlands—for a price. If a little greed would conceal their real intentions, so much the better. And the peddler's partial payment, of strange, jewel-studded silver balls, had only added to the sincerity of their interest in his future plans.

Wim glanced over at the peddler, walking beside him near the dappled cart horse. Up close, the stranger seemed even more peculiar than at a distance. His straight black hair was cut with unbelievable precision at the base of his neck; Wim wondered if he'd set a bowl on his head and cut around it. And he smelled odd; not unpleasant, but more like old pine-needles than man. The silver thread stitched into the peddler's soft leather shirt was finer than Wim had ever seen. That would be a nice shirt to have— Wim tugged absently at the loops of bead and polished metal hanging against his own worn linen shirt.

Though short and heavy, the stranger walked briskly and didn't seem to tire; in fact, became friendlier and more talkative as the afternoon passed. But when they reached Witch Hollow he fell silent again, looking first at the unusual smoothness of the path, then up at the naked bedrock wall that jutted up at the side of the narrow trail.

They had walked for about half a mile when Wim volunteered, "This here's called Witch Hollow. There's a story, how once folk had magic to fly through the air in strange contraptions. One of them lost his magic hereabouts—up till twenty years ago, there was still a place you could see the bones, and pieces of steel, they say, all rusted up. Some say this trail through the holler ain't natural, either."

Jagit made no reply, but walked with his head down, his pointy black beard tucked into his chest. For the first time since they had begun the journey he seemed to lose interest in the scenery. At last he said, "How long you figure it's been since this flying contraption crashed here?"

Wim shrugged. "My granther heard the story from his own granther."

"Hmm. And that's all the . . . magic you've heard tell of?"

Wim decided not to tell the peddler what he knew about Fyffe. That might scare the little man into turning back, and force a premature confrontation. "Well, we have witches in these hills, like Widow Henley's cousin, but they're most of them fakes—least the ones I seen. Outside of them and the bad luck that folks claim follows sin"—a grin twitched his mouth—"well, I don't know of no magic. What was you expecting?"

Jagit shook his head. "Something more than a piddling failed witch, that's sure. The more I see of this country, the more I know it ain't the place I started out for."

They walked the next mile in silence. The trail pierced a granite ridge; Wim glimpsed Hanaban high up on their left, paralleling the wagon. Red-faced with exertion, he waved briefly down at them, indicating no problems. Wim returned the signal, and returned to his thoughts about the peculiar little man who walked at his side. Somehow he kept remembering yesterday, Hanaban whining, "Wim, that there little man smells rotten to me. I say we should drop him," and the unease that had crept back into his own mind. Angry at himself as much as anything, he'd snapped, "You going yellow, Han? Just because a feller's strange don't mean he's got an evil eye." And known it hadn't convinced either of them . . .

Perhaps sensing the drift of his silence, or perhaps for some other reason, the peddler began to talk again. This time it was not of where he was going, however, but rather about himself, and where he had come from—a place called Sharn, a land of such incredible wonders that if Wim had heard the tale from someone else he would have laughed.

For Sharn was a land where true magicians ruled, where a flying contraption of steel would be remarkable only for its commonness. Sharn was an immense land—but a city also, a city without streets, a single gleaming sentient crystal that challenged the sky with spears of light. And the people of Sharn by their magic had become like gods; they wore clothing like gossamer, threw themselves across the sky in lightning while thunder followed, spoke to one another over miles. They settled beneath the warm seas of their borders, the weather obeyed them, and they remained young as long as they lived. And their magic made them dreadful warriors and mighty conquerors, for they could kill with scarcely more than a thought and a nod. If a mountain offended them they could destroy it in an instant. Wim thought of his Highlands, and shuddered, touching the bone hilt of the knife strapped to his leg.

Jagit had come to Sharn from a land still further east, and much more primitive. He had stayed and learned what he could of Sharn's magic. The goods he brought to Sharn were popular and had brought high prices; during the time he had spent in the enchanted land he had acquired a small collection of the weaker Sharnish spells. Then he left, to seek a market for these acquisitions—some land where magic was known, but not so deeply as in Sharn.

As the peddler finished his tale, Wim saw that the sun had nearly reached the ridge of the hills to the west before them. He walked on for several minutes, squinting into the sunset for traces of lost Sharn.

The trail curved through ninety degrees, headed down across a small valley. Half hidden in the deepening shadow that now spread over the land, a precarious wooden bridge crossed a stream. Beyond the bridge the pines climbed the darkened hillside into sudden sunlight. Along the far ridgeline, not more than a mile away, ten or twelve immense, solitary trees caught the light, towering over the forest.

"Mr. Jagged, you're the best liar I ever met." Stubbornly Wim swallowed his awe, felt the peddler's unnerving eyes on his face as he pointed across the valley. "Just beyond that ridgeline's where we figure on putting up tonight. A place called Grandfather Grove. Could be you never seen trees that big even in Sharn!"

The peddler peered into the leveling sunlight. "Could be," he said. "I'd surely like to see such trees, anyhow."

They descended from the sunlight into rising darkness. Wim glimpsed Ounze's high felt hat as he walked out of the shadow on the other side of the valley, but none of the other gang members were visible. Wim and the peddler were forced to leave Witch Hollow Trail, and the going became more difficult for horse and wagon; but they reached the edge of the Grandfather Grove in less than half an hour, passing one of the soaring trees, and then two, and three. The dwarfed, spindly pines thinned and finally were gone. Ahead of them were only the grandfather trees, their shaggy striated trunks russet and gold in the dying light. The breeze that had crossed the valley with them, the roaring of the stream behind them, all sounds faded into cathedral silence, leaving only the cool, still air and the golden trees. Wim stopped and bent his head back to catch even a glimpse of the lowest branches, needled with pungent golden-green. This was their land, and he knew more than one tale that told of how the trees guarded it, kept pestiferous creatures away, kept the air cool and the soil fragrant and faintly moist throughout the summer.

"Over here." Hanaban's voice came muted from their left. They rounded the twenty-foot base of a tree, and found Hanaban and Bathecar, setting a small fire with kindling they had carried into the grove—Wim knew the bark of the grandfather trees was almost unburnable. The struggling blaze illuminated an immense pit of darkness behind them; the gutted trunk of an ancient grandfather tree, that formed a living cave-shelter for the night's camp.

By the time they had eaten and rotated lookouts, the sun had set. Wim smothered the fire, and the only light was from the sickle moon following the sun down into the west.

The peddler made no move to bed down, Wim noticed with growing irritation. He sat with legs crossed under him in the shadow of his wagon; motionless and wearing a dark coat against the chill, he was all but invisible, but Wim thought the little man was looking up into the sky. His silence stretched on, until Wim thought he would have to pretend to sleep himself before the peddler would. Finally Jagit stood and walked to the rear of his wagon. He opened a tiny hatch and removed two objects.

"What's them?" Wim asked, both curious and suspicious.

"Just a bit of harmless magic." He set one of the contraptions down on the ground, what seemed to be a long rod with a grip at one end. Wim came up to him, as he put the second object against his eye. The second contraption looked much more complex. It glinted, almost sparkled in the dim moonlight, and Wim thought he saw mirrors and strange rulings on its side. A tiny bubble floated along the side in a tube. The peddler stared through the gadget at the scattering of pale stars visible between the trees. At last he set the device back inside the wagon, and picked up the rod. Wim watched him cautiously as the other walked toward the cave tree; the rod looked too much like a weapon.

Jagit fiddled at the grip of the rod, and an eerie whine spread through the grove. The screaming faded into silence again, but Wim was sure that now the front of the rod was spinning. Jagit set it against the moon-silvered bark of the cave tree, and the tip of the rod began to bore effortlessly into the massive trunk.

Wim's voice quavered faintly. "That . . . that there some of your Sharnish magic, Mr. Jagged?"

The peddler chuckled softly, finishing his experiment. "It ain't hardly that. A Sharnish enchantment is a lot craftier, a lot simpler *looking*. This here's just a simple spell for reading the Signs."

"Um." Wim wavered almost visibly, his curiosity doing battle with his fear. There was a deep, precise hole in the cave tree. *Just because a fellow's strange, Han, don't mean he's got an evil eye* . . . instinctively Wim's fingers crossed. Because it looked like the peddler might not be the world's biggest liar; and that meant— "Maybe I better check how the boys is settled."

When the peddler didn't answer, Wim turned and walked briskly away. At least he hoped that was how it looked; he felt like running. He passed Ounze, half-hidden behind a gigantic stump. Wim said nothing, but motioned for him to continue his surveillance of the peddler and his wagon. The rest stood waiting at a medium-sized grandfather tree nearly a hundred yards from the cave tree, the spot they had agreed on last night in Darkwood Corners. Wim moved silently across the springy ground, rounding the ruins of what must once have been one of the largest trees in the grove; a four-hundred-foot giant that disease and the years had brought crashing down. The great disc of its shattered root system rose more than thirty feet into the air, dwarfing him as he dropped down heavily beside Hanaban.

Bathecar Henley whispered, "Ounze and Sothead I left out as guards."

Wim nodded. "It don't hardly matter. We're not going to touch that peddler."

"What?" Bathecar's exclamation was loud with surprise. He lowered his voice only slightly as he continued. "One man? You're ascared of one man?"

Wim motioned threateningly for silence. "You heard me. Hanaban here was right, that Jagged is just too damn dangerous. He's a warlock, he's got an evil eye. And he's got some kind of knife back there that can cut clean through a grandfather tree! And the way he talks, that's just the least . . ."

The others' muttered curses cut him off. Only Hanaban Kroy kept silent.

"You're crazy, Wim," the hulking shadow of Shorty said. "We've walked fifteen miles today. And you're telling us it was for nothing! It'd be easier to farm for a living."

"We'll still get something, but it looks like we'll have to go honest for a while. I figure on guiding him down, say to where the leaf forests start, and then asking pretty please for half of what he promised us back at the Corners."

"I sure as hell ain't going to follow nobody that far down toward the Valley." Bathecar frowned.

"Well, then, you can just turn around and head back. I'm running this here gang, Bathecar, don't you forget it. We already got something out of this deal, them silver balls he give us as first payment."

Something went *hisss* and then *thunk*; Hanaban sprawled forward, collapsed on the moonlit ground beyond the tree's shadow. A crossbow bolt protruded from his throat.

As Wim and Bathecar scrambled for the cover of the rotting root system, Shorty rose and snarled, "That damn peddler!" It cost him his life; three arrows smashed into him where he stood, and he collapsed across Hanaban.

Wim heard their attackers closing in on them, noisily confident. From what he could see, he realized they were all armed with crossbows; his boys didn't stand a chance against odds like that. He burrowed his way deeper into the clawing roots, felt a string of beads snap and shower over his hand. Behind him Bathecar unslung his own crossbow and cocked it.

Wim looked over his shoulder, and then, for the length of a heartbeat, he saw the silvery white of the moon-painted landscape blaze with harshly shadowed blue brilliance. He shook his head, dazzled and wondering; until amazement was driven from his mind by sudden screams. He began to curse and pray at the same time.

But then their assailants had reached the fallen tree. Wim heard them thrusting into the roots, shrank back further out of reach of their knives. Another scream echoed close and a voice remarked, "Hey, Rufe. I got the bastard as shot Rocker last fall."

A different voice answered, "That makes five then. Everybody excepting the peddler and Wim Buckry."

Wim held his breath, sweating. He recognized the second voice—Axl Bork, the oldest of the Bork brothers. For the last two years Wim's gang had cut into the Bork clan's habitual thievery, and up until tonight his quickwittedness had kept them safe from the Borks' revenge. But tonight—how had he gone so wrong tonight? Damn that peddler!

He heard hands thrusting again among the roots, closer now. Then abruptly fingers caught in his hair. He pulled away, but another pair of hands joined the first, catching him by the hair and then the collar of his leather jerkin. He was hauled roughly from the tangle of roots and thrown down. He scrambled to his feet, was kicked in the stomach before he could run off. He fell gasping back onto the ground, felt his knife jerked from the sheath; three shadowy figures loomed over him. The nearest placed a heavy foot on his middle and said, "Well, Wim Buckry. You just lie still, boy. It's been a good night, even if we don't catch that peddler. You just got a little crazy with greed, boy. My cousins done killed every last one of your gang." Their laughter raked him. "Fifteen minutes and we done what we couldn't do the last two years."

"Lew, you take Wim here over to that cave tree. Once we find that peddler we're going to have us a little fun with the both of them."

Wim was pulled to his feet and then kicked, sprawling over

the bodies of Hanaban and Shorty. He struggled to his feet and ran, only to be tripped and booted by another Bork. By the time he reached the cave tree his right arm hung useless at his side, and one eye was blind with warm sticky blood.

The Borks had tried to rekindle the campfire. Three of them stood around him in the wavering light: he listened to the rest searching among the trees. He wondered dismally why they couldn't find one wagon on open ground, when they'd found every one of his boys.

One of the younger cousins—scarcely more than fifteen—amused himself half-heartedly by thrusting glowing twigs at Wim's face. Wim slapped at him, missed, and at last one of the other Borks knocked the burning wood from the boy's hand. Wim remembered that Axl Bork claimed first rights against anyone who ran afoul of the gang. He squirmed back away from the fire and propped himself against the dry resilient trunk of the cave tree, stunned with pain and despair. Through one eye he could see the other Borks returning empty-handed from their search. He counted six Borks altogether, but by the feeble flame-cast light he couldn't make out their features. The only one he could have recognized for sure was Axl Bork, and his runty silhouette was missing. Two of the clansmen moved past him into the blackness of the cave tree's heart, he heard them get down on their hands and knees to crawl around the bend at the end of the passage. The peddler could have hidden back there, but his wagon would have filled the cave's entrance. Wim wondered again why the Borks couldn't find that wagon; and wished again that he'd never seen it at all.

The two men emerged from the tree just as Axl limped into the shrinking circle of firelight. The stubby bandit was at least forty years old, but through those forty years he had lost his share of fights, and walked slightly bent-over; Wim knew that his drooping hat covered a hairless skull marred with scars and even one dent. The eldest Bork cut close by the fire, heedlessly sending dust and unburnable bark into the guttering flames. "Awright, where in the motherdevil blazes you toad-gets been keeping your eyes? You was standing ever whichway from this tree, you skewered every one of that damn Buckry gang excepting Wim here. Why ain't you found that peddler?"

"He's gone, Ax', gone." The boy who had been playing with Wim seemed to think that was a revelation. But Axl was not impressed; his backhand sent the boy up against the side of the tree.

One of the other silhouetted figures spoke hesitantly. "Don't go misbelieving me when I tell you this, Axl . . . but I was looking straight at this here cave tree when you went after them others. I could see that peddler clear as I see you now, standing right beside his wagon and his horse. Then all of a sudden there was this blue flash—I tell you, Ax', it was *bright*—and for a minute I couldn't see nothing, and then when I could again, why there wasn't hide nor hair of that outlander."

"Hmm." The elder Bork took this story without apparent anger. He scratched under his left armpit and began to shuffle around the dying fire toward where Wim lay. "Gone, eh? Just like that. He sounds like a right good prize . . ." He reached suddenly and caught Wim by the collar, dragged him toward the fire. Stopping just inside the ring of light, he pulled Wim up close to his face. The wide, sagging brim of his hat threw his face into a hollow blackness that was somehow more terrible than any reality.

Seeing Wim's expression, he laughed raspingly, and did not turn his face toward the fire. "It's been a long time, Wim, that I been wanting to learn you a lesson. But now I can mix business and pleasure. We're just gonna burn you an inch at a time until you tell us where your friend lit out to."

Wim barely stifled the whimper he felt growing in his throat; Axl Bork began to force his good hand inch by inch into the fire. All he wanted to do was to scream the truth, to tell them the peddler had never made him party to his magic. But he knew the truth would no more be accepted than his cries for mercy; the only way out was to lie—to lie better than he ever had before. The tales the peddler had told him during the day rose from his mind to shape his words. "Just go ahead, Ax! Get your fun. I know I'm good as dead. But so's all of you—" The grip stayed firm on his shoulders and neck, but the knotted hand stopped forcing him toward the fire. He felt his own hand scorching in the super-heated air above the embers. Desperately he forced the pain into the same place with his fear and ignored it. "Why d'you think me and my boys didn't lay a hand on that peddler all day long? Just so's we could get ambushed by you?" His laughter was slightly hysterical. "The truth is we was scared clean out of our wits! That foreigner's a warlock, he's too dangerous to go after. He can reach straight into your head, cloud your mind, make you see what just plain isn't. He can kill you, just by looking at you kinda mean-like. Why"—and true inspiration struck him— "why, he could even have killed one of your perty cousins, and be standing here right now pretending to be a Bork, and you'd never know it till he struck *you* dead . . . ."

Axl swore and ground Wim's hand into the embers. Even expecting it, Wim couldn't help himself; his scream was loud and shrill. After an instant as long as forever Axl pulled his hand from the heat. The motion stirred the embers, sending a final spurt of evil reddish flame up from the coals before the fire guttered out, leaving only dim ruby points to compete with the moonlight. For a long moment no one spoke; Wim bit his tongue to keep from moaning. The only sounds were a faint rustling breeze, hundreds of feet up among the leafy crowns of the grandfather trees—and the snort of a horse somewhere close by.

"Hey, we ain't got no horses," someone said uneasily.

Seven human figures stood in the immense spreading shadow of the cave tree, limned in faint silver by the setting moon. The Borks stood very still, watching one another—and then Wim realized what they must just have noticed themselves: there should have been eight Bork kinsmen. Somehow the peddler had eliminated one of the Borks during the attack, so silently, so quickly, that his loss had gone unnoticed. Wim shuddered, suddenly remembering a flare of unreal blue-white light, and the claims he had just made for the peddler. If one Bork could be killed so easily, why not two? In which case—

"He's here, pretending to be one of you!" Wim cried, his voice cracking.

And he could almost feel their terror echoing back and forth, from one to another, growing—until one of the shortest of the silhouettes broke and ran out into the moonlight. He got only about twenty feet, before he was brought down by a crossbow quarrel in the back. Even as the fugitive crumpled onto the soft, silver dirt a second crossbow thunked and another of the brothers fell dead across Wim's feet.

"That was Clyne, you . . . warlock!" More bows lowered around the circle.

"Hold on now!" shouted Axl. There were five Borks left standing; two bodies sprawled unmoving on the ground. "The peddler got us in his spell. We got to keep our sense and figure out which of us he's pretendin' to be."

"But, Ax', he ain't just in disguise, we woulda seen which one he is . . . he—he can trick us into believing he's anybody!"

Trapped beneath the corpse, all Wim could see were five shadows against the night. Their faces were hidden from the light, and bulky clothing disguised any differences. He bit his lips against the least sound of pain; now was no time to remind the remaining Borks of Wim Buckry— But the agony of his hand pulsed up his arm until he felt a terrible dizziness wrench the blurring world away and his head drooped . . .

He opened his eyes again and saw that only three men stood now in the glade. Two more had died; the newest corpse still twitched on the ground.

Axl's voice was shrill with rage. "You . . . monster! You done tricked all of us into killing each other!"

"No, Ax', I had to shoot him. It was the peddler, I swear. Turn him over. Look! He shot Jan after you told us to hold off—"

"Warlock!" a third voice cried. "All of them dead—!" Two crossbows came down and fired simultaneously. Two men fell.

Axl stood silent and alone among the dead for a long moment. The moon had set at last, and the starlight was rare and faint through the shifting branches of the grandfather tree far overhead. Wim lay still as death, aware of the smell of blood and sweat and burned flesh. And the sound of footsteps, approaching. Sick with fear he looked up at the dark stubby form of Axl Bork.

"Still here? Good." A black-booted foot rolled the dead body from his leg. "Well, boy, you better leave me look at that hand." The voice belonged to Jagit Katchetooriantz.

"Uh." Wim began to tremble. "Uh, Mr. Jagged . . . is that . . . you?"

A light appeared in the hand of the peddler who had come from Sharn.

Wim fainted.

Early morning filled the Grandfather Grove with dusty shafts of light. Wim Buckry sat propped against the cave tree's entrance, sipping awkwardly at a cup of something hot and bitter held in a bandaged hand. His other hand was tucked through his belt, to protect a sprained right shoulder. Silently he watched the peddler grooming the dappled cart horse; glanced for the tenth time around the sunlit grove, where no sign of the last night's events marred the quiet tranquility of the day. Like a bad dream, the memory of his terror seemed unreal to him now, and he wondered if that was more witchery, like the drink that had eased the pains of his body. He looked down, where dried blood stained his pants. *He'd took care of the remains,* the peddler had said. It was real, all right—all of the Borks. And all of his boys. He thought wistfully for a moment of the jewelry that had gone into the ground with them; shied away from a deeper sense of loss beneath it.

The peddler returned to the campfire, kicked dirt over the blaze. He had had no trouble in getting a fire to burn. Wim drew his feet up; the dark eyes looked questioningly at his sullen face.

"Mr. Jagged"—there was no trace of mockery in that title now—"just what do you want from me?"

Jagit dusted off his leather shirt. "Well, Wim—I was thinking if you was up to it, maybe you'd want to go on with our agreement."

Wim raised his bandaged hand. "Wouldn't be much pertection, one cripple."

"But I don't know the way down through that there Valley, which you do."

Wim laughed incredulously. "I reckon you could fly over the moon on a broomstick and you wouldn't need no map. And you sure as hell don't need pertecting! Why'd you ever take us on, Mr. Jagged?" Grief sobered him suddenly, and realization— "You knew all along, didn't you? What we were fixing to do. You took us along so's you could watch us, and maybe scare us off. Well, you needn't be watching me no more. I—we already changed our minds, even before what happened with them Borks. We was fixing to take you on down like we said, all honest."

"I know that." The peddler nodded. "You ever hear an old saying, Wim: 'Two heads are better than one'? You can't never tell; you might just come in handy."

Wim shrugged ruefully, and wondered where the peddler ever heard that "old saying." "Well . . . ain't heard no better offers this morning."

They left the grandfather trees and continued the descent toward the Great Valley. Throughout the early morning the pine woods continued to surround them, but as the morning wore on Wim noticed that the evergreens had given way to oak and sycamore, as the air lost its chill and much of its moistness. By late in the day he could catch glimpses between the trees of the green and amber vastness that was the valley floor, and pointed it out to the peddler. Jagit nodded, seeming pleased, and returned to the aimless humming that Wim suspected covered diabolical thoughts. He glanced again at the round, stubby merchant, the last man in the world a body'd suspect of magical powers. Which was perhaps what made them so convincing . . . "Mr. Jagged? How'd you do it? Hex them Borks, I mean."

Jagit smiled and shook his head. "A good magician never tells how. What, maybe, but never how. You have to watch, and figure how for yourself. That's how you get to *be* a good magician."

Wim sighed, shifted his hand under his belt. "Reckon I don't want to know, then."

The peddler chuckled. "Fair enough."

Surreptitiously, Wim watched his every move for the rest of the day.

After the evening meal the peddler again spent time at his wagon in the dark. Wim, sprawled exhausted by the campfire, saw the gleam of a warlock's wand but this time made no move to investigate, only crossing his fingers as a precautionary gesture. Inactivity had left him with too much else to consider. He stared fixedly into the flames, his hand smarting.

"Reckon we should be down to the valley floor in about an hour's travel, tomorrow. Then you say we head northwest, till we come to Fyffe?"

Wim started at the sound of the peddler's voice. "Oh . . . yeah, I reckon. Cut north and any road'll get you there; they all go to Fyffe."

" 'All roads lead to Fyffe'?" The peddler laughed unexpectedly, squatted by the fire.

Wim wondered what was funny. "Anybody can tell you the way from here, Mr. Jagged. I think come morning I'll be heading back; I . . . we never figured to come this far. Us hill folk don't much like going down into the Flatlands."

"Hm. I'm sorry to hear that, Wim." Jagit pushed another branch into the fire. "But somehow I'd figured it you'd really been to Fyffe?"

"Well, yeah, I was . . . almost." He looked up, surprised. "Three, four years ago, when I was hardly more'n a young'un, with my pa and some other men. See, my granther was the smith at Darkwood Corners, and he got hold of a gun—" And he found himself telling a peddler-man things everyone knew, and things he'd never told to anyone: How his grandfather had discovered gunpowder, how the Highlanders had plotted to overthrow the lords at Fyffe and take the rich valley farmlands for themselves. And how horsemen had come out from the city to meet them, with guns and magic, how the amber fields were torn and reddened and his pa had died when his homemade gun blew up in his face. How a bloody, tight-lipped boy returning alone to Darkwood Corners had filled its citizens with the fear of the Lord, and of the lords of Fyffe . . . He sat twisting painfully at a golden earring. "And—I heard tell as how they got dark magics down there that we never even saw, so's to keep all the Flatlanders under a spell . . . Maybe you oughta think again 'bout going down there too, Mr. Jagged."

"I thank you for the warning, Wim." Jagit nodded. "But I'll tell you—I'm a merchant by trade, and by inclination. If I can't sell my wares, I got no point in being, and I can't sell my wares in these hills."

"You ain't afraid they'll try to stop you?"

He smiled. "Well, now, I didn't say that. Their magic ain't up to Sharn, I'm pretty sure. But it is an unknown . . . Who knows—they may turn out to be my best customers; lords are like to be free with their money." He looked at Wim with something like respect. "But like I say, two heads are better than one. I'm right sorry you won't be along. Mayhap in the morning we can settle accounts—"

In the morning the peddler hitched up his wagon and started down toward the Great Valley. And not really understanding why, Wim Buckry went with him.

Early in the day they left the welcome shelter of the last oak forest, started across the open rolling hills of ripening wild grasses, until they struck a rutted track heading north. Wim stripped off his jerkin and loosened his shirt, his pale Highland skin turning red under the climbing sun of the Valley. The dark-skinned peddler in his leather shirt smiled at him, and Wim figured, annoyed, that he must enjoy the heat. By noon they reached the endless green corduroy fringe of the cultivated Flatlands, and with a jolt they found themselves on paved road. Jagit knelt and prodded the resilient surface before they continued on their way. Wim vaguely remembered the soft pavement, a bizarre luxury to Highland feet, stretching all the way to Fyffe; this time he noticed that in places the pavement was eaten away by time, and neatly patched with smooth-cut stone.

The peddler spoke little to him, only humming, apparently intent on searching out signs of Flatlander magic. *A good magician watches* . . . Wim forced himself to study the half-remembered landscape. The ripening fields and pasturelands blanketed the Valley to the limit of his sight, like an immense, living crazy-quilt in greens and gold, spread over the rich dark earth. In the distance he could see pale mist hovering over the fields, wondered if it was a trick of witchery or only the heat of the day. And he saw the Flatlanders at work in the fields by the road, well-fed and roughly dressed; tanned, placid faces that regarded their passage with the resigned disinterest that he would have expected of a plowmule. Wim frowned.

"A rather curious lack of curiosity, I'd say, wouldn't you?" The peddler glanced at him. "They're going to make bad customers."

"Look at 'em!" Wim burst out angrily. "How could they do all of this? They ain't no better farmers 'n Highlanders. In the hills you work your hands to the bone to farm, and you get nothing, stones— And look at them, they're fat. How, Mr. Jagged?"

"How do *you* think they do it, Wim?"

"I—" He stopped. *Good magicians figure it out* . . . "Well—they got better land."

"True."

"And . . . there's magic."

"Is there now?"

"You saw it—them smooth-bedded streams, this here road; it ain't natural. But . . . they all look as how they're bewitched, themselves, just like I heard. Mayhap it's only the lords of Fyffe as have all the magic—it's them we got to watch for?" He crossed his fingers.

"Maybe so. It looks like they may be the only customers I'll have, too, if this doesn't change." The peddler's face was devoid of expression. "Quit crossing your fingers, Wim; the only thing that'll ever save you from is the respect of educated men."

Wim uncrossed his fingers. He walked on for several minutes before he realized the peddler spoke like a Flatlander now, as perfectly as he'd spoken the Highland talk before.

Late in the afternoon they came to a well, at one of the farm villages that centered like a hub in a great wheel of fields. The peddler dipped a cup into the dripping container, and then Wim took a gulp straight from the bucket. A taste of bitter metal filled his mouth, and he spat in dismay, looking back at the merchant. Jagit was passing his hand over—no, dropping something *into* the cup—and as Wim watched the water began to foam, and suddenly turned bright red. The peddler's black brows rose with interest, and he poured the water slowly out onto the ground. Wim blanched and wiped his mouth hard on his sleeve. "It *tastes* like poison!"

Jagit shook his head. "That's not poison you taste; I'd say farming's just polluted the water table some. But it is drugged."

He watched the villagers standing with desultory murmurs around his wagon.

"Sheep." Wim's face twisted with disgust.

The peddler shrugged. "But all of them healthy, wealthy, and wise . . . well, healthy and wise, anyway . . . healthy—?" He moved away to offer his wares. There were few takers. As Wim returned to the wagon, taking a drink of stale mountain water from the barrel on the back, he heard the little man muttering again, like an incantation, "Fyffe . . . Fyffe . . . Dyston-Fyffe, they call it here . . . *District Town Five?* . . . Couldn't be." He frowned, oblivious. "But then again, why couldn't it—?"

For the rest of that day the peddler kept his thoughts to himself, looking strangely grim, only pronouncing an occasional curse in some incomprehensible language. And that night, as they camped, as Wim's weary mind unwillingly relived the loss of the only friends he had, he wondered if the dark silent stranger across the fire shared his loneliness; a peddler was always a stranger, even if he was a magician. "Mr. Jagged, you ever feel like going home?"

"Home?" Jagit glanced up. "Sometimes. Tonight, maybe. But I've come so far, I guess that would be impossible. When I got back, it'd all be gone." Suddenly through the flames his face looked very old. "What made it home was gone before I left . . . But maybe I'll find it again, somewhere else, as I go."

"Yeah . . ." Wim nodded, understanding both more and less than he realized. He curled down into his blanket, oddly comforted, and went soundly to sleep.

Minor wonders continued to assail him on their journey, and also the question, "Why?"; until gradually Jagit's prodding transformed his superstitious awe into a cocky curiosity that sometimes made the peddler frown, though he made no comment.

Until the third morning, when Wim finally declared, "Everything's a trick, if'n you can see behind it, just like with them witches in the hills. Everything's got a—reason. I think there ain't no such thing as magic!"

Jagit fixed him with a long mild look, and the specter of

the night in the Grandfather Grove seemed to flicker in the dark eyes. "You think not, eh?"

Wim looked down nervously.

"There's magic, all right, Wim; all around you here. Only now you're seeing it with a magician's eyes: Because there's a reason behind everything that happens; you may not know what it is, but it's there. And knowing that doesn't make the thing less magic, or strange, or terrible—it just makes it easier to deal with. That's something to keep in mind, wherever you are . . . Also keep in mind that a *little* knowledge is a dangerous thing."

Wim nodded, chastened, felt his ears grow red as the peddler muttered, "So's a little ignorance . . ."

The afternoon of the third day showed them Fyffe, still a vague blot wavering against the horizon. Wim looked back over endless green toward the mountains, but they were hidden from him now by the yellow Flatland haze. Peering ahead again toward the city, he was aware that the fear that had come with him into the Great Valley had grown less instead of greater as they followed the familiar-strange road to Fyffe. The dappled cart horse snorted loudly in the hot, dusty silence, and he realized it was the peddler with his wagon full of magics that gave him his newfound courage.

He smiled, flexing his burned hand. Jagit had never made any apology for what he'd done, but Wim was not such a hypocrite that he really expected one, under the circumstances. And the peddler had treated his wounds with potions, so that bruises began to fade and skin to heal almost while he watched. It was almost—

Wim's thoughts were interrupted as he stumbled on a rough patch in the road. The city, much closer now, lay stolidly among the fields in the lengthening shadows of the hot afternoon. He wondered in which field his father—abruptly turned his thoughts ahead again, noticing that the city was without walls or other visible signs of defense. *Why?* Mayhap because they had nothing to fear— He felt his body tighten with old terrors. But Jagit's former grim mood had seemingly dropped away as his goal drew near, as though he had reached some resolution. If the peddler was confident, then Wim would be, too. He looked on the city with magician's eyes; and it struck him that a more outlandish challenge had most likely never visited the lords of Fyffe.

They entered Fyffe, and though the peddler seemed almost disappointed, Wim tried to conceal his gaping with little success. The heavy stone and timber buildings crowded the cobble-patched street, rising up two and three stories to cut off his view of the fields. The street's edge was lined with shop fronts; windows of bull's-eyed glass and peeling painted signs advertised their trade. The levels above the shops, he supposed, were where the people lived. The weathered stone of the curbs had been worn to hollows from the tread of countless feet, and the idea of so many people—5,000, the peddler had guessed—in so little area made him shudder.

They made their way past dully-dressed, well-fed towns-folk and farmers finishing the day's commerce in the cooling afternoon. Wim caught snatches of sometimes heated bargaining, but he noticed that the town showed little more interest in the bizarre spectacle of himself and the peddler than had the folk they dealt with on their journey. Children at least ought to follow the bright wagon—he was vaguely disturbed to realize he'd scarcely seen any, here or anywhere, and those he saw were kept close by parents. It seemed the peddler's business would be no better here than in the hills after all. *Like hogs in a pen* . . . He glanced down the street, back over his shoulder. "Where's all the hogs?"

"What?" The peddler looked at him.

"It's clean. All them folk living here and there ain't any garbage. How can that be, less'n they keep hogs to eat it? But I don't see any hogs. Nor—hardly any young'uns."

"Hmm." The peddler shrugged, smiling. "Good questions. Maybe we should ask the lords of Fyffe."

Wim shook his head. Yet he had to admit that the city so far, for all its strangeness, had shown him no signs of any magic more powerful or grim than that he'd seen in the fields. Perhaps the lords of Fyffe weren't so fearsome as the tales claimed; their warriors weren't bewitched, but only better armed.

The street curved sharply, and ahead the clustered buildings gave way on an open square, filled with the covered stalls of a public marketplace. And beyond it—Wim stopped,

staring. Beyond it, he knew, stood the dwelling of the lords of
Fyffe. Twice as massive as any building he had seen, its
pilastered green-black walls reflected the square like a dark,
malevolent mirror. The building had the solidity of a thing
that had grown from the earth, a permanence that made the
town itself seem ephemeral. Now, he knew, he looked on the
house for magic that might match the peddler and Sharn.

Beside him, Jagit's smile was genuine and unreadable.
"Pardon me, ma'm," the peddler stopped a passing woman
and child, "but we're strangers. What's that building there
called?"

"Why, that's Government House." The woman looked
only mildly surprised. Wim admired her stocking-covered
ankles.

"I see. And what do they do there?"

She pulled her little girl absently back from the wagon.
"That's where the governors are. Folks go there with peti-
tions and such. They—govern, I suppose. Lissy, keep away
from that dusty beast."

"Thank you, ma'm. And could I show you—"

"Not today. Come on, child, we'll be late."

The peddler bowed in congenial exasperation as she moved
on. Wim sighed, and he shook his head. "Hardly a market for
Sharnish wonders here, either, I begin to think. I may have
outfoxed myself for once. Looks like my only choice is to
pay a call on your lords of Fyffe over there; I might still have
a thing or two to interest them." His eyes narrowed in
appraisal as he looked across the square.

At a grunt of disapproval from Wim, Jagit glanced back,
gestured at the lengthening shadows, "Too late to start
selling now, anyway. What do you say we just take a look—"
Suddenly he fell silent.

Wim turned. A group of half a dozen dour-faced men were
approaching them; the leader bore a crest on his stiff brimmed
hat that Wim remembered. They were unslinging guns from
their shoulders. Wim's question choked off as they quietly
circled the wagon, cut him off from the peddler. The militia-
man addressed Jagit, faintly disdainful. "The Governors—"

Wim seized the barrel of the nearest rifle, slinging its
owner into the man standing next to him. He wrenched the

gun free and brought it down on the head of a third gaping guard.

"Wim!" He froze at the sound of the peddler's voice, turned back. "Drop the gun." The peddler stood unresisting beside his wagon. And the three remaining guns were pointing at Wim Buckry. Face filled with angry betrayal, he threw down the rifle.

"Tie the hillbilly up . . . The Governors require a few words with you two, peddler, as I was saying. You'll come with us." The militia leader stood back, unperturbed, as his townsman guards got to their feet.

Wim winced as his hands were bound roughly before him, but there was no vindictiveness on the guard's bruised face. Pushed forward to walk with the peddler, he muttered bitterly, "Whyn't you use your magic!"

Jagit shook his head. "Would've been bad for business. After all, the lords of Fyffe have come to me."

Wim crossed his fingers, deliberately, as they climbed the green-black steps of Government House.

The hours stretched interminably in the windowless, featureless room where they were left to wait, and Wim soon tired of staring at the evenness of the walls and the smokeless lamps. The peddler sat fiddling with small items left in his pockets; but Wim had begun to doze in spite of himself by the time guards returned at last, to take them to their long-delayed audience with the lords of Fyffe.

The guards left them to the lone man who rose, smiling, from behind a tawny expanse of desk as they entered the green-walled room. "Well, at last!" He was in his late fifties and plainly dressed like the townsmen, about Wim's height but heavier, with graying hair. Wim saw that the smiling face held none of the dullness of their captors' faces. "I'm Charl Aydricks, representative of the World Government. My apologies for keeping you waiting, but I was—out of town. We've been following your progress with some interest."

Wim wondered what in tarnation this poor-man governor took himself for, claiming the Flatlands was the whole world. He glanced past Aydricks into the unimpressive, lamp-lit room. On the governor's desk he noticed the only sign of a lord's riches he'd yet seen—a curious ball of inlaid metals, mostly blue but blotched with brown and green, fixed on a golden stand. He wondered with more interest where the other lords of Fyffe might be; Aydricks was alone, without even guards . . . Wim suddenly remembered that whatever this man wasn't, he was a magician, no less than the peddler.

Jagit made a polite bow. "Jagit Katchetooriantz, at your service. Merchant by trade, and flattered by the interest. This is my apprentice—"

"—Wim Buckry." The governor's appraising glance moved unexpectedly to Wim. "Yes, we remember you, Wim. I must say I'm surprised to see you here again. But pleased—we've been wanting to get ahold of you." A look of too much interest crossed Aydricks' face.

Wim eyed the closed door with longing.

"Please be seated." The governor returned to his desk. "We rarely get such . . . unique visitors—"

Jagit took a seat calmly and Wim dropped into the second chair, knees suddenly weak. As he settled into the softness he felt a sourceless pressure bearing down on him, lunged upward like a frightened colt only to be forced back into the seat. Panting, he felt the pressure ease as he collapsed in defeat.

Jagit looked at him with sympathy before glancing back at the governor; Wim saw the peddler's fingers twitch impotently on the chair-arm. "Surely you don't consider us a threat?" His voice was faintly mocking.

The governor's congeniality stopped short of his eyes. "We know about the forces you were using in the Grandfather Grove."

"Do you now! That's what I'd hoped." Jagit met the gaze and held it. "Then I'm obviously in the presence of some technological sophistication, at last. I have some items of trade that might interest you . . ."

"You may be sure they'll receive our attention. But let's just be honest with each other, shall we? You're no more a peddler than I am; not with what we've seen you do. And if you'd really come from the east—from anywhere—I'd know about it; our communications network is excellent. You simply appeared from nowhere, in the Highlands Preserve. And it really was nowhere on this earth, wasn't it?"

Jagit said nothing, looking expectant. Wim stared fixedly at the textured green of the wall, trying to forget that he was witness to a debate of warlocks.

Aydricks stirred impatiently. "From nowhere on this earth. Our moon colony is long gone; that means no planet in this system. Which leaves the Lost Colonies—you've come from one of the empire's colony worlds, from another star system, Jagit; and if you expected that to surprise us after all this time, you're mistaken."

Jagit attempted to shrug. "No—I didn't expect that, frankly. But I didn't expect any of the rest of this, either; things haven't turned out as I'd planned at all . . ."

Wim listened in spite of himself, in silent wonder. Were there worlds beyond his own, that were no more than sparks in the black vastness of earth's night? Was that where Sharn was, then, with its wonders; beyond the sky, where folks said was heaven—?

". . . Obviously," the governor was saying, "you're a precedent shattering threat to the World Government. Because this is a *world* government, and it has maintained peace and stability over millennia. Our space defense system sees to it that—outsiders don't upset that peace. At least it always has until now; you're the first person to penetrate our system, and we don't even know how you did it. That's what we want to know—*must* know, Jagit, not who you represent, or where, or even why, so much as *how*. We can't allow anything to disrupt our stability." Aydricks leaned forward across his desk; his hand tightened protectively over the stand of the strange metal globe. His affability had disappeared entirely, and Wim felt his own hopes sink, realizing the governor somehow knew the peddler's every secret. Jagit wasn't infallible, and this time he had let himself be trapped.

But Jagit seemed undismayed. "If you value your stability that much, then I'd say it's time somebody did disturb it."

"That's to be expected." Aydricks sat back, his expression relaxing into contempt. "But you won't be the one. We've had ten thousand years to perfect our system, and in that time no one else has succeeded in upsetting it. We've put an end at last to all the millennia of destructive waste on this world . . ."

Ten thousand years—? As Aydricks spoke, Wim groped to understand a second truth that tore at the very roots of his comprehension:

For the history of mankind stretched back wonder on wonder for unimaginable thousands of years, through tremendous cycles filled with lesser cycles. Civilization reached highs where every dream was made a reality and humanity sent offshoots to the stars, only to fall back, through its own folly, into abysses of loss when men forgot their humanity and reality became a nightmare. Then slowly the cycle would change again, and in time mankind would reach new heights, that paradoxically it could never maintain. Always men seemed unable in the midst of their creation to resist the urge to destroy, and always they found the means to destroy utterly.

Until the end of the last great cyclical empire, when a group among the ruling class saw that a new decline was imminent, and acted to prevent it. They had forced the world into a new order, one of patternless stability at a low level, and had stopped it there. ". . . And because of us that state, free from strife and suffering, the world has continued for ten thousand years, unchanged. Literally unchanged. I am one of the original founders of the World Government."

Wim looked unbelievingly into the smiling, unremarkable face; found the eyes of a fanatic and incredible age.

"You're well preserved," Jagit said.

The governor burst into honest laughter. "This isn't my original body. By using our computer network we're able to transfer our memories intact into the body of an 'heir'; someone from the general population, young and full of potential. As long as the individual's personality is compatible, it's absorbed into the greater whole, and he becomes a revitalizing part of us. That's why I've been keeping track of Wim, here; he has traits that should make him an excellent governor." The too-interested smile showed on the governor's face again.

Wim's bound hands tightened into fists—the invisible pressure forced him back down into the seat, his face stricken.

Aydricks watched him, amused. "Technological initiative and personal aggressiveness are key factors that lead to an unstable society. Since, to keep stability, we have to suppress those factors in the population, we keep control groups free from interference—like the hill folk, the Highlanders—to give us a dependable source of the personality types we need ourselves.

"But the system as a whole really is very well designed. Our computer network provides us with our continuity, with the technology, communications, and—sources of power we need to maintain stability. We in turn ensure the computer's continuity, since we preserve the knowledge to keep it functioning. There's no reason why the system can't go on forever."

Wim looked toward the peddler for some sign of reassurance; but found a grimness that made him look away again as Jagit said, "And you think that's a feat I should appreciate; that you've manipulated the fate of every being on this planet for ten thousand years, to your own ends, and that you plan to go on doing it indefinitely?"

"But it's for their own good, can't you see that? We ask nothing from this, no profit for ourselves, no reward other than knowing that humanity will never be able to throw itself into barbarism again, that the cycle of destructive waste, of rise and fall, has finally been stopped on earth. The people are secure, their world is stable, they know it will be safe for future generations. Could your own world claim as much? Think of the years that must have passed on your journey here—would you even have a civilization to return to by now?"

Wim saw Jagit forcibly relax; the peddler's smile reappeared, full of irony. "But the fact remains that a cycle of rise and fall is the natural order of things—life and death, if you want to call it that. It gives humanity a chance to reach new heights, and gives an old order a clean death. Stasis is a coma—no lows, but no highs either, no *choice*. Somehow I think that Sharn would have preferred a clean death to this—"

"Sharn? What do you know about the old empire?" The governor leaned forward, complaisance lost.

"Sharn—?" Wim's bewilderment was lost on the air.

"They knew everything about Sharn, where I come from. The crystal city with rot at its heart, the Games of Three. They were even seeing the trends that would lead to this, though they had no idea it would prove so eminently successful.''

"Well, this gets more and more interesting." The governor's voice hardened. "Considering that there should be no way someone from outside could have known of the last years of the empire. But I suspect we'll only continue to raise more questions this way. I think it's time we got some answers."

Wim slumped in his seat, visions of torture leaping into his mind. But the governor only left his desk, passing Wim with a glance that suggested hunger, and placed a shining band of filigreed metal on Jagit's head.

"You may be surprised at what you get." Jagit's expression remained calm, but Wim thought strain tightened his voice.

The governor returned to his chair. "Oh, I don't think so. I've just linked you into our computer net—''

Abruptly Jagit went rigid with surprise, settled back into a half smile; but not before Aydricks had seen the change. "Once it gets into your mind you'll have considerable difficulty concealing anything at all. It's quick and always effective; though unfortunately I can't guarantee that it won't drive you crazy."

The peddler's smile faded. "How civilized," he said quietly. He met Wim's questioning eyes. "Well, Wim, you remember what I showed you. And crossing your fingers didn't help, did it?"

Wim shook his head. "Whatever you say, Mr. Jagged . . ." He suspected he'd never have an opportunity to remember anything.

Suddenly the peddler gasped, and his eyes closed, his body went limp in the seat. "Mr. Jagged—?" But there was no response. Alone, Wim wondered numbly what sort of terrible enchantment the metal crown held, and whether it would hurt when the computer—whatever that was—swallowed his own soul.

"Are you monitoring? All districts? Direct hookup, yes." The governor seemed to be speaking to his desk. He hesitated as though listening, then stared into space.

Wim sagged fatalistically against his chair, past horror now, ignoring—and ignored by—the two entranced men.

Silence stretched in the green room. Then the light in the room flickered and dimmed momentarily. Wim's eyes widened as he felt the unseen pressure that held him down weaken slightly, then return with the lighting. The governor frowned at nothing, still staring into space. Wim began ineffectually to twist at his bound hands. However the magic worked in this room, it had just stopped working; if it stopped again he'd be ready . . . He glanced at Jagit. Was there a smile—?

"District Eighteen here. Aydricks, what is this?"

Wim shuddered. The live disembodied head of a red-haired youth had just appeared in a patch of sudden brightness by the wall. The governor turned blinking toward the ghost.

"Our reception's getting garbled. This data can't be right, it says he's . . ." The ghostly face wavered and the voice was drowned in a sound like water rushing. ". . . it, what's wrong with the transmission? Is he linked up directly? We aren't getting anything now—"

Two more faces—one old, with skin even darker than the peddler's, and one a middle-aged woman—appeared in the wall, protesting. And Wim realized then that he saw the other lords of Fyffe—and truly of the world—here and yet not here, transported by their magic from the far ends of the earth. The red-haired ghost peered at Wim, who shrank away from the angry, young-old eyes, then looked past to Jagit. The frown grew fixed and then puzzled, was transformed into incredulity. "No, that's impossible!"

"What is it?" Aydricks looked harassed.

"I know that man."

The black-haired woman turned as though she could see him. "What do you mean you—"

"I know that man too!" Another dark face appeared. "From Sharn, from the empire. But . . . after ten thousand years, how can he be the *same* . . . Aydricks! Remember the Primitive Arts man, he was famous, he spent . . ." the voice blurred. ". . . got to get him out of the comm system! He knows the comm-sat codes, he can—" The ghostly face dematerialized entirely.

Aydricks looked wildly at the unmoving peddler, back at the remaining governors.

Wim saw more faces appear, and another face flicker out.
The same man . . .

"Stop him, Aydricks!" The woman's voice rose. "He'll
ruin us. He's altering the comm codes, killing the tie-up!"

"I can't cut him off!"

"He's into my link now, I'm losing con—" The red-haired
ghost disappeared.

"Stop him, Aydricks, or we'll burn out Fyffe!"

"Jagged! Look out!" Wim struggled against his invisible
bonds as he saw the governor reach with grim resolution for
the colored metal globe on his desk. He knew Aydricks meant
to bash in the peddler's skull, and the helpless body in the
chair couldn't stop him. "Mr. Jagged, wake up!" Desperately Wim stuck out his feet as Aydricks passed; the governor
stumbled. Another face disappeared from the wall, and the
lights went out. Wim slid from the chair, free and groping
awkwardly for a knife he no longer had. Under the faltering
gaze of the ghosts in the wall, Aydricks fumbled toward
Jagit.

Wim grabbed at Aydricks' feet just as the light returned,
catching an ankle. The governor turned back, cursing, to kick
at him, but Wim was already up, leaping away from a blow
with the heavy statue.

"Aydricks, stop the peddler!"

Full of sudden fury, Wim gasped, "Damn you, you won't
stop it this time!" As the governor turned away Wim flung
himself against the other's back, staggering him, and hooked
his bound hands over Aydricks' head. Aydricks fought to pull
him loose, dropping the globe as he threw himself backward
to slam his attacker against the desk. Wim groaned as his
backbone grated against the desk edge, and lost his balance.
He brought his knee up as he fell; there was a sharp *crack* as
the governor landed beside him, and lay still. Wim got to his
knees; the ancient eyes stabbed him with accusation and fear.
"No. Oh, *no*." The eyes glazed.

A week after his seventeenth birthday, Wim Buckry had
killed a ten-thousand-year-old man. And, unknowingly, helped
to destroy an empire. The room was quiet; the last of the
governors had faded from the wall. Wim got slowly to his
feet, his mouth pulled back in a grin of revulsion. All the

magic in the world hadn't done this warlock any good. He moved to where Jagit still sat entranced, lifted his hands to pull the metal crown off and break the spell. And hesitated, suddenly unsure of himself. Would breaking the spell wake the peddler or kill him? They had to get out of here; but Jagit was somehow fighting the bewitchment, that much he understood, and if he stopped him now— His hands dropped, he stood irresolutely, waiting. And waiting.

His hands reached again for the metal band, twitching with indecision; jerked back as Jagit suddenly smiled at him. The dark eyes opened and the peddler sat forward, taking the metal band gently from his own head with a sigh. "I'm glad you waited. You'll probably never know how glad." Wim's grin became real, and relieved.

Jagit got unsteadily to his feet, glanced at Aydricks' body and shook his head; his face was haggard. "Said you might be a help, didn't I?" Wim stood phlegmatically while the peddler who was as old as Sharn itself unfastened the cords on his raw wrists. "I'd say our business is finished. You ready to get out of here? We don't have much time."

Wim started for the door in response, opened it, and came face to face with the unsummoned guard standing in the hall. His fist connected with the gaping jaw; the guard's knees buckled and he dropped to the floor, unconscious. Wim picked up the guard's rifle as Jagit appeared beside him, motioning him down the dim hallway.

"Where is everybody?"

"Let's hope they're home in bed; it's four-thirty in the morning. There shouldn't be any alarms."

Wim laughed giddily. "This's a sight easier than getting away from the Borks!"

"We're not away yet; we may be too late already. Those faces on the wall were trying to drop a—piece of sun on Fyffe. I think I stopped them, but I don't know for sure. If it wasn't a total success, I don't want to find out the hard way." He led Wim back down the wide stairway, into the empty hall where petitioners had gathered during the day. Wim started across the echoing floor but Jagit called him back, peering at something on the wall; they went down another flight into a well of darkness, guided by the peddler's

magic light. At the foot of the stairs the way was blocked by
a door, solidly shut. Jagit looked chagrined, then suddenly
the beam of his light shone blue; he flashed it against a metal
plate set in the door. The door slid back and he went through
it.

Wim followed him, into a cramped, softly glowing cubicle
nearly filled by three heavily padded seats around a peculiar
table. Wim noticed they seemed to be bolted to the floor, and
suddenly felt claustrophobic.

"Get into a seat, Wim. Thank God I was right about this
tower being a ballistic exit. Strap in, because we're about to
use it." He began to push lighted buttons on the table before
him.

Wim fumbled with the restraining straps, afraid to wonder
what the peddler thought they were doing, as a heavy inner
door shut the room off from the outside. Why weren't they
out of the building, running? How could this— Something
pressed him down into the seat cushions like a gentle, insistent
hand. His first thought was of another trap; but as the pressure continued, he realized this was something new. And
then, glancing up past Jagit's intent face, he saw that instead
of blank walls, they were now surrounded by the starry sky of
night. He leaned forward—and below his feet was the town
of Fyffe, shrinking away with every heartbeat, disappearing
into the greater darkness. He saw what the eagle saw . . . he
was flying. He sat back again, feeling for the reassuring
hardness of the invisible floor, only to discover suddenly that
his feet no longer touched it. There was no pressure bearing
him down now, there was nothing at all. His body drifted
against the restraining straps, lighter than a bird. A small
sound of incredulous wonder escaped him as he stared out at
the unexpected stars.

And saw a brightness begin to grow at the opaque line of
the horizon, spreading and creeping upward second by second, blotting out the stars with the fragile hues of dawn. The
sun's flaming face thrust itself up past the edge of the world,
making him squint, rising with arcane speed and uncanny
brilliance into a sky that remained stubbornly black with
night. At last the whole sphere of the sun was revealed, and

continued to climb in the midnight sky while now Wim could see a thin streak of sky-blue stretched along the horizon, left behind with the citron glow of dawn still lighting its center. Above the line in darkness the sun wore the pointed crown of a star that dimmed all others, and below it he could see the world at the horizon's edge moving into day. And the horizon did not lie absolutely flat, but was bowing gently downward now at the sides . . . Below his feet was still the utter darkness that had swallowed Fyffe. He sighed.

"Quite a view." Jagit sat back from the glowing table, drifting slightly above his seat, a tired smile on his face.

"You see it too?" Wim said hoarsely.

The peddler nodded. "I felt the same way, the first time. I guess everyone always has. Every time civilization has gained space flight, it's been rewarded again by that sight."

Wim said nothing, unable to find the words. His view of the bowed horizon had changed subtly, and now as he watched there came a further change—the sun began, slowly but perceptibly, to move backward down its track, sinking once more toward the point of dawn that had given it birth. Or, he suddenly saw, it was they who were slipping, back down from the heights of glory into his world's darkness once more. Wim waited while the sun sank from the black and alien sky, setting where it had risen, its afterglow reabsorbed into night as the edge of the world blocked his vision again. He dropped to the seat of his chair, as though the world had reclaimed him, and the stars reappeared. A heavy lurch, like a blow, shook the cubicle, and then all motion stopped.

He sat still, not understanding, as the door slid back in darkness and a breath of cold, sharp air filled the tiny room. Beyond the doorway was darkness again, but he knew it was not the night of a building hallway.

Jagit fumbled wearily with the restraining straps on his seat. "Home the same day . . ."

Wim didn't wait, but driven by instinct freed himself and went to the doorway. And jerked to a stop as he discovered they were no longer at ground level. His feet found the ladder, and as he stepped down from its bottom rung he heard and felt the gritty shifting of gravel. The only other sounds were the sigh of the icy wind, and water lapping. As his eyes

adjusted they told him what his other senses already knew—
that he was home. Not Darkwood Corners, but somewhere in
his own cruelly beautiful Highlands. Fanged shadow peaks
rose up on either hand, blotting out the stars, but more stars
shone in the smooth waters of the lake; they shivered slightly,
as he shivered in the cool breeze, clammy with sweat under
his thin shirt. He stood on the rubble of a mountain pass
somewhere above the treeline, and in the east the gash between the peaks showed pinkish-gray with returning day.

Behind him he heard Jagit, and turned to see the peddler
climbing slowly down the few steps to the ground. From
outside, the magician's chamber was the shape of a truncated
rifle bullet. Jagit carried the guard's stolen rifle, leaning on it
now like a walking stick. "Well, my navigation hasn't failed
me yet." He rubbed his eyes, stretched.

Wim recalled making a certain comment about flying over
the moon on a broomstick, too long ago, and looked again at
the dawn, this time progressing formally and peacefully up a
lightening sky. "We flew here. Didn't we, Mr. Jagged?" His
teeth chattered. "Like a bird. Only . . . we f-flew right off
the world." He stopped, awed by his own revelation. For a
moment a lifetime of superstitious dread cried that he had no
right to know of the things he had seen, or to believe— The
words burst out in a defiant rush. "That's it. Right off the
world. And . . . and it's all true: I heard how the world's
round like a stone. It must be true, how there's other worlds,
that's what you said back there, with people just like here: I
seen it, the sun's like all them other stars, only it's bigger . . ."
He frowned. "It's—closer? I—"

Jagit was grinning, his teeth showed white in his beard.
"Magician, first-class."

Wim looked back up into the sky. "If that don't beat
all—" he said softly. Then, struck by more practical matters,
he said, "What about them ghosts? Are they going to come
after us?"

Jagit shook his head. "No. I think I laid those ghosts to
rest pretty permanently. I changed the code words in their
communications system, a good part of it is totally unusable
now. Their computer net is broken up, and their space defense system must be out for good, because they didn't

destroy Fyffe. I'd say the World Government is finished; they don't know it yet, and they may not go for a few hundred years, but they'll go in the end. Their grand 'stability' machine has a monkey wrench in its works at last . . . They won't be around to use their magic in these parts any more, I expect.''

Wim considered, and then looked hopeful. "You going to take over back there, Mr. Jagged? Use your magic on them Flatlanders? We could—''

But the peddler shook his head. "No, I'm afraid that just doesn't interest me, Wim. All I really wanted was to break the hold those other magician sorts had on this world; and I've done that already.''

"Then . . . you mean you really did all that, you risked our necks, for nothing? Like you said, because it just wasn't right, for them to use their magic on folks who couldn't stop them? You did it for us—and you didn't want *anything?* You must be crazy.''

Jagit laughed. "Well, I wouldn't say that. I told you before: All I want is to be able to see new sights, and sell my wares. And the World Government was bad for my business.''

Wim met the peddler's gaze, glanced away undecided. "Where you going to go now?'' He half expected the answer to be, Back beyond the sky.

"Back to bed." Jagit left the ballistic vehicle, and began to climb the rubbly slope up from the lake; he gestured for Wim to follow.

Wim followed, breathing hard in the thin air, until they reached a large fall of boulders before a sheer granite wall. Only when he was directly before it did he realize they had come on the entrance to a cave hidden by the rocks. He noticed that the opening was oddly symmetrical; and there seemed to be a rainbow shimmering across the darkness like mist. He stared at it uncomprehendingly, rubbing his chilled hands.

"This is where I came from, Wim. Not from the East, as you figured, or from space as the governor thought.'' The peddler nodded toward the dark entrance. "You see, the World Government had me entirely misplaced—they assumed I could only have come from somewhere outside their control. But actually I've been here on earth all the time; this cave has been my home for fifty-seven thousand years. There's a kind of magic in there that puts me into an 'enchanted' sleep for five or ten thousand years at a time here. And meanwhile the world changes. When it's changed enough, I wake up again and go out to see it. That's what I was doing in Sharn, ten thousand years ago; I brought art works from an earlier, primitive era; they were popular, and I got to be something of a celebrity. That way I got access to my new items of trade—my Sharnish magics—to take somewhere else, when things changed again.

"That was the problem with the World Government—they interrupted the natural cycles of history that I depend on, and it threw me out of synch. They'd made stability such a science they might have kept things static for fifty or a hundred thousand years. Ten or fifteen thousand, and I could have come back here and outwaited them, but fifty thousand was just too long. I had to get things moving again, or I'd have been out of business."

Wim's imagination faltered at the prospect of the centuries that separated him from the peddler, that separated the peddler from everything that had ever been a part of the man, or ever could be. What kind of belief did it take, what sort of a man, to face that alone? And what losses or rewards to drive him to it? There must be something, that made it all worthwhile—

"There have been more things *done*, Wim, than the descendants of Sharn have *dreamed*. I am surprised at each new peak I attend . . . I'll be leaving you now. You were a better guide than I expected; I thank you for it. I'd say Darkwood Corners is two or three days journey northwest from here."

Wim hesitated, half afraid, half longing. "Let me go with you—?"

Jagit shook his head. "There's only room for one, from here on. But you've seen a few more wonders than most people already; and I think you've learned a few things, too. There are going to be a lot of opportunities for putting it all to use right here, I'd say. You helped change your world, Wim—what are you going to do for an encore?"

Wim stood silent with indecision; Jagit lifted the rifle, tossed it to him.

Wim caught the gun, and a slow smile, filled with possibilities, grew on his face.

"Good-bye, Wim."

"Good-bye, Mr. Jagged." Wim watched the peddler move away toward his cave.

As he reached the entrance, Jagit hesitated, looking back. "And Wim—there are more wonders in this cave than you've ever dreamed of. I haven't been around this long because I'm an easy mark. Don't be tempted to grave-rob." He was outlined momentarily by rainbow as he passed into the darkness.

Wim lingered at the entrance, until at last the cold forced him to move and he picked his way back down the sterile gray detritus of the slope. He stopped again by the mirror lake, peering back past the magician's bullet-shaped vehicle at the cliff face. The rising sun washed it in golden light, but now somehow he really wasn't even sure where the cave had been.

He sighed, slinging his rifle over his shoulder, and began the long walk home.

Lord Buckry sighed as memories receded, and with them the gnawing desire to seek out the peddler's cave again; the desire that had been with him for thirty years. There lay the solutions to every problem he had ever faced, but he had never tested Jagged's warning. It wasn't simply the risk, though the risk was both deadly and sufficient—it was the knowledge that however much he gained in this life, it was ephemeral, less than nothing, held up to a man whose life spanned half that of humanity itself. Within the peddler's cave lay the impossible, and that was why he would never try to take it for his own.

Instead he had turned to the possible and made it fact, depending on himself, and on the strangely clear view of things the peddler had left him. He had solved every problem alone, because he had had to, and now he would just have to solve this one alone too.

He stared down with sudden possessive pride over the townfolk in the square, his city of Fyffe now ringed by a sturdy wall . . . So the West and the South were together, for one reason, and one alone. It balanced the scales precariously against plenty of old hatreds, and if something were to tip them back again— A few rumors, well-placed, and they'd be at each other's throats. Perhaps he wouldn't even need to raise an army. They'd solve that problem for him. And afterward—

Lord Buckry began to smile. He'd always had a hankering to visit the sea.

AFTERWORD—
THE PEDDLER'S APPRENTICE

This is the only collaboration I've attempted so far; it was the second story I sold, after "Tin Soldier." It was conceived by my first husband, Vernor Vinge, who is also a writer, and who had written about half of the story and then gotten stuck on it. I'd read the fragment before I'd begun to write seriously, and had liked it and wished that he'd find the inspiration to write the rest of it. But then he got a job teaching mathematics at San Diego State University and didn't have time to do any writing for a number of years. Meanwhile, he had been encouraging me to take my own writing seriously, and I had written "Tin Soldier" and sold it. I was casting around for something to work on next, and he offered me the novelette fragment of "The Peddler's Apprentice." He said that he felt my writing style and inclinations seemed more suited to writing the second half of it than his did; the fact that he had that much confidence in my ability was something that did a great deal for my own confidence as a writer.

I began writing the second half, attempting to match my writing style to his style, which is basically sparer and more straightforward than my own. (I find that if I read enough of someone else's work, I can begin to pick up their style almost instinctively, rather like doing voice imitation—which is something I have no ability at. It's a skill that can be both useful and dangerous, depending on what books you happen to be reading. I have to be very careful about reading other people's work when I'm writing something of my own.) I felt that I had a responsibility to maintain both Vernor's tone and his intentions about how the story should develop, since it was his idea in the first place. Generally he was quite pleased, although we had a number of disagreements at the very end of the story, where I kept insisting that I had made exactly the point he'd wanted made, and he kept insisting that I hadn't; eventually we both agreed about what was really said on the page.

I rewrote the rough draft of his half and mine to make everything consistent and sent the finished novelette to Analog, which had published a number of Vernor's stories previously. They bought this one too, and we were both delighted; but they ignored our request that our names be listed separately, and lumped us together like a nightclub act. We both felt that if I was going to seriously pursue a writing career, I needed to keep my identity independent, even in a collaboration. (The story was chosen for two Best SF of the Year anthologies, and both got our separate names correct.)

A note for the curious reader: I took up writing the story at the point where Wim realizes that "Mr. Jagged" is posing as Axl Bork, and has just gotten rid of the entire Bork gang.

Vernor had originally envisioned "The Peddler's Apprentice" as one of a series of stories about Jagit Katchetooriantz, the trader through time. It's quite possible that one or the other of us (or even both) may do more of his strange life history someday.

PSIREN

I don't know why she came that evening. Maybe it was for the reasons she gave me, maybe not. If I'd known her mind the way I used to, when I was really a telepath, maybe everything would have come out differently.

But I might as well have been a blind man, falling over furniture in silent rooms, with just glimmers of gray to show me there was still a world outside my own head. And so I didn't even know she was there until I heard her voice, "Knock knock." Jule never used the stairs, so I never heard her coming. She didn't need to. She'd just be there, like some nightwisp who'd come to grant you a few wishes. I didn't mind that she came in first and knocked afterwards; we'd shared too much for that.

I climbed down from the sleeping platform high up under a constellation of ceiling cracks. "How're you?" There was a time when I wouldn't have needed to ask.

"Lonely." She smiled, that quirky, half-sad smile. I stared at her, my eyes registering her for my mind because my mind couldn't see her. Black hair falling to her waist, gray eyes deeper than the night; the bird's nest of shawls and soft formless overshirts wrapping her long thin body. Protection . . . like mind layers. At least they were in bright colors now, pinks and purples and blues instead of the dead black she'd worn when I first met her. She was pushing thirty standards, had more than ten years on me, but she was still

the most beautiful woman I'd ever seen. Because I'd seen
her from the inside. Nothing would ever change the feeling I
had for her—not the future, not the past, not the fact that she
was married to another man.

"Doc will be back in a couple of days."

"I know, Cat." Her forehead pinched; she was angry—at
herself, for letting need show.

"Somebody's got to mind the mindreaders," I said. "And
you're better at it than he is." She glanced at me, surprised
and questioning. "I remember how your mind works," I
shrugged. "So does Doc. You've got the empathy, he's got
credentials. So he hustles the cause, you hold the fort." *And I
sit up here pretending to be one of his healers, instead of one
of the cripples.* "You're lucky you miss him . . . and so's
he." I moved two steps to the window set in the thick slab of
wall. Looking out I saw the building straight across the alley
staring back at me, black ancient eyes of glass sunk deep in
its sagging face. I listened to the groans and sighs of the one
we stood in; the real voice of buried Oldcity, not the distant
music in the streets. I refocused on my own reflection, a
ghost trapped inside the grimy pane—dark skin, pale curly
hair, green eyes with pupils that were vertical slits; a face that
made people uneasy. I looked away from it.

"Sometimes it feels like the Center is becoming my whole
life, consuming me," Jule was saying. "I need to break away
for a while and let my mind uncoil. I wondered if maybe you
felt that way too." She wondered: Jule, who was an empath,
who knew how everyone felt; who *knew,* who didn't just
guess. Everyone but me.

It wasn't just the Center that was consuming me, even
though I spent all my time here watching over it. It was the
rotting emptiness of my mind. "I don't have anything to
uncoil."

She looked at me as though she'd expected to hear that.
But she only said, "You have a body. You ought to let that
out of here once in a while."

"And do what?" I tried to make it sound interested.

"Go out into Oldcity, see the parts I've never seen . . .
parts you know."

My skin prickled. "You don't want to do that."

"Prove it."

"Damn it, Jule, it ain't—*isn't* anything you want to see. Or anything I want to see again."

She nodded, folding her arms, drawing herself in. "All right. Then can you take me somewhere I do want to see? Give me a fresh perspective for a few hours, Cat."

I dropped the print I'd been reading onto the windowsill. "Sure. Why not?"

She picked it up as I moved away, looked at the title. "CORPORATE STRUCTURE AND THE DEVELOPMENT OF THE FEDERATION TRANSPORT AUTHORITY." She looked back at me, half smiling.

" 'Not bad for a former illiterate'?" I said. She blushed. She was the one who'd taught me to read and write. I picked up my jacket from a corner of the floor. *Only a year ago. A lifetime. Forever.* "You know something?"

She raised her eyebrows.

"Stupidity is easier."

She laughed. We went down the creaking stairs, through the silent rooms of the Center for Psionic Research, and out into the street.

The streets of Oldcity were bright and dark: the bars and gambling places and whorehouses were lit up like lanterns; the heavy glass pavements were inlaid with lights that followed you wherever you walked, down the narrow alleyways between the walls of buildings almost as old as time. None of the light was real light, it was all artificial. Only the darkness was real.

Oldcity was the core, the heart of the new city called Quarro, the largest city on the world Ardattee. Every combine holding on Ardattee had grown fat when the Crab Nebula opened up and made it the gateway to the Colonies. Then the Federation Transport Authority moved its information storage here and picked Quarro to set it down in, and Quarro became the largest cityport on the planet by a hundred times. Earth atrophied, and Ardattee became the trade center of the Human Federation, the economic center, the cultural center. And somewhere along the way someone had decided that the old, tired colonial town was historic, and ought to be preserved.

But Quarro was built on a thumb-shaped peninsula between

a harbor and the sea; there was only so much land, and the
new city kept growing, feeding on open space, always needing more—until it began to eat up the space above the old
city, burying it alive in a tomb of progress. The grumbling,
dripping, tangled guts of someone else's palaces in the air
shut Oldcity off from the sky, and no one lived there any
more who had any choice. Only the dregs, the losers and the
users. It was a place where the ones who wouldn't be caught
dead living there came to feed off the ones who couldn't
escape.

I walked with Jule through the wormhole streets that ten-
driled in toward Godshouse Circle, the one place in Oldcity
where you could still see the sky. For years I'd thought the
sky was solid, like a lid, and at night they turned the sun off.
I didn't mention it, as we pushed our way through the
Circle's evening crowds of beggars and jugglers and staggering burnouts. But I looked up at the sky, a deep, unreachable
indigo; down again at the golden people slumming and the
hungry shadows drifting beside them, behind them, a hand
quicker than the eye in and out of a pocket, a pouch, a fold. I
felt my own fingers flexing, and my heartbeat quickening.

I pushed my hands into my jacket pockets, made fists of
them. Once a Cityboy, always a Cityboy. . . . I felt Oldcity's
heavy rhythms stir my blood, make dark magic in my head;
my body filling with the hunger of it. Hot with life, cold as
death, raw like a wound, it left its scars on your flesh and its
brand on your soul. A hollow-eyed dealer was sliding between us, selling the kind of dreams that don't come true in a
voice like iron grating on cement. *It still shows. They can
smell me.* I shoved him away, remembering too many times
when it had gone the other way.

I turned off of the Circle into another street, not saying
anything; my face stiff, my mind clenched, hardly aware of
Jule beside me. The dark, decaying building fronts faded
behind walls of illusion: Showers of gold that melted through
your hands, blizzards of pleasure and sudden prickles of pain,
fluorescent holo-flesh blossoming like the flowers of some
alien jungle. The heart of the night burst open here in sound
that took your sight away, hard and blistering, sensual and
yielding, shimmering, pitiless. You could drown in your

wildest fantasies right there in the street, and I heard Jule
crying out in wonder, joy, disgust, not knowing her own
emotions from everyone else's.

But it was all a lie, and I'd lived it too many times, hungry
and cold and broke; seen the ones who went through the
images, through the doors where the fantasy turned real, and
left me standing there—all beauty, all pleasure, all satisfaction running through my hands. Reality was no one's dream
in Oldcity. Suddenly I knew why I'd never made this trip,
why I'd stayed like a monk in a monastery at the Center since
I'd come back here . . . suddenly I was wondering why the
hell I'd done it now.

A hand was on my arm, but Jule was drifting ahead beyond
my reach. I turned, wanting to see a stranger; the past looked
me straight in the face. The hand ran down my sleeve, a
heavy hand with sharp heavy rings; the soft ugly mouth
opened, showing me filed teeth. "Dear boy," it said, "you
look familiar."

"I don't know you." Panic choked me.

"Boy . . ." wounded.

"Get away!" I jerked free, ran on through the phantoms of
flesh until I collided with Jule.

She steadied me, staring at me and past me, frightened.
(What's wrong?)

"Nothin'. It's nothing. I just—" I shook my head, swallowed, "Ghosts."

Without another word she took my arm and pulled me
through incense and pearls: The nearest door took our credit
rating and fell open, letting us past into the reality. And
suddenly there was no floor beneath us, no walls, no ceiling;
just an infinity of deepening blue like the evening sky, shot
with diamond chips of light tracking away toward an endless
horizon. Our feet moved over a yielding surface that didn't
exist for my eyes, and with every step my body came closer
to the dizzy brink where my mind swayed now. But we
reached a low table, with seats like cloud; all around us other
cloudsitters watched us walk on air. The sound of their
voices, their laughter, was dim and distant. Patternless music
flowed into the void, a choir of spirit voices weaving their
conversation into its fabric.

As we settled at the table a slow mist rose, curling between us; I felt it tingling against the skin of my face, rising deeper into my head with every breath. The pungent cold of glissen was in it, along with a flavor I couldn't name, that made my mouth water. You could get arrested for this out on the street. My hands were trembling on the transparent table surface; I watched the trembling ease as the glissen began to make me calm. "What is this place?" I took deeper breaths, letting it work.

"It's called Haven." Jule was still searching the room with her eyes. She sighed, as if her inner sight saw only peace and quiet. She looked back at me. "I thought you needed one."

I smiled, half a grimace, pulling at a curl behind my ear. "I didn't—didn't know it would—come back at me like this. Like . . . I don't know." I looked up again. "I've never been in one of these places. Never." My eyes traveled. "Maybe that's the problem. Everything's changed for me, Jule, but I don't believe it. I could *leave* Oldcity—" My hand clenched.

She didn't answer, only looked at me with her storm-colored eyes, until I almost thought I could feel her mind tendril into mine the way it used to. I felt it soothe me, felt her sharing without question.

"Cat, you heard me, outside."

The way she said it made me say, "What?"

"When I asked you what was wrong, I didn't speak it."

"Yes, you did."

She shook her head. "I never got it out of my mouth; you answered me first."

"But I—" I looked away, back, dizzy with infinity rushing at me. "It—happened? I read your mind? And I didn't even know?" I felt cheated.

She nodded. "That's why it did: because you lost control."

"The first time—" *since I killed a man,* "since we came back from the Colonies. More than a year." *Of living in solitary.* . . . I let my mind reach, trying to feel it: the unfolding, the opening out—

She frowned, straining. "You're cutting me off, Cat. Don't—"

"I'm not trying to!" I hit the table edge; my voice made

heads turn. I sank back into my seat. My mind was like a knot.

"Sometimes I've felt you let go, for a second; sometimes you almost—"

"I don't want to talk about it."

"You can't keep it buried. You've got to start facing up to the fact that you are a telepath—"

"Not any more."

"—and you work with me, with us, helping others like us. You're making yourself a martyr to problems we're all trying to face. I want to help you, but you aren't doing a damn thing to cooperate!" The anger and frustration startled me; I couldn't feel them.

"It's not the same!" My own frustration fed on hers. "The rest of them live in a hell made by somebody else, just because the deadheads hate our guts. Nobody else made my hell."

Jule's eyes dropped. "I'm sorry. It's just that I can't help feeling—responsible for the way things are for you now. It's just that when I remember what you had—"

"You think I don't remember?" A silence apart from the music and the room settled on us. I remembered times we'd sat like this in the past, when I was a thief, and she was afraid; before we'd learned to trust each other more than any two human beings had the right to. Before I'd saved her life and Siebeling's by ending someone else's—and lost it all. The music and the awareness of unreal distances around us came back to me slowly, as the glissen numbed my memory. "What do you do in this place, anyhow?"

Jule lifted her head, tension still in the half-smiling corners of her mouth. "I don't know. Meditate?"

I glanced down at the data bracelet covering the old scar on my right wrist. My credit balance had dropped a hundred points. I looked at it again. "Whew. It better be more than sitting on clouds."

Jule glanced down at her own bracelet; her fist pressed the center of her chest. There must have been a time when a hundred credits didn't mean anything to her. But that was somewhere in another life, and now whenever she thought of money she thought of the Center first. "I guess you don't do

anything in Oldcity without considering the consequences,''
rueful.

I nodded. "That's your first lesson. The second one is that
most of the time you don't get the chance to think about it."
She started to get up, and I thought about going out into the
street again. "Wait—till we know if there's anything else.
We're paying for it."

She didn't object. She settled back into her seat; we began
to talk, but not about what had just happened. The glissen
began to make our words slur and our minds wander. After a
while the murmuring choir music faded. In the blue distance
ahead of me a dark opening appeared like a wormhole from
another universe. A figure came through it, walking softly on
air to a place in the center of the cloudsitters. "We welcome
you to the Haven." The figure bowed, wrapped in dark folds
glittering with stars; I couldn't tell whether it was male or
female, even from the voice. "We hope your time here has
been one of tranquility and peace. To further deepen your
experience we give you the Dreamweaver, who will open to
you the secret places of your soul."

I glanced at Jule, rolling my eyes; but she sat half turned
away, watching the act as though it mattered. The figure
raised its arms and folded in on itself, disappearing. The
crowd gasped. I jerked, wondering whether we'd seen a
teleport. But Jule turned back and said, "Just a projection."

I shrugged. All done with mirrors. As I sat watching, a light
began to fall from above us, a captive star drawn down out of
the night. It settled where the projection had been, and as the
light faded there was total silence in the room. I waited for
more cheap tricks, wondering how they ever got enough of
the audience back to this place twice to make it pay.

As the light faded I began to make out another form inside
it, a human body. I kept blinking, trying to clear the dazzle
out of my eyes. It was a child . . . it was a tiny, fragile
woman, lost in a shining silver robe. Her arms were bare,
hung with bands and bracelets showing colored fire; her skin
was no color I'd ever seen before, burnished brass. But her
arms were as thin as sticks, and the bones stood out like a
scream along their length; her face was a shadowed skull.

Her head twisted like a doll's head until she was looking

toward me, at me alone. The touch of those sunken eyes was a blow. I shut my own eyes, not knowing what I was seeing, afraid to see it. I kept them shut for a long minute.

It was the light—the light playing tricks on me. When I looked at her again there was no ugliness, no suffering in that face. But there was a strangeness—something alien about its flat planes, the coloring, about the way her body fit together. *Alien.* I leaned forward, trying to meet her eyes. She looked at me, and they were green, impossibly, translucently green. Our eyes locked; in my mind I saw her seeing the same eyes, like jewels trapped in the matrix of a face that was too human, my face. . . .

I read confusion, a silent cry in her look. She twisted her head away again, searching the crowd as if she needed a hiding place. But infinity was an illusion; the audience held her captive with its anticipation. I almost thought she shimmered, began to disappear . . . caught herself, in control again. Jule murmured something across from me, but I didn't listen.

The Dreamweaver put her hands up to her face, but it was only a gesture, a sign of beginning. Something like a sigh moved through the crowd . . . something like a whisper formed in my mind. I shut my eyes again, trying to hear the image clearly: the soft, fragile-colored dream that echoed palely as a ghost in my mind's darkness. I strained toward it, trying to make it clear, to share what made even the blind, deaf, and empty deadheads all around me gape and dream and squirm in their seats.

"Cat. Cat!"

I opened my eyes again, blinking; whispered, "Damn it, Jule—"

Her face twisted with pain. "I want to leave. I have to leave."

I couldn't focus on her; the echoes wouldn't leave my mind alone, calling, promising—"I can *feel* her, I can almost—"

Jule put her hands to her head, and tears started in the corner of her eyes. "I can't stand it, Cat. Please!"

Laughter rippled across us and through us: the cloudsitters, lost in another world, one I wanted to share so much it hurt.

"It hurts!" Jule gasped.

"Block it, then," trying to keep my voice down, trying to ignore hers.

And suddenly she was gone. Into the air. "Jule!" The one or two people nearest me jerked and swore. I stared at the empty seat across from me. She'd teleported, she'd left me behind; she'd wanted to get away that much. *Why?* Why would she run from this? But the whispers were smokey and seductive now, I couldn't keep my mind on her, couldn't keep it away from them. . . .

The Dreamweaver held the room inside a spell for what seemed like hours, but wasn't. A part of my own mind felt the passing of time, a dim clock marking seconds to the beating of my heart. My concentration and my need fell inward until I was as lost in seeking as the dreamers around me were lost inside themselves.

But dreams end, and the time came when the mindsong faded like dawn, growing fainter, paler, farther away . . . until all that was left to me was my own mind lying. The light in the room was brightening into sunrise; feeling it through my lids, I opened my eyes. The Dreamweaver was drowning in light until I couldn't look at her, couldn't see her, felt the light wash me with physical heat— And she was gone. The light imploded, left my eyes dancing with phosphenes. The other cloudsitters began to shake themselves out, murmuring and gesturing toward the empty center. There was no applause, no calling out for more. Dazed by glissen and drugged with wonder, they stood on air and began to drift toward the door.

Someone passed through my line of sight like a rainbow. I caught at his arm without thinking; felt the electric prickle of the charged cloth and let go of it again. He turned to look at me, seeing worn jeans and a leather worker's jacket, the only kind of clothes I felt comfortable in; seeing the plain tight curls of my hair, the half-homely strangeness of my face. He couldn't make me fit in. . . . I saw him figure me for some rich eccentric. I realized he was right, in a way, and I grinned. He smiled, a little uncertain.

"Is—uh, is the show always like that?"

He nodded. "But the dreams are always changing."

"Is there anyone here besides us? I mean, who runs this place? Who owns it? Where are they?"

He shrugged. "I never see anyone. But I've no doubt they watch over us all from the other side of the sky." He waved vaguely at infinity. His eyes were glassy.

"What about the Dreamweaver? Who is she? Where does she go? I want to . . . want to . . . thank her."

He laughed. "She sees into our minds; no doubt she sees our gratitude there. Who knows where she goes, or who she is? It's all a part of her mystery. Knowing too much would spoil it." He leaned forward, sharing a secret. "Anyway, she's not human, you know."

I felt my face close. "Neither am I."

He half frowned. "That's not funny."

"I know." I looked back again at the emptiness where she'd been; feeling the empty place in my mind. He drifted away. The room was darkening around me, infinity reaching an end, walls closing in with almost a physical pressure. I followed the rest of them out into the street, not thinking about where I was this time, but only about tomorrow—about remembering this place, and coming back to it again, and again.

I walked back to the Center through Oldcity's night without seeing any of it. I climbed the ancient circling stairs at the rear of the quiet building to my room. And as I opened the door I remembered Jule again, remembered her coming here and how our evening had started; how it had ended, when she left me at the Haven without a goodbye. *Why?* But I wasn't ready yet to go to her and find out. Because it would mean sharing what had happened to me, and I wasn't ready for that; not even with Jule.

I stretched out on my sleep platform, staring at the ceiling. My long-pupiled stranger's eyes tracing every crack, even in the darkness. *Alien.* She was an alien, the Dreamweaver— and that was why she'd been able to reach into every mind in that room at once and start them all into fantasies. Why she'd even been able to crack the tomb I'd buried my own mind in. No one else I'd met since I'd lost my telepathy had even come close—because I was only half human. The other half was Hydran, like she was, and that half came with psionic ability that no one I knew could touch. All human psions had some Hydran blood, but in most of them it was generations thin—from the time before humans had decided to hate the only other intelligent race they'd ever encountered.

My mother had been Hydran; my mother was dead. My life after that had been living proof that nobody wanted a Hydran halfbreed—until I'd met Jule and Siebeling. But even they hadn't been able to make me a telepath again.

And yet the Dreamweaver had looked at me and known, and even holding dozens of other minds, she had made a blind man see.

I rolled onto my stomach, pushing the heels of my hands into my eyes; seeing stars, *God, oh God!* feeling tears. I ground them out. After more than a year working with other psions crippled by human hate, proving to them just by existing that they could be worse off than they were . . . to have this happen! To feel alive again, to *feel* the presence of another mind reach into mine. The pain of returning life was the sweetest torture I'd ever known. The Dreamweaver . . . I had to find her; had to let her know . . . *let her know* . . . a heavy peace began to settle on me as I touched the memory again . . . *find her*. . . .

It was daylight when I opened my eyes again; another artificial day of Oldcity street-lighting. I blinked and squinted in the band of glare that lay across my face; sat up, feeling excitement hot and sudden in my chest as I remembered. I tried to remember how long it had been since I'd felt anything but a dim, tired ache, morning after morning. I pulled on a clean smock over my jeans and went downstairs.

I'd overslept. Jule was already there, passing out hot drinks to the day's first handful of miserable-looking psions who'd come for their ration of human contact—something I should have been doing for her. She jerked as I came up beside her, catching her by surprise. I took the drinks out of her hands, keeping a mug of bitter-root for myself. "Sorry. Why didn't you call me?"

She looked at me with an expression I couldn't read. "I didn't know you were here."

"Jule, I want to take the day off."

Her face pinched. "Cat, not today. It's half crazy around here without Ardan. Mim and Hebrett can't handle it without you."

The hell they can't. I opened my mouth to say it, changed my mind. I sighed, and shrugged. "If you need me. . . ."

She smiled. The smile stopped. "Yes, I want to talk about last night. Later. . . ."

I nodded and went back to work. The morning passed in a haze of going through the motions, setting up control exercises, watching them happen, listening to a new day's complaints from the 'paths and 'ports and teeks who were trying to come to terms with the freak mind talents that were tearing up their lives.

And then I was alone with Jule in Siebeling's broom-closet office, sitting on the corner of his perfectly organized desk and drinking soup. I watched Jule sipping at her own cup, sitting in his chair; watched the kinetic sculpture on his desk, afraid to let my mind focus. The sculpture was lifeless, nothing more than a tangle of metal without Siebeling here to make it dance with his mind the way he did. You could tell what sort of mood he was in by what it was doing.

"Last night . . ." Jule said finally.

"Why did you leave?" The words sounded hard.

She leaned back, the chair re-formed around her. "Because it was . . . *painful.*" She bit her lip. "I felt a—"

"It was beautiful! Everyone there, everyone in the room—she made them let her into their minds and love her for it! And she—she—"

"Touched you." Jule nodded.

"Yeah." I looked down.

"The strength of her sending—"

"She's Hydran."

"Yes." Jule's eyes traced my profile. "Even you couldn't resist her."

"You couldn't either." I leaned forward. "But why run away from it? It ought to make you happy to see a psion in control, strong, proud."

"She wasn't in control; she was afraid! She was there out of fear, need, helplessness, compulsion . . ." Jule's knuckles whitened against the cup. "All that and more, inside the pretty lies. Cat, I know what you felt last night, and how much it meant to you. But inside she was screaming, she couldn't stop it; and I couldn't listen to it.'' Her body shuddered, and soup spilled.

I lowered my own cup slowly onto the desktop. "I don't believe it.'' But Jule wouldn't lie—wasn't lying. I shook my head. "Why?''

"I don't know.''

"Then if anybody ever needed our help, she does. But she appears and disappears—how can we reach her?''

"There is a way," meaning mind to mind. She took a deep breath. "But I can't face it, Cat. I can't block her sending. And I'm not even sure she'd listen. There's something else she needs more.'' Her hand moved in an empty circle through the air.

"Does that mean you won't try?'' My hands tightened.

"It means that I want someone else to try. Someone she might respond to, who's protected from what's inside her.''

Me. I was the one she meant. There was something I might be able to do that no one else here could. . . .

There was a knock at the door. Jule called, "Come in," and Mim came in. She looked from Jule to me and back again. Mim was a telepath, a student psi tech; she could have told Jule anything she needed to without ever opening the door. But they did it the hard way, because of me.

"What now, Mim?'' Jule looked tired suddenly.

Mim rubbed her hands on her pants, frowning. "There's a Corpse out front, who wants to speak to Whoever Runs this Freakhouse. He's going to ask us about corporate crime and using psionics for brainwashing. He's also scared we'll rape his mind while he's here.'' Her mouth twitched, her blue-green eyes were as cold as the sea.

"All right: I'll make him feel like we're all angels.'' Jule pushed her head into her hands, leaning on the desktop. "Corporate Security looking for blood, that's all we need. Damn it! Why don't the deadheads leave us alone? . . . Cat, where are you going?'' She called after me as I started for the door.

"Hunting.'' I pushed past Mim and went out.

* * *

I spent the rest of the day, and as much time as I could steal of the days that followed, searching and asking around the Oldcity streets . . . getting nowhere. I'd known all my life how the information root system grew in Oldcity, thick and tangled; sending shoots up into the light among the shining towers of Quarro. Now I had money to back me, something I'd never had before; a key to Oldcity's hidden doors that had always been closed to me. But still I got nowhere. Whoever controlled the Haven, and the Dreamweaver, wanted it kept a secret.

And meanwhile I went back again and again, like an addict, to drop another hundred credits at the Haven's door and sit on clouds and needles, waiting. Until infinity would open once more and show her to me, let her reach out to me and into me, touching my need. And every night I tried to catch her eyes, complete the circuit, give her something in return—just my name, just my gratitude, *Ask me, ask me for anything*. But there was never an answer, never a sign that she felt anything. Her control was complete, and I was a blind man asking her to let me guide her. I wondered if she laughed at me, somewhere behind the inhuman peace of her face. If she was suffering there was no sign of it. Any suffering was mine, anger and frustration eating at me until it was all I could do not to get up from where I sat night after night and cross the space that separated us like the barrier in my mind. Always knowing that if I ever tried it she'd disappear, and I'd never see her even this way again.

There were other regulars in this place. I got to know them by sight, although none of them ever talked about why they came, or what they felt, sharing the forbidden fruit of telepathy. Some of them were even combine or Transport Authority officials, wearing power and arrogance like their fine upside clothes. And they were all perverts. Most of them probably swore they hated psions when they were back in the daylight; most of them probably did. Jule said they hated psions because they were afraid—and because they wanted what we had. I'd never believed her, until now. You could satisfy any hunger in Oldcity, if you had the price. If you were willing to pay enough, you could even call it entertainment. I tried to find a little pleasure in watching their faces get soft and slack from glissen and psidreams.

And one night, watching, I saw something happen I'd never seen before. At the end of the regular show, after the Dreamweaver had disappeared and the crowd was drifting toward the door, the hologram host came back through the crack in space and caught one of the guests with a word. The man nodded, lighting up like a lottery winner, and followed it into somewhere else. I started after them when I saw them disappear. But as soon as I did infinity went black ahead of me; a soft, clammy wall of nothing was suddenly between me and the place I was trying to reach. I turned back, disgusted, and went out with the rest.

The lucky winner was back the next night, as if nothing had happened; but he wore a strange smile when he watched the Dreamweaver appear. And a couple of nights later I saw the same thing happen to someone else. Again I tried to follow; again I ran into a soft wall. Somehow, a few of the ones who came here were being chosen for something extra; but no one would tell me what, if I didn't already know. And no matter how often I asked her with my mind, the Dreamweaver never answered me.

Siebeling had come back to the Center, in the meantime. I figured when he finally called me into his office that it would be to tell me what Jule had begun telling me with looks and frowns, if not with words: That I was spending too much time and money and getting nowhere. That maybe I'd taken on something impossible, and was too damn stubborn to admit it. Jule was with him when I entered his office; standing, looking uncomfortable. Just like I felt. "Doc?" I said, making it half a question.

He glanced up at me. His face was the same as ever; only more tired. He was a plain-looking man, and the clothes he wore were even plainer—but there was something about him, a quiet determination that made you pay attention. "Jule told me about your experience with the Dreamweaver. I take it the two of you had very different reactions." He leaned forward; his hazel eyes searched my face.

I nodded, leaning against the closed door, running my fingers along the seams of my smock.

"You want to talk about it?"

"You've heard it all." I glanced at Jule, not able to keep the accusation out of it. She met my eyes; something darker and more confused than resentment was in her own.

"I've heard that the Dreamweaver is Hydran. That for Jule her sendings are a cry of pain. That you can't feel the pain—but you feel something. And so you keep going back for more. True?"

"Yeah." I stared at my feet, at braided straps of scuffed leather. Resentment was pushing hard inside my chest, the sound of his voice taking me back suddenly; making me remember old times, bad times, before we'd seen the inside of each other's minds, and our own.

"Why?"

What's it to you? I almost said, almost let my own doubt turn me back into a scared street punk. I took a deep breath and raised my head. "I want to help her. Jule says she needs help—and nobody else wants to try."

"*Can* try," Siebeling said softly. Jule's face was turned away, and I understood a little more.

"Then why do you want me to stop?"

"I didn't say that." Siebeling leaned further across the hard, shiny desk top, and I could see his tension. The kinetic sculpture was tumbling and ringing softly. I remembered his first wife, who'd been Hydran too, who'd died when he wasn't there to help her. "I just want to know what you're getting out of this for yourself." It wasn't an accusation. Only a question.

I shrugged. "I dunno, I . . . that is, it's what we're here for. It makes me feel like I have a purpose. A reason. It makes me feel alive—"

"Knowing someone exists who can prove that you are."

"Yeah." I looked down again.

"There's nothing wrong with that. You're only letting her help you." He glanced at the sculpture; it reversed direction. "But what's going to happen if you can't help her? If she won't be helped? Can you let it go, or is this thing an obsession?'' I finally began to let myself believe that he only meant what he said.

"I can handle it." I let my hands hang loose at my sides. "If I have to forget her, I will." *But I won't have to.* My fingers twitched.

Siebeling smiled at Jule. She matched the smile without really meaning it, because she knew he wanted her to. I wondered if we were all thinking about his first wife then, and what had happened to her. "Then I don't see any reason not to continue; at least until you've reached a decision. As you say, it's what we're here for." Several kinds of longing were in his voice.

"Thanks." I opened the door and went out, not wanting any of us to have more time to think.

But that night the Corpses came back; three deadheads in matching gray, looking more like businessmen than police. The Transport Authority had taken what had once been separate corporate police forces and made them its own here in Quarro. The Corpse who asked most of the questions was a Transport Special Investigator named Polhemas; his coming in person meant that the matter under investigation was making a lot of people upside sweat. . . . And it meant that even though Dr. Ardan Siebeling was a teek who didn't try to cover it up he was still Dr. Siebeling, who had a few friends Up There.

But the Corpses were looking for someone who could pick the brains of important officials and researchers and sell what they found to the most interested party. Not just the usual combine political backstabbing, but something with underworld roots. They were looking for psions; and here we were in the middle of Oldcity, right where they'd expect us to be.

We spent hours arguing the truth and our right to exist; the way we'd had to do so many times since we'd begun the Center, and probably would have to do forever. They didn't leave until the time of the Dreamweaver's show was long past. I went up to my room and stayed there staring into the darkness, like a burnout aching for a fix.

And the next night it happened again. Just as we were closing Polhemas showed up, his hired help pushing the door back into my face. This time they'd come to pick on me. They wanted to blame their troubles on the Center, because that was easier than thinking; they were going to pry into the cracks until they could. And I had a record that matched just about anybody's opinion of bad. Jule and Siebeling wouldn't leave me alone for the questioning, which meant that Polhemas was going to give us three times the grief; but I was grateful anyway. We stood together in the office while Polhemas sat in Siebeling's chair, daring someone to object; while he demanded to know what I was doing here, what I was *really* doing here, what I did in my spare time, whether anybody could prove that, prove I wasn't moonlighting, prove I was really a mental burnout and not a galactic arch-criminal. . . .

Some other time I might have enjoyed watching a Corpse on the wrong track making an ass of himself. But the questioning went on and on, he talked down to and over and through me, while I watched the minutes crawl past up on the wall until I'd missed the Dreamweaver's show again. Until I couldn't sit through one more insulting question, couldn't listen to Jule or Siebeling make one more soft answer in my place—

I pushed away from the wall. "Listen, Polhemas, maybe you never get sick of this shit, but I do. So I've got a record: if you know that, you know it's been sealed. If you've got anything fresh on me, then do something about it. Otherwise, try a different datafile. I've got a Corpse commendation on record too—just like they do," nodding at Siebeling and Jule. Just saying it made me stronger. "That means I don't have to—"

"Shut up, freak," one of the other Corpses said.

Polhemas glared at him. "Is that true?" He asked Siebeling the question.

Siebeling nodded, with a smile only I could see in the corners of his mouth. Once we'd worked together for the Federation—been used by it—against a psion renegade who kept slipping through its hands. We'd stopped him; that was how I'd learned what I could really do with my mind. I'd killed him . . . and that was how I'd lost it all. "Even we have served justice in our small way," Siebeling said. His smile said we were still waiting for justice to give us something in return.

Polhemas glared at Siebeling then and back at me. "I don't like your attitude."

I opened my mouth, saw Jule stiffen. I closed it again; watched the sculpture clattering on Siebeling's desk. "The matter isn't closed. I may still close this place down before it is." Polhemas gestured his men into line and went out into the Oldcity night.

"He knew about the commendations," Jule said finally. "There was no surprise in his mind . . . he knew all about us before he came here. But it didn't matter to him."

Siebeling grunted in disgust.

I looked up at the time again, and didn't say anything.

The third day was business as usual; I went through the motions, counting the hours until the Center closed and the Haven opened. But then Jule was beside me, her face drawn with a strange tension, as if she were holding her breath. "Cat, there's someone here to see you."

I followed her out to the front reception area, holding my own breath, somehow knowing without knowing who it was I'd see there.

The Dreamweaver stood near the entrance, melting into the dark-beamed wall while the Center's regulars circled past, some of them not even seeing her, some of them staring and edging away as though they were seeing a crazy woman. My skin prickled. One of the telepaths across the room started to moan; Hebrett pulled him through into another room and closed the door. Jule's face was rigid when I glanced at her.

But I didn't feel anything except hope swelling inside me; didn't see anything but a tiny frightened woman holding herself together with her arms. She wore a loose cowled smock and pants, rich cloth, all in brown. Her hair that had been a haze of spun gold was buried under a heavy beaded net. Only her face, the color of burnished brass, showed her alienness. Her eyes were waiting for mine, as green as emeralds.

We stood face to face at last, and suddenly my mouth was too dry for words. I nodded.

"This is Cat," Jule said, because something had to be

said. She caught my eye, asked me, begged me with her look to *Go away, take her away, far away from here please*—

"What are you doing here?" I got the words out at last.

The Dreamweaver kept her eyes on my face, hugging herself, as if it was all she could do to hold herself here. "You didn't come. Twice."

I felt myself blush, hot and sudden. "I—I couldn't. I wanted to, but I couldn't. I would've come tonight."

She blinked, her arms wrapping her harder. "Truly?"

I nodded again. Jule turned and walked away too quickly. "That's why you came here? How did you know—how did you find me?"

"You told me. Every night I heard you. Showing your self to me, showing this place. Saying, 'Come, come please'—"

"You heard." I swallowed a hard knot of joy. "I—listen—I mean, do you want to go somewhere? Somewhere we can— talk?" *But talking is so hard, useless, when two minds can share the space of one and you only have to know.* "Somewhere else, quiet, away from here." I waved a hand, wishing that somehow I could make the whole Center disappear.

"Yes." Her face eased and turned eager to be gone all at once.

"Is there a place—?"

"Yes," almost impatiently. She led me outside and along the street to a cab caller. One of the upside bubbles was drifting toward us over the crowds almost before the silence started to make me feel like a fool. We got in, she said, "Hanging Gardens" into the speaker. I felt something I couldn't name, that almost choked me. We were going up—out of Oldcity, into Quarro. I'd never been upside in all the time I'd worked at the Center—hardly been more than a kilometer from the place itself, even here in Oldcity. I swallowed and swallowed again, as the cab carried us in toward Godshouse Circle and then rode an invisible updraft into the light of day, the real world. The air brightened around us as the shadowed, twisted underside of the city fell behind and below. The air got sweeter, clearing the stench of a thousand different pollutants out of my lungs. I only knew them now by the fact that they were gone. The corporate crown of Quarro shone around us, the silvered, gilded, blued towers mirroring endlessly flowing images of more reflecting more and somewhere the sky caught up in it, bluer-on-blue and cloud-softened. I thought about the first time I'd seen the city I'd spent my whole life inside of, out the window of a Corpse flyer, under arrest . . . not even two years ago.

The cab set us down again almost before I'd finished the thought; the Hanging Gardens were above Godshouse Circle, like the rim of a well whose waters had gone bad. We climbed out; the cab docked me for the whole fare, and I realized that she wasn't even wearing a data bracelet. If I hadn't had mine on no cab would have taken us up from Oldcity.

The gardens rose and dropped away on all sides of us; manmade tiers of living land growing, flowering, spreading, shading. Islands in the sky, worlds-in-a-bottle, each of them a living miniature of a homeworld somewhere in the Federation. I followed the Dreamweaver along the curving walkways that spiralled through the air between one suspended island and another. The spring breeze was sharp and biting, the arch of sky above us was bruised with purple clouds. There weren't many other walkers on the paths.

Her silence began to get on my nerves until I remembered that a Hydran didn't need the useless small talk humans needed to bridge the emptiness between them. Words were an emphasis, or an afterthought—the contact was already, always, there. Knowing she didn't need the words when I did didn't make it easier. But she seemed to be moving toward something, not just moving for its own sake, and so I kept my words and my thoughts to myself.

We came out at last in a garden where the green of tendrils and crescent leaves was shot with veins of silver, the wind making them shimmer, fade, brighten as though reality was something always just beyond the limit of my eyes. I looked back at the Dreamweaver, seeing that she'd reached the right place at last. *The right place* . . . because there was something of this place in her, about her, something not-quite-seen.

"Your homeworld," I said. My own voice startled me. "A piece of it. Koss Tefirah," squinting at the plaque beneath a silver-skinned treeshrub.

She nodded. She sat down on a low bench sculptured out

of stone, touching the crystal-flecked surface with copper-gold hands.

I stood a minute longer watching her, thinking about how small she looked, how fragile, cupped in the hands of stone; how much like a child or a flower or a piece of down carried on the wind. Nothing like Jule, who was tall, taller than I was, thin but with a man's kind of lean strength. . . . And yet everything like Jule on the inside, lighting my darkness and making me see hope again. Sharing a strength with me that she couldn't afford to give, but gave anyway because I needed it . . . even when her own need, her own fear, were more than she could live with.

I jerked out of the thought, not knowing where it had come from—from what Jule had said or from something lying deep in my own mind. The Dreamweaver looked at me, her green eyes shifting like the green on every side. I looked down into them, seeing the same healing strength that had held Jule together when the world was pulling her apart. Seeing the strength that had been my mother's once, too, and the eyes. . . . And seeing those things, knowing someone like this should never have to use that kind of strength just to keep herself sane, I knew that I would do anything for her, anything at all— My knees got weak and I sat down on the bench, keeping just out of reach, hers or mine, I wasn't sure. I looked away across the floating glade in a half-blind glance; seeing the swaying boneless treeshrubs and the flowering vines that softened the hard underside of the next tier above us. The air was sweet and musky with the scent of them, like the scent of a woman's skin—I swallowed, wondering if it was her doing this to me, or the place, or if I'd just gone a little crazy hiding from life down in my Oldcity room. "How—how long've you been gone? From Koss Tefirah, I mean?" still not looking at her. *Oh God, can she hear me? Stop it stop it you damn fool—*

"Many years." Her voice was suddenly small and dreary.

"And so you come here, trying to hold onto the memories." I twisted my hands on the stone seat. "Doesn't it make you sad?"

She turned toward me abruptly. "Yes. Yes—" turning

away again. "It makes me sad. But still I come . . . I don't know why."

"Because you think someday you'll find what you're looking for here. What you lost."

She stared at me, and out of the corner of my eye I could see that she was afraid.

"No. I'm not reading your mind. Just my own." I shrugged. She didn't speak but I knew she was asking. My hands hung onto each other in the space between my knees. "I—I miss a place, a life, a right, a—a—" hating my stupid, clumsy words, "—*belonging*. Me, too."

"How long are you gone?"

"A long time. A lifetime."

She frowned her confusion. "Where is your home?"

"I don't know." My hands fisted. "Here: Oldcity! I mean, I was born here. I lived my whole life here . . . thinking I was only human, and wondering why people kicked my ass all the time. But I went away, to the Colonies, and I met—some of our relatives. And they made me proud of what I really am—half Hydran." I looked back at her finally, letting her see my eyes that were as green as emeralds, as grass, as her own. "But that half of my life, I lost it before I ever had a chance to learn. . . . And now I've come back to Oldcity, and I keep waiting for some kind of magic to show me the way home. Only it never happens. Because it's not Oldcity I'm looking for, and it won't ever give me what I want." Every word of it was true, and I wondered why I'd never seen the truth before. "But it's all I've got."

She nodded, her face pinched, her eyes shimmering, drowning. I noticed something wrong with the eyes then—the pupils were open almost halfway, black depths pooling in the green. We were sitting in bright sunlight, and they should have been no more than slits, barely visible.

What are you on? I almost asked it . . . but no matter where either of us thought we belonged, we belonged to Oldcity now, and in Oldcity you didn't ask. Instead I said, "Why? Why did you come here, why do you stay?"

"Relocation." The smallness, the dullness, the loss came back; the single word hit me like a fist.

Relocation. One indifferent, empty word that held a world

of rage and suffering and loss—the grief of a life and a whole people torn apart. Once Koss Tefirah had been her people's world; the way Earth had been home to humans. But Earth hadn't been enough for humanity; like roaches, like flies, they'd spread out across the galaxy to other worlds. Some of the worlds already belonged to another people, the ones the humans called Hydran; naming them for the system Beta Hydrae where first contact was made—and for an ancient Terran monster with a hundred heads.

The Hydrans were humanoid enough that they could even interbreed with humans; their only real difference was in having psi talents that made most humans deaf and blind by comparison. Some early xenobiologists even called the human race a world of defective Hydrans, psi mutes. It wasn't a very popular idea with the rest of humanity, especially when some empire-building combine wanted to strip the resources of a Hydran world. The FTA would oblige them, one way or another, and because the Hydrans' psionic ability had made them nonviolent, getting rid of them was easy. They lost their lives, their rights, their homes . . . they lost everything. And they couldn't—wouldn't—fight back. I took a deep breath, and another, before I could say anything more. "I'm sorry." Something stupid. "At least—at least you're the Dreamweaver. At least you make them come to you hungry for the dreams they've lost themselves, and willing to pay. Even if it'll never be enough."

She didn't say anything. Her fingers traced the folds of her smock over and over. Twitchy. Mindless. Not in peaceful silence, any more. Birds were calling somewhere far below us. I noticed again that she didn't wear a data bracelet. Without a data bracelet, you didn't exist on this world.

"How do you get here on your own?"

"I teleport." Her lips barely moved.

"Oh." Pure-blooded Hydrans could do nearly any form of psionics there was a name for. Most human psions couldn't. I couldn't. All I'd ever been any good at was telepathy. But once I'd been *good* . . . better . . . the best.

"What happened to you?"

"What?" I looked up.

"Why is your mind like that? What have they done to you?"

I felt my own eyes drowning suddenly, blinked them clear. "Somebody made me see myself without illusions, once. I killed him for it."

"Murder?" Her voice filled with thick horror.

I shook my head. "Self-defense." I made myself go on looking at her, knowing that no true Hydran could kill another being and survive. Their own empathy destroyed them. "I'm human enough to klll. But I was Hydran enough to pay for it." *And pay, and pay* . . . knowing I would never forget the white agony of death that had burned out my senses and left my mind a wound that would never completely heal. "Scar tissue. That's all I have now . . . except when you send your dreams out to me. I've been trying for so long just to . . . thank you." It died in whispers. "Why . . . how . . . all those others and still you knew, you touched *me*." I almost touched her, but only with a hand. "Why?"

"You were different, you and the woman. Not like the rest—" I heard her disgust. "I looked at you, and I felt you different from all the rest, even from her, and so alone, more alone than anyone could be."

"It's not so bad," lying.

"But you came back, over and over. I felt you thanking me, and calling me, and asking me things I could not answer. Until you stopped coming."

"You heard me—" I straightened, feeling the stone grate against my back, "and I heard you. Could we be that way now—talk mind to mind, not words?" *Please, please.*

"No." She shut her eyes. "You aren't like the guests, the empty minds. You focus sharply, clearly. But then your own mind's hand covers its mouth, and you make less than a whisper. And your mind's hands cover its ears, even though I am shouting. . . . Even to talk like humans with you is easier. Forgive me."

"It's all right . . . I shouldn't have asked." My hope curdled, and I was glad then that it wasn't easy for her to see my thoughts. We sat together without thoughts or words, listening to the wind speak and the leaves answer.

"You are called Cat. Why?" Change of subject.

"It's my name." I relaxed finally, smiled a little, settling into the seat.

"Is that all?" She bent her head; beaten-gold earrings winked at me. "Cat?"

"It's all I need." I shrugged.

"But it is an animal." Curiosity and protest.

"Have you ever looked at a cat, at their eyes? They see in the dark. Their eyes are green, and the pupils are long slits. Like mine; like ours." I laughed once. "I picked it up on the streets. It fits."

She nodded slightly to herself. "I see. You keep your real name hidden. The humans don't do that, because their minds are hidden already."

"Real name?" I shook my head. "I don't have any other. Maybe once . . . but not any more." I felt an old loss cut deeper. "I'm not hiding anything." *But you are, damn it, you are.* "What about you? I don't know any of your names."

"Ineh. Call me that."

"Is that your real name?"

"No." Her hands stroked the bench, never quiet.

My mouth twitched. "Oh."

"I could not show you that name. You would have to see it in my mind's heart."

"Oh," again. I couldn't decide whether to get annoyed or get angry, so I didn't. "You're telling me that I'll never know you that well."

She didn't answer.

"Why did you come to see me, anyway?"

"You stopped coming to see me." She glanced up, her pupils wide and black. "And then I had a sending that you would help me."

I opened my mouth, but nothing came out. A sending . . . precognition. The wild card power. Nobody who had it could control it; they could only learn to sift images when they came, try to pick the true ones out of the static. "How? How can I help?"

"I don't know."

"What's wrong that should be right?"

"Nothing." Her pupils like black pools of emptiness swallowing the sun said, *liar, liar.*

I laughed again, frustrated. "Is it the Dreamweaver, the Haven—do you want out of it?" I remembered what Jule had said. No answer again. "What is it, are you afraid to tell me? I owe you a debt. Let me pay it."

"I have no right." She looked away, searching the glade for enemies, or an escape.

"I want this. Ineh—" I caught her hand, like a handful of bones; jerked, but then it was only a hand, soft-skinned, pulling free. "Who owns the Haven? Have they got something on you, is that what you're afraid of?"

"Stop it! Stop!" She held herself rigid like a shield.

I stopped.

"I should not have come to you. If they find out they would keep you from seeing me." Her face fell apart. " You can't help me, I was wrong to speak of it. Promise me that you will not ask me any more."

"It's drugs, isn't it?" It had to be the answer; how else could any human hold someone like her, and make her obey?

"No." *Yes, yes,* her eyes said.

"Yes."

She wavered, losing substantiality, going—

"No, no wait! Don't—" I reached out, caught her arm, felt it solidify into flesh again. I let her go, sitting back. "I'm sorry, I should've known better. We are what we are. It won't happen again." I kept watching her body still held like a shield, her closed face; my own face promised her.

She let herself loosen, nodding. "I cannot share with my own people, or with the humans. But you are both and neither . . . when I see you I will not feel so alone. Will you come in the evenings to my show?"

I moved against the bench, feeling uncomfortable. "Look, Ineh . . . this is hard to say, but I can't keep coming forever. I don't have that kind of money."

"No?" She looked at me as though she couldn't understand why not.

"No." I shook my head. "Do you even know what it's like to be poor?"

"Yes." She looked through me. "My people were poor when I came here. But that was a long time ago. . . ." As if it didn't matter any more.

"And you're not poor any more. What about the rest of them? What about your family?"

"I don't know. I don't know where they are."

Anger rose in me again. I swallowed it, and said, "That doesn't seem to bother you much either."

"No. It is a long time. . . ." She shifted listlessly. "Before my people came here we shared a life, we shared our minds' hearts. But the humans took our life away, and in this place no one shares anything. There was nothing left for us. We stopped sharing. We stopped wanting to. Because what was the use? There are better ways to stop pain."

And you know the best. I grimaced. It wasn't hard to see where her life had gone from there; or to see the possibilities some Oldcity user had seen in her, that had put her into this trap. But I only said, "I know."

Her eyes came back to me.

"I'll come to the Haven when I can. But I can come here too, it'll be better that way. Just let me know, somehow. I'll get the time off."

She nodded. "Come to the Haven soon. I'll know then."

I stood up, not needing to be told that she was leaving. "Promise me this isn't the last time."

(I promise.) The words whispered into my mind. And then she was gone.

When I got back to the Center, Siebeling called me into his office again. Jule came with me, and together they asked about what had happened. And suddenly I didn't want to tell them. "We talked. About things—you know," shrugging. "What we are, who we are. She's lonely, she's lost her people."

"Where is she from?" Siebeling asked. I couldn't know what he was thinking, but he must be thinking about his dead wife not about Ineh. He couldn't see *her,* he wouldn't understand her kind of trouble the way I could. . . .

"Koss Tefirah. She was relocated here."

His face turned down.

Jule said, "Did she tell you why she came to the Center?"

"She missed me." Somehow even that was too personal, too much. I could imagine what I would have been getting from her mind: she couldn't cope with this, she couldn't understand any more than he did, maybe she was even jealous of me for doing what she couldn't. . . .

"Is that all?"

"I guess it's something," I said, resenting it. "It's a beginning." I knew then that I wouldn't say the rest, the whole truth. This was my affair, *mine,* and I'd handle it myself because I was the right one, the only one who could. "I'll be seeing her again; and not just at the Haven." Daring them to stop me. "I'm going to help her, I know it. She knows it." *Everybody knows it!* wishing that everyone could.

Siebeling glanced at Jule and back at me. They didn't say anything. The kinetic sculpture on his desk stopped dead in the air.

I met Ineh in the Gardens more than once in the next couple of weeks, and watched her at the Haven. Watching her now, knowing that drugs fed her the dreams she was feeding to the crowd, I hated the place; hated myself for still needing them, even while I was trying to stop them. But nothing else changed. When we were together she never let me any closer.

Then one afternoon at the Center Mim came up to me with a strange, glazed look on her face. "Message for you."

"Huh?" I straightened up from the storage cabinets. Her hands were empty. "Where is it?"

She tapped her head. "In here. What are you, deaf?" The joke had teeth and it bit me hard. "Somebody's screaming her brains out for you, trying to tell you she wants you *now.* Make her stop, damn it! And tell her not to use my head for a call box in the future." She started to turn away.

"Where's Jule?"

"Out."

I let out the breath I was holding. "Mim—"

She turned back, still frowning.

"I'm sorry."

She grimaced. "Just find her before she puts every 'path in the building into an epileptic fit. When I say this is a pain, I'm not kidding."

"I'm going out." I left the uncalibrated meters lying helpless on the table and started toward the door.

"Hurry!" She threw it after me.

I left the building and headed for the cab caller. Ineh was waiting there for me. I hadn't expected it.

"Why didn't you come to the Center?" It came out more sharply than I'd meant it to.

She shook her head. "They don't want me there. So I called you."

"Next time use the phone." I pushed the call button.

She stared at me, looking tiny and miserable and alone.

"I'm sorry." I bent my head. "It's just that when you call me I'm the last to know, in a place like that."

She still stared at me. The cab came finally, and I was glad.

We sat together in the Koss Tefirah garden. I asked her, finally, "Why did you call me, anyway?" Hoping there was a good reason, afraid of what I was going to feel like if there wasn't.

"I was unhappy."

My hand tightened over the stone arm of the bench. "About what?"

She shivered like a plucked string. "Nothing." Her own hands twisted, always moving.

"About what?"

She didn't answer. (Nothing.)

"Damn it, Ineh! You can't tell me 'nothing' forever! Either you trust me or you don't and if you don't I don't know what the hell I'm here for!"

"I can't. I can't tell you. I'm afraid—"

"For you or for me?"

"I'm afraid!" She crushed her eyes shut, and her fists, and her mind.

I unlatched my data bracelet, let it fall into my hand. "Open your eyes. There's something I want you to see; I want to show you something."

Slowly her eyes opened, and her fists. She looked at me, tensing.

I held out my wrist. A band of scar tissue circled it, naked and alien. "See that?"

She nodded.

"A bond tag did that." I turned away from her, pulled my

jacket up and my shirt loose. The sun felt warm on my skin; I remembered the feel of another sort of fire on my back. . . . I let her look at the scars. "That's what it means to wear one." I pulled my shirt down again, turned to face her. "I was shipped to the Colonies as contract labor. If it hadn't been for the people who run the Center I'd still be there. I've been somebody's slave, Ineh."

She touched my wrist with cold fingers.

"Tell me what's wrong."

"I must give a private performance."

The words hung in the air between us like crystal beads. I felt the answer to the question complete its circle before I could even ask. The strangers I'd seen at the Haven, disappearing after the show, going on to something more—a private performance.

"It's different than what you do in the show?"

"Different . . . the same . . . more." Her hands pressed her arms inside her long sleeves.

"When is this next 'performance'? After the show?" It was dusk already.

"Yes." Her fingers dug into the flesh of her arms. "I don't want to go. I don't want to—"

"Then don't go. Stay with me. We'll protect you."

"No, they'll come for me. They'll find me; nowhere is safe from them!"

"Ineh, that's what they want you to think. It's not true, not if you don't want it to be."

"It is! I see it in their minds."

I broke off, not sure any more whether she was fooling herself, or I was. "What about the Corpses? We could go to them—" Even the word left a bad taste in my mouth.

"No!"

I could have argued it, but I didn't. Suddenly I was remembering Polhemas, and why he'd come to the Center.

Ineh stiffened where she sat, looking past me. There was no one else anywhere near us. "They're coming. They'll find us together. I have to go—"

"There's no one—"

"I feel them!" She stood up, and I knew that in another moment she'd disappear.

"Wait, where—? Where can I find you?"

"In Ringer's End. Thirty-five—" She wavered, and was gone. I sat on the bench alone, waiting for whatever happened next. The stars were starting to show through, and a sliver of the lower moon. About five minutes later a middle-aged man and woman, upside gentry, came into the glade, walking slowly. They looked at me a little longer than they might have; but no longer than anyone dressed the way they were would look at someone dressed like me, in a park at dusk. They went on, murmuring something I couldn't hear. Thinking thoughts I couldn't hear. Were they the ones? Or were they just her fear showing; or just an excuse? I sat twitching until they'd passed, and then I went looking for a cab.

I got to Ringer's End as fast as I could. For Oldcity it wasn't a bad looking street; at least it was clean, and almost quiet. I could hear the sea. I found the building entrance, but no one answered when I buzzed. It was almost time for the Haven show; I couldn't make myself stay there waiting, with no proof that she'd ever even been there. I left Ringer's End and went to a weapon shop, where I got myself a stungun. Then I chased the hour across town to the Haven.

I went through the Haven's doors again, hiking across infinity, not even noticing any more that I walked on thin air. Time mattered, not space—and time was shrinking in on me all the time. I sat down, leaning back away from the glissen mist, not wanting anything to dull my mind. My fingers beat seconds on the empty tabletop, out of rhythm with the gibbering background voices. I'd never noticed before how much like a dirge the music sounded.

At last the usual show began, and I held my breath until I saw Ineh coming out of her cloud of light. As soon as she was a solid reality I started, (Where were you? Where the hell did you go? What's happening; tell me what to do!)

And in the frozen moment before she began, my waiting mind filled with an echo of numbers, a combination . . . I saw that it unlocked the secret of the invisible walls and would let me pass through. (Why? Why?) But she didn't answer, and I couldn't let myself wonder too much. There weren't any answers now, only the soft whispering of her soul reaching out to me, the knowledge that in another hour someone might be using it for a private playground. The seconds crawled past me, space-time warped out of shape in this strange dreamland; her performance went on forever—and was over before I had time to realize it. The guests were on their feet, shuffling out, the room was darkening behind them.

I got up, stood trying not to look like I was waiting, until most of them were gone. The invisible wall was moving up on me, pressuring me to leave. . . . I said the numbers, and the wall of darkness swallowed me up.

Beyond it there was nothing but a corridor—blank, gray, empty. I blinked, shaking off the feeling that I'd walked through a wet, open mouth. At the far end of the hall was a door. I walked toward it, still not quite believing that I'd come this far. I put my hands into my pockets, feeling the stungun cool and smooth in my palm. The door at the end of the hall didn't have a knob or a plate. I pushed it, and it swung open. Beyond it was more darkness—an alley.

I turned, looking back over my shoulder. Behind me, the entrance I'd come through had become a solid wall. I had the feeling it wouldn't let me back again. And there were no other doors; at least none that I could see. (Ineh!) I shouted her name with my mind, but there was no answer. This time I wasn't expecting one. I'd been shown the door, and Ineh—Ineh. . . . The door was still open. I went through it.

A heavy fist came down across my shoulders, clubbing me to my knees. Grease and grit skidded under my hands, scraping my palms, and then it was somebody's foot in my side throwing me back against the wall. The hands on my jacket dragged me up, knocking me against the cold peeling surface until my brains rattled, pulling away and coming back to hit me again, everywhere, and I couldn't seem to make any part of me work well enough to stop them. . . . Until the hands let go again at last and I slid down into the trash.

"Keep away from her, freak—" His foot in my ribs, underlining the word. "Or the next time they won't find your body." The foot came after me one last time.

Somehow I brought up my hands and caught his leg, twisted under him with his own motion and jerked him off his feet. He fell past me onto the pavement, coming down like a

condemned building. I thanked God he hadn't landed on top
of me. I hauled myself up, the stungun in my hands; revers-
ing our positions and a lot of other things. "Hold it."

He was trying to get his feet under him. He stopped when
he saw the gun.

"Where is she?"

"Who?"

"You know who." I tried to stand straighter and not listen
to my body. "I ain't got much time. Are you gonna make this
easy or hard?"

He laughed, giving me the answer.

I could see the features of his face clearly now. It looked
like he'd landed on it. I wondered how much he could see of
mine. I grinned and spat blood. He knew what I was. If he
was like most psi-haters—"Did they tell you what kind of
'freak' I am—did they tell you I'm a 'path, like she is? I can
turn your brains inside out, read everything you ever thought
of, back to the day you were born. It hurts like hell . . . I'll
make sure it does." I grinned wider, hurting like hell. "You
gonna give me what I want, deadhead, or do I rip it out of
your skull?" I frowned like I was concentrating hard; watched
his face turn to jelly.

"All right, all right!" His head dropped, but he was still
staring up at me with white eyes from under his brows.
"They took her to Kinba's."

"Where's that?" I knew the name; I tried to keep my voice
steady.

"Outside the city."

"What's the co-ords?"

He told me.

"Access codes?"

He told me that too; his own voice wasn't too steady.

I spat again. "You sure about that? Maybe I should take a
look."

"It's true!" He threw his hands up again, shielding his
face, as if he thought that could stop me. "Jeezu."

I nodded. "Okay. I think I believe you." I hugged my
aching stomach with my arm. "Thanks, sucker."

His own arms came down, and already his face was hard-ening again. "You ain't a 'path! You didn't even sense me waiting. You can't—"

"I know." I pressed the button on the stungun with my thumb, and he went to sleep.

I went out to the street to find a cab. No one looked twice as I pushed my way through the crowds; a stumbling punk who drooled blood was business as usual in Oldcity. And the cab didn't ask questions when I shoved the woman aside and got in, just, "Destination?" I let myself collapse as it took me up over the crowds, heading for the world upside; heading for trouble.

The cab carried me out a long way beyond the southward limit of Quarro, on along the thin peninsula between pincers of sea gleaming like gunmetal under the light of the two moons. I tried to keep count of the wealthy estates winking like stars, hiding in the darkness down below. I remembered seeing mansions on the threedy somewhere a long time ago. I ached all over and felt lonelier than I'd thought I knew how to.

After a while the cab dropped down again, and the world came back at me in a rush. An estate opened out below, like a holo-still blown up out of all proportion: I couldn't quite make myself believe what I saw tumbling down the steep hill slope, layer on layer of broken crystal pulsing with light. The cab didn't veer off as it came down; the codes worked.

And then I was standing on the landing flat, staring at my own reflection haloed by the cab lights—tiny and shattered, repeating over and over in the crescent of facing walls. A lens opened in the smooth surface, and someone came through. It was the hologram host from the Haven. There was no cloak this time, and I decided finally that it was a woman. "Are you real this time?"

She half-smiled. "You've seen my show. You didn't like it?" She hesitated, as if she was listening to something I couldn't hear. "That stungun you carry is useless here. This house is weapon-sealed, of course. So why don't you toss it away." She flicked a hand. The words were all hard surfaces and sharp edges, like the house behind her.

I shrugged, and took the gun out of my pocket. I threw it away into the dark, bloodstain-colored grass. I wondered how many other eyes were looking me over, all up and down the spectrum.

"This is a private estate, boy. Why are you trespassing here?" Her voice swatted me like a bug: not even worth a threat. I had to admire her ice.

I had to match it: "Ineh wants to see me."

The flat line of one brow quirked. "Ineh? You've come to see Ineh? Then you're that one . . .?" Her fingers darted out at me like a snake's head. "All right. Come in and see her, then." Her smile ripped me to shreds.

I smiled back, tasting a little more of my own blood. "Thanks." I followed her in through the opening iris, jaws full of glass teeth; heard it ring shut behind me. I took a deep breath. She led me through room after room that probably made the Five Worlds Museum look sleazy. "You know, I used to be a thief myself. What did I do wrong?"

She looked at me; she didn't smile.

There didn't seem to be anyone else in any room we passed. This was the private estate of Farheen Kinba, one of the dark gods who ruled Oldcity's underworld. I thought about what it would be like to live in a place like this all alone . . . knowing all the time that alone was the last thing we were right now.

We took a lift down and down into a part of the house sunk deep into the hillside. And there were all the rest of the bodies, the rest of the eyes that weren't already watching me; there was even Kinba himself. They were watching someone else, through a wall of mirror-backed glass: Ineh.

The room she sat in was almost empty of anything else; the walls were a silent gray-green, and so was the carpet. She sat in a hard, straight-backed chair, its arms and legs carved with eye-twisting tangles of vine until it almost seemed to be growing up and over her, holding her prisoner.

And across from her in a cushioned recliner, not touching her in any way, lay a man. They both wore long white robes, like shrouds; but from what I could see of his heavy face and his soft, thick hands, he was somebody who was used to having too much of everything. His eyes were shut, but he wasn't asleep. He was dreaming. . . . I watched his face, the expressions that stretched it, warping rubber; his body tight-

ening, jerking once, shifting. Ineh's face moved with her own
shaping and sharing of his dream, but the emotions that
moved it weren't the same. Her body was as rigid as the chair
that held it, trembling with strain. Her eyes were shut, and I
saw the wetsilver tracks of tears lying on her cheeks.

I closed my own eyes, shut off all the outside senses I
could—trying to reach what was happening out there with the
one left inside. I felt whispers and mutterings, muffled cries,
pressing my mind against the wall of glass that lay inside my
own head. I held my breath, forgot my body and where it
was. . . . Ghost images began to form, began to pull at me.
Cold raw hands began to dig into my brain: This was a man
with hungers that had never been satisfied, never could be.
Hungers that had driven him to a position of power only a
few others ever reached, given him all the pleasures that still
weren't enough. And now he had the powers of the Dreamweaver to play with. She wasn't leading his dreams, she was
following them, letting him fix the rules and being forced to
play by them. The power he'd always wanted, to domin: te
and humiliate and use—the freedom that the laws of society
kept him from ever really getting his fill of—all that was his
now, his to dream about, with Ineh as his tool and his victim.

(Ineh! Ineh!) I screamed her name silently, trying to break
through. But she was caught up in his nightmare; her mouth
opened in her own silent scream. I pushed through the knot of
watchers to the transport wall, beat my fists against it. "Ineh!"
but the surface was solid, the sound recoiled. Ineh didn't
move.

Hands caught my arms, dragging me back into the real
world. The group of watchers around me were suddenly all
watching me, their faces half slack, half ugly. I realized
they'd all been listening to what I'd just heard; a bunch of
goddamn voyeurs peeping through the keyhole into somebody
else's mind. Two or three of the faces I recognized from the
past, Kinba himself and a couple of Oldcity's other first
citizens, all looking businesslike and respectable in drapes of
watercolor silk. There was a stranger dressed the same way,
but looking uneasy. The rest I didn't recognize; but I recognized the type.

And there was someone else in the room, sitting to one side

while the others stood, with a remote on his knees. Right now
he was leaning forward, muttering some kind of message into
it. He stopped, looking up, not at me but at Ineh again, and
his eyes got glassy. He didn't seem to fit in with the rest, and
I knew the look on his face too well. He was a telepath—a
corporate telepath. Some combines used them for security,
though most were too paranoid to use a 'path who was good
enough to really pick brains, including their own.

And this one was communicating with Ineh, getting mes-
sages that no one else here was getting. . . . I looked back at
the stranger who was dressed for business, and suddenly it all
fit. The Corpses were right: Somebody was using psionics to
pick brains. It was happening right here in front of me, and
the victim never even knew it. Ineh must have screened every
crowd at the Haven, picked out the customers whose minds
were crammed full of secrets to be sold to the highest bidder.
And this was how she pulled them out.

Kinba turned to the woman. "Hedo, what is this?" He
waved a hand at my face. He was wearing a sapphire as big
as a cockroach on his middle finger. "Why did you bring him
here?"

"It's Ineh's freak; he got past Spoode. I thought such
determination ought to be rewarded. And I thought you might
like to ask him how many others know he's here."

I saw Ineh slump over the far arm of her chair. I tried to
pull free, but Kinba's bodyguards held me with no trouble. I
felt something slip over my wrists behind my back and
tighten, pinning them together. Kinba smiled at me, a tiny
twitch pulling his mouth against his perfect teeth.

"You son-of-a-bitch," I said.

The hand with the sapphire ring slapped me. I shook my
head, feeling fresh blood in a warm trickle down my cheek.
"Mind your tongue or I'll have it cut out." His voice was
white and cold like his face. "If you prefer to keep it, you
half-breed abomination, perhaps you'll consider telling us
who else knows you're here?" The rest of them had stopped
watching Ineh, and their faces were grim.

I kept my own eyes on her, felt my body trembling. "The
Corpses know. They know about the Haven and what you're
doing with it—"

He held up his hand. I stopped. "We'll see." Some of the faces began to look worried; but not his. The combine man kneaded his hands together. A door was opening in the next room. Two men were shaking the slug awake, hauling him off his couch. The woman called Hedo went to Ineh, helped her to stand, leading her out after the others were gone. The corporate telepath stared at me as if he'd just noticed I was there; glanced at his boss, who frowned. He looked back at me, confused, and I tried to make him react somehow. He looked down again at the remote in his lap, his shoulders hunching. Kinba's bodyguards led me out of the room.

We went back up in the lift, back into the main part of the house; into a room looking out on the night and the long ruddy slope of the hill. Ineh was already there. She sat gulping something from a cup, her robe soaked and stained, her movements jerky. And yet she was more beautiful, almost shining; not because of what had happened, but somehow in spite of it. I shook my head again, not understanding what I was seeing. She looked up then and saw me, froze as she saw what I looked like.

"Ineh," the woman said, "see who came for your performance."

Ineh still sat frozen. She didn't answer. Her mouth quivered.

"I'm okay," I said. "I've come to take you back with me. The Corpses know everything. If anything happens to me or you, they know who to blame."

"Ineh, is he telling the truth?" Kinba strolled past me to where she sat, ran his maggot fingers through her hair, massaged her neck.

I felt her touch me with her mind: a hard clumsy blow that tore the tight-woven defenses I couldn't control apart. I tried not to resist, holding out trust, hope, reassurance, not even bothering to hide my lie. Trusting her—

"He told no one." Her voice was flat. "He is here alone, no one knows what he's done."

Kinba's hands dropped to her shoulders, patted her lightly; all the hidden tension had gone out of them. His laughter was loose and easy. I was just exactly as stupid as he'd figured I was. "You see, good people, there was nothing to worry about," heavy on the *nothing*.

I looked down at the floor, twisting my hands against the hard edges of the binder.

"Ineh, I'm disappointed." His hands squeezed her shoulders. "Is this quixotic idiot really your idea of someone who's going to change your life?" She grimaced, but didn't answer. "Well, here he is. You did well enough for us just now. But you seem to detest it, you resist it so. That impairs your usefulness. I always said our relationship was one of mutual need, not slavery. You could leave any time you chose. Would you like to go away with him?" She looked up, her face caught in the middle of half a dozen different emotions. "You've given us years of loyal service. Shall I repay you now . . . let you go away with him? Of course if you do, you'll be losing the—privileges of our partnership. Are you ready to lose all that? Or do you want to stay on, safe and protected, and . . . let us get rid of him?"

I couldn't believe that she was really listening to what he said, any more than I believed for a second that he was offering her a real choice. But she stared up at him like she was seeing God. Then she looked at me for a long minute, without letting me through into her mind. She looked out the window at the empty night, and the minute stretched into two, into eternity. My mind ached, waiting for her to choose, even while I knew it was no choice and at least one of us was going to die.

I looked after her out the windowed wall at the sky . . . just in time to see the windows dissolve like a film of ice in the sun, the sun bursting in on me, my sight going redgoldwhiteblack before I could shut my eyes. Then all hell broke loose—shouting and curses and noises I didn't recognize, bodies slamming into me, knocking me down. By the time I blinked my eyes clear, there was a Corporate Security cruiser hanging beyond the slagged windows and the room was filling up with Corpses.

And Ineh was on her knees beside me, pulling at my arm. Her voice was high and broken, I could barely make out what she said. "Cat, Cat . . . they come to arrest us, to take us away!"

I sat back, trying to get my feet under me. "Get out of

here, Ineh! Now, while you can—'' A Corpse had spotted us, was starting toward us through the forest of shifting bodies.

"Where, where can I go? I'm afraid—"

"Somewhere they won't be looking! Anywhere. Go on!"

"You—?"

"I'll be all right. Go on!"

She disappeared; I felt the soft inrush of air that followed. Neat gray legs stopped short beside me. I heard the Corpse swear, and looking up I saw Polhemas. I started to get up. He reached down and caught the front of my jacket, hauling me onto my feet.

"Where did she go?"

"Who?"

"Don't play brain-damaged with me." The polite official front was gone. "You're in enough trouble as it is."

"Me?" I jerked at my cuffed hands. "Come on, Polhemas, you think I did this to myself? You know I didn't have anything to do with them—" I bent my head at the rest of the room.

His hand was still clenched on my jacket front. "I knew you were lying when you told me you didn't know anything, back at the Center. That's why I had a tracer put on you. And it led us right to the answer."

"You think I didn't know you were following me? It would've been damn stupid to walk into this all by myself if I wasn't involved; that's what you figure, isn't it?" I tried to stare him down. I hoped he couldn't see my ears burning. "I'm not stupid," *just crazy,* "and I wasn't lying to you. But I was smart enough to see a few things you overlooked, while you were spending all your time trying to blame this on the Center. Face it, Polhemas, I'm the hero here. You can't turn it inside out."

His face turned redder than my ears, and his hand on my jacket jerked me forward. But then he grunted and let me go. He was going to be hero enough himself to keep him from making a case of proving I was wrong. I let my own breath out in a sigh. He looked me over again, looking hard at my bruised face. Then he turned me around and released the binder on my wrists. "Why didn't you just tell us what you learned? If you wanted to be a hero that would've been enough. Why risk being a dead one?''

I pulled my hands forward and rubbed them. ''Why should I do you any favors? What have you done for the Center for Psionic Research lately?''

He ignored that. ''It was the Dreamweaver, wasn't it? Where did you send her—where is she?''

''I don't know. Somewhere you won't find her. You can drug me all you want but I can't tell you more than that.''

''We'll find her.'' It was a threat.

I caught his arm. ''Why don't you leave her alone? They made her do it, she didn't want to. That's why she came to me, for help. She's suffered more than that mindfucker ever did—'' pointing at her ''guest'' standing sullen and confused while two Corpses questioned him. ''He's the one you ought to send up. If you'd seen the inside of his head you'd kill him on the spot.''

Polhemas looked at the slug and back at me without saying anything. His eyes were still cold and empty.

''Look, you've got what you want. Leave us alone. . . . Maybe it never occurred to you, but we're just trying to live like everybody else. Give us a goddamn break! We gave you what you want; we've earned it.''

He didn't answer.

I let go of his arm and turned away. The corporate telepath was looking at me from across the room, where his boss's voice was getting louder and louder. His face was full of fear and despair; I could see it, but I couldn't feel it. I started to walk away.

''Nobody said you could go anywhere,'' Polhemas said.

''Try and stop me.''

He did.

It was hours later before I was free again, walking back through the streets to the Center, feeling the steel and stone of all Oldcity weighing down my heart. Polhemas had asked me a thousand questions about everything I'd seen, heard, overheard, thought or guessed. I'd told him everything I could, because it didn't matter any more and I only wanted to get out of there. It was only after I'd left the detention center that I let myself realize he hadn't tried to force anything more out of me about where Ineh had gone. It surprised me, because it meant that he must have listened to something I'd said before. But either way it didn't really matter; because Ineh was gone, and I didn't know where. How the hell would I find her; what would she do—what would I do?

The Center had long since closed for the night when I reached it. But there was still a light on somewhere inside, so I went in the front entrance instead of taking the back way up to my room. Jule and Siebeling stood waiting for me in the empty hall; I almost walked past them without seeing them.

"Cat?"

I stopped, shaking my head. They came toward me when I didn't move. Siebeling lifted his hand, and across the room the lights brightened. Their faces showed pools and lines of shadow, their tired eyes looked me up and down. Siebeling caught my jaw with his hand, gently, turning my face right and left.

"Did Corporate Security do that to you?"

"No."

"What happened?" Jule asked. The question didn't stop with my face.

"I fell down." I tried to pull away, but Jule held my arm.

"Wait, Cat." She stood in front of me. "You've been trying to pretend that you're the only one who's involved with the Dreamweaver's problems; but you're not. You're not alone in this. You're not alone in the world—for better or worse."

"You weren't exactly killing yourself to help me out."

"That's hardly fair," Siebeling said. "You didn't give us any information. You didn't tell us the kind of problems that were really involved, the kind of people, the danger. You went off on a suicidal crusade against Evil, and you damn near got just what you were asking for! Didn't it ever occur to you that—that—" he broke off, "that we can't read your mind, Cat."

"I never thought about anything else. That's the trouble." I looked down, my arms hanging heavy at my sides. "I'm sorry. Maybe I'll start appreciating what I've got left, now."

Now that it doesn't matter any more, now that it's too late.
"How'd you know what happened? Were the Corpses here?"

"No." Siebeling leaned against a seat-back. "They haven't been here."

"They haven't? Not at all?"

He shook his head.

I laughed, a choked sort of sound. It meant there might be something decent in Polhemas after all, and I wasn't ready to believe it. "Then how did you know?"

"Ineh told us," Jule said.

Ineh? The word wouldn't form in my mouth. "Where—where is she?"

"Up in your room. I had to give her a sedative to help her keep control; she's sleeping now." He touched his head. "You know she's an addict, Cat—?"

I flinched. "I know. What's she on, Doc?"

"Trihannobin."

"Nightmare." I felt the blood drain out of my face. "They call it nightmare."

He nodded. "And it takes you for a hard ride. It's a kind of nerve poison. Most people don't use it for long; they generally stop when it kills them." His face was as empty as my own.

"I went for a ride once." The memories came without my wanting them to. "I thought I was in heaven. I didn't eat or sleep for three days. And then it wore off." I kept my eyes open, kept looking at their faces: proving that I was here in the present, that I'd really come through it. *Nightmare . . . that's why they call it nightmare.* I could still see the hospital ward through their faces, the nutrient bath shining on my skin like sweat, the straps. . . . They hadn't cared enough to make it easier. "Give her something to make it easier—"

He shook his head, looking down.

"Why not?"

"She's Hydran, Cat . . . I can't predict how it would affect her. She doesn't react to the drug the way a human does, or she'd be dead by now. If I tried to counteract it without doing an analysis, I could make it worse for her. . . ." He sounded helpless; I wasn't used to hearing him sound that way.

"I guess I want to see her now."

He nodded, and the three of us went upstairs.

I was the first one into the room. Ineh sat waiting, watching, from my bed platform. Her arms were locked around her knees, her fists were clenched tight. Her face was clenched too; I couldn't tell what she was thinking.

"We may need restraints," Siebeling murmured to Jule.

"No." I looked back. "If she needs it I'll do it; I'll hold her." I realized as I said it that I was going to do more—that I was going to do everything. Not because I wouldn't share it with them, this time, but because I couldn't. Ineh would lose control again, and when she lost it completely I'd be the only one left who could stand to be near her. "You'd better get out of range while you can."

They looked at each other, and at me. This time they didn't argue. They left the room.

"Hello, Ineh," I said softly. She didn't answer. I moved across to the bed platform, climbed up and sat beside her, trying to keep my face calm and easy. "Thank God you came here," thinking that she had more sense than I did, to trust Jule and Doc when I hadn't. "I just about went crazy wondering how I'd find you." I reached out to touch her arm. Her body jerked away; I didn't know whether she'd meant it to or not. "Sorry." I looked down at my hands, up again. A hard knot was forming in my throat. "I know, it's already starting. Don't be afraid."

Her eyes fixed on me, wild and glassy, as though she was listening to a lunatic. She licked her lips. "I need my dream tonic. Help me."

I shook my head. "Not that way. I've been through this, Ineh, and I came out the other side. I'll help you. Trust me. Let me in, let me share the—"

Something blinding hit me behind the eyes, fed back along the nerve-paths to the ends of my senses—all her power, focused on me and driven home by fear. I cried out, holding my head. And I saw her clearly, at last: not the Ineh I thought I knew, but the Ineh I'd seen in ghost glimpses when her concentration slipped, when she couldn't make me see her the way she wanted the world to see her, and I'd fallen through it into the way she was. The nightmare Ineh, brittle bones, sunken eyes, wasted flesh. *The nightmare.* The nightmare already beginning— Disgust and hatred filled me up like the urge to vomit: Ineh's loathing for the thing she'd become in her mind, was becoming with her body; a filthy, crawling, drug-infected ruin, born to pain, deserving pain, terrified of pain but trapped inside it with no escape, trapped—

Trapped. I'd be trapped with her in this nightmare journey of pain and more pain, pain until you wailed, howled, beat yourself senseless against walls to get away from it. Your hands ripped your own flesh, your legs wouldn't hold you up, your body betrayed and humiliated you in ways you never dreamed of and you didn't even care. . . . When I could sit up again in the hospital there was a corpse in the mirror, I saw a corpse and I screamed and I can't go through it all over again I can't—!

I threw myself down from the platform, away from the sight of her. I almost shouted for the others, almost started for the door; almost ran—out of the room, away from her and the power of her pain and myself.

But instead I turned back, and looked at her. She hunched forward, burying her face in the stained whiteness of her robe, dragging isolation over herself like a shroud. There was no reaching from mind to mind now; I'd shut her out of myself, and she wasn't trying to get back in.

And I was going to leave her that way. I was going to leave her alone and prove to her that there was nobody on this world who wouldn't betray her; that there was no one she could count on; that no matter what she tried to do, because of what she was it would turn against her. . . . That if she reached the other end of this road through hell she'd only find that it hadn't been worth the trip. I was the only one who could share the journey, who knew the roadmarks, who could make her believe there was a reason to survive it. But I was going to leave her here alone and run from her problems; just like I'd done to myself. . . .

I climbed back onto the platform. I kneeled beside Ineh, put my arms around her huddled body, feeling her muscles knot and quiver. "I'm here, I won't leave you. You can count on me—" My voice broke.

A wall of blind hatred slammed into me, locking me out. Hopeless pain was all that was left, all that was real to her

now, eating her alive from the inside. She wanted to die; and
she would. I had to break through to her again, somehow,
before everything imploded.

And there was only one thing still working her mind. If I
could turn the rage that was holding me out into a tool to let
me in. . . . "All right!" I shouted it into her face. "You hate
me, you want to blame it all on me. But you dragged me into
this, you set me up to do what you didn't have the guts to do
yourself. Then you lost your nerve, and I got the shit beat out
of me. If I was going to stop believing in you, that should've
done it. But I didn't; I didn't give up on you. I kept on until
you were free. You're *free*.

"If you have to hate, remember where you were before
you came here tonight! Remember who did it to you, who
turned your gift into something sick and dirty. If you want to
shut somebody out of your life, shut them out. If you want
something enough to die for it, make it your freedom. If you
want to hate somebody let it be Kinba!" I shook her. "Don't
let them win. We don't have to let the goddamn scum of this
universe destroy us. Let it out, the hate . . . the pain will go
with it. Let me in—" *(Let me share your pain,)* pushing
myself aside, trying to loosen my mind, to forget any other
thought, and just once let the emptiness go unguarded.

Ineh jerked upright, tears streaming down her face. She
opened her mouth. And screamed. The scream went on and
on, pouring out of her like blood.

My mind burst open as the images smashed into me, losing
all control as she lost all control. Not even my own mind any
more, but a stage in darkness for the Dreamweaver's nightmares: Agony from a million neurons like live wires snapping
. . . the taste of gall, the stench of putrefying flesh, my ears
screaming, knives of light slashing my eyes, agony that filled
all time and went on and on and on. . . . Cancer flowers
spreading, the face of the torturer with a thousand faces,
petals opening endlessly changing out of control controlling
body, soul . . . Kinba, white yielding *inevitable* cajoling
soothing *strangling striking tearing destroying/*flash shatter*
hot blades broken glass*/Hedo, oblivion's water food of gods
of dreams *hands of ice edge of knives/*screaming blackness*
eyes torn from sockets*/ Body of a slug mind full of worms

bursting like a boil, endless floods of diseased image that went on and on, no escape from filthy minds, stupid, greedy, blind, empty empty minds—mutilating *her* gift denying her self, suffocating her soul in their soul-darkness until she was only a thing used by things. . . .

(*I know, I know.* . . . Struggling up out of her nightmares, dazed, torn, falling back, into my own: In the mines, breathing poisoned air, beaten starved buried alive in the freezing guts of an alien world. No rest, no hope, no night or day . . . no escape, no end except a dead end. Warm bodies, cheaper than cold machines. No one caring if you lived or died, until finally even you didn't care, betrayed, abandoned, a thing used by things. . . .)

Hate them I hate them!!!/*Stars*/ Kinba, Hedo, an endless wheel flickering changing *offering betraying humiliating tormenting* . . . no one in all the space of the living who was not there to torture/*ripping forcing* violation death*/ Let me go oh let me die! die! die! Ruined, infected, weak degraded coward!! No reason to live no reason no no

(*Her hands* from another world, the real world, flailing, clawing, reaching for my throat; *my body* sprawled against her own, holding it down, holding the hands away from her face, from finding a weapon. The false light of a new day breaking, showing me the truth—life was the nightmare, and there was no waking out of it. This was real, and reality was no one's dream. They sang it in the streets . . . the streets of Oldcity, the faces of a lifetime glaring down like floodlights, smothering me in spit and blows and ugly laughter: City-boy, halfbreed, bondie, scum. All *shouting* whispering thinking it . . . their hands fists, their feet on my neck; taking what they wanted, over and over, and never giving a word, a touch, no friendship, no kindness, no reason—

("Let me help you." *Jule* . . . Jule, saying four words that I'd never heard from anyone before, touching my mind with gentleness, making me see the world in the mirror and not hate it any more. There was a reason, there *was*. . . . *Ineh! Listen, listen to me*, fighting upstream against the flood of two rivers. *It doesn't matter what happened, none of it, none of them. What they did to you, or me, it isn't us, it hasn't changed the truth*— Repeating it over and over and over and getting nowhere; losing strength, losing— *You have a gift, reaching out to the world, reaching out to me, so many that need it, really need it. Not sick, only like you are or I am, sick of hatred and pain—)*

Hatred pain/*nails thorns iron*/ nothing else real, no one not evil ugly empty *human!* . . . herself, evil ugly human corrupted . . . I want to die! let me let me go—

(Not human! No, you aren't, you never will be—they'll never let you be; be glad of it. Remember who you were, remember your real people, everything you shared with them—)

Nooo! wild anguish, denial, terror— *(Yes! You belong to your people, you can help them, share with them—)*

No no *gone* lost abandoned betrayed— Herself, themselves, betrayed, lost. . . . Faces, loved faces torn away; torn apart by parting, minds torn apart families torn apart, lost in the endless darkness of space lost forever, forever, pain going on forever lost in pain. . . .

(Lost in my own pain, my people lost to me, lost in the endless darkness, lost forever . . . No! stop . . . terror, pain, memories, screams echoing in an alley-end—in a child's ears, in a child's mind. . . . Stop, stop it!)

New world harsh ugly gray prison walls gray minds hunger hatred fear . . . minds sharing *shriveling breaking sealing shut, closing out hunger hatred loss each other* giving *giving less, giving nothing, giving out giving in* . . . *betraying, abandoning, surrendering*—

(It doesn't matter. It doesn't matter. Find your way back, they'll take you back; they have to. Only one thing, one thing could never be forgiven.)

Too far! Too long, too much shame filth ugliness! Never return, never forgiveness enough for so much shame. Only death only death forgives!

(No. Not death—only death never forgives. Only death is never forgiven. . . . Choking, suffocating, fluid: my mind filling up with blood—no no— No forgiveness. No death for a killer no help for a cripple—*me, not you! My punishment, my guilt, my shame!* The weapon lying in my hands and the hatred in my soul and an enemy inside my mind showing me that I had no right to pride or love or loyalty, halfbreed scum I ought to be dead! Like my dreams my memories *my mother*

in an Oldcity alley, screaming and screaming inside my head
until I can't hear anything at all. . . . She died, and I couldn't
save her. She died inside my head and I didn't, and that made
me human enough to hate and kill. No matter that it saved a
life, two lives, three—my own. . . . I could, I had to, I
wanted to—*I did*.

(Mind inside mind exploding like a star, burning out cir-
cuits senses soul . . . lost in a rain of black ashes falling
through silence. Silence and blackness—no light no sound no
way back to the land of life . . . dead inside my own body.
Lie down and die, murderer, betrayer, failure! black ashes to
drown in, ashes blood death only death forgives, darkness,
darkness soft and deep, drowning. . . .)

Light breaking like sunrise, streaming through the choking
fall of death. *See death,* see it for Nothing, absence denial
loss fear escape—lifeless beautyless emptiness . . . *Light*
growing stronger, surrounds crystalizes dissolves darkness—(*I
remember, I remember* being wrapped in light, Jule, Siebeling,
mind joining mind strong enough to drive out any pain) . . .
Light rising suffusing, golden, opening onto sky, endless
rumpled fields of whiteness, clouds (*snow* the snowfields of
another world, remembered world, spring green mountains
rising impossibly from snow against a sapphire rain-washed
sky: proving beauty still existed, trust, friendship, love). . . .
Death destroys us, hate/pain makes us blind; but those things
still exist, still live and are true within us without us. True
beyond us—true because of us, true between us, nothing hidden
now, my name written on my heart, read it, read it and show
me your own, let me in. . . . *Light* growing stronger brighter
incandescent, dissolving pain, hatred grief, loosening bonds
setting free, dissolving into the universal heartbeat promise
refuge peace, peace, peace. . . .

I woke, and waking was like a dream. I moved through
slowtime, the room flowed around me like honey as I lifted
my head. Ineh was beside me, eyes shut, barely breathing.
Nothing reached me now from her mind, but one of her hands
was locked inside my own like a double vise; my arm was
raw with scratches. Slowly I knew that my hand was aching
with cramp, my whole body was locked in a cramp, my skin

burned and the room stank of sweat and sickness. Ineh's face was bruised and hollow, her hair snarled like weeds; her own genuine body lay beside me, wasted by drugs. There was nothing hidden now; but I couldn't be sorry, only glad. Nothing was hidden between us; nothing hidden from ourselves. She had shown me the name hidden in her soul, and shown me my own; we had shared the understanding that surpassed all truth. I could see again—and everything I saw was beautiful. I let my head fall back, my empty mind was full of peace, and I slept.

When I came to again there was no one beside me. I reached out with my mind, groping, and found nothing. Then I believed it. I dragged myself to the edge of the platform and looked down—had to shut my eyes. There was a sound like a sigh, and when I opened them again Jule was standing there. *Jule* . . . I kept trying to see Ineh.

"She's safe," Jule said, and smiled. "She's all right."

I grunted, and let an arm drop down.

She squeezed my hand, helped me down from the platform and into the bathroom. I drank six cups of water while she peeled off my stinking clothes. Then she pushed me into the fresher and disappeared again. I stood inside until it turned my raw skin numb and tingling, until I could tell that I had legs to stand on. It felt like a long time since I'd used them.

It was a long time. The readout on the clock said three days. I pulled on a tunic and drank some more water, trying to sort out my mind.

Then Jule was back again, with food. Eating it gave me a little extra time. Finally I said, "Is she with you?"

She nodded. "With us, yes. Ardan's treating her; she's in bad shape physically."

"I know. It's all right? She doesn't—?" I touched my head, looking at her.

Jule shook her own head. "It was her suffering that I couldn't bear. The worst of that is past; I can protect myself from what's left. But it will be a long time before she believes she has any control—over herself or her life. She's going to need all the help we can give her; all the shared strength."

Do any of us really control anything? But I only said, "Half a lifetime doesn't heal in a night. Nothing's that easy. But the worst is over, like you said. And I'll—we'll be here, to show her how much good she can find in . . ." Something in Jule's face made me stop. But I didn't ask. With my heart beating too quickly, I let my mind go loose, trying to feel what was wrong. And got nothing. Nothing.

"Cat? What's the matter?"

"Nothing. I mean—*nothing*," feeling my face collapse; feeling my mind as tight and hard as a fist. "Did you—was there anything?"

She looked at me, confused. Then, "Oh." No.

"It didn't last." *Didn't last, didn't last, didn't.* . . . Echoes, was that all she'd left me? (Jule, feel it, for God's sake, *feel* it!)

She blinked, twitched.

I leaned forward, tilting my stool. "Did you . . . ?"

She nodded slowly, starting to smile. "I felt something. I felt something."

"Yeah?" I settled back; knowing I should have realized that Ineh wasn't the only one whose healing wouldn't finish in a night. . . . "At least there's something. Hope." *A crack in the wall.* A beginning, now that I'd finally accepted that guilt would only die when I did. I sighed, looking back at Jule. "What did I say wrong about helping Ineh?" Asking; just asking.

Jule stood up, turning away from me. "She doesn't want to see you again."

"What?"

"She doesn't want to see you." Her voice got weaker instead of stronger.

"Why? Why not?" I stood up, following her. "We shared—everything."

"That's why." She turned to face me, finally. "She isn't ready, she isn't strong enough to deal with what that meant to both of you. You saw things about her that made her wish she was dead, Cat. Things she'll be working to forget for the rest of her life."

"But she knows things about me—" *things that made me wish I was dead,* "things even you don't know. She doesn't need to feel any shame with me. What she knows about me—''

"Is more than she can bear. Not added to her own problems. Not right now." She frowned, not with anger, not at me.

"So she needs time, you mean. In time she'll want to see me again. . . . A long time?"

She nodded.

"I see." A long time before a Hydran could face a halfbreed who couldn't face himself. A long time before he'd ever be able to do even that. A long time, a long cure, a lot of memories like bandages . . . a lot of proving I had a right to be alive. "I can't stay here anymore." Jule didn't say anything. I went to the window, stared through the dark ghost trapped there in the dirty pane. "At least I'll know she's got you—at least she'll have the best friends anybody could ask for, to help her through if I can't." I traced lines in the dust on the deep sill. Glancing down, I saw that I'd written C-A-T.

"You've already done the most important part, alone. You saved her sanity, Cat."

I shook my head, wiped my name out in the dust. "You've got it backwards. She saved mine. I thought I could handle it, I thought I could make her believe in herself. But I couldn't. I was the one who broke. And she had to come after me and drag me out of my own death wish."

"But you showed her she could use her talent in ways that were healing, not degrading. And then you gave her a chance to prove it. You showed her that she isn't the only one who's suffered . . . and survived." Her voice touched me softly.

I glanced over my shoulder. "How much did you—did you—?"

She shook her head. "None of it. I couldn't. We're all afraid of something in our lives . . . of meeting the past head-on. But Ineh knows that, and I understand it, now. We've begun to find common ground. She showed me enough . . . she showed me how much you gave back to her."

I took a long breath, leaning against the casement. I could hear Oldcity's voice through the window: feel its reality gritty under my hands. I looked out and up, seeing nothing but walls. Somewhere up there was a garden where the sweet breath of spring moved silver crescent leaves; farther above two moons, hanging in the sky like lanterns. . . . "She's got a gift, Jule. For healing, for reaching even somebody like me. She could help her people here, who've lost everything. Maybe she could give them back some of what they lost—not their life, but maybe their pride. Make her believe that, will you?"

"I'll try. And so will Ardan."

I remembered his first wife, his own common ground, and nodded. "Yeah. That's fine. She'll do fine. . . ." I turned around, to look back at the room Ineh and I had gone through hell in together: Cracked, cramped, peeling; with a couple of cheap holos of somewhere better on the walls to make it even more depressing. Only one thing in the room that was beautiful, besides Jule; one thing that was beautiful and mine—a small Hydran crystal globe sitting on the bookshelf table, that Siebeling had given to me. An image of a nightflower bush lay inside it, black petals striped with silver repeating like a starry night.

I went to it and covered it with my hand. It was warm, not cool; it always was. I closed my eyes and felt for it with all my mind, felt it tingle and stir with the psi-tuned energy I was calling. . . . But when I opened my eyes the nightflower was still there. Once I'd only needed to touch the warm surface and wish, to change the image inside. The nightflower had been there for most of a year, ever since Siebeling had given it to me. *A promise,* he'd called it. "Give this to Ineh for me. Say it's—a promise." I cupped the ball in my hands.

Jule came to my side, put her arm around my shoulders. Dimly I knew that she was trying to reach me. I held my mind as loose as I could . . . felt warmth belief hope sorrow trust love; a drop of nectar, a whisper of a poem where before there had only been the silence of the grave. Feeling what they had only been able to tell me: that they loved me, that they wanted to help me; that they were responsible for the way I was, and they would be responsible for making it right again.

"But it's not your responsibility." I moved away from her,

gently. "It was my choice; I killed a man. I have to pay for it, I have to make it right with myself."

"You can't give up now, Cat, just when you've—"

"Jule," I said; she stopped. "You don't understand. You want to help me; I know that. You tried—you did help. But now I know I'm the only one who can make the trip. You can't carry me; you don't need to: I'm not a cripple. I can walk." *Someday I'll run.* I looked down. "And I guess it's about time I got started."

"You're really going to leave here, then." Not a question; a dim barb of dismay caught in my mind.

I nodded, not really sure of the answer until I'd made it; realizing then that I'd been certain all along. "It's better if I do. Better for Ineh. Better for me. Better for everyone."

She shook her head, but she didn't deny it. I moved back to her and put my arms around her. We held each other for a while, not saying anything. Her body was warm against mine, made real by the touch of her mind. "I'm sorry. . . ." she said finally; but I wasn't sure why.

I let her go at last and moved back to the window; looking out again because I had to.

"Where will you go?" she asked.

"I don't know. I don't care. Maybe it doesn't even matter." I shrugged. "I mean, what have I got to lose?" Up there somewhere two moons were hanging like lanterns in the sky; and beyond them were the stars.

AFTERWORD—
PSIREN

"Psiren" is actually a sequel to a novel I wrote, Psion. Publishing schedules and story commitments being what they are, however, it got published before the novel did. I had promised George R. R. Martin that I would do a story for the fourth volume of his New Voices anthology, in which I was due to appear, having been nominated for the award in 1976. Committing yourself to writing stories to a deadline is a lot like making a deal with the devil (although the editor and the author probably disagree about which role they're in), especially if you happen to be a very slow writer, like I am. I had made the mistake of agreeing to do several stories for different editors around the time I was due to write this one, and I'd also committed myself to attending a number of science fiction conventions. My personal life was also in a lot of turmoil, not a little of which was due to planning a wedding (my own). I needed a story idea that I thought would flow easily.

At the time I was also preparing to start revising Psion, a classic "trunk novel"—something I'd written long ago, before I had any ambitions about becoming a published writer. (I'd had the "restless urge to write" for years.) For some reason, I couldn't forget about the characters, and after nearly half a lifetime I still wanted the novel published—although not in the form it was in.

I'd sold Psion with the understanding that it would be extensively revised, but I hadn't realized how much revision I would really decide to do when I sat down and reread it. (It's gratifying to a writer to look back on old work and see exactly what's wrong with it—it's proof that you're improving.) I'd always felt that I'd like to write a series of stories about the protagonist of Psion, following him through his life; the idea for "Psiren" was to be the first of them. I thought that it would be simple to write "Psiren" because I had the background and the main character already.

But as I tried to write it, I realized that, if it was going to be consistent with the revised novel, I had to do all the background work for the novel before I could finish the novella. As a result, it took a lot longer to finish the story than I'd anticipated. (I wasn't alone in causing George to do a lot of groaning. I once got into a good-natured debate with one of the other writers from the anthology about whose story was really the one that held it up the longest. "Mine!" "No, mine—" Strangely enough, it was very comforting. But it has made me cautious about how quickly I agree to sell stories that I haven't written yet. It's a luxury to be able to finish something before you sell it, but sometimes it's also a necessity.)

And despite the amount of backgrounding I did before finishing "Psiren," there were still some discrepancies that occurred by the time I finished Psion. As a result, I've made some minor revisions in this version of the story to make it consistent with the novel and to make the background clearer for readers who haven't read the novel already. (I strongly believe that sequels should stand on their own as stories as well and not have to depend on anything else for the reader's comprehension and enjoyment.)

MOTHER AND CHILD

Part 1: The Smith

All day I have lain below the cliff. I can't move, except to turn my head or twitch two fingers; I think my back is broken. I feel as if my body is already dead, but my head aches, and grief and shame are all the pain I can bear. Remembering Etaa . . .

Perhaps the elders are almost right when they say death is the return to the Mother's womb, and in dying we go back along our lives to be reborn. Between wakings I dream, not of my whole life, but sweet dreams of the time when I had Etaa, my beloved. As though it still happened I see our first summer together herding shenn, warm days in fragrant upland meadows. We didn't love each other then; she was still a child, I was hardly more, and for our different reasons we kept ourselves separated from the world.

My reason was bitterness, for I was *neaa*, motherless. The winter before, I had lost my parents to a pack of kharks as they hunted. My mother's sister's family took me in, as was the custom, but I still ached with my own wounds of loss, and was always an outsider, as much from my own sullenness as from any fault of my kin. I questioned every belief, and could find no comfort. Sometimes, alone with just the grazing shenn, I sat and wept.

Until one day I looked up from my weeping to see a girl,

with eyes the color of new-turned earth and short curly hair as
dark as my own. She stood watching me somberly as I wiped
at my eyes, ashamed and angry.

—What do you want? I signed, looking fierce and hoping
she would run away.

—I felt you crying. Are you lonely?

—No. Go away. She didn't. I frowned. —Where did you
come from, anyway? Why are you spying on me?

—I wasn't spying. I was across the stream, with my shenn.
I am Etaa. She looked as if that explained everything.

And it did; I recognized her then. She belonged to another
clan, but everyone talked about her: Etaa, her name-sign,
meant "blessed by the Mother," and she had the keenest
eyesight in the village. She could see a bird on a branch
across a field, and thread the finest needle; but more than
that, she had been born with the second sight, she felt the
Mother's presence in all natural things. She could know the
feeling and touch the souls of every living creature, sometimes even predict when rain would fall. Others in the village
had the second sight, but not as clearly as she did, and most
people thought she would be the next priestess when she
came of age. But now she was still a child, minding the
flocks, and I wished she would leave me alone. —Your shenn
will stray, O blessed one.

Old hurt pinched her sun-browned face, and then she was
running back toward the stream.

—Wait! I stood up, startled, but she didn't see my sign. I
threw a stone; it skimmed past her through the grass. She
stopped and turned. I waved her back, guilty that my grief
had made me hurt somebody else.

She came back, her face too full of mixed feeling to read.

—I'm sorry. I didn't mean to make you unhappy too. I'm
Hywel. I sat down, gesturing.

Her smile was as sudden and bright as her disappointment,
and passed as quickly. She dropped down beside me like a
hound, smoothing her striped kilt. —I wasn't showing off . . .
I don't *mean* to. . . . Her shoulders drooped; I had never
thought before that blessedness could be a burden like anything else. —I just wanted to— Her fingers hesitated in mid-

sign. —To know if you were all right. She looked up at me through her long lashes, with a kind of yearning.

I glanced away uncomfortably across the pasture. —Can you watch your shenn from here? They were only a gray-white shifting blot to me, even when my eyes were clear, and now my eyes were blurred again.

She nodded.

—You have perfect vision, don't you? My hands jerked with pent-up frustration. —I wish I did!

She blinked. —Why? Do you want to be a warrior, like in the old tales? Some of our people want to take the heads of the Neaane beyond the hills for what they do to us. I think in the south some of them *have*. Her eyes widened.

The thought of the Neaane, the Motherless ones, made me flinch; we called them Neaane because they didn't believe in the Mother Earth as we did, but in gods they claimed had come down from the sky. We are the Kotaane, the Mother's children, and to be *neaa* was to be both pitiful and accursed, whether you were one boy or a whole people. —I don't want to kill people. I want to be farsighted so I can be a hunter and kill kharks, like they killed my parents!

—Oh. She brushed my cheek with her fingers, to show her sorrow. —When did it happen?

—At the end of winter, while they were hunting.

She leaned back on her elbows and glanced up into the dull blue sky, where the Sun, the Mother's consort, was struggling to free his shining robes once more from the Cyclops. The Cyclops' rolling bloodshot Eye looked down on us malevolently, out of the wide greenness of her face. —It was the doing of the Cyclops, probably.

Etaa sighed. —Her strength is always greatest at the Dark Noons, big Uglyface; she always brings pain with the cold! But the Mother sees all—

—The Mother didn't see the kharks. She didn't save my parents; She could have. She gives us pain too, the Great Bitch!

Etaa's hands covered her eyes; then slowly they slid down again. —Hywel, that's blasphemy! Don't say that or She will punish you. If She let your parents die, they must have offended Her. She lifted her head with childish self-righteousness.

—My parents never did anything wrong! Never! My mind saw them as they always were, bickering constantly. . . . They stayed together because they had managed to have one child, and though they'd lost two others, they were fertile together and might someday have had a fourth. But they didn't like each other anyway, and maybe their resentment was an offense. I hit Etaa hard on the arm and leaped up. —The Mother is a bitch and you are a brat! May you be sterile!

She gasped and made the warding sign. Then she stood up and kicked me in the shins with her rough sandals, her face flushed with anger, before she ran off again across the pasture.

After she was gone I stood throwing rocks furiously at the shenn, watching them run in stupid terror around and around the field.

And because of it, when I had worn out my rage, I discovered one of my shenn had disappeared. Searching and cursing, I finally found the stubborn old ewe up on the scarp at the field's end. She was scrabbling clumsily over the ragged black boulders, cutting her tender feet and leaving tufts of her silky wool on every rock and thorn bush. I caught her with my crook at last and dragged her back down by her flopping ears, while she butted at me and stepped on my bare feet with her claws out. I cursed her mentally now, not having a hand to spare, and cursed my own idiocy, but mostly I cursed the Mother Herself, because all my troubles seemed to come from Her.

Scratched and aching all over, I got the ewe down the crumbling hill to the field at last, whacked her with my crook, and watched her trot indignantly away to rejoin the flock. I started toward the stream to wash my smarting body, but Etaa was ahead of me, going down to drink. Afraid that she would see me for the fool I was, I threw myself down in the shade of the hillside instead and pretended to be resting. I couldn't tell if she was even looking at me, though I squinted and stretched my eyes with my fingers.

But then suddenly she was on her feet running toward me,

waving her arms. I got up on my knees, wondering what crazy thing—

And then a piece of the hill gave way above me and buried me in blackness.

I woke spitting, with black dirt in my eyes, my nose, my mouth, to see Etaa at my side still clawing frantically at the earth and rubble that had buried my legs. All through her life, though she wasn't large even among women, she had strength to match that of many men. And all through my life I remembered the wild, burning look on her face, as she turned to see me alive. But she didn't make a sign, only kept at her digging until I was free.

She helped me stand, and as I looked up at the slumped hillside the full realization of what had been done came to me. I dropped to my knees again and rubbed fistfuls of the tumbled earth into my hair, praising Her Body and begging Her forgiveness. Never again did I question the Mother's wisdom or doubt Her strength. I saw Etaa kneel beside me and do the same.

As we shared supper by my tent, I asked Etaa how she'd known when she tried to warn me. —Did you see it happening?

She shook her head. —I *felt* it, first . . . but the Mother didn't give me enough time to warn you.

—Because She was punishing me. She should have killed me for the things I thought today!

—But it was me who made her angry. It was my fault. I shouldn't have said that about your parents. It was awful, it was—cruel.

I looked at her mournful face, shadowed by the greening twilight. —But it was true. I sighed. —And it wasn't just today that *I* have cursed the Mother. But I'll never do it again. She must have been right, to let my parents die. They hated staying together; they didn't appreciate the blessing of their fertility, when others pray for children but can't make any.

—Hywel . . . maybe they're happier now, did you ever think? She looked down self-consciously. —To return to the Mother's Womb is to find peace, my mother says. Maybe She knew they were unhappy in life, so She let them come back, to be born again.

—Do you really think so? I leaned forward, not knowing why this strange girl's words should touch me so.

She wrinkled her face with thought. —I really think so.

And I felt the passing of the second shadow that had darkened my mind for so long, as though for me it was finally Midsummer's Day and I stood in the light again.

Etaa insisted on staying with me that night; her mother was a healer, and she informed me that I might have "hidden injuries," so gravely that I laughed. I lay awake a long time, aching but at peace, looking up past the leather roof into the green-lit night. I could see pallid Laa Merth, the Earth's Grieving Sister, fleeing wraithlike into the outer darkness in her endless effort to escape her mother, the Cyclops, who always drew her back. The Cyclops had turned her lurid Eye away from us, and the shining bands of her robe made me think for once of good things, like the banded melons ripening in the village fields below.

I looked back at Etaa, her short dark curls falling across her cheek and her bare chest showing only the softest hint of curves under her fortune-seed necklace. I found myself wishing that she would somehow magically become a woman, because I was just old enough to be interested; and then suddenly I wished that then she would have me for her man, something I'd never thought about anyone else before. But if she were a woman, she would become our priestess and have her pick of men and not want one without the second sight. . . . I remembered the look she'd given me as she dug me out of the landslide, and felt my face redden, thinking that maybe I might have a chance, after all.

Through the summer and the seasons that followed I spent much time with Etaa and slowly got used to her strange skills. I had never known what it was like to feel the Mother's touch, or even another human's, on my own soul; and since I had few close friends, I didn't know the ways of those who had the second sight. To be with Etaa was to be with someone who saw into other worlds. Often she started at nothing, or told me what we'd find around the next turn of the path; she even knew my feelings sometimes, when she couldn't see my face. She felt what the Earth feels, the touch of every creature on Her skin.

Etaa's second sight made her like a creature of the forest (for all animals know the will of the Mother), and, solitary like me, she spent much time with only the wild things for company. Often she tried to take me to see them, but they always bolted at my coming. Etaa would wince and tell me to move more slowly, step more softly, breaking branches offends the Earth . . . but I could never really tell what I was doing wrong.

The next year on Midsummer's Eve I was initiated into manhood. During the feast that followed, while I sat dripping and content after my ducking in the sacred spring, Etaa sat proudly at my side. But when midnight came I left the celebration to walk in the fields with Hegga, because for that one could only ask a woman, and Etaa was still a child. Which she proved, by sticking her tongue out at Hegga as we passed. But it made me smile, since it meant she was closer to being a woman, too.

Now that I was a man, Teleth, who was the village smith, asked me to be his apprentice. Smithing is a gift of the Sun to the Fire clan, and a man of that clan is always the smith, whatever clan he marries into. Teleth, my mother's cousin, had a son who would have followed him, but his son was farsighted, and not much good at the close work smithing required. I was Teleth's closest nearsighted kin; but he signed that I was good with my hands and quick with my mind too, which pleased him more. And pleased me too, more than I could tell him; because besides the honor, it meant that I'd have a better chance of impressing Etaa.

Though she was still a child, whenever I saw her passing in the village, or watched her sign to the people who came to see her, the grace of her manner and her words left me amazed; especially since for me words never came easy, and my hands showed my feelings better by what they made from metal and wood. But often I saw her, from the smithy, going off alone on the path to the Mother's Glen, and I remembered the burden she always carried with her, and how she had lightened mine. And then I'd go back to work, and work twice as hard, hoping Teleth would take pity on me and let me go early.

But usually Teleth kept me working every spare minute; he was young, but he had a lung sickness that made him cough up blood, and he was afraid he wouldn't live long. When I could be with Etaa at last, my hands tangled with excitement while I tried to set free the things I could never share with anyone else. With me Etaa was free to be the child she couldn't be with anyone else; and though sometimes it annoyed me, and I thought she would never grow up, I endured it, because I saw it was something she needed; and because she would pull my head down and kiss me sometimes as lightly as the touch of a rainbow fly, before she ran away.

We were always together at the Four Feasts and for other rituals, because until she became a woman she wouldn't be our priestess. We saw each other in the fields at planting and harvest too, when everyone worked together, and sometimes in the summer she'd come foraging and berry picking with me. Having eyes that saw both near and far, she could choose whatever task she liked; and, she said, she liked to be with me.

Usually our berry picking went crazy with freedom, and more berries got eaten and stepped on than ever went into our baskets. But one windless, muggy day in the second summer after my initiation, we went in search of red burrberries and Mother's moss for healing. All through the morning Etaa was strangely reserved and solemn, as though she were practicing her formal face in front of me now too. I tried to draw her out, and when I couldn't, I began to feel desperate at the thought that I'd offended her by something I didn't know I'd done—or worse, that she was finally losing interest in me.

—Mother's Tits!   I jerked back from a thorn, cursing and fumbling all at once, and lost another handful of berries.

Etaa looked back from the stream bank, where she was peeling up moss, sensing sharp emotions as she always did. —Hywel, are you all right?

I nodded, barely able to make out her signs from where I stood. —Just save some of that moss for me. I'm being stabbed to death.

She came scrambling up the bank. —Let me pick, then, and you get the moss. It will soothe your hands while you work.

—I'm all right. I felt my old sullenness rise up in me.

—I don't mind. My scratches are better already . . . Look! There's a rubit. It's the Mother's bird; She wants you to change places with me.

—How do you know what it means? You're not the priestess yet. I squinted along her pointing finger. —And that's not a rubit, it's a follower bird.

—Yes, it is a rubit, I can feel its—

—It is not! I crossed my arms.

—Hywel— She stared at me. —What's wrong with you today?

—What's wrong with *you*? All day you've acted like you barely know me! I turned away, to hide the things my face couldn't.

At last she touched my shoulder; I turned back, to see her blushing as red as the burrberries and her hands twitching at her waist. —I didn't mean to . . . but I couldn't tell you . . . I thought . . . Oh, Hywel, will you walk in the fields with me on Midsummer's Eve? Her face burned even redder, her eyes as bright as the Sun.

Laughter burst out of me, full of relief and joy. I caught her up in my arms and swung her, my body saying *yes* and *yes* and *yes,* while she hung on and I felt her laugh her own relief away. I set her down, and straightened the links of my belt to cover my speechlessness. Then I looked her over, grinning, and signed, —So, brat, you've finally grown up?

She stretched her face indignantly. —I certainly have. So please don't call me "brat" anymore. As a matter of fact, my mother hasn't cut my hair for nearly six months, and you never even noticed!

I touched the dark curls that reached almost down to her shoulders now. —Oh. I guess I didn't. I'll have to make you a headband, to go with your necklace.

Her hand rose to the string of jet and silver beads I had made for her. —My necklace doesn't hang straight anymore, either.

—I noticed that. I grinned again, moving closer.

She caught my head and pulled it down to kiss me, as she always did; but this time she didn't pull away, and her kiss was more like fire than a rainbow fly's wing.

I jerked away instead. —Hai, I never taught you that! Who
have you been with?

—Nobody. Hegga told me you liked that! She danced
away, and hands waving wildly, slipped and fell down the
bank into the bed of moss.

I leaped down the bank after her, landing beside her in the
soft, gray-green moss. —Gossip about me, will you? I signed.
And then I taught her a few things Hegga hadn't told her
about.

It seemed to me that Midsummer's Eve would never come.
But it came at last, and I found myself laying my cape out on
the soft earth between the rows of wheat. I drew Etaa down
beside me, her woman's tunic still clinging wetly against her.
And then we made love together for the first time, asking
fertility for the fields and for ourselves, while I wondered if I
was dreaming, because I'd dreamed it often enough.

After, we lay together in the gentle warm night, seeing
each other's smiles bathed in green glow, watching the Cyclops like a great striped melon overhead. I gave her the
earrings I'd made for her, silver bells shaped like winket
blossoms, the symbol of a priestess of the Mother. She took
them almost with awe, stroking them with her fingers, and
signed that they had a beautiful soul. And I thought of how
she would become our priestess tomorrow on Midsummer's
Day, and pulled her close again, wondering what would
happen between us then. Etaa wiggled her hands free, and
asked if she was really a woman now, in my eyes. I kissed
her forehead and signed, —In every way, feeling her heart
beating hard against me. And then, proudly, as if she had
read my mind, she asked me to be her husband. . . .

We didn't return to the village until dawn; and the harvest
that year was bountiful.

But cold drizzling rain falls now, the sky is gray with grief,
I lie below the cliff and even yesterday is beyond the reach of
my crippled hands. Only yesterday . . . yesterday Midsummer's Day came again, the Day of Fruitfulness, the greatest
of the Mother's sacred feasts—and the day that should have
been our joy, Etaa's and mine. Yesterday our Mother Earth
escaped the shadow of the envious Cyclops, and was united

again with her shining lover the Sun, once more defying
darkness and barren night. And yesterday the priestess of our
village took the Mother's part in ritual, and a man of the
appointed clan was her consort, to ensure a safe passage
through the seasons of Dark Noons and a better future for our
people. Because the priestess of a village is the woman most
blessed by the Mother, each Midsummer's Day by tradition
she joins with a man of a different clan, in celebration, and in
the hope of creating a child blessed as she is, who will
strengthen the blood of its father's clan.

This year, as in the past seven years, Etaa was our priestess; but this year my own clan had chosen her consort, and
they had chosen me. Etaa's face mirrored my own joy when I
told her; because though I was smith now, and though I was
her husband, that highest honor usually went to the clansman
most gifted with the second sight.

And then on Midsummer's Day Etaa shook me awake at
dawn, her eyes filled with love. She wore only her shift, and
already her Midsummer garlands twined in the wild dark curls
of her hair. She smelled of summer flowers. —Hywel, it's
Midsummer!

I felt myself laugh, half a yawn. —I know, I know, priestess! I could hardly forget—

—Hywel, I have a surprise. She glanced down suddenly,
and her hands trembled as she signed. I saw her silver earrings flash in the light. —I missed my monthly time, and I
think—I think—

—Etaa! I touched her stomach, still flat and firm beneath
the thin linen of her shift.

—Yes! Her smile broke into laughter as I pulled her down
beside me into the hammock. Eight years of marriage and
seven Midsummer's Days had passed, and we had begun to
think Etaa was barren, like so many others; until now—

I held her tightly in the soft clasp of our hammock,
swaying gently side by side. —We're truly blessed, Etaa.
Maybe the Mother was waiting for this day. I began to kiss
her, pulling at her shift, but all at once she pushed me away.

—No, Hywel, today we have to wait!

I grinned. —You take me for an old man, me, the father of

your child? I won't slight the Mother today—but neither will I slight my wife!

Yesterday was all it could have been, the Sun's glory dazzling the sky, the bright fields of grain . . . Etaa's radiant face in the Mother's Glen, on the day when she became Wife and Mother to us all, and I was her chosen.

But then, this morning, she asked me to let her ride with us when I went to trade with the Neaane. We have traded with the Neaane since we first settled on their border, longer ago than anybody can remember. They are a strange, inward people who have lost all understanding of the Mother. Their lives are grim and joyless because of it; they even persecute their people who are blessed with the second sight, calling them witches. They believe in gods who live in the sky, who abandoned them, and, they say, caused the plague that took the Blessed Time from all people.

We never liked their beliefs, but we liked their possessions: soft-footed palfers to carry burdens or pull a plow, new kinds of seed for our fields—even a way to keep the fields fert'le over many years, which gave us a more settled life. They wanted our metalwork and jewelry, and the hides of wild animals, because they like to show wealth even more than we do, especially the ones who have most of it. Settled farming has given them time to develop many strange customs, including setting some people above all others, often for no good reason as far as we could see, not wisdom or courage or even good vision.

Still, our trade was good for both of us, and so we lived together in peace until, in the time the elders still remember, the Neaane's gods returned to them—or so they believed. With the gods' return the Neaane turned against us, saying it proved their beliefs were the only truth, and we, the Kotaane, were an abomination to their gods. Ugly rumors had come to the village of incidents farther south, and even here ill-feeling hurt our dealings with the local lord and his people at Barys-town. I didn't want to see it grow into war, because I had never wanted to kill anyone, and because a war with the powerful Neaane could only bring us death and pain. I also didn't want to expose my priestess-wife with her unborn child to the hostility and insults I'd gotten used to in Barys-town.

But she insisted, saying she wanted adventure. She was as irresistible as the summer day, and as beautiful, and I gave in, because I wanted to share it with her.

When we reached Barys-town, we found it choked with the soldiers of the king, the most powerful lord in their land. He was making a rare visit to his borderlands, probably to make certain they were secure against us. I saw the king himself, not thirty feet away but hardly more than a blur to my eyes; he sat on his sharp-footed horse, watching with his nobles as we began to barter. But then his soldiers crowded around us, waving at Etaa and mocking her, calling her "witch" and "whore." One tried to pull her from her palfer, but she hit him with an iron pot. The king made no sign to stop them, and angrily I ordered my goods taken up, not caring who my nervous palfer stepped on in the crowd. I had taken too many insults from the people of Barys-town in the past, and while they gathered sullenly around I told them this insult to my wife was the last one, and they would get no more metal from me. We turned and rode away, passing the fat local priest of the sky-gods, who had come for the jeweled god-sign he had commissioned from me. Seeing him, I threw it onto a dung-hill. I didn't look back to see whether he ran to fetch it out. Etaa was very pale, riding beside me; she signed that it was an evil place behind us, and begged me to keep my promise and never go back, because she'd seen hatred in too many eyes.

Then horror froze her face, though I didn't see anything; she turned in her saddle, looking wildly back at the town. —Hywel!

My palfer lunged sideways as an arrow struck its flank. I jerked its head back, saw the mounted men coming fast behind us, the sunlight sparkling on chain mail. Etaa pulled at my arm and we kicked our palfers into a gallop, getting drenched with spray as we plunged through the stream that crossed the trail.

We rode for the hills that separated our village from the Neaane, hoping to lose the soldiers in the rough brush where our palfers were surer-footed. But the Neaane seemed to know our every move; again and again we lost sight of them, but they never lost us, and always they cut us off from escape. We knew nothing about the broken uplands. Soon we were lost and scattered until only Etaa and I still rode together; but the soldiers followed like hounds on a trail.

Until at last the rigid black-striped hands of a stream-cut gorge brought us to the end of our run—the edge of a cliff where the snow water dashed itself down, down to oblivion, and there was nowhere left to go. My palfer sank to its knees as I slid from its back and went to look down. The drop was sheer, a hundred feet or more onto the wet-silvered rocks below. I turned back, stunned with despair. —They still follow?

—Yes! Etaa threw herself off her palfer, her dappled gown mud-smeared, the summer blossoms torn from her hair. She clung to me, breathing hard, and then turned back to face the brush-filled gorge. —Mother, they're coming, they still come! How can they follow us, when they can't *see*? She trembled like a trapped beast. —Why, Hywel? Why are they doing this?

I touched her cheek, bloody with scratches, with my own scratched hand. —I don't know! But . . . My hands tried to close over the words. —But you know what they'll do, if they take us.

Her eyes closed. —I know . . . Her arms closed in fear around her body.

—And burn us alive then, so that our souls can never rest. I glanced toward the cliff, trembling now too. —Etaa— Her eyes were open again and following my gaze.

—Must we— Her hands pressed her stomach, caressed our child.

I saw the riders now, a shifting blur down the shadowed canyon. —We have to; we can't let them take us.

We went together to the cliff's edge and stood looking down, clinging together, dizzy with the drop and fear. Etaa threw out a quick handful of dirt and prayed to the Mother, as it drifted down, that She would know and receive us. And then she looked up at me, shaking so that I could barely understand her. —Oh, Hywel, I'm so afraid of heights . . . Her mouth quivered; she might have laughed. She drew my head down then and we kissed, long and sweetly. —I love you only, now and always.

—Now and always— I signed. I saw in her eyes that there

was no more time. —Now! I fumbled for her hand, seeing soldiers at the mouth of the gorge, her stricken face, and then—nothing. I leaped.

And felt her hand jerk free from mine at the last instant. I saw her face fall upward, framed in dark hair, through cold rushing eternity; and then my body smashed on the rocks below, and tore the bitter anguish from my mind.

Why I ever woke again at all I don't know; or why I still live now, when I would gladly die and be done with my pain. But I woke into nightmare, trapped in this broken body with my shame: knowing I had jumped and Etaa had not. I had let her be taken by the Neaane. I tortured my eyes for some sign, some movement above the face of the black-striped cliff; but there was nothing, only the glaring edge of day, the red Eye of the Cyclops. Etaa was gone. The falling river leaped and foamed beside me, mocking my grief and my aching mouth with cold silver drops. I strained my head until my metal collar cut into my throat, but nothing moved. And so I lay still finally, and prayed, half in dreams and half in madness, and couldn't even form her name: Etaa, Etaa . . . forgive me.

Overhead the clouds gathered purple-gray, darkening the noon; the Mother in Her grief drew Her garments close and rejected Her Lover. The crops will fail. She had cursed Her children for this abomination; for the unbearable sacrilege of the Neaane, for the pitiful weakness of Hywel, Her Lover and son. She tears the clouds with knives of light, crying vengeance, and Her tears fall cold and blinding on my face. I drown in Her tears, I drown in sorrow . . . Mother! If I could move one more finger, to make Your sign . . . Giver of Life, let me live! Give me back my body, and I will give You the heads of the Neaane. I will avenge this desecration, avenge Your priestess . . . my Etaa . . . Mother, hear me—

Who touches my face? Work, eyes, damn you . . . Smiling, because I'm still alive . . . they wear black and red. They are the king's men! And they will take my soul. Mother, let me die first. No. Let me join my Etaa, on the wind. And have pity on us. . . .

Part 2: The King

It's hardly an army fit for a king. . . . But Archbishop Shappistre tells my people openly these days that King Meron is bewitched—and they believe him. They believe anything the Church tells them. My poor people! Though with my only child lost, and the Kedonny eating away Tramaine while the Gods do nothing, who can blame them? But if I angered the Gods by wanting the Kedonny Witch, if I brought myself ruin, it wasn't because my mind was not my own. It was because it was too much my own, and I knew exactly what I was doing.

And yet, when I look back and remember how I came to this, perhaps there was a kind of bewitchment about it. For it was on the day I first saw her that the plan came into my mind, as I watched her ride into the border village with the Kedonny traders: my Black Witch, my Etaa. . . . The Earl of Barys' priest pointed her out to me, signing she was a pagan priestess, his fat hands trembling at how these godless Kedonny worshipped wantonness and *hearing;* at which point he spat religiously. I fumbled for my lenses to get a better look, and was surprised to see, not some debauched crone, but a fresh-faced girl with masses of dark hair falling loose across her shoulders.

The Kedonny believe that hearing is a godly blessing, and not a curse, as our Church considers it to be; and for my own part, all my life I've questioned the practices that teach us to suppress it. Why should any gods who had our best interests in mind ask us to weaken ourselves? Why, when my own father had passing good vision, had he felt guilty about it, and chosen for my mother a woman who could barely see his face—so that without the lenses so kindly presented me by the Gods, I must stumble into doorframes in a most unkingly manner? Now, watching the Kedonny priestess, revered as the most gifted of her people, my old discontent was transformed. Suddenly I realized that my own heirs didn't need to suffer the same weakness and dependency. I would get them a mother who could give them the strengths I could not. . . .

I snapped out of my thoughts to see the Kedonny traders riding abruptly away, their faces set in anger, while my men-at-arms gestured curses and the villagers shuffled sullenly between them. Almost without thinking, I summoned my carriage and gave orders to my men for pursuit.

As my carriage rose into the air over the heads of the gaping locals, I looked down on the earl's priest digging inexplicably in a dunghill. If I were a religious man, I might have taken it for a sign.

My carriage was made by the Gods, a smooth sphere with a texture like ivory that not only moved over land without using palfers but could take to the sky like a bird. From the air I could track the fleeing Kedonny easily, and guide my men in separating the woman from the rest—all except one man, who stayed stubbornly at her side even when we drove them into a trap. But in the end he was no problem, because he flung himself from the cliff, apparently afraid of being burned alive. I saw his body smashed on the rocks below, and turned away with a shudder, thinking how close I had come to losing what I sought—for my men said that the woman had pulled back from the edge at the last second, and they had barely gotten to her in time. Some of them had thrown her down on the ground, with obvious intent, and I disciplined those with the flat of my sword, in a fury edged with shame. Then I took her up myself, her face the color of hearth ash, and carried her to my carriage.

Being king, I had no need to explain my behavior to anyone at Barys Castle, though there was a flutter of knowing amusement among the nobles as I said an early good-night. I went directly to my chambers, where the Kedonny priestess waited, and left orders with my watch that they were not to disturb me.

The woman sat huddled at the window slit, staring out into the sodden twilight; but as I entered she jerked around, fixing her wide, burning eyes on me. I smiled, because it proved she could hear, and because I saw again that she was a beauty. But seeing me, she pressed back against the cold stone slit as though she wanted to throw herself out.

"Your lover is dead—"

She hesitated, her face blank, and I realized she couldn't read lips. I repeated with my hands, —Your lover is dead. You tried to follow him, and failed. I wouldn't try it again.

She understood the common sign-speech at least, for she sank back down on the seat with her face in her hands. I brought my own hands together sharply, and she glanced up again, startled. I noticed a meal, untouched, on my carven chest beside her. —Will you eat?

She shook her head, her face still frozen.

—Stand up.

She rose stiffly, her hands clutching at her torn gown, her slender arms bare except for bracelets and burned as dark as any peasant's. Her unbound hair gleamed black in the flickering firelight, tangled with wilting flowers and twigs. On her face the dust of flight was smeared and tracked by tears, but I was relieved to see she wasn't the dirt-encrusted barbarian I had half expected; she looked cleaner than some members of my own court. Her ragged dress was coarsely woven and dull-colored, but somehow it brought to my mind the pattern of green leaves and the muted light of deep woods. . . . This was my wanton priestess, the fertile Earth incarnate, who would strengthen the royal line. And even now her witchy beauty went to my head like wine.

It must have shown, for she shrank back again. I pulled off my cloak, amused. —What, priestess, am I so hard to look at? They say a Kedonny priestess will lie with any man who wants her. I touched my crown. —Well, I'm king in this land; surely that makes me as good as any Kedonny shennherd. I caught her arms, and suddenly she came to life, fighting with a strength that stunned me. She struck at my face, knocking off my lenses, and I felt more than saw them shatter on the floor. Angry, I dragged her to the bed and threw her down, pulling off the rags of her dress.

And then I forced her, ruthlessly, in the way I thought befitted a whore of the uncivilized Kedonny. On the bed she did not struggle, but lay limp as a corpse under me, biting her lips while fresh tears of humiliation ran down her face, staining the satin pillows. Her eyes were as brown as peat, the only part of her that showed life, and they tore at me in grief and outrage and supplication. But I looked away, too angry and too eager to admit I had no right to make her mine.

And whatever else may come to pass, that is the one thing I will never forgive myself. Because I did not use a pagan slut that night: I raped a gentle woman, on the day she saw her husband die. Because later I came to love her; but I could never undo the wrong, or hope to change the bitterness I had caused in her heart.

She slept far into the next day, the sleep of exhaustion; but she sat waiting, clad in her rags, when I came back to my chamber after making ready for our departure. She looked as if she hadn't slept at all, or as if she had wakened to find herself still caught up in a nightmare. But she lifted her hands and made the first words I had seen from her, strangely accented: —Will you let me go now?

It took me a moment to realize that she thought I had done all this merely for a night's pleasure. —No. I'm taking you with me to Newham.

—What do you want of me? Her hands trembled slightly.

I pushed my new lenses higher on my nose. —I want your child.

Her hands pressed her stomach in an odd gesture of fear, then leaped into a series of words that meant nothing to me; I guessed she was pleading with me in her own language.

I shook my head and signed patiently, —I want you to bear me sons. I want your—your "blessings" for them. They will be princes, heirs to the throne of Tramaine. They'll have luxuries you can't imagine—and so will you, if you obey me.

She twisted away hopelessly to gaze out the window slit. I could see the line of hills that separated us from the Kedonny, gray land merging into gray sky in the silver rain. Her hands pressed her stomach again.

I clapped and she looked back at me. —What is your sign, priestess?

—Etaa.

—The serving women will bring you new clothes, Etaa. My fingers tangled on the unfamiliar word. —We leave within the hour.

We returned to the palace at Newham, since continuing in the marches would only have made an incident likely; our return took several days, because my carriage had to go more slowly than usual for the sake of my retinue. But we outdistanced the rain at last, and though the roads were mired, the fresh rolling green of the land, the fertile fields and dappled groves of horwoods filled me with pride. Looming Cyclops, which the peasants called the Godseye, merged its banded greens with the green of the earth, and to one side I could see the gibbous outer moon paled by its magnificence. The outer moon was swirled with white that the court astronomer said was clouds, like the ones on Earth. When I was young I had thought of taking the Gods' carriage and flying out to see it, having been told that men once lived there too. But the Gods said the air grew thin as you went higher, and told me I would suffocate if I tried. I tried anyway, and found they were right.

The Kedonny woman accepted the matter of flight without the terror I had expected, only asking, —How does it do this?

—The Gods give it power. It was a gift to my grandfather on their return to Earth.

—There are no gods; there is only the Goddess. A small defiance flickered on her face.

I glanced briefly at the forward compartment, where my coachman tended our flight. —I agree: there are no Gods. But never say it again, priestess, since you know well enough what happens to heretics. You're under my protection, but my archbishop will not welcome a pagan at court.

She settled back into the velvet cushions, and into her quiet resignation, confined and incongruous in the stiff, brocaded gown and the modesty of her headdress. Small silver bells shaped like winket blossoms dangled from wires piercing her ears; she toyed with them constantly. Sometimes as she did she would almost smile, her eyes fixed on nothing.

As I watched her, the image came to me of a pitiful wild child I had seen as a boy, kept in a cage at a fair. The kharks had stolen human children and raised them as their own, until the Gods came and destroyed the kharks. The wild humans could never adjust to normal life again, and I had wondered if there was something about being wild that was better than being a prince, and it saddened me to think that all the kharks were gone. I looked away from Etaa, falling into another memory of my childhood and the Gods: of the time I had inadvertently spied on them during hide-and-hunt with the pages—and seen the grotesque, inhuman thing they treated as a brother. And somehow I knew that this *thing* was the Gods'

true form, and that the too-perfect faces they showed to us
were only enchantments. I slipped away and ran to tell my
father, but he was furious at my blasphemy, and beat me for
it, forbidding me ever to speak against our Gods again. I
never did, for I realized quickly enough that whatever they
weren't, they had powers even a king dared not question. I
often wondered if my father had realized that too. But pri-
vately I never gave up my heresies, and because of that I
found less and less that was deserving of reverence in the
teachings of the Church. Which is why my cousin, Archbishop Shappistre, and I have never been much in accord.
Why, indeed, he would gladly see me dead and damned.

The archbishop was quick to inform me of his displeasure
in the latest instance, after my arrival at the palace at Newham.
My good wife, the queen, did not come out to meet us,
sending word that she was indisposed. I wondered if she had
heard that I was bringing back a mistress; but since through
fifteen years of marriage she had rarely been disposed to
come and greet me, it hardly mattered. I espied her brother
the archbishop among the nobles, however, marking my progress across the banner-bright courtyard from the carriage,
with Etaa at my side. He alone was not amused; but then, like
his sister, he rarely was. I anticipated a visit from him before
the day was out.

I was not disappointed, for early in the evening my watchman entered the room, standing patiently with his face to the
door until I should happen to notice and acknowledge him.
Etaa started at his entrance, and I caught her motion in the
mirror I had fixed at the side of my lenses; it occurred to me
that her very presence could be a useful thing. I went to touch
the watchman's shoulder, giving him audience, and was informed that the archbishop desired to speak with me. I sent
for him, and returned to the table where I was laboriously
reviewing the reports sent to me by my advisers. Etaa watched
from the long bench where she befriended the fire, avoiding
me. Even though she did, after so many years alone I found
that the constant presence of a woman was oddly comforting.

The archbishop did not appear to share my feelings, however. His gaunt, ascetic face had always seemed at odds with
the flaming richness of his robes; but the look of pious

indignation that he affected on seeing Etaa touched on the absurd. "Your majesty." The modish sleeves of his outer robe swept the flags as he bowed low. "I had hoped I might speak with you—alone."

I smiled. "Etaa does not read lips, my lord. You may speak freely in her presence." I gained a certain pleasure at his discomfort, having been made uncomfortable by him often enough in my youth . . . and more recently.

"It is about—this woman—that I've come to your majesty. I strongly protest her presence at court; it's hardly fitting for our king to take a pagan priestess for a leman. Indeed, it smacks of blasphemy." I fancied seeing hungry flames leap behind his eyes; or perhaps it was only firelight reflecting on his lenses. "The Gods have expressed their displeasure to me. And the queen, your lawful wife, is extremely upset."

"I daresay the queen, your sister, has little reason to be upset with me. I have allowed her all the lovers she wants, and the Gods know she has enough of them."

The archbishop stiffened. "Are you saying she is not within her right?"

"Not at all." Divorce was forbidden by the Church, which places duty far above pleasure. As a result, it was common that childless couples would seek an heir from formalized liaisons; though most of the queen's were far from being that. "But we were married, as you know, when I was sixteen, and in all the years since she has not produced a child. If I couldn't give her one, I would gladly acknowledge someone else's. But she is ten years my senior—frankly, my lord, I've begun to give up hope." I didn't add that I'd even given up trying—our marriage had been arranged to bind factions, and it had never been a love match. "This woman pleases me, and I must have an heir. Her beliefs will not affect her childbearing."

"But she is not of noble breeding—"

"She is not a Shappistre by blood, you mean? You would do well to contemplate the scriptures and the law, my lord. The relationship between church and state is a two-edged blade; take care that you don't cut yourself on it."

He bowed low again, his bald head reddening to match his jeweled cap. "Your majesty . . ." Abruptly he glanced at

Etaa and clapped his hands. Etaa, who had returned to her firewatching, started visibly and turned. A smile of triumph crossed his face. —She hears. I must request that your majesty have her ears put out as soon as possible . . . in accordance with the scriptures, and the law. His hands moved carefully in the common signing.

My fists clenched over an angry retort. Then, evenly and also by hand, I replied, —She is a foreigner. While under my protection she is subject to neither the religion nor the laws of Tramaine. And now, good night, Archbishop; I am very weary after my long journey. I crossed my arms.

My archbishop turned without another word and left the room.

I joined Etaa by the fire, noting how she drew away as I sat down, and asked if she had understood us.

Her eyes met mine briefly, and wounded me with their misery, before she signed, —He would hurt me. He fears the blessings of the Mother.

I nodded, reminding her that here her "blessings" were sins, but assuring her that she would not be hurt while she was under my protection. —Tell me, Etaa, what did you think of the archbishop? He's the high priest of my people.

—He does not like you.

It surprised a laugh out of me.

—And he is a poor man to be priest, who cannot feel another creature's soul. To deny the second sight is to deny one's—gods.

—But the Gods say they wish it that way.

—Then they are false gods, who do not love you.

Then they are false Gods. . . . I watched the flames eat darkness for a long moment. —But they're here, Etaa, and powerful; and so is their Church. The archbishop would gladly see you burn as a witch, and so would almost anyone. But I believe as you do, that hearing is a blessing—and I want to share it. You will give my children the "second sight." And you can give it to me.

—From now on, if you hear anyone come into my presence you will tell me immediately, wherever we are. It's not an easy thing to be king in these times, or any times. I need your help . . . and you need mine. If anything should happen to

me, there's no one who would protect you. You'd be burned
alive, and suffer terrible agony, and your soul would be lost
to your Goddess forever. Do you understand me? I knew that
she had understood everything, from the changes that crossed
her face. Slowly she nodded, her hands pressing the stiff,
gold-embroidered russet that covered her stomach.

Unthinking, and somehow ashamed, I reached out in a
gesture of comfort, only to have her wither under my touch
like a blossom in the frost. Gently I went on touching her, but
to no avail, and when at last I took her to the bedchamber,
she lay as limp and deathly unresponsive as ever. As she
turned her face from a final kiss I caught her shoulders and
shook her, saying, "Damn you, you heathen bitch!" I let her
fall back against the pillows, remembering that she didn't
understand me, and raised my hands into the lamplight. She
lifted her own defensively, as though she thought I was going
to strike her, and I brushed them aside. —Watch me! Do you
think a man enjoys taking a corpse to bed? I know what you
are with your own people; why should you turn away from
me? I'll have an heir from you whatever you do; you're mine
now, so why not enjoy it—

Her fist flew out and struck me across the jaw. I jerked
back in painful disbelief, while her hands leaped in hysterical
fury.

—I serve my Goddess in holiness, I am not a Neaane
whore! You have stolen a priestess, you have defiled Her,
murderer, and She will never give you heirs. Neaa, you
murdered my husband, whom I loved. Soul-stealer, I would
burn a thousand times and weep forever in the wind before I
would give you pleasure! Never will I . . . never . . . Hywel
. . . She crumpled into sobbing and meaningless gestures,
and buried her face in the cover.

Slowly I rose from the bed, and groping for my lenses,
forgave the only woman who had ever struck a king of
Tramaine.

I still took her to my bed as often as I could, although her
wretchedness had driven all the pleasure from it; for, priestess
of fertility though she might be, and king though I might be,
children are a rare gift of fortune since the plague. And the

Gods have done nothing to change that. I was away from her much of the time after our arrival in Newham, though, being engrossed as usual in affairs of state. And so I could scarcely believe my eyes when fat old Mabis, whom I had sent to serve Etaa, informed me gleefully of seeing signs that I was going to be a father. She was my nurse as a child (and so accepted most of my quirks, including a godless mistress), and assured me that if anyone could tell, it was Mabis. Giddy with pride, I forgot the quarreling of my nobles and the complaints of the burghers; I left even my watchman behind and ran like a boy to find Etaa.

She sat as she so often did, gazing out the high windows, her hair hanging at her back in a heavy plait, for Mabis couldn't get her to wear a covering. She looked up in amazement as I entered; composing myself with an effort, I managed to keep from destroying the moment by lifting her up in my arms. She seemed to know why I had come, and I thought, relieved, that maybe traces of pride hid behind her dark eyes as I bent my knee before her. I gave her my heartfelt thanks and asked what gift I could give her, in return for the one she had given me.

She glanced out the open window for a moment, her face lit with rainbows from the colored glass; when she looked back, her hands were stiff with emotion. —Let me go outside.

—That's all you want?

She nodded.

—Then you shall have it. Carefully I took her hand, and ordering my watch to keep well behind, led her outside into the palace gardens. Etaa somehow belonged in the beauty of roses and pale marisettes, her own wild grace set free from the gray stone confines of the palace walls. I took her to the limit of the green slopes overlooking the placid Aton and the edge of Newhamtown on the river's farther shore. I tried to describe for her the city that was the heart of Tramaine, the bright, swarming mass of humanity, the marketplaces, the pageantry of New Year's and the celebrations of Armageddon Day. She gazed and questioned with a hesitant wonder that pleased me, but I thought she seemed glad when the peaceful bowers closed her in again.

We made our way along drowsy, dappled paths heavy with

the heat of a late summer's afternoon, and I found it hard to believe the sun was already half hidden as it sank behind Cyclops. And as we walked I saw the drawn, anguished look fade from Etaa's face for the first time since midsummer. At one point, we unexpectedly came upon young Lord Tolper and his sweetheart, in a compromising position on the grass. I took Etaa's arm and led her quickly away, before the blushing lord felt required to rise and make a bow; as we turned to go I saw a quick, sweet smile of remembrance touch her lips, and felt a pang of envy.

Because I had so little time to myself, I instructed Mabis to accompany Etaa in the future into the gardens—and to do anything else that might be required for her health and comfort. Mabis confided that she had already been gathering healthful herbs for the babe at Etaa's request; for, bless her pagan soul, the girl had the skill of ten Newham physicians, and had even told her of a poultice to ease the ache in an old woman's back. Mabis was deeply religious in her own way, but she had never liked the queen, and Etaa's thoughtless kindness and lack of vanity had won her heart.

Etaa had little contact with the court in the beginning, partly at my wish and partly at her own. Yet she found another friend in the palace before long, a fellow outcast of sorts: young Willem, who was one of my pages. He was a strange, nervous boy, his hair as flaxen as her own was black, who seemed to be constantly starting at unseen sights and sometimes even to see around corners. He stuttered in both noble and common speech, as though not only his lips but even his own fingers wouldn't obey him. One afternoon I came to call on Etaa in her chambers and found him sitting at her feet before the fire, their faces half in the green light of waning eclipse, half ruddy with fireglow. They looked up at me almost as one, and Willem scrambled to his feet to bow, barely concealing his dismay at the arrival of his king. I gathered that Etaa had been telling him a story, and asked her to continue, feeling that I would be glad of a little diversion too.

She took up her story again almost self-consciously, a Kedonny tale of how a wandering people had come to settle and find a home at last. I grew fascinated myself by the

realism of it, even though it was riddled with allusions to the
supernatural powers of the Mother. It struck me that this must
be the story of how they had come to our borders, in the time
of the second Barthelwydde king, nearly two hundred years
before.

I was fascinated too by the motions of her hands, so quick
and bold compared to the refined gestures of the court poets,
whose graceful imported romances usually left me yawning.
Occasionally she would stumble, breaking the trancelike rhythm
of her tale, and I remembered that she had to translate as she
told, a feat that would leave my poets ill with envy.

When her tale was finished I sent Willem away to his
neglected duties, and, impulsively, asked Etaa if she would
come with me to see our own collected lore. She nodded,
politely curious. The child growing within her seemed to have
given her a thing to love in place of the man she had lost;
perhaps because of it—and because I no longer touched her—
she tolerated me now, and sometimes almost seemed glad of
my company.

I led the way into the part of the palace given over to the
Gods; it was hung with gilt-framed paintings and ornate
tapestries of religious scenes. I went there often, not for
homage, but to visit the repository for the holy books. It had
taken all the power and influence of the kingship to defy the
clergy successfully, but I had been determined to study on my
own those remnants of the Golden Age that the Gods deemed
too complex—and possibly too heretical—for the layman.
The priests who were entrusted with the books spent the
greater part of their lives studying them, since they were
presumably protected by their faith (or, I sometimes suspected, by their ignorance). I had had the best possible educa-
tion, but even I found to my frustration that most of the
learning from before the plague time was far above me. The
Gods would give me no clues, of course, though they claimed
omniscience, since they opposed my right to study the sacred
lore. But then, they also refused to give guidance to the
priests.

As we entered the corridors of the Gods a viridian-robed
priest came to meet us, and I recognized him as Bishop
Perrine, the archbishop's chief lackey. His bow was scarcely

adequate, his lips moving in rigid formality. "Your majesty. You cannot possibly bring that—that woman here! It would be sacrilege to reveal the holy works to a—a pagan."

I smiled tolerantly, suspecting that after the morning's usual strife with the archbishop, this very scene had been secretly taking shape in my mind. "Bishop Perrine, this woman is acting as my watchman. I am quite sure she can't read—"

Etaa started, and I glanced past the bishop's shaven head to see one of the very Gods coming toward us down the hall. Bishop Perrine turned, following my gaze, and together we dropped down on one knee. Too late I noticed that Etaa still stood, defiantly facing the towering, inhumanly beautiful figure in robes lit with an unearthly inner glow. I signaled her to kneel but she ignored me, caught up in fearful amazement.

I waited while God regarded priestess in return, my knee grating on the unaccustomed hardness of the floor and my head thrown back until a crick began to form in my neck. At last an expression passed over his face that I almost took for appreciation; and remembering us, he gave us permission to rise, signing, —My pardon, your majesty, for causing you discomfort; but I forgot myself, at the sight of the opposition.

Bishop Perrine began apologies, his fingers knotting in nervous obsequiousness, but the God stopped him. —No need, Bishop Perrine—I understand. And she is charming, your majesty. I see why they say the Black Witch has enchanted you.

I inclined my head while I mastered a frown, and signed with proper deference, —She is no witch, Lord, but merely a handsome woman. Her beliefs are of no consequence; only primitive superstition.

—I am relieved to learn that. His hands expressed a faint mockery, each move slightly too perfect. —Etaa, can you deny the presence of the true Gods, now that you see one before you?

Slowly she nodded. —You are beautiful to see. But you are a man, and so you cannot be a god. There are no gods other than our Mother. Her face was serene, her eyes shone with belief. I had often envied unshakable faith, but never more than now.

Bishop Perrine shuddered visibly beside me and clutched his god-sign, but I saw the God laugh. —Well signed, priestess. Your belief may be misguided, but not even I can deny its purity. Bishop Perrine, I take it you sought to keep this woman from entering here. I commend you—but I think you should let her pass. Perhaps some further exposure to our beliefs would do her soul good.

Bishop Perrine dropped to the floor, and I sank grudgingly down beside him as the God passed. And as I led Etaa on to the repository, I wondered that a God should have treated us so affably. I knew that the various Gods who called on us had different manners, just as they had different faces when you were used to their splendor. But they were seldom so kindly disposed toward heretics, or anything that threatened the stability of their Church.

Etaa brushed the blue velvet of my sleeve. —Meron— She seldom called me by name, although it pleased me. —How is it that you do not believe in your own gods, when you've seen them all your life? Her hands moved discreetly, half hidden by her wide fur-trimmed sleeves.

I remembered my comment to her in the carriage, so long ago. —You don't believe in them because you say they look like men. Our scriptures tell us that they *are* like men; but I've seen them when they were not. I told her what I'd seen as a child. —So whatever they are, they're *not* the Gods of the scriptures who abandoned us long ago. But they control the lives of my people, and the peoples of all the adjoining lands, through the Church: these—false Gods.

She frowned. —It was only after the gods came that your people began to hate us. Are they cruel, then, to make your people cruel? Her eyes stole glances at the dark scenes displayed along the walls.

I shook my head. —No . . . they're not cruel to us. But they don't condemn cruelty toward nonbelievers. They want no competition, I think. I looked away from a woven witch-burning. —They've done good, useful things for us—driven the wild kharks from the countryside, helped us grow better crops, shown us how to control the shaking fever . . . they've made us—comfortable. Too comfortable, I sometimes think. As though . . . as though they wanted us to stay here forever, and be content never to regain the Golden Age again. And there *was* a Golden Age, I've seen proof of it, in the volumes we go to see now.

—Volumes? Books? Excitement lit her face. —We have a book in our village, that I've studied with the elders; it's said to be from the Blessed Time, when all people knew the touch of the Mother.

—You have that legend too? I stopped moving. —Then it must have been widespread—perhaps the whole world! Think of it, Etaa! But what knowledge we have left, the Gods keep hidden from anyone who could use it. My bitterness made my hands tighten. —The Church teaches us "humility"—not to strive, not to tempt fate, or the Gods, but follow the old worn path to sure salvation. It teaches the people to hate the "second sight" that could give them such freedom, and to hate your people most of all, because you make a religion of it. The Gods make us comfortable, but not because they love us. Damn th—

Etaa caught my hands suddenly, in a graceful grip that was like a vise; she forced them to her lips in a seemingly effortless kiss. I stared at her, astounded, and caught movement in the mirror at the side of my lenses. Down the hall, the archbishop stood watching us intently; she had kept me from cursing the Gods in his presence. I let her know by my tightened hands that I understood. She freed me, and I signed, —Come, love, first go with me to see the holy relics. We continued to the repository; the archbishop did not follow us. I wondered if he had seen enough.

I thanked Etaa, and for a moment she touched my hands again; but then she only looked away, signing stiffly, —Your life is my life, and my child's, as you have said. You need not thank me for that.

But I felt she had been repaid when her hands rose in wonder as we entered the repository and she saw the books— thirty-five volumes resting on yellow satin, above the elaborately embellished study table. Two priests were at their contemplation; not having attendants with me, I went myself and tapped them on the shoulder, asking them to leave. Their faces flashed surprise, acceptance—and a hint of scandal as they passed Etaa and left us alone. Etaa went to stand by the sloping desk, looking down reverently on the smooth, time-less pages of the open books. And then I learned one more thing about the barbaric Kedonny—that their priestess read the printed words of the old language as well as any man of our own priesthood.

And so, though I had taken her with me originally out of a certain obstreperous pride, and because I valued her as a watchman, I began taking her with me for her opinions as well. Word of the pagan woman studying the holy books got rapidly back to the archbishop, and when he came to make his complaint I was forced to remind him sharply that he spoke to his king. I think despite his hunger for personal power he believed in the Church's tenets and its Gods, and was torn by the dilemma they created for him: He believed I committed sacrilege, but because a God had approved it there was nothing he could do to stop me. Or so I thought, even though I knew well enough he would do anything to get at the kingship, for the aspirations of his family and the furtherance of Church power.

As the dark noons of autumn passed into the bright, snowblind days of true winter, I continued to take Etaa with me to study the books, and to have her beside me as my watchman and companion whenever the occasion allowed. Her coming motherhood grew obvious to all, and was the target for much discreet levity, and also more serious specula-tion. Also for some unpleasant and ugly rumors revolving on witchcraft, whose sources I thought I knew. I didn't bother to deal with them, however, being more concerned with other matters; particularly with the rebellious Kedonny, who stub-bornly harried our borderlands even though the snows lay heavy on the earth. There were rumors that a new leader had emerged, using the defiling of a priestess to rally them, and so I sent messengers to my most trusted border lords, telling them to be on guard. But the Kedonny would strike whenever a back was turned, and then fade away into the hills, and their Mother shielded them in Her snowy cloak, as Etaa would have signed—if she'd known. My best leaders seemed help-less against the determined fanaticism of the Kedonny chief, a man called only "the Smith," who was becoming a bogeyman in Tramaine fit to compete with the Godseye that looked down on my people's sinful lives.

At last came Midwinter's Day—a day I would not have marked except that I found Etaa kneeling awkwardly at her hearth, wearing dappled green velvet. She was tossing stalks of ripened wheat into the fierce blaze and reciting a ceremony of the Mother. Pale Willem crouched watching as if hypnotized, while his spotted pup chewed unnoticed at the tail of his jerkin. Mabis sat spinning in the far corner of the chamber, her round chill-reddened face set in righteous disapproval. I was mildly disturbed to see Willem so caught up in Kedonny ways; but his friendship with Etaa cheered them both, and lately I found it hard not to prefer Etaa to our own dour ways myself. But I chided Willem, and he disappeared, ghost-like as always, when I took Etaa away to visit the holy books.

That day she sat beside me as usual, though lately she found it hard to bend forward at the ornate table's edge. (Mabis had said my son—for I was sure it would be a son, just as I was sure he would hear like his mother—must be a strapping babe, perhaps even twins.) Her ungainly roundness charmed me even more than her former grace.

I had taken my lenses off in order to read close up, for with Etaa there, I had no fear of being caught unawares. She glanced down as I set the lenses on the table, and then suddenly she caught at my arm. —Meron, look— She picked up the end of the thin, dark strip that lay pinned under them, curling it between her fingers. —What is this? It's like glass, but soft as paper. And look—look! Tiny words, under your lens—

I squinted, unable to make them out, and reached for a magnifying glass. —It's plastic, that the Gods use . . . and that we used, once, in the Golden Age.   A strange excitement filled me as Etaa pulled the rest of the tape out from under the shelf into the lamplight. —How did it get here? Could the Gods have forgotten—

Etaa took up the glass and held it over the plastic strip. —Can you read it?

She didn't see me, but sat frowning, breathless with concentration, her hand toying with the silver bell at her ear. At last she looked up, her fingers barely moving as she signed, —I

can read it. It is part of a book in the old language. . . . But
it's from *before* the plague time.

—Are you sure? All our holy books had been written after
the plague; though they mentioned the wonders of the Golden
Age, they were clouded with the despair of a failing people,
and many references were unclear. My hands shook. —Read
it to me.

I held the glass and Etaa translated, until her eyes were red
and her hands trembled with fatigue. And though many things
were still unclear, because they were so far above us, one
undeniable truth stood out: —All men *could* hear, in the
Golden Age. I was right! Men weren't meant to be less than
the Gods—men *were* Gods. The Church has lost the truth in
fear since the plague time, and these false "Gods" use our
superstition to control us. I took Etaa's weary hands and
kissed them. —But our son will be the beginning of a new
Golden Age, he'll hear and see clearly, and show my people
the truth. He will be our greatest king. Etaa smiled, caught
up in my dreams, and if she smiled for her son and not for
me, it didn't lessen the fullness of my joy.

And then the moment was torn by a lash of pain that raked
my back, a blow that knocked me from my seat. My useless
eyes met billows of indigo as I rolled, and a streak of light
arcing down at my face; desperately I threw up my hands.
But before the blade could find me again, a sweep of green
velvet blocked my sight as Etaa flung herself on the attacking
priest. Fair hands dimmed the shining blade, and somehow
she drove him back from me while I got to my feet. I caught
up my lenses and drew my dagger, only to see him fling her
against the wall and bolt toward the door. I brought the priest
down as he tried to get past me; his skull cracked against the
flags, and the knife flew from his grasp.

And beyond him I saw Etaa curled on her side on the floor,
racked with a spasm of pain. She pressed her stomach, staining the velvet with blood from her slashed hands. I looked
down again into the face of my attacker, full of terror now as
my dagger rested on his throat. And saw that he was no
priest: dirty hair slipped from under his cap, his face was
young, but grimy and pinched with hardship. He was a paid
assassin out of the Newham stews, and I was sure he was a

hearer as well. And I couldn't touch him—or his master—for the Church claimed jurisdiction here. My hand tightened on the dagger hilt, and I would have slit his throat. But as blood traced my blade across his neck I felt Etaa's eyes on me, and I sickened. "Let the archbishop try you, then, for your failure, 'priest,' " I said. "And I pity you—" I struck him on the head with the dagger's butt, and felt him go limp.

Then I went to Etaa and fell on my knees beside her, raising her head. Her eyes sought me almost with hunger, and for a moment they filled with wild joy as her wounded hands brushed my face. But they tightened into fists with another spasm as she tried to form signs. —Meron . . . my child. My child . . . comes—

My throat tightened with despair. It was scarcely half the year since her conception, and that was too soon, too soon . . . I felt the back of my tunic soaking with blood, but the assassin's knife had caught in the folds of my cape and the wound was not deep. I picked Etaa up in my arms, gasping with pain, and started back through the endless halls.

Halls that were endlessly empty, until suddenly I came on the archbishop and Bishop Perrine. The archbishop saw us first, and laughter fell from his face, leaving blank horror. He hurried toward me, arms outstretched, until he met my eyes; then, and only then, did I ever see my cousin afraid. He stopped. "Your majesty—" His lips quivered; Bishop Perrine's eyes went to the trail of red on the stones behind us, and he dropped to his knees, babbling incoherently.

"My Lord . . . bishop." I staggered against the wall to save my precious burden. "If my son dies, my lord, not even the Gods will find sanctuary from me." I pushed grimly past him, and saw in my mirror that he was hurrying on toward the repository.

I found a guardsman and friendly halls at last, and summoned aid. My physicians swarmed around me like flies, binding my wound and begging me to rest; but I stood at the door of the chamber where they had taken Etaa, until finally my knees buckled and I could not stand. And then I remember little except my helpless fury, at events and my own weakness, until I woke in my canopied bed, hemmed in by kneeling attendants, to face a God. I struggled toward the only thing of real importance: —Etaa . . . my child—?

I thought the God smiled, though I couldn't focus. —I have been with them—

"No!" I lunged at him, and was pulled back by my horrified attendants.

They gibbered apologies, but he waved them aside. —The lady is well, and asks for you. And your son—yes, your majesty, your son—will live. He is well grown for one born so early, and we will watch over him.

I sank back into the pillows. —Forgive me, lord, I—I was not myself. I thank you. And now, doctor, with your aid I would go to see my Etaa . . . and my son.

The Church proclaimed that my assailant was a mad priest, who had wrongly believed me guilty of sacrilege concerning the Church's holy books; he had been summarily excommunicated and put to death for his treason, upon order of the archbishop. There were mutterings in the Church faction at court that the priest was hardly mad, but in the celebration at the birth of a royal heir they were scarcely heard. I named my son Alfilere, after my father, and to me he was the most beautiful sight on Earth. And second only to him was his mother, her own face shining with pleasure as she gazed down upon him in his golden cradle or caressed him with bandaged hands.

I began to take her with me everywhere now, seeking her impressions of the things she saw at court; and though she protested, I seated her openly beside me at table. The queen still sat at my other hand, unwilling to give up any of her position, though her eyes drove daggers into my back. Her brother absented himself from the great hall these days, and I wondered if he was sharpening a new blade of his own. But he would never dare such a blatant attack on me again, and though my advisers knew of his treason and urged me to act against him, I refused. If I attacked my cousin I would risk civil war, and I would not bring that on my people for the sake of personal revenge. But I no longer went anywhere without attendants, and I saw that my guard kept watch at all times over Etaa and her child.

But though tension whispered in the halls like the chill
drafts of winter, it could not discourage the spring that brightened my heart at the thought of my newborn son, or the
nearness of Etaa. For the Armageddon Day festivities, I
taught her, amid much laughter, to dance. I had always hated
memorizing intricate patterns and steps, the watching of ceiling mirrors, the need to be constantly keeping count. But she
was enchanted at this new challenge to her imagination, and
her enthusiasm caught me up and made me feel the beauty of
the dance.

The Armageddon celebrations, mirrored in Etaa's delighted
eyes, had not seemed so bright since I was a boy, and as I
carried my son in my arms I imagined how the same wonders
would delight him too: the poets and jugglers and acrobats,
the trained hounds and morts, the magicians flashing colored
fire, even the Gods who presided, resplendent in their shining
auras. All the gaudily clad folk feasting and dancing, driving
away the cold bleakness of dark noons that marked the equi-
nox and the grating end of a cruel winter beyond the walls.

I think, looking back, that I had never been happier than on
that evening, when Etaa danced beside me. Gowned in the
fragile colors of spring, her shining hair bound with pearls,
she was the very goddess of the Earth. Her cheeks were
flushed with excitement and her dark eyes radiant; after the
last dance I took her in my arms and kissed her, and she did
not pull away. Anything seemed possible to me then, even
that someday she might come to love me . . . as I had come
to love her, this captive goddess, in a way that I had never
loved any woman.

But, as I have always known in my saner moments, not all
things are possible, even for kings. And not long afterward
Etaa turned cold eyes on me as I entered her chamber,
looking up over Alfilere's dark curly head as he fed at her
breast.

I hesitated. —Etaa, is something wrong?

Mabis got up heavily from her stool. She moved to sit
facing away from us, still knitting, her ruddy face showing
trouble and concern.

Etaa did not answer me for a moment, but rose and took
Alfilere to his cradle near the fire, where she stood smiling

and rocking him gently. She had refused a new nurse, prefer-
ring to feed and care for her own babe, another virtue which
had pleased old Mabis. And indeed, my son's mother was
better than any nurse, for she could "feel" his needs; she
grew uneasy if he was ever beyond her hearing. At last she
came back to me, the smile fading again, and I repeated my
question.

Her pink-scarred hands snapped up with accusation. —Meron,
I know the truth now, about my people. That they're making
war on Tramaine, and being killed, because you've stolen
me. I know that they demand my return—and beyond that,
only to be left in peace by your witch-burners. But instead
you send them soldiers, to kill and burn all the more. And
you have kept it from me! And made me . . . made me forget
. . . A strange emotion tormented her face, her hands twitched
into stillness.

—Where did you learn this, Etaa?

She shook her head.

—Willem—

—You will not hurt him!   Anger and fear knotted her fingers.

—I would not hurt a child for repeating gossip.

—But it's true?

—Yes.

Her fingers searched the rough edge of the tapestry that
swayed in the draft along the wall.

—Then let me go home to my people.

I looked away, feeling disappointment stab me like an
assassin's blade. —I . . . I cannot do that. You wouldn't leave
your child. And I will not give up my son. Are you so
unhappy here? Can't you tell your people you're content to
stay? I'll make peace with them, pay whatever restitution . . .
I—need you, Etaa. I need you here with me. I depend on you
now, I—

She shut her eyes. —Meron. The man who leads my
people, who demands me back, the man you call "the Smith":
He is my husband.

—Your husband is dead!

—No!   Her foot stamped the floor.

—You saw him yourself, broken on the rocks! No man
could survive that. He was a coward; he killed himself, he

abandoned you to me, and I won't let you go. I drew a breath, struggling for control. —Your people raid and slaughter mine, and take their heads. You damn *our* souls—by our beliefs dismembered spirits cannot be freed by cremation. If there's war, then the Kedonny bring it on themselves!

Etaa drew herself up stiffly. —If you won't release me, he will come and take me!

I frowned. —If he can rise from the dead, then perhaps he will. But I doubt if even you can expect that of the Mother.

She crossed her arms, her eyes burning.

I left the chamber.

She stayed in her rooms from then on, refusing to accompany me anywhere, the drawn look of grief she had first worn returning to her face. When I came to see my son she would sit by the fire and turn her back on me, wordless. Once I came and sat beside her on the cushioned bench, with Alfilere squirming bright-eyed on my knees, wrapped in a fur bunting. I clapped my hands and saw him laugh, and as I offered him ringed fingers to chew on, looked up to see Etaa smile. I took back my fingers and signed, —Who could ask for a handsomer son? But he doesn't favor his father, I fear, little dark-eyes— I smiled hopefully, but she only looked away, brushing the silver bell at her ear, and tears showed suddenly on her cheeks.

Angry with Willem, at first I had forbidden him to visit her again; but I'd relented, knowing her solitude and sorrow. Not long after, I found him with her, his pale head in her lap, his thin shoulders shaken with sobs. She looked up as I came toward them, her eyes filled with shared pain; but Willem did not, and so she lifted his head from her lavender skirts. He rose unsteadily to make a bow, then sank exhausted onto the wine-red cushions beside her, wiping his face on his sleeve.

But I stood frozen in my place, because I had seen the thin tracks of drying blood that ran down his neck and jaw. Suddenly all his strange, frightened prescience fitted into place, and I realized the truth: my own page was a hearer, and somehow until now his family had managed to keep it a secret. Until now. My stomach twisted: His ears had been put out by the Church.

As though she had followed my thoughts, Etaa signed bitterly, —It was your Archbishop Shappistre. He hounded Willem for being with me, until he learned that Willem felt the Mother's touch—and see what he's done! He persecutes all who have Her blessings, he almost killed my child—he almost killed you! Your own kinsman! How can you let him go free, if you are king; why don't you challenge him?

I reached to the crooked scar along my back, caught in my own bitter outrage. The archbishop's open attempt to destroy me had failed, and now he waged a subtler war, spreading rumors, subverting those I trusted, tormenting those I loved. I had the power to strike him down, even in the face of the Gods; but I could not. —Etaa, it's not that simple. This isn't some villager's dispute, I can't take him out on the mead and thrash him! The royal line is split in two, and with it the loyalties of the nation; I rule a land at peace because I have tried to keep them reconciled. The archbishop is my counterbalance, but he'd upset the scales if he could, with his dreams of a Church-ruled state. He would throw this country into civil war to achieve it; he cares nothing for consequences. If I charged him with treason I'd do the same. He will stop at nothing; but I stop a long way before that.

Etaa stroked Willem's drooping head. —I don't understand the needs of nations, Meron . . . and you don't understand the needs of women and men. Suddenly she looked up at me, her face anguished. —He'll destroy you, Meron! Don't let him, don't . . . Her hands dropped hopelessly into her lap; she rose and turned away, going to the baby's cradle to comfort her gentle son.

Two days later, Willem was gone. The other pages said he had run away home. But one of Etaa's earrings, the tiny silver bells that she always wore, was missing too. I asked her where it was, and too carelessly she signed that she had lost it. And so I knew that Willem had gone east to find the Smith.

Slowly, with all the pain of birth, winter gave way at last to spring, while the Kedonny raided on our borders. Etaa mourned in her chambers, and the New Year's revels on the green were a bright, shallow mockery of the past.

And while I slept that night and dreamed of happier times, Etaa and my son disappeared.

Frantic with loss, I had the countryside searched and searched again, but there was no sign of them. There was no rumor, no clue; it was almost as if they had never been. I could get no rest, and my own lords said openly that I looked like a man possessed. The archbishop, smiling, said that perhaps the Earth had swallowed them up—and I almost came to believe him. But I learned my coachman had disappeared on the same night as Etaa, and some said they thought my carriage had gone in the night, and come back carrying no one. And so I wondered if the truth lay not in the Earth but in the sky . . . and the Gods had taken their revenge on me.

But the Kedonny ate deeper into my lands, and finally I was forced to abandon my search. I planned to raise a full army and put them to rout; but as I sent out calls to gather men, I discovered how well my archbishop had done his ungodly work. His rumors of my bewitchment had taken hold: My own people believed the Black Witch had snared me in a spell and addled my mind, then disappeared like the accursed thing she was, stealing even my son to be put to some terrible blasphemous use. They believed I would betray them to the Kedonny in battle, and that the Gods themselves had abandoned me.

Even lords who were always loyal to my father's line have deserted me for the archbishop, and those who still support me get little support themselves for the raising of an army. The word is abroad in the land that it is suicide to ride with me to war—that if I am denied, and destroyed, then the forces of Right will be served, and the Gods will save them from the pagan hordes. Damn the Church! The Gods have never intervened in a war of men; I doubt they'll do it now.

And so I leave today, with what forces I can gather, to go and save my kingdom myself, if I can. Perhaps then this new storm of ignorance will pass, and not inundate us all. Perhaps. Or perhaps it is already too late. . . .

If so, then maybe it is best that Etaa has gone, and taken my son. I only pray, to whatever true Gods may be, that they are safe, and that some day her son will return to claim his throne, and be the greatest of our kings. If she chose to leave me, I cannot blame her, for I never had the right to take her as I did. But I loved her, and I pray she will remember that too, and forgive me a little.

I often wonder if she ever loved me. If so, it was more than I deserved. But sometimes there was a look, or a sign— The hands of the summer wind are as warm and light as your touch, Etaa; it may be that your Mother has stolen you home after all. Watch over my son, and forgive his father. Give him your blessings, as you gave them to me. Etaa . . . I think I will not see you again.

But come, my lords; the Godseye keeps watch on us, and the sun is already high. They say a smith may look at a king: Then let it be the last thing he ever sees!

Part 3: The God

I understand that I'm speaking today because you wondered how a "naïve kid" in the Colonial Service was inspired to solve the Human Problem. The answer is simple—I loved Etaa, and Etaa was the mother of Alfilere.

You probably all remember the situation at the time. The Colonial Service had come upon the Humans not long before: an intelligent life form based on carbon rather than silicon, but oxygen breathers and compatible with roughly the same temperature range that we are. That made them another competitor, but only marginally; and if they were anything else but Humans, we could have expected to coexist with them. But our studies of their ongoing culture, and the scanty records of their past, indicated they were the most unrelentingly and irrationally aggressive species we'd ever encountered. Combined with a high technology, it would have made them the most dangerous, too. We'd live in peace with them willingly enough, under the circumstances, but the question I'd always heard was whether *they* would live in peace with *us*. The majority Conservative opinion was that it wasn't likely, and so our sector council ordered us to intervene, and stall their cultural progress. The Liberal faction in the Service objected, doing their best to prod the Human status quo, and that was how the trouble started.

I'm a xenobiologist, and at the time I was just beginning my career; I was also too inexperienced to question policy then, and so I blindly supported the majority's stand on

Humans. Especially since I'd had to live among Humans, to study (and watch) them, as the "coachman" for the God-hating king of Tramaine. When the Libs gave restricted records to the king, and then openly incited the neighboring Kotaane to war, we Conservatives retaliated by kidnapping Etaa, the king's Kotaane mistress, and her son, his heir. I was chosen to do the actual deed, because of my strategic position—and, frankly, my naïveté. All I had to do was keep the pair safely out of the way, they told me, and at the same time I could experience my first change-study of an unknown world. . . . All I had to do was spend an eternity alone, I discovered, on a desolate abandoned world with no one for company but a superstitious alien woman and a squalling alien brat. I didn't know whether to feel honored by the responsibility, or ashamed of being used. But I did my duty, and stole her away to the outer moon.

I sent Etaa drugged wine, and shuttered all the ports; she never knew what had happened, even when I brought the shuttle down near the ruins of the dead colony and opened the lock. I watched her on the screens as she stepped outside, waiting while the first rush of stunned dismay took her. She stumbled back, clutching her child protectively against her as the cold wind gusted, swirling the drab rust-brown grit into stinging clouds. Beyond us the naked, stony slope swept upward toward the ruins of the Human town, fangs of bitterness snapping at the clouds. I'd seen it once before, but never like this, knowing I couldn't leave it. My own eyes burned with the bleakness and the memory of the stinging wind. It would be hard to learn the unity of this world . . . it was easy to see why the Humans had failed to.

I don't know what thoughts were in Etaa's mind then; only that they probably weren't the ones I expected. But confusion and despair were on her face as she started down the ramp, the wind tugging at her long cape and stiff, ungainly skirts. Her baby had begun to cry, wailing with the wind. For the first time she was real for me, touching my emotions and stirring—pity. This was the stolen woman, used by a ruthless king, whose misery I seemed to be tied to from the start, when I'd piloted the king's carriage in her capture. She was only another victim of the cruel and senseless schisms that

divided these wretched Humans, and she'd suffer more now
and never understand why, because of them, and because of
us. . . . I felt unease pull down pity: Did I have the right—?
But she'd been a pawn, she would be a pawn; maybe that was
her destiny, and this was mine.

I left the controls at last, bracing myself to deliver the final
horror to her. I'd gotten rid of my Human makeup, and knew
my form would be starting to slip after the stress of the flight.
And no Human had ever seen a "God" unmasked, even a
God who passed for a coachman. Avoiding the velvet cushions on the floor, I went to stand at the lock.

—Meron—? She turned with a gasp to stare up at me, her
hands asking the question. I remembered she was a Kotaane
priestess, and could hear; the speculation was that the king
had taken her precisely because she *could*, out of his hatred
for tradition. Her eyes had brightened with hope and something more as she turned. It froze into terror as she saw me,
and she backed away, her fingers stiffening out in a sign to
ward off evil. It was too much like an obscenity popular with
the king's retainers; I almost laughed. That would have been
the final cruelty. I caught it in time and only spread my hands
in a peace gesture. I signed, —I will not harm you, Lady
Etaa. Have no fear. She shook her head, keeping her distance. I wondered what I must look like to her—a mockery of
a Human made of bread dough, or clay. I ducked back into
the king's "carriage" to get my hooded jacket, thinking the
more I covered the better. But as I disappeared I heard her
startled cry and footsteps behind me on the ramp. She appeared at the lock in a swirl of dust, and dropped to her knees
at my feet. —Oh, please, don't leave me here! The baby
whimpered as her signing jostled him, inside her cape. I
stared down at her, stunned; but seeing my face again she
faltered, as if she saw her own doom instead. Looking away,
she placed her wriggling child tenderly on a red velvet cush-
ion, then forced her eyes back to mine, signing, —Then have
mercy on my child. Take him with you, he's no harm to
anyone! He is a prince, return him to—to his father, King
Meron. You'll be rewarded! Give him to anyone . . . but let
him live—

I bent down and picked up the child; he gazed at me in

fascination, and suddenly he began to laugh. Inexplicably delighted, I held him close; then, slowly, I passed him back to his mother's arms. Hope shattered on her face, and she flinched when I touched her.

I stepped back. —Etaa, you aren't being abandoned in this godforsaken place. I am your guardian; I'll stay with you here, to look after you and your child. You've been . . . exiled, and it will be a hard life for us both. But it won't last forever, only until—certain matters are settled in Tramaine. But it has to be this way until then; you have no choice. This is your new home.

She watched rigidly, the need to ask a hundred questions struggling against the certainty that she didn't need to ask, but only accept, and endure, this new trial. She looked down at last, and I saw the trembling lines of her face grow quiet with resolve; she would adapt. I felt relieved, and somehow surprised.

—Who has ordered this? Not . . . not the king? Her dark eyes flickered up again with a kind of urgency.

—No. I reassured her, thinking how she must hate the man, and not wanting the truth to seem any harsher than it was. —It—is the will of the Gods, Etaa.

Her flush of relief turned to a sudden frown, and she looked hard at me for a moment. But she pulled back into her silence, and signed nothing more, waiting for me.

I gave her a clingsuit and boots like my own to replace her awkward gown, then waited outside the craft in the wind, knowing the preoccupation with bodily shame that these heterosexuals had. She appeared at last, with her hair bound up and her child slung at her back in the folds of her cape. The heavy jacket flapped around her like a tent, but I could see that the suit had adapted to her well enough to keep her warm. I sealed the clasps on her jacket while she watched me, intent and suspicious. Then I unloaded supplies, and sealed the hatch behind us. The lifeboat rose silently; the king's carriage would be home before he missed it. I wished we could have been, too.

We struggled up the hill toward the ruined town, battered by blowing grit and dead, unidentifiable vegetation. The ragged maze of the tree-eaten ruins broke the back of the wind as

we reached the summit; we stood panting and rubbing our
burning eyes while the wind moaned and clattered in frustration overhead. I led Etaa through the rubble to a shelter that
stood intact, a prefabricated box that still had its roof. As we
stumbled along the street she watched with awe, but without
the sickly dread Tramanians had for the cities of their dead
past. I wondered if she had ever seen a pre-plague Human
city even on her own world, not knowing she didn't understand that this wasn't her own world.

The Humans had colonized the inner, major moon of a gas
giant they had named Cyclops, which circled the yellow star
Mehel. This outer, barely smaller moon was just marginally
habitable, and they had only tried to establish a colony here to
escape from the disease that decimated them at home. They
had failed, and all that remained was this town, under skies
that were endlessly gray with clouds. Etaa never saw the
change in the heavens, and never knew there had been one
because she never asked a question: We communicated as
little as possible, and often I caught her staring at me, her
eyes somewhere between fear and speculation.

But once she insisted that she needed to gather healthful
herbs for the baby, and when I tried to tell her that our
supplies had everything she would need, she gathered him up
protectively inside her jacket and slipped out the door. I went
after her, armed, because I still wasn't sure exactly what else
was making its home in this dead city. For over an hour I
watched her search for a trace of the life she knew, but
nothing had survived the departure of the Humans. At last,
shivering and defeated, she brushed past me without meeting
my eyes, and returned to the shelter. After that she communicated less than ever, only glaring at me as if this terrible
strangeness were somehow my doing too. She never ventured
outside again by choice, and never left her son alone with me.

I spent most of my time outside, struggling with equipment
in the bitter wind as I tried to gather background data for my
ecological change-study. The deserted Human town crouched
like a tethered beast on the rim of the plateau, waiting with
un-Human patience for the return of its masters while time
and the gnarled hands of the tree-shrubs worried it toward

oblivion. Beyond the plateau's rim eons of sediment from some murky forgotten sea lapped away to grim distant peaks. But closer in, the stone had been shattered by countless faultings, eroded by the winter rains and the sand-sweeping wind until a network of twisting sheer-walled canyons had been eaten into its undulating plain. The eternal wind sang through the maze, whipping the iron-reddened dust of the washes, where flashing water roared and passed with every drowning downpour. The wind was a bully, tumbling the slow, heavy clouds, breaking them open for a sudden glimpse of burnished heaven and shutting them again before you found it. Land and sky merged at the dusky horizon, and everywhere the colors repeated, shadow-violet and rust, burnt orange and fragile lavender, all merging toward gray in the somber light.

What flora there was was carbon-based, mainly lichen and an omnipresent hummocky dark moss. The sparse scatter of higher forms climaxed in the tree-shrub that dotted the ruins, a grotesque thing that looked like it was growing upside down. I knew almost nothing about the animal life, the preliminary survey having been so cursory; from time to time dark things scuttled at the edge of my vision, and in the updrafts above the canyons I could sometimes glimpse a shadowy, undulating form. As I began to watch these "gliders" in flight, I first felt the change stir within me, a blind groping toward understanding, a restlessness, a formless need to seek the new equilibrium . . . for the first time I wasn't being forced into a preset mold, this time my body would find its own place freely in the unity of a new unknown. I was fulfilled in the knowledge that now I knew nothing of the life on this world . . . but soon, in a way, I would know everything.

And I wondered whether that was the true reason why we feared the Humans: For all the studies we'd done, we had never been to their origin place or really "gone native" among them. Because we were forced to non-natural imitation among this transplanted stock, we had never really *felt* what it was to be Human. We wore false faces, false bodies; We saw them act and react around us, but never knew what moved them to it.

Exploring the dead Human town, I found myself thinking

of how it would feel to colonize an unknown world, to think you were secure and settled—and then to be struck by an alien epidemic: to see half the population die, the survivors left genetically mutilated, sterile and deaf and blind . . . to lose contact with the rest of the Human kind, to see your proud civilization torn apart by fear and your technology crumble to barbarism . . . to lose everything.

And then to come back, to begin again from nothing in a treacherous, silent universe, and come so far—only to be stopped again, by us. They had adapted; and there was nothing we admired more. Yet the Colonial Service held them back; we counted ourselves lucky that they had suffered so much. And I'd never had any doubt about the morality of our position.

But then I shared a deserted world with Etaa, and passed through the change, and was changed in ways I had never meant to be.

The changes were resisted, in the beginning, as change always is. My physical deterioration of form had slowed, while my body chemistry fumbled toward an understanding of its new environment; but I stayed longer and longer out in the bitter days of the alien spring. My physical change was also slowed by the presence of Etaa; I went on instinctively mimicking the form of my closest companion—my only companion, for dreary weeks on end, until the return of Iyohangziglepi with supplies, and with them, the chance to hear a spoken word again and see a friendly face. And heard the gradually more agonizing reports that things in Tramaine continued unresolved. The Liberals had aroused the Kotaane, and now there seemed to be no stopping them. And as long as the uncertainty lasted, the king's son had to be securely out of it.

I began to worry sometimes that Etaa would break down in her endless solitude, since she rarely even had my escape into the greater world around the dead town. But she came from a people used to long, buried winters; and if she sometimes tended the fire below the window needlessly, or slept too long, and cried in her sleep, I tried to leave her alone. We all cope however we can, and she wouldn't have listened anyway. But I watched her with her child, as I watched the gliders by day wheeling over the maze, and again I felt an indefinable shifting in my soul.

Her thoughts were wrapped in her eternal cloak of silence, and only the baby, Alfilere, could draw her out. She would sit rocking him for hours while rain dinned on the roof, the silver bell she wore on one ear singing softly. She made him toys from scraps, smiled when he pulled her hair, tickled him while he played naked on her cloak by the fire, until their laughter filled the bleak room with light. She made the best of their new captivity, and so her son thought the world was a delightful place.

But sometimes as he fed at her breast her gaze would drift out of the present; a wistfulness would fill her eyes like tears and pass into a deeper knowledge that was wholly alien, and wholly Human. Sometimes too she would look into her child's face as though she saw someone else there, and then cover his face with longing kisses. She called him by a Kotaane name, "Hywel," and never "Alfilere," and I suspected that she knew he was her husband's child, and not the king's—this child of hope and sorrow. This child who was the center of her world—to whom Etaa, who was named "the blessed one," could never give the most unique and wonderful "blessing" she possessed, the gift of speech. Because she would never know she possessed it.

Her Alfilere was a bright, gentle baby who smiled more than he cried, and only cried when he had a reason. His awareness of the world grew every day, and soon I shared Etaa's fascination at each change. But when he first found his voice, babbling and squeaking to himself for hours on end, she only watched him with perplexity. Her people believed that hearing was the manifestation of another's thoughts and soul, and I knew this was her first child. Though she clapped her hands to get his attention, she never made another sound for him except her laughter, only moving her hands over and over while he watched, repeating the signs for simple words. Usually he would only catch her fingers and try to stuff them into his mouth.

And watching this woman, who was strong and fertile and gifted with full hearing and sight, who represented everything a Human could be . . . or should be . . . I suddenly realized what it would be never to find fulfillment, because you had even lost the sound of the word . . . *the feel*— In desperation I began to recite, "I am the eye that meets my gaze, I am the limb . . ."

Etaa started and stared at me; I'd never spoken before in front of her. Surprise and consternation pulled at her face; she looked back at her son, whose cheerful babbling must have made as much sense as mine, and then across the room at me again. On an impulse I repeated the lines, and she frowned. She picked up the baby and moved to the far corner, huddling inside her tentlike jacket on her ruined mattress . . . touching her throat. She coughed.

It wasn't long before I caught her mimicking the sounds her baby made. In a week or so more she had learned to hum for him. At first I was half guilty about what I had done; but gradually I convinced myself that it wouldn't come to anything. Though I wasn't even sure anymore that I'd done anything wrong.

And then the day came when the clouds parted. As I prowled the rim of the canyons, grateful for the slowly warming weather, brilliance suddenly opened up around me and all across the canyonlands a shower of golden sunlight was falling. For a moment I stood gaping at the incomprehensible glory until, glancing up, I saw the red "eye" and the banded green face of Cyclops peering back at me, filling a ragged piece of sky so bright it was almost black. I had taken off my braces to free my legs for change—running had gotten to be awkward and nearly ridiculous—but I ran back to the shelter and ducked in the open doorway. "Etaa, come and look!"

She stopped Alfilere in mid-whirl as she danced him around the room, and blinked at me, her smile fading. I realized I'd been shouting. I repeated it in sign language. —You can see the sky.

She followed me outside, and set Alfilere down to roll in the springy moss while she stood beside me, entranced by the sun-brindled, golden land and sky. I had almost forgotten the majesty of Cyclops wearing the sun for a crown, only a little diminished even from this outer moon. I remembered again that the sky the Humans took so much for granted was the

most beautiful one I had ever seen. —Look, Etaa, can you see
that dark spot against the face of Cyclops? That's your Earth.

She reddened as if I had insulted her. Only then did I
realize that she had no idea we were on another world, and in
my blind inexperience I had no idea of what that could really
mean. —We traveled to Laa Merth, the moon you see from
Earth, in the king's carriage; the Gods can make it travel
between the worlds. You can see your Earth, up in the sky
now instead; both these worlds are moons of—

She shut her eyes angrily, refusing me. —The Mother is
the center of all things. *This* is the Earth! She folded her
arms, then turned away toward the edge of the cliff, a small,
stubborn figure plucked by the wind. She was still the Mother's priestess, and I suddenly realized that she was as true a
believer as any Tramanian, and that her chthonic Goddess
was just as tangible and real. As if by her will, the clouds
closed over the last shining piece of the sky and rain splat-
tered down, pocking the russet dust with spots the size of
kiksuye buds.

Etaa turned back from the cliff's edge as the rain began,
her eyes scanning for her child—and screamed. I jerked
around, following her gaze, to see the shadow-form of a
glider plummeting like dark death out of the clouds toward
little Alfilere. She came running, her arms waving desperately. I pulled my stunner and fired, not knowing where a
glider was vulnerable, but hoping the shock would divert its
strike. I ran too, and saw the incredible, leathery balloon of
the glider billow with the shock, heard myself shouting,
"Here, here—damn you!" And heard the piercing shrill of
outrage, saw the sky darken as the glider swerved to strike at
me. Warty mottled skin flayed me, I staggered with the
impact of its shapeless bulk. I heard my own scream then and
the glider's moaning wail as a pincer beak closed over my
arm, sank in, and snapped my body like a whip into the air.
The glider shuddered at my weight, and hysterically I saw
myself being crushed where it fell. . . . But then suddenly my
arm was free, the air brightened—and I slammed back down
onto the earth. The glider soared out over the canyon's rim,
still keening.

I lay in the patch of blessed moss staring up into the rain,

feeling as if a stake had been driven through me, pinning me
to the ground. My torn arm throbbed with the beating of my
heart, and I drew it up, strangely light, to see that the end was
gone, bitten through. I studied the oozing stump where my
hand had been, somehow unimpressed, and then let it drop
back to my side.

But it didn't drop, for Etaa caught it in her own hands,
making small moans of horror while Alfilere wailed his fright
against my leg.

" 'S all right, 's all right . . ." I said stupidly, wondering
what had happened to my voice, and why she didn't seem to
understand me. I managed to sit up, shaking her off, and then
stand. And then finally to realize that I didn't know what I
was doing, before I fell to my knees again, weeping those
damn sticky silicon-dioxide tears and cursing. But strong
arms pulled me up again, and with Alfilere on one arm and
me on the other, Etaa led her two weeping children home out
of the rain.

I collapsed on my bedding, just wanting to lie in peace and
sleep it through, but Etaa badgered me with frantic solici-
tude. —I'm a healer, let me help you, or you will die! The
blood—

And I discovered that with a hand missing, there was no
way I could explain. I frowned and pushed her away, and
finally I held up my wounded arm and shook it at her; it had
closed off immediately, and there was no more blood, nothing that needed to be done. She pulled back with a gasp of
disbelief and looked at me again, her eyes asking the questions I couldn't answer. Then she brushed my cheek gently
with her fingertips, and there was no revulsion in her touch.
At last I let her bury me in warm covers and build up the fire,
and then I slid down and down into darkness, through layers
of troubled dreams.

I slept for two days, and when I woke my mind was clear
and fully my own again, and I was starving. As if she knew,
Etaa plied me with hot soup that I almost gulped down,
though it probably would have poisoned me. I rejected it
unhappily, unable to explain again. She looked down, hurt
and guilty, as though I were rejecting her. I touched her face,
in the gesture of comfort I'd seen Humans use, and signed,

one-handed, —Can't . . . can't. Mine . . . cans— I waved at
my own food supply, stacked by the Human supplies on the
dusty shelves by the door. Her head came up, as if she should
have known, and she left me. I looked at my wound and saw
signs that the tissue was regenerating already. But it only
made me realize the bigger problem: I'd been slowly reab-
sorbing all my limbs. Now that there was a need, and a
reason, how could I communicate anything?

Etaa returned with an armful of cans and dropped them
beside me on the floor. Then, kneeling, she held out the pad
and stylus I'd been using for my sketches outside. I took
them; she signed, beaming with inspiration, —Write for me.

I'd heard the king had taught her to read the archaic "holy
books," but I hadn't believed it. I printed, clumsily, "Can
you read this: 'My name is Etaa.' " I handed back the pad.

She smiled and signed, —My name is . . . She glanced up
at me, puzzled. We used an arbitrary sign/symbol system
based on the Human alphabet to record the Human hand-
speech, and she had never seen her name written down at all.
I pointed at her. She smiled again. —My name is . . . The
middle fingers curled and straightened on her left hand, she
held her right hand turned palm down, toward the earth.
—Etaa. I am a priestess, I can read it.

I smiled too, in relief, and showed her how to pull open
cans.

After I had eaten she brought Alfilere to me, half asleep,
and gently sat him in my lap. I cradled him in the crook of
my wounded arm; he settled happily, trying to nurse my
jacket. Etaa laughed, and a feeling both strange and infinitely
familiar came to me like spring, and left me breathless . . .
and content.

—Thank you for saving my child. Etaa's dark eyes met
mine directly, without loathing. —I was afraid of you, before,
because of your strangeness. I think there was no need to be
afraid. You have been . . . have been very kind. Again her
eyes dropped, heavy with guilt. I thought of the king.

I printed laboriously, shamed by my own hidden prejudices,
"So have you; though you had every right to be afraid, and
hate me. Etaa, my strangeness will keep growing with time.
But believe me that it will never harm you."

She nodded. —I believe that. . . . Can't you eat the food I make? It's better than those— Her wrist flicked with faint disdain at the emptied cans; I wondered if they looked as disgusting to her as the coarse Human meals did to me.

I hesitated before I wrote an answer. "I can't eat meat." I didn't add that I couldn't eat anything at all that wasn't on a silicon base like my own body.

—The Gods do many things strangely, besides changing their shape. Meron was wiser than he knew; you are false gods indeed to his people.

She watched me coolly, almost smug in her conviction. I remembered hearing of her confrontation with another God, back in the dreary halls of the royal palace.

She was probably gratified by my stupefaction. I wrote, "How did you know?"

—The king knows. He saw a God once in an inhuman form; he knows you are not the ones promised to his people.

I frowned. So that was why the king scorned the Gods: He had discovered the truth. Suddenly his repressed anger and his ill-concealed hatred of the Church fell into perspective, and I realized there could have been more to the man than royal arrogance and consuming ambition. But that hardly mattered now. "Who does the king think we are?"

—He doesn't know . . . and neither do I. We only know your power over us, over our people. She studied me, and her dark-haired child blissfully asleep again in my lap. —Who *are* you . . . what are you? Why do you interfere in our lives?

"Because we're afraid of you, Etaa."

Her eyebrows rose as she read the answer, and her hands rose for more questions, but I shook my head.

She hesitated, and then her face settled into a resigned smile. She signed, —Why is it that you don't wear golden robes like the other Gods?

I laughed and wrote, "I'm a young God. We don't have all the privileges." Besides which, it was impossible for a biologist to make valid observations of any xenogroup while wearing golden robes.

She smiled again, the conspiratorial smile of one who was herself a Goddess incarnate. —What shall I name you?

"Name me Tam." I gave her my name-sign among Hu-

mans, since Wic'owoyake would have been unmanageable. I
felt myself yawn, a trait I'd picked up from the Humans too,
and reluctantly gave up Alfilere's sleeping form to my own
need for sleep. He clung to me with his strong, tiny hands as
his mother lifted him away, and I felt a rush of pleasure that
he had taken to me so. I slept again, and had more dreams;
dreams of change.

I don't know exactly when I decided to teach Etaa to speak.
The desire arrived on a wave of exasperation, as it got to be
more and more trouble to write out every word of every
answer I made. My hand regenerated, but the change over-
took it, and my other hand was getting too stiff and stubby to
make signs or hold a stylus. Teaching Etaa speech meant
going against the rules in a way I had never even considered
before, interfering with Human society by adding a major
cultural stimulus. But then, I thought, what was I doing here
with her in the first place, and what were the Libs doing
waging war back in Tramaine? I'd be guilty of Liberalism
too, but I had to be able to communicate—and so I convinced
myself that even if she could learn to speak, it would never
come to anything among a people who were still mostly deaf.

And so while the final drenching storm of the rainy season
battered the helpless land and rattled on the roof, I explained
to Etaa how she knew there *was* rain on the roof, when other
Humans didn't. I called her attention to the sounds her child
made, and the ones I'd made—and the ones she had begun to
make herself. I showed her the patterns they could weave, as
her hands wove patterns in the air. I sang her a song from one
of the pre-plague Human tapes, and twice again she asked me
to sing it, her whole body tight with excitement—and, almost, fear. The third time I sang it she began to hum along,
tonelessly at first, while Alfilere sat in her lap chewing a strip
of plastic and adding his own delighted babysong. But abruptly
she broke off, glancing from side to side nervously. Wrapping her cloak of silence around her again, she signed, —This
is not right! The Mother tells us that we feel—hear—the inner
soul of all things. This "voice" is not from the soul, not real
. . . perhaps we weren't meant to use it, or we would *know*.
Her earring jingled with her desire and uncertainty.

"Etaa," I scrawled patiently, "your people did know, once; all Humans did. But after the plague they forgot how to use their voices, because no one could hear them. You've seen the Tramanian nobles move their lips, and understand each other—they've forgotten their voices too, but they remember how a mouth was used to make signs. A voice was given to every Human, so they could let people know how they felt. Think how much more you know about other creatures because you can hear their voices—feel their souls. Think how much more you'd know about people, too, if they knew how to use their voices fully!"

She stared at the message for a long time, and then she made a series of signs in Kotaane; I realized she was praying. She gathered up a handful of dust from the floor and let it drift between her fingers. At last she took a long breath, and her eyes told me before her hands did, —I will learn it.

Once she had decided, she was never silent, practicing her sounds to me or to Alfilere, or to the gliders on the warming winds of summer if no one else would listen. She immediately learned to tell one sound from another as she heard it, to my relief, and I put away my pad and stylus once I had taught her the phonemes of the pre-plague speech. Making them herself was harder, and in the beginning she answered in an earnest singsong of slurred and startling imitations, making her own translations by hand as she went along. But slowly her instinct for forming sounds sharpened; she laughed and marveled at the endless surprises hidden in her own throat. And so did I, as though together we had triumphed over ignorance and fear, and had begun to find our own private unity.

We began to spend more and more of our time together in conversation, too. She told me of her people and her life as their priestess, and about the man she loved, who had been her other half and made her whole. And that she had lost him . . . but no more than that. She kept Alfilere close in her arms as she spoke, the living symbol of her lost joy. It moved me in ways I couldn't explain, that would have made no sense to her; and somehow for the first time I began to feel the real nature of heterosexuality, and sense the kinds of love and desire that made it possible, the ties that could bind such a terrible wound of dichotomy.

I almost told her then that I had seen her husband, and that I knew he was still alive. She had asked me often for news of the king, and of the Smith, who led her people against Tramaine. When she asked about the Smith, sorrow and longing for the past made her tremble. But I thought she couldn't know that the Smith and her man were the same: that the Libs had found him broken at the bottom of the cliff and saved his life, and had used his own love and outrage to make him their tool for change. He fought for her now like a hero out of Kotaane legend . . . and he might still die for her in the end. And so, though I told her what I'd heard about the Smith and the king, to spare her further anguish I never told her what I knew.

Etaa pressed her curiosity about my nature too, as we began to feel more free with one another. Who was I? What was I? Why were we here among Humans? I was forbidden by my training to give her the answers; but I gave them to her anyway. Cut off from everything, with even my own form getting unfamiliar, this separate world I shared with Etaa and her son was suddenly more important than my own—and in a way, more real. If I had been less impulsive, or more experienced, maybe I wouldn't have become involved; but if I hadn't, this galaxy would be a different place today.

But Etaa had been open with me, and so I opened myself in return. I told her about my "home" far off among the stars, farther away than she could ever imagine—so far away that I had never even seen it; how I had been born in space, and followed my parents into the Colonial Service. I tried to tell her how many worlds there are, and of the limitless varieties of form to be found upon them, all lit by the unifying fire of life. How much of it she believed, I'll never know, but her eyes shone with the light of other suns, and she always pressed for more.

I never intended to be fully open about our purpose on her world, but I felt she had a right to know something about why she had been stolen into exile. So I told her we had come to make things comfortable for people on Earth—so that they would never want to leave it and intrude on our stars. We had helped the Tramanians to lead better lives, and if the Kotaane ever "needed" us we'd help them too. I explained to her

about the starfolk faction that wanted to stir up trouble among
her people (and stir up progress too, but that I didn't say):
How they had encouraged the Kotaane to fight a painful,
vicious war they could only lose, and caused endless suffering and misery, when the rest of us wanted only to bring
peace to her Earth. But Tramaine's king had begun the war
by stealing her, and so we had rescued her from him, to help
stop the ill-feeling (but primarily to keep the king from
raising an heir to the throne who would be hostile to us, but I
didn't say that, either). Let the angry king win the battle with
the Kotaane but lose the war for progress, and the Libs would
suffer a policy setback it would be hard to get over.

Etaa listened, but when I finished I noticed her dark eyes
fixed on me, as bright and hard as black diamonds in the
firelight. She said, "If you have taken me to save me from
the king, then why won't you let me go to my people? You
say it would stop the war—"

I hesitated. "Because the war wouldn't stop now, Etaa.
Too much else is involved. When the war is over you can go
home; it's not safe for you now, while the king could still
search for you." And so could the Liberals, and they would
have found her.

She set her silver bell ringing softly, with fingers that were
still nervous to form a reply. "I *know* why the war will not
stop. You say starfolk want peace for us, and comfort, and
only a few wish us trouble. Then tell me why the 'Gods' urge
the Neaane to burn my people and persecute them! My people
are not fools to be misled, they fight because they have good
cause, and the cause is you! The Neaane were our friends
until you came to them, and now they spit on us. You offer
us your help, 'God.' Spare us, we've had enough of it.'' She
caught up Alfilere, who had been placidly stuffing a rag doll
into my empty boot, and stood glaring at me before she
turned away to her pallet in the corner.

"You've learned to speak very well, Etaa," I said weakly.

She glanced up at me from the shadows, disappointment
softening her words. "Better than you do, Tam."

I settled down in my own darkened corner, listening to the
sounds of Alfilere nursing himself to sleep, and his mother's
sighs. And thought about the strains on a culture when new

ideas come too fast, and the need for an escape valve to ease the pressure, a catharsis . . . the Humans had needed a lot of them, in their past, and the Tramanians had needed one now, so we let them have it. We let them kill the Kotaane. It was a vicious escape, but they were vicious creatures. . . . But did that make it right? Not by our philosophy of unity; not by our standards. And we upheld those standards, or I thought we did. All life is our life, and so we do not wantonly destroy any species, no matter how repulsive or threatening it is to us. We meddle, yes, to protect ourselves. But how far should it go? What about the kharks, the wholesale destruction of so many, for the "comfort" of the Humans? The kharks were the most highly developed species indigenous to the planet. Was it right to put them so far below the Human intruders? Had the Human lust for destruction infected us too—or did this politic blindness to the philosophical ideal go on everywhere?

I hadn't been everywhere—I'd hardly been anywhere, and I'd never questioned my teachings; I'd never had cause. The Liberal faction argued for more xeno self-determination, and I couldn't see the point, because with Humans it was suicide. The Libs tampered with Human society to overthrow our settled status quo, to force the sector council to accept a "better" one, and to do it caused Human bloodshed and chaos. The Libs revolted me—but had we been more honest, or only bigger hypocrites? Suddenly there were no answers; there were only Humans who suffered and died for their "Gods," and the words "More atrocities are committed in the name of religion than for any other reason." A Human quotation. I fell asleep at last, aching with fatigue and indecision, and dreamed that I met the Human empire, come to reclaim its lost colony: a colony of the deaf and blind, living in ignorant stagnation. And with the guns of their warships trained on me the Humans said, "What have you done to our children . . . our children . . . our children . . . ?"

While Etaa went through the greatest change in her life, the evolutionary changes my body was undergoing speeded up, as though my instincts had finally become attuned to the rhythm of this new world, and my body had chosen its most suitable form. Etaa never referred to the change at first, too unsure even to ask me questions. But at last, one evening, she came to stand beside me while I played with Alfilere, now more awkward than he was, and making him bounce with sudden baby laughter. Cool, dry breezes fingered her dark hair, and she asked with lips and hands, "Must you change?"

I nodded as much as I could. "I'm committed, now."

"Why?"

"Why must I change? Because it was planned that I would, for the protection of us both on an unknown world. It helps me know what to expect." The specter of a glider struck behind my eyelids: I'd recorded that this world was too unknown, that the adaptation had left me vulnerably in-between for too long. "Or why do I change?" I opened my eyes. "Because . . . every living creature changes as its environment changes, that's called evolution; but my people have the ability to change very fast. What takes most creatures many lifetimes to do, we can do in months, instinctively—in a way, like your rainbow flies change the colors of their wings in an instant, to match a flower. We've learned to control the changes when we want to, and freeze them—but when we need to understand the system behind the form, nature has to take its own course."

"Her course," Etaa said mildly. "Will—will you still speak with me when you are changed?"

I smiled, and Alfilere giggled, blinking up at me with wide brown eyes. "I think so. I need my voice now."

Her smile broke apart, her speech broke down into gestures. —I wish I could change, as you do! Mother, let me change my being and start again; let me lose my memories, and . . . and my sins— She rubbed her hand across her mouth like a child, pressing back the bitter misery.

"Etaa . . ." I raised myself up, holding Alfilere. "However you changed, your mind and soul would still be the same—with all the bonds to hold you. But however you changed, you couldn't choose better than to be who you are." I remembered how I'd looked forward to my change, my hope and anticipation, and said, "If you knew the truth, I wish I didn't have to change. I—I'd rather stay Human with you." I laughed. "I never thought I'd hear that—but it's true. It's true."

She took Alfilere from me and slipped open her clingsuit as he nuzzled her in hunger. She stroked his curly head and smiled again at me, her eyes so strong with feeling that I could barely meet them. "Thank you," she said, very clearly; and I knew I had been given my reward.

The change reabsorbed and reformed my Human limbs, and I settled squatly to the ground. My skin mottled rust and gray, expansible air sacs made my leathery hide sag into whispering folds: I was becoming a glider—a creature of the air, bound to the earth by my own unsureness. To be an earthbound glider was clumsy and exasperating; it was difficult even to use a recorder for my observations, and worst of all, I itched all over with the changes, and couldn't scratch. Etaa reconciled herself with her usual determined grace; she spent her evenings singing off-key to her child while she sat beside me scratching my back with a stick, and my alien body sang with relief.

During the days I haunted the cliffs, watching the gliders swing and soar, hunting far out over the maze—or sometimes closer in. Seeing me, they would set up a moaning that started tonal vibrations in my own air sacs; they lured and cajoled . . . until at last my alien desires slipped free of my inhibitions and I threw myself from the cliff and joined them. My flaccid body ballooned as the sacs expanded and filled with air: I could fly. Battered and caressed by the wind, my elemental god, mindless with exhilaration and terror, I probed the limits of the constant sky. I was one with the wind and the cloud-shadow; without thought, with only the flow of light into darkness, time into eternal timelessness, motion to rest to motion.

At last I came back to myself and remembered my duty, and my reality. I returned to the shelter, to find the hot, rising winds had turned cold in the long shadows of evening. Etaa looked at me strangely, as if somehow she knew where I had been. For a moment I saw envy in her eyes, the envy of one who could feel the unity of all things for one who could share in it.

But as I grew apart from Etaa in one way, suddenly and unexpectedly I found that I had become much closer to her in another, more profound way: I discovered that I had become pregnant. I was very young for that, barely twice her age, and separated from my own people, everyone I cared for; there was no stimulus—and yet I was pregnant. And then I realized my stimulus had been Etaa and her laughing Alfilere. But they were aliens. There was no one here of my own people to share a birth with, no one I loved, not even a pregnant stranger. How could I bring a child into the world without conjugation, to be a part of no one but me: a solitary-child, not a child of shared love, and without namesakes or a family? I struggled alone with my despair, hiding it from Etaa behind the growing strangeness of my face, until the supply shuttle came again. But Iyohangziglepi could only report ''no change'' in Tramaine, and sharing my misery only seemed to deepen it in the end, as I watched the shuttle climb toward the sullen clouds and turned back alone to the ruined town.

But like all natural things, I was prepared by nature to be glad, and when finally I was ready for the first partition, my fears disappeared and astonished pride filled the void they left behind. A secret pride, which I kept hidden from Etaa as I had hidden my pain, because I didn't know what her reaction would be. She had accepted everything until now—because Human culture had not progressed to the point where ''miracles'' were impossible—but my protective instincts kept me silent. I only made her promise to avoid a darkened back room of our shelter, and hoped she would obey.

Not trusting her with that one secret of the differences between us, thinking that one mother of a child could not learn to understand another, was the worst thing I could ever have done. And somehow I knew it, when I heard her shriek of horror; knew it, as I struggled frantically back to the shelter from the fields: She had entered the forbidden room and found my child.

''Etaa, no!'' I floundered to the doorway, wild with frustration and grief.

''Tam, hurry, help me, a beast—!''

''Etaa!'' My voice broke with fury—she froze with the stick in her hand, over the formless bleeding lump of gray still quivering on the floor. Its piteous cries shrilled in the range that only I could hear, fading now as its life faded.

"Etaa"—the words burned my mouth—"what have you done?"

Etaa dropped the stick and backed away from me, frightened and confused. She lifted Alfilere, crying now with his own confusion and fright, and stood staring from me to the bundle of living parts that cowered on their nest, all that remained of my half-finished child. Her lips trembled. "Hywel . . . Hywel crawled into this room. And when I came after, I found—I found—*that* creeping around him."

"Etaa, that . . . is my child."

"No!" Revulsion flared in her eyes, against the truth, or against her deed, or both.

"Yes . . ." I moved to the quivering cluster, avoiding the part that lay still and silent now, and the rest gathered close, mewing for comfort and warmth.

An anguished cry tore itself from Etaa; I looked up to see her bury her face against her own child. She sank down on the dusty floor, sobbing her desolation.

I held my little ones close, and groped for the strength, the words, to help us both. "I should have told you . . . I should have warned you. They're helpless, Etaa, they wouldn't harm your son. Among—among my people, we don't have children the way you do, all in a finished piece. We form them a part at a time, by duplicating each part of ourselves; the way I was able to grow another hand, when I needed one. Some parts serve an extra purpose, protecting the rest, that are more specialized; they might have stung him . . . but it's harmless."

She looked up at me, shaking her head, her mouth drawn too tight for words.

"I should have told you, Etaa."

"They . . ." She took a long breath. ". . . they are—yours?"

"Yes."

"But, I th-thought . . . ?"

"You thought I was a man? I am. But I'm also a woman. We don't come together with another to form a child; we form our own and choose someone we love for sharing: a part of our child for a part of theirs, after the birth."

She groaned again, softly, fighting for acceptance. "Oh, Mother, help me . . . Oh, *Tam*, what have I done to you?" She clutched Alfilere against her so hard that he squalled in protest.

I looked away. She had done what all Humans did, acted
from fear, reacted with violence, inflicted pain and death
blindly out of ignorance. I had been a Human once, and had
despised them; but only now, after I'd lost Human form, had
I really learned anything about the Human mind and spirit—
and now, in the face of this most terrible act, I found I could
only blame it on myself. "It—wasn't your fault. And this
hurt can be mended . . . we're more fortunate than you that
way. It would never have happened, if you'd known all
along."

But she only sat rocking her child, the bell on her ear
singing softly with her helpless grief.

Etaa spent long hours alone in the days that followed,
gazing out across the sighing, broken world from the doorway
of the shelter or walking the rim of the cliffs with her baby at
her back. The clouds that filled the sky now were only wind
clouds, dark and licked with lightning, never dripping enough
moisture to settle the endless dust. The wind had grown hot
and parched, shredding the clouds and sweeping the dust high
into the upper air, to fade the brazen blue that sometimes
broke through into this land of somber hues. She watched the
sky with yearning as Midsummer's Day approached, and
when it came she performed makeshift Kotaane rituals; but
clouds hid the triumph of the Sun, and she left them unfin-
ished, her eyes haunted and empty.

At dusk she came to me where I crouched in the doorway
watching the luminous fantasy-face of billowing Cyclops wink
behind the clouds. I heard Alfilere murmur as he slept,
somewhere in the firelight behind us. She pushed a dark curl
back from her eye, brushed at it irritably as it slipped down
again. At last she said, "It's true, isn't it, Tam?"

"What?" I waited, knowing there was more troubling her
than the secret of my child.

"What you told me: that we're not on the Earth anymore.
That we're on Laa Merth? And"—she struggled to keep her
voice steady—"and that little speck that you see, passing
over the face of the Cyclops like a fly . . . that's the Earth?
I've watched the sky, and it is different; the Cyclops is
shrunken, the bands on her robe are twisted . . . everything is
different here. I think it must be true."

"Yes. It's all true."

"Our legends tell how Laa Merth once had children of her own, but the Cyclops destroyed them. This must be their town, and so that must be true too."

"Yes." I wondered if there was any truth in the Kotaane myths about the source of the Human plague.

"But our legends say that the Mother is the center of all things, She is greater than all things. How can She be a speck on the face of the Cyclops!"

My throat tightened with the pain that shook her voice, and I couldn't answer.

"Tam." Her fingers reached down, scraping my rough hide. "I know nothing; it is all lost on the wind. Tell me what is true, Tam." She sank down beside me, her voice wheedling and her eyes wild. "What shall I believe in now?"

"Etaa, I—can't . . ." Her fingers convulsed on my back, telling me that I *had* to, now: that my pitiless, self-centered world had torn her world away and thrown her into the darkness of the void. Her faith was her strength against adversity, and without faith she would shatter, we would all shatter. "Etaa, the Mother is—"

"There is no Mother! Tell me the truth!"

I closed my eyes, wondering what truth was. " 'Mother' and 'Earth' . . . are the same to you, in your language, in your mind. But the Earth is also the world where you live, and a mother is what you are, and I am, a bearer of life. And those things are both still real, and wonderful. Your Earth looks very small now, but only because it's far away; like Laa Merth, in your sky at home. When you return you'll see again how large it is, and beautiful—full of everything you need for life. It's like a mother, and that will still be true. The Kotaane are very wise to call themselves the children of the Earth, and be grateful for its gifts."

"But the Cyclops is greater, and stronger."

"Greater in size. But only another world." And only a brightness behind the clouds now. "Your myths are right; it doesn't love your people—it would poison you to live on Cyclops; but the Earth is strong enough to stay out of its reach, and will always care for you. And the sun will always defy its shadow, making the Earth fertile, able to give you life. You see, you've known the truth all along, Etaa."

"But . . . the worlds are not alive . . . they do not see all, or *choose* to interfere in our lives as you do—"

"No. But really in the end they are more powerful than any of us. All our lives depend on them; even starfolk need air, and water, and food to survive. We're very mortal, just as you are. Everything we know of is mortal, even worlds . . . even suns."

"Isn't there anything else, then? Is there no God, or Goddess, to give us form?"

"We don't know."

Etaa gazed out into the growing darkness, silent, and her hands formed signs I didn't know. And then, slowly, she reached up to her ear and removed the silver bell. She dropped it into a pocket of her jacket as if it burned her fingers.

"Oh, Meron," she whispered, "how did you bear it for so long, never knowing what was true, or whether anything is, at all?"

I glanced over at her, surprised; but she only got up and went to her pallet, seeking her answer in the closeness of Alfilere. I slipped into my darkened nursery to see my own child, thinking of the sorrow we two had given to each other, and the joys. And as I lay beside my forming child, I wished there could have been a way for us to give each other the greatest gift of all.

We stayed on Laa Merth for more than a third of a Cyclopean year, nearly half a natural Human year. Bright-eyed Alfilere took wobbling steps hanging onto his mother's fingers, and my own baby, full-born now, soft and silvery and new, opened enormous eyes of shifting color to the light of the world. I marveled to think that I could have been so beautiful once, for S'elec'eca was both my child and my perfect twin.

Etaa loved "her" on sight (Humans have only gender terms reflecting their basic dichotomy, and she refused to call my baby "it"); and if it was partly out of guilt and need at the start, I saw it grow into reality, while she watched both children and I studied the world outside. She called my child "Silver," her term for S'elec'eca, the name I had chosen. She said nothing more about religion or belief, and her love for the children filled her empty days; but when she absently invoked the Mother a painful silence would fall, and her eyes would flicker and avoid me. Sometimes I noticed her touching her throat, as if in finding her voice she had eaten the bitter forbidden fruit of a Human myth far older than her own and found the cost of knowledge was far too high.

When the supply shuttle came again I slithered and slid down the hill to meet it, oblivious to everything but the chance of good news for us; Iyohangziglepi nearly stunned me, thinking I was an attacking alien beast, before I remembered to call out to the ship.

But after the initial shamefaced apologies, I finally heard the news I had been waiting for so long: the war between Tramaine and the Kotaane was over. But the Kotaane had won—and not just won concessions as the Libs had planned, but won Tramaine. The king had been killed in battle, fighting to save his people; because, thanks to our Archbishop Shappistre, the people wouldn't fight, cursing the king and expecting us to take their side when we couldn't. And so the Liberals had won too, and the Service would have to support the Kotaane; but the Kotaane didn't know what to do with their victory now that they had it. They wanted only their priestess, and their peace, and the shattered Tramanians filled them with disgust: so signed the warrior Smith. Once I would have said that he was lying or insane, or else he wasn't Human. But he was Etaa's husband, and I believed him.

But if it was true, then nothing was settled, and Etaa's world teetered on the brink of more chaos. Iyohangziglepi said bitterly that even the Libs were appalled at their success in changing the world: because of it, we were faced with leaving the Humans to worse grief than we had caused already, or interfering in their culture to a degree that would destroy all that was left of our faltering integrity. Etaa could go home at last, and so could I. But to what kind of a future?

Etaa was still waiting eagerly at the top of the hill, watching my return from the ship. She held a child in each arm, masked against the blowing sand, and I could almost see hope lighting her eyes as I scrabbled back up the gravelly hill and the shuttle stayed on the ground behind me.

"Tam, are we going home? Are we?"

"Yes!" I reached her side, puffing.

She danced with delight, so that one baby laughed and one squeaked in surprise. "It's true, it's true, little ones—"

"Etaa—"

She stopped, looking at me curiously.

"The ship will wait for us. Let's get our things, and—and I'll tell you the news. But let's get out of the wind."

We threw together our few belongings in minutes, and then she settled with the children on the piled moss beside the ashy fire-ring. I crouched beside her, and our eyes met in the sudden realization that it was for the last time. Taking a long breath, I said, "The war is over, Etaa. Your people have beaten the Tramanians."

She shook her head, wondering. "How can it be—?"

"Your people are brave warriors. King Meron is dead, because the Tramanians wouldn't fight them anymore; they expected the Gods to—"

"The king is dead?"

I nodded, forgetting it wouldn't show. "Long live the king." I finished the Human salute as I smiled down at Alfilere, who had come over to me and was trying to climb up my face. Etaa cradled my own little rainbow-eyes in her lap, as I longed to do, and would do, soon, at last. "Your suffering has been avenged, and the suffering of your people."

"How—how did he die?"

"Struck by an arrow, in battle against your people."

A spasm crossed her face, as if she felt the arrow strike her own heart; her head drooped, her eyes closed over tears. "Oh, Meron . . ."

"Etaa," I said. "You weep for that man? When your people hate him for taking you, and defiling their Goddess? When his own people hate him for keeping you, and bringing the wrath of their Gods? Even the Gods have hated him . . . But you, who deserve to hate him more than any of us, for ruining your life—you weep for him?"

She only shook her head, hands pressing her eyes. "I am not what I was. And neither is the world." Her hands dropped, her eyes found my face again. "One's truth is another's lie, Tam; how can we say which is right, when it's always changing? We only know what we feel . . . that's all we ever really know."

I felt the air move softly in the cavities of my alien body and the currents of alien sensation move softly in my mind. "Yes. Yes . . . I suppose it is. Etaa, do you still want to return to your husband, and your people?"

Her breath caught. "Hywel . . . he is alive? Oh, my love, my love . . ." She picked up her curly-haired son, covering him with kisses. "Your father will be so proud! . . . I knew it must be true, I knew it!" She laughed and cried together, her face shining. "Oh, thank you, Tam, thank you. Take us to him now, please! Oh, Tam, it's been so long! Oh, Tam . . ." Her face crumpled suddenly. "Will he want me? How can he want me, how can he bear to look at me, when I betrayed him? When he jumped from the cliff to save his soul from the Neaane, and I pulled back? How can he forgive me, how can I go home again?"

"Why did you pull back?" I said softly.

"I don't know! I thought—I thought it was because of my child." She held him close, resting her head on his while he squirmed to get free. "For half a second, I drew back—and then it was too late, the soldiers . . . But how can I know? I was so afraid, how can I know it wasn't for *me*? To let him die, thinking . . ." She bit her lip. "He will never look at me!"

"But who was the coward, Etaa? Who threw himself from the cliff and left you to the Neaane? Was it you who betrayed, or Hywel?"

"No! Who says that—"

"Hywel says it. He is the Smith, Etaa, the victor in this war, and whatever the reasons that others fought, he fought for you. All he wanted was to find you, and to repay you for his wrong. He wants you brought to him, that's all he wants— but only if it's what you want, too. He cannot send you his feelings, but he sends you this, and asks you to—remember." Carefully I produced, from a pouch in my hide, the box Iyohangziglepi had given me.

She took the box from me and opened it, lifting out a silver bell formed like a flower, the mate to the one she had worn on her ear. She searched in her pockets for the one she had taken off, and laid them together in the palm of her hand. Her fist closed over them, choking off their sound; her hand

trembled, and more tears squeezed out from under her lashes.
But then, slowly, a smile as sweet as music grew on her face,
and she pressed them to her heart.

Alfilere had drawn Silver off her lap, and they rolled
together in the moss beside her, sending up a cloud of dust.
Etaa's exile and sorrow were ended at last; she would return
to her people, and I would return to mine. Probably we would
never see each other again, and the children . . . I looked
away. What sort of a life would Alfilere have, in the world
we had left him? The son of the Smith, the heir to Tramaine,
the strong, gifted child of Etaa, the Blessed One . . . who
would have been my child too if there had been a way; who
was as dear to me as my own child. The child of unity in a
broken world. The child of unity—

And suddenly it was so obvious: The answer to everything
had been here in my keeping, all along. We could raise
Alfilere to inherit his birthrights, and be a leader such as his
people had never known—one who could give them back
their rights and give us back our pride.

"Etaa?" She looked at me vaguely, still half lost in rev-
erie. I tried to keep my voice even, not knowing if she felt the
same way I did, or what her reaction would be. "You know
the situation back on your Earth is very unstable right now.
The Kotaane have won a war they didn't expect to win, and
they don't know what to do about it. Your husband wants
only to go home with you, not to rule a kingdom. Your
people despise the Tramanians, and now the Tramanians
despise themselves. They don't even know what to think
about their Gods, they have no leadership; all the nations that
surround Tramaine will be shaken, and there'll be more war
and hardship that could involve your people, unless something is done—"

She frowned, and reached to catch up the escaping children.

I released air from my sacs in a sigh. "Yes, I know. *We've*
done too much already. Even the Service can see that, finally.
But if some new answer isn't found, some compromise,
things will keep on getting worse. We could destroy you,
Etaa, with our meddling, unless somehow you stop being a
threat to us. And if we did that to you, we would have
destroyed ourselves as well."

She shifted the babies uneasily on her knees. "You have a plan to stop it?"

"I do . . . I *think* I do. . . . When I met you, I thought all Humans were violent and cruel without reason. That's why we were afraid of you, why we wanted you to stay where you were. But now I don't believe it. Your people are more aggressive than we are, and you have to learn there are responsibilities to progress that can't be ignored; you have to grow in understanding as you grow in strength.

"But your cultures are still young, and maybe if you begin to learn now how to live with one another, when you come to us as equals between the stars you'll be able to live with us as well. The time is perfect now, in the balance of change, for a religion to show Humans the unity of all life, and how to respect it—as your people do, when they follow the teachings of the Mother. And there is the perfect sign of that unity, the perfect *Human* to begin it: your son." I shifted nervously, trembling with hope and love. "Etaa, will you give me your son? Let me raise him, among my people, and give him the chance to change your world forever."

Her eyes stabbed me with incredulity and betrayal. "My son? Why should you take my son?"

Blindly I said, "Because he's the child of the Kotaane and the child of the Neaane. Let him inherit his father's throne, and close the wound between your peoples forever."

"He is not the king's son! He is mine, and my husband's."

"Only you know that, Etaa. The Tramanians believe he's the heir to their throne."

"My husband knows. He would never agree, he would never give up his son and clan-child."

"Hywel would be proud to give his child such an honor! I know he would, I . . ." I faltered, in my terrible need to be right.

"No!" Her hand rose in a fist. "I will not! Do you think we're less than animals, that you can take our children and we'll never mind?" Her voice broke. "Tam, eight years we waited for this child—eight *years*. How can you think we could give him up?" She looked down at me, her eyes changing. "But I forget; you aren't even Human." It was the first time she had made that an insult.

And I suddenly remembered that I wasn't, that we were still two totally alien beings who would never really know each other's needs or share each other's dreams; and there would never be an answer that was right for both our peoples. "I didn't know what I was asking, Etaa. I'm sorry, I—"

"Would you give up your child, Tam?"

I saw Silver from the corner of my eye, and tiny mock hands contentedly exploring Etaa's real one. I forced my eyes to meet Etaa's. "For this, I would give up my child, Etaa. Even if it was the only child I would ever bear. If it meant the future of my people, I would. And it *can* mean the future of both our peoples."

Coldly she said, "Would you give me Silver, Tam, if I gave you my son? To raise in his place?"

"Yes . . . *yes!*" I wondered wildly what emotions showed on my glider's face. "Etaa, if you could only know how you honor me, how much it means, to share a child with you. If you knew how much I've wanted you to love my child the way I love yours—it's all I could ask; to share with you, and bind our lives together."

She searched my eyes desperately, holding the children, and the future, in her hands. At last she looked down, into the two small flower faces peering up from her lap, and asked, "Would you teach him to use his voice?"

"And write, and read; and hand-sign, too. And to respect all life, and make others want to do the same. He's a good, beautiful baby, Etaa; let him be a great man. Let him be all he can be. He could save your world."

She shook her head aimlessly and no silver song answered now to give her comfort. "Is this true? Is it the only way to help? Will it help everyone in the world?"

"It's the only way, if you want the Humans to have any say in their own future, Etaa. If you want to save yourselves from our meddling." The knowledge tore at me that I was the biggest meddler of all, not shifting the fates of anonymous aliens, but tearing apart the life of someone I knew about and cared about, who had suffered so much—for a dream that might never come true. And what if I was wrong? "Etaa—"

"All right," she said softly, not even listening. "Then it must be, if we are to have our future. If you will love my

son, if my son will be all he can be; if the *world* can too, then
. . . I will share my child with you." The final words fell
away to nothing. But she looked up, and for a moment her
voice was strong and sure. "There is no one else I would do
this for, Tam. Only for you. Don't let me be wrong."

I kept my un-Human form hidden in the shuttle when we
returned to Tramaine, to the town by Barys Castle where it all
began. Etaa rose from her seat as the lock opened; beyond, in
the darkened afternoon of early autumn, I could see the
congregation of resplendent artificial gods—and goddesses,
our "manifestation" of the Mother's willingness to accept
this new union of beliefs. Beyond them were the milling
Human representatives, and somewhere among them, a dark-
haired warrior who only wanted his wife. Etaa took Alfilere
up in her arms for the last time wrapped in a royal robe, and I
saw her shiver as he nuzzled her neck, cooing. Her face was
the color of chalk, frozen into a mask too brittle to melt with
tears. She left Silver squirming forlornly alone on the foam-
cushioned seat.

"Etaa—?" I said. "Won't you share my S'elec'eca?"

In a voice like glass, she said, "I couldn't take Silver,
Tam. I love her, I *do*—but how could I teach her what she
was meant to be? And my people wouldn't understand her. It
wouldn't be fair. I will try . . . try to help them be ready for
my son. And maybe someday for Silver, too. Will you bring
her to see me then?"

"I will," I said, wanting to say something else. Tears crept
down my face like glue.

"Will you always be with him, and Silver too?"

"Yes, always . . . and never let him forget you." I hesitated, looking down. "Etaa, you'll have more children. And
it doesn't have to be eight years again. There are ways, we
can help you, if you want us to."

Her mouth stiffened in angry refusal; but then, softening,
she bent her head to kiss Alfilere and said very faintly, "I
would like that . . . Tam, I should hate you too, for everything you've done. But I don't. I can't. Good-bye, Tam.
Take care of our children." She knelt and stroked my mottled
hide, while I caressed her with the sighing hands of the wind,
the only hands I had.

Etaa left the cabin, and Iyohangziglepi came to pick up Silver, who began to cry at being held in a stranger's arms. Together we watched the viewscreen as Etaa presented Alfilere to the waiting deities, with the small speech I had trained her to recite for effect. She delivered it flawlessly, standing as straight and slender as a rod of steel, and if there was any sign on her face of the agony inside her, I couldn't see it. But Archbishop Shappistre stood nearby, still tolerated by the grace of the Gods, watching with an expression that surprised and disturbed me. And then after one of the Goddesses had accepted Alfilere, Etaa turned on him with pointing finger and charged him in sign language with treason, in the name of Alfilere III and his father Meron IV before him. The archbishop turned pale, and the Gods glanced back and forth among themselves. Then one of them made a sign, and guards appeared to lead King Meron's betrayer away. Fleetingly, as if for someone beyond sight, I saw Etaa smile.

But already she was searching the Human crowd, and I saw it part for the tall dark man in Kotaane dress, the warrior known as the Smith—Etaa's husband. A fresh puckered scar marked his cheek above the line of his beard, and he still walked with the small limp that bespoke his terrible fall. He stopped beyond the crowd's edge, across the clear space from Etaa, and his grim, bespectacled young face twisted suddenly with uncertainty and longing.

Etaa stood gazing back at him across the field, a bizarre figure in a flapping dusty jacket, her face a mirror of his own. Two strangers, the Mother's priestess who had found her voice and lost her faith, the peaceful smith who had taken heads; strangers to each other, strangers to themselves. And between them they had lost the most precious possession this crippled people knew, a new life to replace the old. The frozen moment stretched between them until I ached.

And then suddenly Etaa was running, her dark hair flashing behind her. He found her and they clung together, so lost in each other that two merged into one, as though nothing could ever come between them again.

AFTERWORD—
MOTHER AND CHILD

People often ask me, "Where do you get those weird ideas?" And they frequently go on to ask if I get them from dreams. Most of my dreams are not all that interesting, unfortunately. (I find far more inspiration for my work in the world around me when I'm awake.) I do get bits and pieces of image from dreams that I can sometimes work into my stories, but "Mother and Child" is the only thing I've written that comes entirely out of a dream.

In the dream I happened to be reading a story in an anthology; I had begun browsing somewhere in the middle of it and became more and more engrossed as I went along, until I was reading the second half of the story very carefully. (This is something I have a habit of doing when I'm awake, as well.) The story was illustrated, and, in the way of dreams, it began to have more and more illustrations, until at the end it had actually become a kind of animated film instead of a story. When I woke up I wrote down what I remembered and then set out to plot for myself what had happened in the "first half" of the novella. (The dream began *where Etaa and Tam are stranded on the second moon together.)*

I couldn't remember the name that I'd seen at the top of the pages while I was "reading" it in my dream, but I remembered that the name had begun with an O. After I wrote the novella, I ended up selling it to the anthology Orbit—which led me to wonder a little about precognition.

A lot of fantasy readers tell me that they really enjoyed this "fantasy"; like some of my other stories, the anthropological backgrounding I did in "Mother and Child" gives it something of a fantasy feel. (I'd been reading a lot of historical fiction just before I began the novella, and some of what I'd read influenced its tone, as well.) But unlike "The Storm King," I consider this to be strictly science fiction. One of my favorite aspects of this story is the way that many of the characters regard hearing, which under normal circumstances is a perfectly normal sense, as a kind of extrasensory magic. I'm also particularly fond of Tam, the alien, who is probably my personal favorite among all the alien characters who have appeared in my work.